THE ENCHANTER'S TORMENT

Phillip L. Ramsay

THE ENCHANTER'S TORMENT

DEDICATION

For Gail, who has put up with me for so many years and been a constant source of strength; and for all those people who had faith in me when I had none in myself. To everyone who has helped me directly or indirectly — many thanks.

This second (revised) version of 'The Enchanter's Torment' came about quite unexpectedly for me. Many people were enthusiastic about the project, and I am grateful to them for their support. I'd like to add thanks, in this second version, to: Alex Lewandowski, Marion B., Lisa P., Becca C., Cinda W., and especially to Mary, my Mother-in-Law, with all my love and affection, always.

Phill Ramsay

Chapter One: Musings

The car swept along the rain-streaked road, at times its grip on the road surface less than perfect. The weather was lousy and only promised to get worse; rain had begun to pour heavily two hours earlier, the temperature dropping rapidly, the rain turning to sleet. The sky, almost mocking all those of humankind who wished to travel this day, was heavy with grim clouds and soon snow would fall, with the rising wind helping to create blizzard conditions.

Inside the car, in stark contrast to the whims which Nature delighted in manifesting, was a warm, smoke-filled atmosphere, created both by the car's heater and the two occupants. The woman sat restlessly in the passenger seat; her expression might have indicated that she was on a day trip to the local cemetery, but in fact she was simply bored by the long drive. The man driving the car was in his mid-twenties, blond haired, a determined look upon his features. When not concentrating upon matters which he, rightly or wrongly, considered of supreme importance, his face could light up in a smile which had the effect of attracting people to him. He was aware of this, and exploited it when necessary.

Tony Baron was disappointed. He knew that they would have to stop for the night, if only at a country inn but he had reckoned on being much closer to his destination by now. The atrocious weather had made him cautious, but true to his personality, he accepted the fact — even though it *did* annoy him. He smiled at the fact that he could find humour in his annoyance, and at the sometimes contradictory nature of his personality. He shot a quick glance at his companion.

She was a delicate-looking young woman just a couple of years younger than Tony. She had a narrow face, brown hair, blue eyes. Her name was Margaret Hunter. Although she looked delicate, her face could take on an intense expression of self-will, and usually did so when she was certain that she was in the right and anyone else thought otherwise. When Tony glanced at her she was staring dejectedly through the windscreen, the unpleasant weather slightly depressing her.

Bringing her mind from the weather, she thought about this journey, which seemed more than a little absurd to her. She ran the events which had led to it through her mind quickly, from when she first met Tony.

It had been just over seven months ago; Margaret, not really one for nightclubs had been persuaded, by several workmates, to try a night out on the town, but she hadn't found the experience a pleasurable one. The noise, the bustle, the shouting to make herself heard, all combined to give her a pounding headache. She felt in her handbag for her cigarettes, but realised she had forgotten them. Excusing herself, (although her workmates couldn't have heard her), she went to the bar to buy herself some. Whilst waiting, she felt eyes upon her; glancing to her left, she saw two men looking at her. She could feel them mentally undressing her.

Suddenly, her heart began to pound, she began to panic, feeling a claustrophobic atmosphere closing in upon her. Memories she had repeatedly tried to bury struggled to force themselves into her awareness, adding to her panic. Terrified, she turned and staggered away from the bar, cigarettes forgotten, workmates nowhere to be seen. She realised abruptly, with a certainty she had never before felt, that they had gone, moved on without realising she wasn't with them. A low moan escaped her, and, looking over her shoulder, she saw one of the men following her.

Unreasoning terror overtook her, and she began to run toward what she thought was the exit, but it wasn't. She veered to her left, unconscious of the curious looks

8

which she was receiving, and as she rushed around a corner she collided with someone coming in the opposite direction. Arms encircled her, stopping her from losing her balance, and holding her in a close, but non-threatening embrace.

After a few seconds, which seemed to stretch out into long minutes, Margaret recovered sufficiently to realise she was being held by a man who appeared slightly older than she; her immediate reaction was anger at his embrace, but the anger faded as abruptly as it had appeared as she took in his features. He was smiling at her. Not laughing, not angry; he removed his arms from her waist, the smile still playing on his lips — not in a condescending way, which would have made her temper flare, but in a 'This isn't your night either' kind of way.

She stood stupidly, staring at him, at a total loss for words. His smile had somehow broken the ice, made her aware of a curious feeling of affinity with him.

If Margaret was speechless at these occurrences, her companion was not. He flashed his smile again, and, indicating a vacant table with a nod, he asked, "Want to sit down?"

It was such a natural suggestion, delivered so easily, almost as though he had known her for years. His very easiness puzzled her, and an echo of her only recently vanished fear returned. As they walked to the table, Margaret tried to analyse her reaction to his embrace of a few moments ago. Her breathing and pulse rate, already racing, slowed, although not by much. Her fear had gone — not faded, but disappeared completely. A pleasant, unfamiliar feeling rushed through her, confusing her anew.

Throughout that first meeting, Margaret could never afterwards remember speaking, yet she knew that she must have done. She answered questions about herself, her likes and so on. A long time passed before she even thought of looking for the men who had frightened her at the bar, and especially for the one who had started following her and caused her panic, although she saw neither.

From being a total disaster, the evening seemed to have been salvaged. Margaret felt relaxed, calm, and was thoroughly enjoying herself, thanks to her companion. She felt a perverse sense of gratitude to the man who had frightened her, felt that her terror had been worth enduring.

It was so natural for her to agree to a second meeting that she did so without the hesitation such a request would normally have caused. Margaret sighed. Things had seemed so straightforward back then, but were so uncertain now. Although she didn't like to, she thought about the psychic link which had established itself between them. Christ, it complicated things at times — and gave Tony certain insights which she felt uncomfortable about. It wasn't as though it was something which she could control.

White. Suddenly focussing on the present, she became aware of snow falling, the driving wind making the night outside the car seem full of rushing white flakes. She stretched, dismissing her previous thoughts, and tried to find a comfortable position in which to sit.

Whilst Margaret was thinking back, Tony was preoccupied with thoughts of his parents. He still missed them, would always miss them, no matter whether time healed the pain or not. He inclined to the theory that it didn't. Perhaps you just got so used to the pain that you noticed it less and less. Over four years, and the pain was still as intense as it had ever been.

His parents had been travelling to Glasgow, his father on business, his mother going along for no better reason than she loved being with her husband, and was nervy and irritable when he had long journeys to make. She always tended to go with him on his trips — he loved her company, too — and she believed that no accident could occur whilst she was with him. Neither had seen the van whose steering had failed, causing it to cross the central reservation and crash obliquely into them. Chaos had ensued. A total of twelve mangled hulks were the end result, but that wasn't the worst of it...

The funeral over, attended only by friends of his parents and a few sympathizers, Tony found himself wondering: 'Is this it? Is this all a person's life is worth? Years of working to succeed, to make your mark on the world, just so you can die prematurely, and be mourned only by a few friends and well-wishers'.

The absence of his Great-Uncle annoyed him. Tony knew that his Great-Uncle had heard about the deaths of his parents. He had received a letter which was short and unfeeling. It read:

> Dear Tony,
> You probably won't remember me, but rest assured that life goes on, every setback may be overcome.
> Great-Uncle Robert.

It was the thought that his Great-Uncle regarded the tragedy affecting Tony as a mere setback which infuriated him. It was this, more than anything that compelled Tony to find his Great-Uncle and confront him with his anger.

However, this was easier said than done; no matter how hard he tried, no matter where he looked, he could find no trace of him. It was almost as though his Great-Uncle didn't want to be found; as if, somehow, he'd managed to slip out of the system, and become an *un*person.

In desperation, Tony had gone to a lawyer who specialised in representing abused and neglected children, and who had successfully traced many runaways.

When Tony explained his problem, the lawyer pointed out that Tony's Great-Uncle wasn't a runaway child, and wouldn't agree to help trace him himself. However, Tony's smile once again worked its charm, and he left with the address of a man named John Peterson, who, he was informed, made his living finding people.

Mr. Peterson agreed to help Tony, but warned that if someone, like his Great-Uncle, really didn't want to be found, then he might be wasting his money. Accepting that possibility, Tony gave his phone number, fully expecting John Peterson to have no more success than himself.

However, Tony remembered his startled reaction when Mr. Peterson rang him two days later and asked to see him. Something in Peterson's tone of voice told him that he had succeeded where Tony had failed.

"It was by accident, really. If I hadn't been digging for information about a totally different matter, I'd never have come across it."

"You know where my Great-Uncle lives? How d'you find out? Where?"

"Yes, here is his address — miles from anywhere, I might add; as to how I found out, you don't honestly expect me to tell you? But I was surprised, to say the least, when I found out who your Great-Uncle is."

"What are you getting at? I don't understand," Tony demanded, not liking the mystery, but intrigued, despite himself.

"Let me ask a rhetorical question: ever heard of George Hayter?"

"Hayter? Of course I have; he's one of the greatest living authorities on the occult — he must make millions from the books he's written; but what's he got to do with my Great-Uncle?"

Peterson grinned, a full ear to ear grin, which at any other time would have been comical to see, but Tony wasn't in the mood for humour.

"Okay, I'll tell you the connection. George Hayter *IS* your Great-Uncle. No—"

Tony had opened his mouth to protest, but closed it again as Peterson raised a cautionary finger. "It's true. I came across the original document of copyright for your Great-Uncle's first book. Both names were there, but at that time George Hayter was only a pen-name. I think that's changed now. Anyway..."

"But I don't..."

"Mr. Baron," Peterson's voice had a hard edge to it, "either listen, or I'll leave." Tony said nothing, and Peterson continued, "As I was saying, although he's become famous, he's a recluse. He hardly ever leaves that mansion," said Peterson, indicating the paper with Hayter's address. "He thinks nothing of prosecuting anyone who enters his grounds — and the ground surrounding the mansion *is* his land — without his express permission, which is rarely given. I don't think he has ever even consented to be interviewed.

"All in all, he's a bit of a riddle. That's about all that I can tell you."

"You say it's difficult to get to see him — how do you know that? What's to stop people just going to the door?"

"When I found out who I was looking for, I asked a few friends, and they provided the information. If you want to try going to his door, fine. From what I've been told, you'll need a battering-ram to force the door open — unless, of course, Hayter invites you there...and if he *does*, I'd think twice before accepting."

"What d'you mean? Is there any reason I shouldn't go there?" Tony was getting caught in the conspiratorial tone adopted by Peterson without even realising it.

"Put it this way. I'd feel more than a little peculiar visiting someone whom I haven't seen since early childhood, who's never taken any pains to be associated with me throughout my entire life, who wouldn't even attend his own nephew's funeral, who lives in seclusion, and is an acknowledged authority on the occult.

"I think I'd stay away: occult mysteries are out of my league. Jesus, the time! I've got a client to meet." He stood abruptly. "Goodbye, Mr. Baron, I hope I've been of some use — I'll send you my bill."

Peterson grabbed his briefcase and fled out of the house, leaving Tony with conflicting feelings. He struggled to take in the knowledge that his Great-Uncle Robert was none other than George Hayter. At the same time, a strange sense of creeping fear began to pervade his mind at the very thought of meeting him.

That fear was to remain with Tony for some time, mostly at a subconscious level, and was to trigger his temper at times when he would normally have let his perverse nature seek humour in adversity. Perhaps its most insidious consequence would be to cause a hesitation. That hesitation, depending on Tony's own reaction, would cause the death of either a hated enemy — or of somebody close. In actuality, it was Tony's equivalent of the Sword of Damocles, although he was completely unaware of it in that sense.

Tony glanced quickly at his watch. The rhythmic *whick-whack* of the windscreen wipers a hypnotic whisper, urging him to sleep. He tried to shut the noise out of his consciousness, concentrating on driving, keeping his speed within reason, given that the snow was still coming down thickly, covering everything with a frozen white glow. Taking advantage of a red traffic light (which, considering the amount of traffic abroad, seemed more than a little redundant), Tony grasped a cigarette, lit it, and breathed out a breath of fog in a gesture which seemed to say, 'I needed that'.

As he accelerated through the junction (although that seemed too grand a name for the crossing where some Council had decided traffic lights should be erected), Tony again glanced at Margaret, and found her looking at him, smiling slightly.

"Thanks for offering me one," she said, punching his shoulder in mock-seriousness. "How much longer?"

"Another hour or so and we should be able to stop for the night." Tony grinned at her, "Bored?"

"Yes, and bloody uncomfortable — my backside feels as though it's flat."

"Cheer up, I'll massage it back into the right shape when we reach an inn or whatever they have around here. Who knows, we might just end up with a single room and a double bed..." The sentence trailed off as he noticed the alteration in her features, the confused frown, the subtle impression that he had reminded her of things that she didn't want to bring to mind. She turned her face away from him, saying nothing, not having to, and looked dejectedly through the window.

Tony sighed; he'd never been able to guard everything he said all day of every day — even when being light-hearted and only half-serious, he knew he had to be careful what he said. Margaret's reaction to his attempt at levity irritated him.

He noticed the snow falling less heavily than it had been, and dismissing Margaret from his thoughts, he accelerated gently, falling back into his musings about George Hayter.

Having his Great-Uncle's location, Tony remembered his reluctance to confront him. He had no reason not to do so, but a weird feeling of reticence constrained him to do nothing.

Indeed, he now felt no real reason to confront Hayter, as he had done at the time of his parents' funeral. His anger had dulled itself into a vague resentment which, strangely, bordered on curiosity.

Tony found it difficult to equate the great George Hayter with his Great-Uncle — it seemed so improbable. For years he had studied occultism. His basic — and a large proportion of his advanced — studies had been completed using Hayter's material as a foundation. Through many a night, grappling with the esoteric mysteries of the Cabbala, Hayter, like a mentor, had shown him the way forward.

It was as though an unseen guardian had suddenly materialised just for him — but Tony didn't believe in such coincidence. Although he didn't understand how or why, he knew, with a deep certainty, that there was a purpose in this discovery.

He dug out the letter which his Great-Uncle had sent to him, seemingly aeons ago. He remembered it as terse and unfeeling; now, as he reread it, he felt as though he could just divine another meaning, to which he had at first been oblivious:

> Dear Tony,
> You probably won't remember me, but rest assured that life goes on, every setback may be overcome.
> Great-Uncle Robert.

True, it had been a setback — and yet, was it after all a message within a message? Was Hayter trying to reach out to his relative after all this time? Could Tony be deluding himself?

Tony had pondered this until his head ached. He went round and round in a circle, and still seemed to get no nearer to the solution.

He grinned as he recalled Margaret's reaction to his studying the occult. She had looked at him as though he should already have a set of horns and a forked tail. Even after he had explained exactly what his studies entailed, it had taken her some time to come to terms with his being an occultist.

16

Several times she had hinted that she would be happier if he dropped the study of what she considered dangerous and sickening practises. Of course, Tony had chosen to ignore her hints, more from stubborn instinct than anything else. The study of the occult came easily to him, as though he were a sponge waiting for the correct liquid to absorb. The occult provided him with that liquid.

Finally, an uneasy equilibrium had been established. Tony only discussed the occult with Margaret when it came up in normal conversation, which wasn't that often. Hayter had been a neutral subject, speculated upon by them both, until that day, three weeks ago. Their uneasy equilibrium had been shattered, and their first serious argument, caused by George Hayter's second letter, had ensued.

Margaret lay back in her seat, gazing out into the windswept night with unseeing eyes. She felt hurt, a mild feeling of betrayal tinged her emotions. She understood that Tony had been joking with his quip about the double bed — but her past experiences had made her hypersensitive and vulnerable, and her reactions tended to be automatic. She realised that her hasty response to Tony's joke hurt him, but she felt unsure and insecure; half of her wanted to talk with him, to explain that she didn't intend to hurt him; but another part of her told her to remain safe and secluded in her silence. Trying to resolve this dilemma was always a problem, which she resolved by refusing to resolve it. Then, feeling guilty at her own cowardice, she reached absently for a cigarette, lit it, inhaled deeply, and allowed her mind to wander.

She felt drowsy, and let her thoughts take what direction they would, as she closed her eyes. Her first meeting — colliding — with Tony; her contradictory feelings of nearness and distance to him; their first argument, the cause of this bloody uncomfortable journey.

She opened her eyes as she drew on the cigarette; she was sure, in a dreamy way, that had she been a moment sooner, she would have caught Tony's eyes on her. Mentally shrugging the thought off, she closed her eyes again, listening to the drone of the car, the rhythmic thumping of the windscreen wipers.

She located the ashtray by touch and crushed the cigarette out, beginning to feel herself drifting, relaxing despite, or because of, the monotonous sounds around her. She thought back to her childhood, repulsed the memory as though it might hurt her, and then, slowly, tentatively, she recaptured the memory, treating it as if it might, after all this time, cause her pain anew.

She thought about her father, and then quickly about the mother she had never known. How different would her life have been, had her mother lived? The very question caused her pain, since it forced her to recognise how unhappy her childhood had been, forced her to bring it into focus, rather than leave it a blank in her memory, as she would do in normal circumstances.

It was her father's brutality she could never fully comprehend; certainly she could never remember being given any cause to love him, and the severity of the beatings which she had been forced to endure had only helped alienate her from him.

As though the sluice gate of a dam had been opened, the memories repressed for so long began to unlock themselves, demanding attention before being either discarded, or examined more closely. Margaret was stunned to find that many memories which she had kept securely hidden for so long seemed to have lost their power over her. The pain associated with them was there — but only as a memory.

Imposing order on her chaotic thoughts, she remembered things that had seemed magical to her, as a child. Her childhood had been an unhappy one, but not one totally devoid of happiness. She remembered watching the birth of kittens, every day visiting the neighbour who owned the cat, to marvel over the furry bundles. She pondered the mysteries of nature, which turned caterpillars into butterflies, with her surprisingly loving and open personality.

These memories, however, were in the minority. Most of the memories she brought to mind were unpleasant. Wanting to push the discovery that these memories no longer had the power to hurt her, she began, more confidently, to focus upon them.

She remembered her father's severity; but it was more than just severe beatings — there was a sadistic element present, of which, as a child, she had not been fully aware. Even at a relatively young age, she had understood that her father enjoyed stripping and hitting her with his belt — and he did so for the most minor crimes.

Unconsciously gritting her teeth, she hesitated, then recaptured one of the memories.

She had been just over ten years old, she recalled. Her father had just cleaned the tiled floor, a job which, along with all housework, he hated doing, but which he would do if Margaret wasn't around to be told to do it. This always resulted in his being more likely to lose his temper with her.

It was a Saturday, and she had run out of the house early, before her father was awake, breakfast ignored. It had been raining during the night, and, when she took a short cut across fields, it was inevitable that her shoes and socks ended up muddy.

An hour or so later, suddenly feeling hungry, she had decided to head back home — and without thinking, she retraced her route across the short cut, making her shoes and socks even worse.

She was humming to herself as she entered the house, and was across the room before she turned to make sure the door had closed after her. Her heart seemed to stop for a second, and then it began pounding, threatening to tear itself from her chest. God, if her father saw the mess her footprints had made...

She hadn't even got half way through trying to clean the mud off the floor when the door opened, and her father stood there, surveying both Margaret and the mess she had brought in with her.

She remembered being told to go to her bedroom; that was the signal that she would be beaten. Climbing the stairs slowly, hoping that the inevitable could be postponed somehow, Margaret began feeling an icy dread building up inside her, exciting her still palpitating heart. She wished it was later, with the punishment just a memory, the pain having died away. The sight of her bedroom made her queasy. That was where it always tended to happen, the room a constant reminder of pain.

She sat on the bed, waiting; waiting. She could never decide which was worse, the actual punishment, or the mental torture of waiting for it to begin. Just as her fear began to ebb away, she detected her father's footsteps. She stood up, swallowing. This was it. God, she wished it was over.

Then he was there; she was told to get undressed, and she felt the humiliation of this part of the ritual as keenly as it was intended. Naked, she was told to bend over the footboard of her bed. Grabbing the bedclothes in her hands, she did as she was told, clenching and unclenching her hands in ghastly anticipation of the pain to which she was about to be subjected.

She understood instinctively, from the expression she had seen on her father's face, that no mercy would be shown, and that, by the time this punishment ended, she would be feeling more than sorry for herself.

She heard her father taking the thick leather belt from around his waist, and tensed. She knew what to expect.

Wave after wave of pain tore into her consciousness. As the agony intensified with each stroke, she struggled to remain in the position which she had been told to assume over the footboard. If she jerked upright, as the pain from every blow demanded, she was only too aware that the next stroke might land anywhere — on her back, or her legs, which she knew from past experience, would be even more excruciating.

The waves of pain became less frequent, as though her father were savouring her punishment; each time the pain flooded into her body, it was accompanied by the sickening *whap* of the belt as it connected with her buttocks.

Through her yelps and tears, and her sobs and screams, the punishment continued. She had stopped counting the strokes after she had reached twenty-five. All she wanted was for it to end, for the torment to stop. Her father, as though reading her thoughts and delighting in thwarting them, and in the pain which he was inflicting upon her, sadistically applied the belt to the backs of her legs.

Although she had been able to control her cries and tears to a limited extent whilst her bottom was being chastised, now that control was impossible. White fire seemed to run from her legs through her body, making her writhe and scream and beg her father to stop; through her tears and torment she thought she heard him chuckle, but she couldn't be sure. The signals of pain which her buttocks were still sending seemed now to be unimportant, by comparison.

It was only when her legs wouldn't support her any more, when they buckled and crumpled completely, that the end of this waking nightmare arrived. As she lay shivering on the floor, two further waves of pain hit her, stinging her side and back, and then, abruptly, she was alone.

Alone with her pain, and her tears, and her sobs, and her hatred, which she could only give utterance to in her pain-wracked mind. Shuddering, crying, she dragged herself to her bed, and heaved herself onto it, covering herself with blankets. There, alone in the darkness, lonely and afraid, she cried again; she sobbed out all her pain and anger, but most of all, her unhappiness.

Gulping a deep breath, Margaret opened her eyes; she realised that tears had been rolling down her cheeks. The memories might not have been as painful as she had feared, but it was an unpleasant experience to relive. She felt in her handbag for a paper handkerchief, dried her face, and tried to swallow the lump which had risen in her throat. She felt an echo of the despair that she had felt as a ten-year-old.

She glanced at Tony, wanting him to understand how she felt; she wanted to confide in him, to tell him about her childhood, but he seemed deep in thought. A frown creased his forehead, then erased itself. In that second, the moment when Margaret could have communicated with him was lost.

She reached for her handbag, wondering how many children were subjected to such physical maltreatment — and to worse. Her maternal instincts cried out against such injustice; but her feelings about her own abuse as a child were strangely difficult to articulate.

Disturbed at her reaction to these memories, she plucked another cigarette from the pack, replaced it in her handbag, and concentrated on what she could see through the windscreen. It wasn't much. The night was dark, the wind buffeted the car, the snow fell steadily. How long was it since Tony had said they would only be travelling for another hour?

Ten minutes? Thirty? She was growing restless, partially due to sitting in a confined space for so long, and partly as a result of her unpleasant memories.

Tony, although concentrating on driving, was thinking back to Hayter's second letter. True, he had discussed Hayter with Margaret lots of times but never had either of them voiced the opinion that it might be Hayter who would take the initiative, and contact them. Tony had made vague suggestions about visiting Hayter, but always in a detached, abstract way.

He thought of the heavy envelope, addressed in bold strokes. He remembered, too, the strange feeling when his fingers came into contact with it. It felt warm to the touch, and a sensation which he could only describe as 'searching' seemed to take hold of him. Then, as it died away, the envelope cooled abruptly and seemed to him to be just an ordinary envelope. Tony had a feeling that he had just passed a test, and had been in danger. But what that test was, or what the danger had been, he couldn't fathom.

He opened it, wondering what the hell it could be, and took out a piece of paper. He recognised the writing before it connected with a name in his mind. His Great-Uncle?

Tony took a deep breath before scanning the lines, and then, incredulous, he reread them, and reread them again. What he read took minutes to sink in.

> Dear Tony,
>
> I know it's been years since you last heard from me, and then not in the happiest of circumstances. I doubt you ever remember meeting me, as you were so young at the time.
>
> It seems to me that, for various reasons, we must meet soon. The time is drawing near. And, as your parents are deceased, I am freed from my

promise; but perhaps I go too fast. This we can discuss when we meet.

I suggest you come here, say, the week after next. You can stay indefinitely, may have to, in fact. But, as you know, deep down, we must get together soon. I will assume, in my arrogance, that this will meet with your approval. Finally, Tony, I am looking forward to meeting you, at long last.

Great-Uncle Robert—George Hayter

P.S.

When I invite you, Tony, I *automatically* extend that invitation to Miss Hunter. I shall expect you both on the twenty-third.

Tony had to keep rereading the letter to prove to himself that what he had read wasn't a figment of his imagination. He was certain that Margaret would be fascinated by it, and by the proposed meeting; he had already made up his mind: he would go.

But when Tony told Margaret of the arrival of the letter, and of the invitation which it contained, she was less than happy. Unknown to either of them, Hayter had come to symbolise to her, at an unconscious level, those aspects of occultism that she found so disturbing. She immediately attempted to use every argument that she could think of to deter Tony from embarking on the proposed visit; but all to no avail.

Finally, she abandoned the subtle in favour of the obvious. She asserted that Hayter and the occult meant more to Tony than she did, even though she didn't believe it, and that precipitated their first serious argument.

It was an argument which Margaret felt she had lost before she began; she was a hopeless liar, and her clumsy attempt at manipulation was quickly seen through. Not only did Tony see through her intentions, but she had ended up agreeing to accompany him on this seemingly endless journey, the object of which seemed as enigmatic as Hayter himself.

Tony contended that here was a mystery which he felt he had to solve. Referring to the letter, Tony paraphrased the sentence which seemed to imply that time was precious. Why time was short, what Hayter wanted to talk to him (and presumably Margaret) about, seemed to be a puzzle. Tony knew, intuitively, that only George Hayter held the solution.

Margaret had given in unwillingly, mentioning that Tony had at one point wanted to confront his Great-Uncle about the message which arrived whilst he was preparing for his parents' funeral. Tony had smiled and said: "I can still mention it, can't I?" Leaving Margaret no answer.

As Margaret had tried to manipulate Tony, Tony felt only a slight hesitation in turning the tables around. Somehow, Tony knew that it was *right* that Margaret should accompany him: he knew it to be so, but couldn't articulate why he felt it so strongly.

Thinking back, he brought from his memory a dim picture of a man; he was sure this man was Hayter. He remembered that the man had spoken to him, but what he had said was lost in the mists of time. He recollected that after he had been put to bed that night, he had stayed awake. Whether it was the excitement of knowing that there was a stranger in the house, or whether he hadn't been able to sleep, he didn't recall.

He *did* remember the drone of voices, which rose in volume and sharpness; the argument, (for such Tony had decided it must be) went on for what seemed like hours. But Tony was asleep long before the stranger left the house. His parents had never afterwards referred to the stranger, or to Great-Uncle Robert, in Tony's hearing.

That seemed to be the only memory of his Great-Uncle (if it had been his Great-Uncle) which had lingered in his memory.

Tony wondered again about the letter which promised so much, but actually said so little. The one thing Tony simply couldn't understand was Hayter inviting Margaret as well. How had Hayter managed to find out about her? They had been together for over seven months, but it was hardly the sort of information that Hayter would have been likely to come across; not unless he had been looking.

Thinking of Peterson, Tony smiled grimly. Perhaps two had played the same game: birds of a feather? The thought brought with it a sense of the ridiculous, causing him to chuckle. Margaret looked questioningly at him.

Well, so Hayter must have checked up on him; it was no more than he'd done to Hayter. Tony found himself wondering how much Hayter knew, or thought he knew, about his relationship with Margaret.

Examining their relationship, Tony found that there were many areas which were grey, unclear. He felt close to Margaret, closer than she knew. But he didn't feel he was as close to her as he wanted to be. Tony felt intense affection for her — but the possibility that he might love her he hadn't even considered.

Margaret herself was a difficult person to know, and even more difficult to understand. Tony felt that, most of the time, he was trying to complete a jigsaw with half the pieces hidden. It was only now that he realised just how much he didn't know about her. He remembered certain question which he had asked which had received only vague and evasive answers.

Further, her negative reactions to any sexual overtures that he might make, had, in the beginning, implied nothing more than she wanted to be certain of him; perhaps wished to remain a virgin until she married. That he could have understood — but he knew that there was more to it. Her reactions, taken with her evasions, added up to what? Something that she didn't feel confident enough to tell him about.

'*Perhaps*,' Tony thought, '*I haven't given her the opportunity that she needs.*' And with this thought, he became aware of the fact that he hadn't been very responsive to her attempts to discuss her past — few though those attempts had been — and he resolved to be ready when the next opportunity presented itself.

Margaret was still trying to come to terms with the rush of emotion which had accompanied her deliberate probing of her early life. She drew again on the cigarette and heard Tony chuckle. She looked at him, her glance both questioning and wary.

Had he shared her memory? She realised quickly that the thought was absurd. The psychic link didn't work that way.

A minute later, catching her glance, he smiled at her. As his eyes returned to the road, she caught herself wishing that he could know about her past, without her having to go through the pain and feeling of degradation she was certain to feel if she told him about it.

Musing on this, her thoughts centred on whether or not she could bring herself to open a window into the shadowy depths of her past for him. She was certain that he suspected there was something that she was keeping from him, but he hadn't probed, hadn't persisted or demanded.

It was the difficulty she felt she would have putting her experiences into words which made her squirm, along with the embarrassment, the fear of being hurt again, and her insecurity. Tony made her feel relaxed and secure. Perhaps, if the right opportunity presented itself, she...

Her thoughts snapped back to the present as the car braked smoothly to a halt. It was only when the engine died that she realised they were outside a large wooden-beamed inn. Its sign declared:

OOMS FU L   ENGLI H   CUIS NE   VA ANCY

"Hungry?" asked Tony.

Chapter Two: Revelations

Margaret nodded, "I could do with a wash first. I feel tired out."

As they stepped out of the car, the wind hit them, slicing through their clothing with knives of ice. They hurried into the inn. Whilst he went to reception (what there was of it), Margaret gazed at her surroundings. Carved wood was evident everywhere — and it was old.

She found herself studying a complicated design, seemingly of squares, circles and triangles inscribed within each other, but intersecting with other such geometrical shapes.

She turned at Tony's approach. "Well, two rooms, but we've got a communicating door, or doors, I suppose. We share a bathroom. Best I could do, honest."

He looked at her so seriously that she had to laugh. His gaze took in the design carved into the wood, intensified, and then, with a puzzled frown, he led the way to the stairs.

The rooms were plainly furnished, but the beds looked comfortable. Once inside, Margaret's first action was to locate the bathroom, fill the sink with tepid water, and wash away what felt like the accumulated grime of weeks.

Feeling much refreshed she went back into her own room suddenly conscious of something not quite right — or not quite usual. She looked at the wooden beams, the wooden walls, even the ceiling, but it wasn't just the wood which caught her attention; it was the carvings which were evident upon them. Frowning, but intrigued at the craftsmanship that had gone into producing them, she examined one wall more closely.

An equilateral triangle inscribed in a circle, its apex pointing to the floor, straight lines radiating from the inverted base to the circle's circumference. Within the triangle was what seemed to Margaret like a badly formed 'n', which was surrounded by a small circle.

She gazed at the carving above it, and saw hemispheres intersecting a full circle, a square inscribed within the circle, and what she took to be a plus sign in the middle. She frowned at what seemed a very peculiar design, and had just moved on to the next carving, when Tony came into her room, a little hesitantly.

She was too absorbed in the carvings to feel in any way threatened by his presence in what was, after all, her bedroom. "Tony, what d'you make of these carvings?"

He glanced at the delicately inscribed figure. Although he had seen many illustrations like it, he was nevertheless unsure about answering her; but her interest seemed to have been aroused, so he replied honestly. "It's a symbol of occult protection — and it's been beautifully carved. I'd bet it took hours to ensure all the angles were accurate, let alone the time the actual carving took."

"You mean all these designs are to do with the occult?"

"It seems like it, and they appear to be almost exclusively on one theme. All the symbols I've seen here have a direct or strong bearing on protection; either of the occupants, or the building itself." Taking in Margaret's look of curiosity, he continued, "It's a strange way to decorate the walls: expensive. Perhaps someone was trying to keep something out."

"Tony!" she remonstrated, "You're just trying to scare me, but it won't work."

"Too bad," he muttered, moving towards her.

"Why?" she demanded.

"Well, if you were scared, I'd put my arm around you, like this," he said, demonstrating the manoeuvre, "and then I'd hold you close to me, stroke your hair, kiss you..."

As he kissed her a pleasant tingle ran through her body. His lips traced a path from her lips to her eyes, her nose, her throat; his breath tickled as he kissed the side of her neck. He pulled away from her a little, his arms still around her.

Margaret gazed into his eyes and saw good humour reflected there. Smiling, she said, "Tony, it might be interesting to know what you'd do to me if I was scared, but I am hungry."

Tony grinned. "Okay, but I reserve the right to scare you later."

All thoughts of her musings in the car forgotten for the moment, she mirrored his movement as he placed his arm around her waist. They made their way down the stairs, Tony grinning as he whispered vague threats concerning what he might do to her later, and Margaret giggling in embarrassed reaction, eventually reaching a room claiming to be the restaurant.

He glanced at a menu as they sat opposite each other at one of the numerous tables. It was a room devoid of people apart from a bored-looking waitress. She hovered impatiently, waiting for them to order so that she could get back to reading her paperback which she clutched, breaking its spine in the process.

"What would you like?" he asked, not being hurried by the hovering waitress.

"Oh, anything, as long as it's hot."

Tony quickly scanned the list and ordered. The food was served surprisingly quickly, and, amazing Tony even more, it was edible.

He ordered a bottle of white wine. The wine, too, tasted better than expected, and they were left alone to enjoy their meal in relative privacy.

Conversation was quiet and intimate — hardly what he had expected. It came as a pleasant surprise, all the same. The meal finished, they sat on, talking about anything but their journey, or Hayter. As they talked, the atmosphere became more relaxed, more intimate, were that possible. He became conscious of the fact that Margaret's presence and the seductive atmosphere were arousing him. As conversation continued, he regarded her; her face, her eyes, her neck. His gaze took in the swell of her breasts, unobtrusively. His arousal intensified, and he moved to sit nearer to her — next to her.

"Wouldn't you like to discover what might happen if you were scared?" Before she could answer, he had her lips gently under his own. As the kiss broke he became aware of her breathing more rapidly, the jump of the pulse in her neck. He smiled, inwardly.

She put her arms around his shoulders and pulled him back to her; the kiss was more passionate this time, and Tony felt a part of his mind beginning to assume...

Margaret jerked away from him as though she had just received an electric shock. It took a second for Tony to work out what had happened. They were no longer alone. A tall man had entered the restaurant and, smiling at Margaret's obvious embarrassment, he strode towards them.

"I hope you enjoy your stay here; I'm the owner." Here, Tony could have sworn that the man winked at him without Margaret being able to observe it. Well, let him think what he liked, as long as he hurried up and got lost. Tony wanted to get back to Margaret and to the seduction which had started so well, and from his point of view promised much more — providing he was careful.

"We're only here for the night," Margaret's voice.

"Well, even so, if there's anything I can do...well, don't hesitate to ask." He turned to go. Tony took Margaret's hand, but her mind had obviously latched onto something else, as she pulled her hand away and called after the owner.

He halted, turned, and walked back to their table. Tony noticed the man's shirt had a button missing. He tried not to laugh; wished Margaret hadn't called him back; wondered what she wanted. When it came, he heard warning bells going off deep inside him, but not for any reason that he could understand.

"I've been wondering," Margaret said, "about the occult symbols carved onto the walls and ceiling in my room — and Tony's. Why are they there? Who put them there? Is there a story behind it?"

Tony groaned involuntarily. His arousal was beginning to fade, and it was the occult which was ultimately responsible. Normally he would have seen the ironic and humorous side of events, but this time the whole thing annoyed him.

He became conscious of the scrutiny of the owner upon both himself and Margaret, as if the question was not really welcomed. "That's nothing to concern yourself about; I don't want to be responsible for giving you nightmares," he smiled.

But Tony knew that the result of this type of evasion was only guaranteed to make Margaret more insistent upon an answer.

"But what happened? Why were these things carved? Tell me; you can't leave me wondering what the mystery is all about. Is it some kind of secret?"

The owner frowned. "No," he said slowly, "it's no secret, but it's not the most talked about event in this neck of the woods." He looked at Tony, as if he might find the answer to his dilemma there, but Tony just lifted his eyes ruefully, as much as to say, '*You should have said that you didn't know a thing about it.*'

The owner pulled a chair to himself and sat down, looking at them both again. He sighed a heavy sigh, one of resignation as well as one of pleasure at being the centre of attention.

"What I'm going to tell you, you might find difficult to accept: maybe impossible to believe. It's a story that's come down to us from word of mouth over hundreds of years. Maybe it's distorted, but even legends have their bases in fact. Where the facts stop and the fiction starts nobody knows, but the story, as I was told it, runs something like this.

"Shortly after being built, this house was purchased — it was then a large house — and occupied by an adept. He was a curious and mysterious person — very little is known of him, who he was, where he came from; but he was a stranger, that much is certain.

"What he did that caused the animosity and suspicion has been lost, but rumours began. It was believed he practised the Black Art; that he could cast the Evil Eye. The villagers, who only lived a half a mile away, ostracised him; not that this bothered him. I think that privacy was exactly what he wanted.

"What, if anything, happened in the next few months who can say? But the story picks up when the recluse attempted to buy the site of a church that had fallen into ruin. Some claim that he actually wanted the church rebuilt, others say that he wanted it for certain unholy purposes: who can tell?

"The Church authorities, however, seemed happy enough to express the sentiment that the sale could be arranged, if the price was high enough. So, all seemed set; the stranger was rich, could easily afford fifty times the sum that the Church asked, but here entered the crux of the events that were to follow.

"At that time, there were several Cults following the 'Old Religion'. They weren't necessarily Satanists, but not believers of the God of Jesus, either. One of these Cults, the most depraved and said to be the most powerful, wanted control of the ruined church. But they didn't want to buy it — they were already using it. Why should they pay for something which they already virtually possessed? And why give money to the *very* organisation which they regarded as their *more* than mortal enemies?

"Obviously, the Cult couldn't bid openly for the church; their society being a great secret, they could trust nobody outside their own ranks for such an undertaking, yet they would not risk any member becoming known to outsiders.

"But this was a secondary consideration. As I said, they did not wish to buy. Instead, they decided that it would be easier to persuade the owner of this house to withdraw from the proposed sale. His refusal angered them, and everything escalated from there; the exact details aren't known, but the end result was war.

"Combined, the Cult was just too powerful for him; on an individual basis he might have stood a chance, who knows?

"He was found by his housekeeper, an old woman he had brought with him — you can believe none from the village would work here — he was paralysed. This caused a sensation, and the proposed sale of the church had to be abandoned.

"It was at this point that, fearing more attacks by the Cult, he gave orders for the walls and ceiling to be covered in the signs of Light — he even had a pentacle burned onto the floor, which is still visible. He sent various messages — and waited.

"But the Cult decided that their objective had been achieved. The sale of the church was halted. They had nothing to fear, as obviously their knowledge of the occult was superior to that of the owner of this house. In their belief of victory, they let him live. It was a grave mistake."

Tony listened with growing interest, his arousal now only a distant memory. He had expected a boring story, but had been drawn into the recounting of events, and was fascinated with what he was hearing.

Paradoxically, Margaret was feeling sorry that she had asked. She had thought that there would be some tame mystery attached to the occult signs — or that they might be just a curiosity from an eccentric owner of the past. Occult battles she didn't want to hear about. She opened her mouth to say that she had heard enough, when she noticed the look upon Tony's face. He would insist on hearing it all, no matter what she said. As the owner continued, she felt her anger mounting.

"About six months later, a change was noticed in the recluse. He regained the use of his limbs, some say by resorting to the occult, but that may or may not be.

"This house became a virtual fortress. Nobody dared come near, but word still got around that the housekeeper had been sent away, and that the owner was expecting a visitor.

"Every stranger appearing around the village was carefully scrutinised — for the villagers didn't understand what was happening around them, they held the owner of this house to blame. They feared him.

"At last, the stranger came, right into the village public house to ask his way. He didn't get a very friendly reception; but at least his name is known, as he introduced himself most politely.

"Anyway, he found this house, and was admitted. He was seen occasionally, but unlike the owner, he was friendly and cheerful. If he hadn't been the owner's friend he might even have become accepted by the villagers.

"But I'm digressing. Both of these men were *very* powerful occultists, and had a great friendship and respect for each other. To attack one was to injure the other; without any warning given, they attacked the Cult and began to wipe it out, member by member.

"It didn't take long for the Cult to realise its extreme danger, and soon battle was joined by both sides, with a savagery beyond description. The two magicians, combining their abilities, were a match and more for the Cult. They *all but* destroyed it."

"All but? What happened?" Tony couldn't stop himself asking the question.

"Well, things get hazy again. The most commonly held theory is that, in a final incantation, the magicians made a mistake in their formulas of protection, or, that they panicked into summoning a force that they couldn't control. It matters little. The result was horrific.

"The next day, all that remained of them was blood spattered on the walls, and pieces of flesh and bone embedded into the wood. There were no bodies — they had been, quite literally, liquidated." The owner paused, hoping that his witty remark would spark some response from his audience, but Tony was too interested to notice the double-meaning, and Margaret felt her stomach turning.

A little put out, he continued his story: "The Cult had all but been destroyed, but it went about re-forming itself. It swore *deadly* vengeance on the lineage of both magicians. It didn't mean much to the owner's relatives, as there weren't any; he was the last of his line.

"But the other — his line continued, and the story runs that the Cult is still at its task of vengeance. The occult signs were left as a reminder; this place was sold. That's about all there is to tell."

"But there must be more — what happened? What form did the revenge take?" Tony asked, insistent on getting an answer.

"Apparently all of that line have died violent and painful deaths at the hands of, or at the instigation of the Cult — and they won't stop until their vengeance is complete, the line annihilated."

Tony pondered this for a moment, whilst the owner got to his feet. "I *do* hope I won't be the cause of unpleasant dreams," he said, looking fixedly at

37

Margaret. He smiled and turned, and walked back the way that he had come.

"What...?" Margaret croaked out. The owner stopped abruptly, turned, and looked questioningly at her.

"What was his name? You said that the name of the second magician was known because he introduced himself. Who was he?"

But Margaret didn't want to know. She knew that she would not like the answer when it came, and yet she had to ask the question. The restaurant was silent, as she and the owner locked eyes.

"I *did* say that, didn't I? Yes, the name of the second magician is known," he hesitated almost imperceptibly. "The man's name was Anton Baron. Good night, sleep well, both of you." He turned and was gone.

Tony closed his eyes to try to make thinking easier. He had sensed danger, but this was uncanny. What did it mean? Did it have anything to do with Hayter, this weird journey? Less than an hour ago, he had been gently attempting to seduce Margaret; he knew by the menacing silence that the intimate atmosphere between them had undergone a subtle yet unmistakable change. He felt her eyes upon him.

Meeting her gaze, he saw the mixture of conflicting emotions running through her: pain, anger, resentment, fear, and love. That last emotion seeming, perversely, to exacerbate the others.

With tears in her eyes, Margaret stood and walked through the door which had been used minutes ago by the owner, leaving Tony alone.

He called after her, tried to catch up with her. She made no reply but walked quickly away, until she disappeared up the stairs which led to their rooms. He walked back to the table that they had shared. He noticed some wine left in the wine bottle: damn.

As Margaret turned and headed for the door, she had difficulty in both keeping her sobs buried deep inside her, and in not running, which was what she really wanted to do. When Tony called after her, she hurriedly made her way to her room. Once there, she collapsed upon the bed, crying out her fears and anguish.

As her tears subsided, she began examining what she had heard about the occult symbols that surrounded her. Suddenly, as though an inner light had shone illumination where it was most needed, she comprehended (as far as she was able) the connection between Hayter, Tony and the story she had just heard.

The implied danger to Tony renewed and sharpened her fears, and before she realised what was happening, her fears and misapprehensions erupted within her. She buried her head in the pillow.

Eventually, as her sobbing eased, she began thinking about Tony's reaction. It seemed as if the story that they had been told had literally stunned him. When she had looked at him, she'd seen his closed eyes, and sensed a tenseness about him she had never noticed before.

When he had looked at her his gaze, although not openly frightened, had a kind of fear written into it; again she realised intuitively that he wasn't terrified for *himself*, he had been frightened for *her*, and that was when she had walked away from him.

She pounded her fists on the bed in utter fury. If the story was true, and Tony was a descendant of Anton Baron, then it followed that he was in danger. She had a chance to show Tony just how much she cared for him and had turned her back on it.

Adding insult to injury, she had walked away refusing even to talk to him, as though he were guilty of some crime. Why had she not stayed with him, rather than running like a frightened rabbit to the loneliness and seclusion of her room?

Fear, hysteria, insecurity. Her anger at Tony for becoming interested in the story as it unfolded had somehow turned into resentment of him — and when

Margaret had asked the question about the name of the magician involved, she already half-knew the answer. When it was confirmed, however, she found herself resenting Tony for being mixed up in a situation which she could only envisage as an incomprehensible nightmare — as if he was to blame, or could alter his parentage.

Feeling angry again, and threatened, and that she could not take any more, she had walked away, attempting to keep her feelings hidden; but Tony's voice had been the catalyst which had forced her emotions to come tumbling out, causing her to hurry to her room.

Feeling lonely and guilty simultaneously, she went through to the bathroom, hoping that Tony had come up to his room. She hadn't heard anything to suggest that he had, but she felt that she couldn't sleep until they had at least talked and made peace. She would apologise for hurting him instantly if, as she feared, he had taken her actions to heart. She caught herself wondering if he cared about her; he hadn't exactly come running after her.

She knocked upon the door connecting his room to the bathroom but received no answer. Thinking that he wasn't there yet, she decided to try again later. Absently, she turned the handle, and immediately realised that the door wouldn't open. It had been locked from Tony's side.

Biting her lip, feeling more despondent than ever, she returned to her room to ponder this. Obviously, Tony didn't want to talk to her — poetic justice? her mind asked her, mischievously.

Smiling at the thought, although she still felt guilty, she undressed slowly, slid into her nightie and got into bed where she lay, arms behind her head, wondering what, if anything, she should do now. She leaned over, reaching for a cigarette which she smoked, her thoughts jumping over recent events.

Tony's reaction to being left alone in the restaurant was more a sense of confusion as to exactly *why* he was alone. If, as he suspected, the story he had heard was basically true, then it sounded as though it was more than his life on the line. The thing which surprised him most, however, was that he wasn't really frightened. He smiled grimly. He'd probably make up for it, eventually.

Like Margaret, Tony now thought he understood the link between Hayter, Anton Baron and himself. But there were gaps in his understanding. He wished that he had Hayter's letter to read again; he was sure that he would be able to read more into what it said now, but that was more trouble than it was worth. He had packed the letter into one of the suitcases still residing in the car.

He sat and drank the rest of the wine; great seduction it had turned out to be: great.

Irritation began to build in Tony; what was the problem with the bloody girl? At that moment he wanted her to be here next to him, just for her company (although he wouldn't have said no if she allowed herself to be seduced); but he was alone. Feeling mildly depressed he left the restaurant and walked slowly to his room.

His first inclination was to go into Margaret's room and demand to know why she had left him alone, but he wasn't in the mood for a row. He eyed the door to the bathroom, noticing the key in the lock. With a humourless smile he turned it, his movements suddenly becoming almost robotic.

"Well, Margaret, you're not going to sneak in here tonight to rape me." Although, perhaps not surprisingly, his mind didn't raise any objections to the idea.

He collapsed onto the bed, his mind going round and round; Hayter, hate her, Baron, hunt her, Hayter hate her Hunter hunt her hateherhunther-huntherhateher...

Sometime later, he stood, went to the door of the bathroom, unlocked it, and hesitated before entering

41

Margaret's room. She had been on the verge of sleep. Her eyes jerked open and she sat up, making sure that the bedclothes still covered her.

"Tony? Are you *very* angry at me? It was stupid of me to walk off like that: I'm sorry — honestly, I am. Forgive me? Please?" She half-smiled at him, although he appeared somewhat distant. His eyes travelled over her face, neck, shoulders, over the shape that she made under the sheets, as though this might have been the first time he had seen her.

"Nice speech," he said finally. "You're very good at making a mess of things and apologising afterwards: must have been born with the talent. Well, quite honestly, I'm sick of it. Do you think nothing exists in the world but you? Do you really expect me to devote every second of every day to making sure that I don't listen to something that you might not like, or trying to be certain that I don't say something that disturbs you? Am I asking too much to be allowed to get close to you, or is that frigid vacuum of yours too important? Are you *that* terrified of being hurt, Margaret?" He turned and stormed out.

The silence was complete, save for the sound of the door, which Tony slammed as he made his exit. She sat stunned in the bed, unable to believe what she had just heard. He wasn't one to overreact like that; she blushed as she thought over what he had said — and wondered whether or not he meant it, or had simply drunk too much.

Confused, tired, she got out of bed and ran to the bathroom and again tried the door to Tony's room, but it was locked. She pounded on it, but as before, he wouldn't answer her. Dejected, she went back to bed, feeling like the little girl she had been when, then as now, she was alone in the darkness; lonely and somehow afraid.

She glanced at the clock: 1:06 a.m. She hoped all this could be resolved; she refused to believe that Tony meant what he said. Restless and anxious now, she repeatedly turned the events of the last few minutes over in her mind. It was no wonder that, when she did sleep, her sleep was restless and fraught with dreams bordering upon nightmares.

Tony opened his eyes. Something was wrong. He knew it: unmistakable. He glared at the digital clock by his bed: 3:17 a.m. He hadn't meant to sleep — remembered only being undecided whether or not to confront Margaret about her actions.

But something wasn't right. Lying quietly, he examined his uneasiness and realised that there was a sense of manipulation, or impending danger, and as he tuned into his feelings more acutely, of terror.

In the same instant, he sensed that Margaret was in danger. He jumped out of bed, wondering vaguely why he was still fully dressed, even to his shoes, and was then wrestling with the door to the bathroom which wouldn't open. Damn, she had locked it from the other side.

Tony took one look at the lock and shook his head in disbelief, seeing the key where it belonged. This had to be some weird nightmare. Unlocking the door he ran, without knocking, into Margaret's room, ready to tackle whatever danger might be there.

There was nothing. She lay in bed asleep; no danger. Margaret's shriek was therefore so unexpected that Tony's heart hit a beat so hard he was sure it could have been heard downstairs. Attempting to control his sudden palpitation, he strode over to her, grabbed her shoulders and shook her. She didn't wake immediately. He began lightly slapping her face, saying, "Margaret, Margaret," in a soft, urgent voice.

Another shriek ripped its way from her throat, and Tony, in despair, shouted, "Margaret, wake up for God's sake," accompanying the shout with a sharp, open-handed slap to her left cheek.

Margaret's eyes bulged open, glaring, not recognising him for seconds, then, as her mind caught up with her body she clutched one hand to her cheek, covering the reddened imprint of his hand. She looked accusingly at him.

"Margaret, are you okay?" he asked, somewhat lamely.

She simply glared at him.

"Y'see, I woke up feeling that you were in some danger, and I ran in here — but the door was locked and I'm still dressed, and you screamed and I tried to wake you up but I..."

"You seem to have made a good job of it," Margaret shouted back, angrily indicating her cheek. She began to tremble with fury.

"Margaret, I didn't mean to hurt you; I was just...concerned."

She was about to hurl back a reply when she realised she could see his concern etched upon his face, could hear it in his voice.

"Tony, why did you lock your door and not let me talk to you?"

"But I didn't."

"And you didn't tell me you were sick of me, and accuse me of demanding all your time and attention? Didn't tell me that you had to be careful what you said to me? Didn't accuse me of keeping myself in what you called a frigid vacuum — whatever that might be?" she questioned, sceptically.

"Of course not — I've been asleep in bed since..." he trailed off, suddenly suspicious.

He looked at her, knew that she was trying not to let him see her fear, the residue of her dream, which was pouring from her in waves. He smiled at her as reassuringly as he could; he didn't realise that his suspicions turned his smile into a sickly parody of what it normally would have been, and that she noticed it.

"All right, Margaret, I think it's time for you to get dressed."

"What? Why?"

"There's something damned peculiar going on here, and I don't like it. I think it's a good idea to get moving." He looked directly at her, "What was the nightmare about?"

She attempted to lower her eyes, to break eye contact, but found it impossible. With mixed feelings, she took a deep breath and said, "I'll tell you in the car — if you're serious about wanting to go?"

"I am. Since we've been here nothing's been going as it should. I can't explain, but it just feels wrong."

"Maybe; perhaps you're right." She hesitated, not getting out of the bed. "You're not going to stand there and watch me, are you?"

"Yes, if the offer's open; if not, I'll make myself useful passing you your clothes." He smiled, the old smile that she remembered. Despite the uncomfortable memories floating in her mind, she caught the look in his eyes.

"No, the offer isn't open; and I can get my clothes myself."

He grinned. "I'll wait for you in my room. Shouldn't take long for you to pack your nightie, there isn't a lot to it; did you know it was see-through?"

She glanced at herself involuntarily — what Tony said was true. Further, in her anxiety, she hadn't noticed that the bedclothes had betrayed her, and fallen below the level of her breasts.

Fighting the crimson blush which rushed to her face, she pulled the bedclothes back to their previous position. "Out, Mr. Baron," she ordered, pointing at the still-open door to the bathroom.

He grinned again, and resisting the impulse to make another remark, meekly turned and went through to his room to wait for her.

She got out of bed and dressed as quickly as she could, replacing her nightie in the small case she had carried in with her — was it only hours ago?

She went through to Tony's room and they walked downstairs together, each feeling a peculiar sense of unreality about the time that they had stayed there. They walked out into the dark night, the snow crisp underfoot.

Less than two minutes later, Tony swung the car out onto the road, leaving behind the sign which boasted:

OOMS FU L ENGLI H CUIS NE   VA ANCY

Settling down in the cold car, a reaction seemed to hit Margaret. Her emotions had been pulled and stretched in every direction, and she felt a sense of relief that they were on their way again.

Trying to examine what had happened to them at the inn, neither of them seemed able to make a coherent whole of the segments that they remembered. Even when they compared memories, they ended up more confused than ever. The story they had been told about the Baron curse seemed vague and unreal, like the memory of a dream.

Margaret put a hand to her swollen cheek; she could just trace the ridges where Tony's hand had landed. It *had* hurt her, but at least it had freed her from the nightmare which she had been having.

She thought of similar blows inflicted upon her throughout her childhood, yet her father had never hit or punished her out of a sense of love; how could he have...

Wrenching the thoughts away, she realised that what had happened after she had been woken up seemed relatively clear in her mind; she found herself blushing as she recalled Tony asking if she realised her nightie was see-through. A flush of embarrassment flooded through her body; she wondered if he really had managed to see anything of her breasts — and was surprised to find that part of her hoped he had caught a glimpse of, well, *something*. The other part of her rebelled with fear at this possibility, and she took a curious pleasure from these two contradictory feelings.

Had he seen anything? Was her nightie see-through? She hadn't realised if it was, and she wore nothing underneath it. Well, it would have to remain one of those unsolved mysteries of life; there was no way on this Earth that Margaret was going to ask these questions of Tony.

Tony went through what he could remember of his time at the inn, but it seemed to be deleting itself from his memory, detail by detail. He wondered vaguely if he was overtired. He knew, but didn't know how he knew, that there was more to it than that. He found that he could remember everything that had happened since he had started awake feeling something was wrong.

He wondered if now would be a good time to attempt to get Margaret to relate something about herself to him. '*Had she been hurt by a previous relationship?*' he wondered. He simply didn't know. Perhaps getting her to confide about her nightmare might unlock some mysteries about her past: at least the opportunity was there, and Tony didn't intend to let it slip by.

"So," he said, deliberately keeping his voice neutral and low, "what was the nightmare about? You said you'd tell me."

She let out a sigh; this was it. Her heart began to pound, her nerves suddenly sent mild spasms through her body. She took several deep breaths, and glanced at him. His eyes were firmly on the road ahead, as though he knew just how difficult this was for her, and was trying to make it as easy as possible; she warmed to him, and this made the unpleasant task ahead that much easier. Her heart slowed its pounding and her nervous agitation became bearable — just.

"I was dreaming about something that happened when I was in my late teens. I suppose, really, I should tell you about my childhood first, or what I dreamed about might seem distorted.

"I've never really told you much about my parents — I don't know much about my mother, anyway. She died long before I ever could remember her, but you already know that.

"I don't know why it was, whether my father blamed me for my mother's death, or whether I was just too painful a reminder of her. I just don't know. Do you know what my first memory of my father is? The earliest?" Not waiting for a reply, now that she had begun, the past became compelling, and she continued: "It's of being smacked for not sitting down the instant I was told to. That might not sound extreme, but other beatings I was put through were.

"It seems to me, that as I got older, my father increased the severity of the — what word do I use? 'Punishment' implies that I'd deliberately done something wrong, and deserved to be beaten; yet I was beaten at times just for my father's pleasure. Anyway, the beatings were increased in severity as I grew older, regardless of whether I'd done something wrong or been a few seconds late when my father called me.

"I remember my ninth birthday," Margaret stated, bitterness beginning to creep into her voice. "Why do I remember it? Because I got lots of lovely presents and cards and had a birthday cake? Not quite. I remember my birthday present because it was from my father. He told me that now I was nine, I was old enough for him to beat me with his belt, rather than using his hand, or a slipper.

"It was a massive belt; made of leather; thick and heavy. And Jesus, when it hit you, you knew about it — even if it was only swung with moderate force, the pain was unbelievable. If he happened to be angry and used

48

his strength, every time it landed I remember being certain that all the skin where it had struck had been ripped away — excruciating wasn't the word.

"That was my birthday present, and I found out what pain it was capable of inflicting that same day; the beatings up to then had been relatively minor, by comparison.

"If a week went by when I'd only been beaten five or six times, I thought it was my lucky week. I thought every child was thrashed to the same extent. But the beatings weren't really the worst part.

"The worst thing, I think, was when I became aware of the presence of a sexual element that corresponded to when I was beaten. I don't mean that I got any thrill out of it, far from it. I somehow realised that it excited my father, beating me, hearing my cries, watching me flinch as every blow landed.

"He always made me strip before beating me, even when I was in my teens. I never knew which was worse, his ogling me while I stripped, or the pain that followed.

"I always had to strip naked — I couldn't just be naked from the waist down — that would have disappointed him, I think. It was part of the ritual. I can't even remember when his stripping me began; when I was about eight, I suppose.

"If I jerked out of the position I was supposed to be in, then it was just luck where the next stroke — I *hate* that word — would land. I soon learned which parts of my body were most sensitive."

"Is he still alive?" Tony asked, as she grabbed a cigarette, her nerves getting the better of her again.

"*Jesus*, I don't know, or care. I'll just be happy if I never see the bastard again."

"You were saying," Tony prompted, as gently as he could.

In a dull, resigned tone, Margaret continued: "Yes, I *was*, wasn't I? The stripping, the physical abuse went on

49

and on; I was terrified of him — still am, I think. It stopped just two months before my eighteenth birthday."

Tony held his breath, and after a moment, Margaret resumed.

"This was what I was dreaming about. My father wanted to beat me again, so he made up an excuse — it doesn't matter what — well, it never did to him. I went through the stripping ritual and ended up sort of bent over my bed. It was only when I heard his zip that I realised what he had in mind.

"I struggled; he punched me, really laid into me. If I hadn't stopped resisting I think he might have killed me. He...Tony, he..."

Margaret's tears rolled down her cheeks, her sobs choking off any words she might have tried to add.

"He raped you?" Tony asked, trying to keep his tone steady.

"He tried, but he couldn't...do it. The realisation made him furious. He began punching me again. He knocked me out; when I came to, he wasn't in the house. For the first time in my life, I made a decision for myself: I ran away.

"I took my clothes with me, and my bank book. I'd been saving money from my job for a long time. It took me nearly two years before I could accept that I was free of him and that it was *my* life. I was lucky, one of my friends from work put me up, gave me a shoulder to cry on."

With more strength in her voice, she added, "After that, things were really uneventful. I always seem to have nightmares about him when I'm upset, or tense."

Her voice trailed off, and the atmosphere in the car became almost strained. Now that she had purged herself of the demon within her, she felt more vulnerable than ever before. She realised that it was simply her insecurity, her fear that Tony might exploit the knowledge which she had given him. However, at another level, she knew she had only told him because she felt that she could trust him. It was her first attempt at trusting anyone with the knowledge of her childhood, and the unfamiliarity of the experience disorientated her.

She stared through the window, not knowing how to break the silence, wondering what his reaction would be. The lull stretched painfully long, and Margaret was just about to break it by asking him anything, anything at all, when he spoke.

"Christ, Margaret, why didn't you tell me earlier? I wish you had; it explains so many things that had me baffled — have you ever told anyone else?"

She shook her head. "No. At the time, I was terrified that he'd find me, and I just wanted to forget that it all ever happened. I did a fairly good job, I'd half-forgotten it, never brought it to mind; not until I met you and I knew that if things began to get serious I'd have to tell you, but I didn't think that I could do it."

"Are you glad you told me?"

"Ask me next year. I was frightened that you might think I led him on to..." She shook her head and continued, "Right now, if you want me to be honest, thinking about it, and talking about it make me feel sick. I think I'm glad I told you, but I'm not sure."

Tony reached out with his left hand and placed it upon her right. "I'll try and make you sure," he said.

It was this simple declaration that unlocked a mass of emotion from her. She sat gulping air, as her throat released a torrent of soundless, tearless sobs. They gradually subsided, and as she became aware of him watching her from the corner of his eye she managed a small smile and nodded at him, "I'm okay."

He smiled back at her, his own thoughts a mixture of disgust, loathing and utter rage towards Margaret's father. He gripped the steering-wheel with a ferocity of which he had not known he was capable.

The difficult thing to do was to lay his feelings to one side. It would do Margaret no good to realise just how her explanation had affected him, the anger it summoned.

Gradually relaxing his hand on the wheel, Tony went back over the time that he had spent with her. Things had suddenly fallen into place; he felt a pang of guilt at the times when he had thought of trying to seduce her, of the times when she had seemed to freeze when she thought he had gone too far. He should have guessed, he told himself, should have realised.

But a more rational part of his mind reminded him that he had been sensitive, hadn't pushed too far. If he had, his mind told him, Margaret wouldn't be sat next to him now.

They drove on in silence, she recovering her composure, he fighting his anger.

Glancing at a sign which seemed to rush past, Tony calculated that they were only about forty miles from Hayter's mansion. About another hour, he thought, looking at the clock on the dashboard. It was 4:56 a.m.

He began to wonder whether or not Margaret had fallen asleep. Her eyes were closed, her breathing seemed regular. Best thing for her, Tony found himself thinking, she must be worn...*JESUS*!

The car plunged into a bank of dense fog; visibility was drastically reduced. Tony was sure that he could not see more than a yard or so beyond the headlights. Braking hard, he reduced speed rapidly. Crawling along, he hoped that this fog bank would clear as quickly as it had appeared.

Margaret opened her eyes. "Fog? I don't believe it."

"You can believe it or not, but it's there. Sorry, I'm just tired. This'll slow us right down unless it's just a local quirk."

Inching their way forward, Tony wondered how it was that he hadn't seen the fog bank before he had hit it.

It was still dark, but he was certain that he would have noticed it normally. '*Must be more tired than I thought*', he argued in his mind. The road they were on was a winding affair, and 'road' was a rather grand title for it. But it was a shortcut — at least, Tony had believed so. Trees lined the road, and glimpsing them through the fog, Margaret thought that they looked evil, were hungry for human flesh. The thought made her shiver. She looked straight ahead from then on.

Twenty minutes later they were still crawling along; Tony began to feel his irritation mounting. At that moment, the fog thinned dramatically, and he couldn't help taking advantage of the renewed visibility to accelerate, hoping to get completely clear of the fog.

However, within a minute or so it descended again as thick as ever. Tony groaned. Margaret felt a vague sense of unease which she couldn't articulate, but it was there, nevertheless.

Again the fog thinned; Tony accelerated carefully, and then instinctively pushed the pedal all the way to the floor. The falling tree missed the car, but some of its smaller limbs hit the boot and rolled off, jolting it sickeningly.

Margaret looked at Tony. "Now I'm scared," she whispered. Tony nodded, tried to smile; failed. The fog thinned to a mist, but even before he could react it had thickened again to make visibility zero. He couldn't even see the road.

"I can't drive in this," he snapped angrily.

He glared at the fog through the windscreen; abruptly, it was gone and visibility could not have been better. Tony took full advantage, accelerating into the dawn light, nerves dictating his reactions.

Over an hour later, he turned into a drive marked as private and warned trespassers that they would be prosecuted. It seemed a long time before the mansion came into view, but when it did, Margaret couldn't believe what she saw.

It was as massive as the term suggested, and dominated a landscape where colours abounded — lawns, gardens, even a wood leading off to the south-east. The whole effect of the scene was breath-taking, and she thought that she had *never* seen anything so beautiful.

They moved closer to the mansion, and she couldn't help feeling that they were being watched; if not by somebody inside it, then by the mansion itself.

Tony pulled up opposite the doors. They were massive, and he was reminded of Peterson's words: "I've been told that you'll need a battering-ram to force the door open." It was true; it didn't look as if anybody would get into this mansion uninvited.

They climbed out of the car, their eyes constantly on the door barring their way inside. Margaret grabbed Tony's hand. Together, they walked to the massive door. As they approached, Tony saw a bell-pull, and shrugging his shoulders, he pulled it.

In the far distance, deep inside the mansion, a faint answering jangling sound could be heard. Both Tony and Margaret felt somehow exposed, standing, waiting for the door to be answered.

Tony reached for the bell-pull again, when the door opened smoothly.

"Yes?" said a voice.

Chapter Three: Determinations

"Yes?" the voice repeated. A tall man held the door open, gazing down at them in what seemed to be a mildly amused manner. His black suit only emphasised his ruddy complexion; his dark blue eyes focussed upon them intently. He was thin, but his body radiated physical strength.

"We've come to see George Hayter, I..."

"Your name, sir?"

"Tony Baron, but..."

"You are expected — both of you." He didn't seem to want to know Margaret's name. She looked at him, not knowing what to make of what she saw. Without saying another word, he motioned them to enter. The door crashed closed behind them.

"If you'll follow me, please."

Feeling that they had little option, they did so. Margaret took in the fact that the door opened onto a small hallway with three corridors leading off it. Through the central corridor she could see a flight of stairs, although where they might lead she could only guess.

Instead of walking straight ahead towards the flight of stairs the man turned towards the left hand corridor, which he followed. They passed numerous doors, until the corridor intersected with another. Turning left again, they followed him to the third door on the right. This door he opened and for the second time, he motioned them to enter.

Margaret looked around the room which she had entered; it was huge. A log fire burned and crackled, a seemingly welcoming sound. Although her apprehension about meeting Hayter had returned whilst getting out of the car, it receded quickly. The room was furnished with four leather chairs which faced a leather sofa larger than any Margaret had ever seen. Away from this, to the left, was a bar — this immediately caught Tony's attention.

Further away, dominating the other half of the room, was a concert grand piano, its lid reflecting the glow of the fire. Margaret looked at Tony, and then at the man who had admitted them, who stood simply watching their reactions.

"I'll take your coats and inform Mr. Hayter of your arrival; his instructions are you should make yourselves comfortable, and he will join you as soon as he is able."

He took their coats as they removed them. Tony wondered who the man was, and what his function was in his Great-Uncle's home. At that moment the man gazed at him and then at Margaret, smiled, and said, "I am John — Mr. Hayter's private secretary." He turned and left the room, closing the door quietly behind him. Margaret sat upon the sofa (trying not to make it squeak), whilst Tony headed straight for the bar.

"D'you want a drink, love?"

"No, thanks. I'm too nervous," she replied.

Tony grinned at her. He, too, was feeling nervous, but not just about meeting Hayter. The whole journey had been weird.

He poured himself a drink; whisky, ice and soda, and then sat next to Margaret on the sofa. He sipped his drink, turned his face to hers and kissed her cheek.

Now that they had reached their destination and could relax, all Margaret could think about was how tired she was becoming. She yawned, letting her eyes close briefly, listening to the comforting spit and crackle of the log fire. She let her head rest on Tony's shoulder, felt his arm ease loosely around her, comforting, yet not threatening or demanding.

Reacting to the various emotions that had troubled her in so short a time, it was little wonder that she felt pleasantly drowsy. She murmured, "Tell me about your Great-Uncle again."

Tony had already told her all he knew about his Great-Uncle, and this request surprised him more than a little. Still, it would do no harm— might even jog a few extra details from his mind. Sipping his drink whilst she listened and drowsed, he began:

"I never really learned much about him from my parents — I think I might have met him once, but I don't know whether or not the man I remember is him. I don't understand why they never referred to him, or what the promise was that Hayter said he made.

"I know more of him from his writings than from anything else. I think that Peterson was right in one thing — I've never heard of George Hayter being interviewed.

"Anyway, Hayter's books tell more about him than you might at first think. He explains occultism with such insight and clarity, it seems that he *must* have a phenomenal understanding of it — his books cover such a vast amount of the differing aspects of occult doctrine. Whether or not he's ever put the theory into practice, I don't know.

"He does have a reputation for having an extensive library of occult literature; whether or not that's true is anyone's guess. His critics, and there are quite a few of them, find it difficult to criticise the man himself, and have to be content with criticising his motives in publishing and simplifying occult literature.

"I suppose that a lot of the gaps will be explained when we meet him; he's taking long enough to get to us, isn't he? It's not as though he didn't know we were coming; we can't be interrupting him.

"This waiting is making me nervous. I feel tense — the atmosphere seems almost oppressive. You feel it?"

When no answer was forthcoming, Tony glanced down at Margaret, her head was upon his chest. Her eyes were closed, her breathing regular. She was asleep.

Sleeping so peacefully, trustingly, he realised that, whether or not she was glad that she had bared her past to him, she felt safe in his arms. He felt a curious urge to protect her from any hurt — the word 'love' dared to present itself to his mind, but he dismissed it immediately.

He glanced towards the door, half hoping that it would open and announce the arrival of his Great-Uncle, but the door remained closed. The silence within the room, save for the crackling of the logs, was strangely relaxing, and Tony suddenly felt very tired.

'*Probably all the driving catching up with me; and I didn't get much sleep*', he thought. He didn't even suspect that there might be more to it than that. He felt relaxed, calm, his eyes slowly looking over the room. Without his realising it they started to close. He began drifting, felt himself floating slowly into a sleep which promised to be incredibly peaceful. The sensation was so pleasurable that he had to savour it for as long as possible.

He forced his eyes open and smiled to himself as he gave Margaret a glance full of affection. Gently moving her, he got up, walked to the bar and poured himself another whisky. He was surprised at the effort it took to stop his eyes from closing; he had never felt so tired in all of his life. He drained his glass in one gulp and wandered back towards her, knowing only that he had to sleep.

He half-sat, half-collapsed onto the sofa; instantly he roused, looking to see whether or not he had woken her. She hadn't even registered the fact that he had fallen heavily next to her; she was breathing evenly, seemed completely relaxed and peaceful.

He grinned inanely. He drew her arm across himself, let her head rest as it had previously. He took a deep breath; only seconds later he was breathing as regularly as Margaret and sleeping just as deeply.

For a few minutes things remained exactly the same in that room. The two occupants slept soundly upon the sofa. The logs upon the fire spat and crackled. The calm atmosphere which the room exuded seemed almost unnatural.

Five minutes passed.

Ten.

Fifteen.

Twenty minutes after Tony had fallen asleep the door opened and two men entered the room. One of them went forward to Tony and then to Margaret, and lifted the eyelids of each. He proceeded to take first Margaret's pulse, and then Tony's. The first man nodded to the second, as he re-joined him at the door. Again they surveyed the unconscious occupants of the room, and both of them smiled.

Chapter Four: Deliberations

About twenty miles away, as the crow flies, a man sat reading in his study. He glanced up at the clock as it struck the hour. His associates would be arriving soon — and he was anticipating the meeting with pleasure.

He frowned, and then smiled. The result was beyond doubt; they were, after all, about to fulfil their curse. Yet the thought gave him a vague feeling of unease.

Abruptly he stood and strode out through the door of his study. He went downstairs, towards the cellar. At the cellar door he paused and smiled again. He opened the door and climbed down into the darkness below. Once at the foot of the stone staircase he strode confidently to the far wall. To all appearances it was exactly the same as the other walls. However this wall served a second purpose in that it concealed the fact that there were further steps cut into the rock behind it, which led down into the earth.

At his touch the wall moved — pivoted — slightly, allowing access to those stairs. He descended them slowly.

At the foot of them he stopped, the dank atmosphere seeming to welcome him back. He gazed around at the rough-hewn passages to which his cellar connected. He knew every turn and blind passage within this maze — and a few which led into deeper caverns.

With this in mind, he set off to the area in which tonight's meeting was to be held. Because of the nature of the meetings the locations were frequently altered, his colleagues only being informed of the meeting-place as little as hours before the assemblies were due to begin.

On reaching the cavern in question he was pleased to see that all necessary preparations had been made. Glancing around he located the niche behind which was a smaller cave. Having entered, he slowly undressed and, opening a small suitcase which lay upon a table in the centre of the cave, he donned the contents. A richly brocaded robe, a mask which covered the upper part of his face, and a ceremonial dagger.

Whilst he was doing this, a hum of noise told him that some of his colleagues had already arrived. Mentally gauging the time, he decided that he would make his appearance in about ten minutes. He removed his mask, wiping his brow; at that same moment another man entered the cave, somewhat more timidly than had the first.

"All are assembled, Supreme Brother," he said, in a servile tone.

"Good: leave me. Instruct our Brothers to be ready."

The second man inclined his head. His master didn't deign to turn and face him, but the other had seen his face enough times to know his leader's everyday identity. It mattered little. Knowing who comprised the Brotherhood didn't constitute a danger; relating that information to others — he shuddered as he thought of the probable consequences. Nothing could have induced him to reveal the Brotherhood's secrets. He needed the Brotherhood, as did they all to a greater or lesser degree, to cater to the darker side of his personality. He thought of the Brothers as his brothers — in practises and depravities, if not in any genetic sense of the word. The Brotherhood satisfied his deepest needs and desires, and demanded relatively little in return. He felt comfortable with the arrangement.

He returned to the cavern where most of the Brothers waited. Interestingly, only the hierarchy were cloaked and hooded, the rest wore every day clothes. The hierarchy apart, the gathering might simply have been there to admire the perfection of the system of caves; in fact, they were there for other purposes that night.

About one hundred and eighty people were assembled. They sat in three semicircles, facing a low dais; the hierarchy in the third circle, closest to it. Talk was spasmodic, but serious. One sound which was conspicuous by its absence was laughter, which had no place here.

All muttering died away the instant that the figure of the Supreme Brother came into view and approached the platform. He stood for a second upon the dais before sitting down; then he glanced at the three semicircles gathered to present the latest information about the various projects which the Brotherhood had sponsored.

Supreme Brother's gaze came to rest upon a cloaked and hooded Brother sitting in the third circle. The Brother moved restlessly under the penetrating stare.

"Brother Paul, how do our overseas affairs, especially the drugs?"

Brother Paul stood, facing the Supreme Brother, and said, "All is as was approved previously. With the co-operation of our American Brothers, we are smuggling massive quantities of illicit drugs into Europe each day. The amount smuggled may be increased with only a few days' notice required — our agents negotiate the sales to interested parties, and," here, he permitted himself the barest of smiles, "I can say that our bank balance is healthy."

This statement was greeted with an amused murmur, The Supreme Brother nodded, and made a gesture for Brother Paul to resume his seat.

"Brother Paul fulfils all my expectations of him — and more besides. Your responsibilities are dangerous ones, and your endeavours — your *successes* — shall be rewarded. The next time we offer human sacrifice, when we torture or defile an outsider for the gratification of our Patron Demons, or for the pleasure of the Brotherhood, this I swear; you shall be the one that tortures, that defiles. Are you content?"

At this point, Brother Paul could have declined the honour without compromising himself in any way;

indeed, he could have chosen his own reward, within reason. But he simply looked at the Supreme Brother, and replied, "You value me too highly, but I am well content."

Ignoring the remark, the Supreme Brother swept his gaze around the circle of robed figures again.

"Brother Jerome, give us your report upon the journalist — he who tried to expose our Brotherhood. Has all been resolved?"

Another man rose to his feet. He stared defiantly at the Supreme Brother, and could get away with this insolence because it was characteristic of his zeal in the Brotherhood's service. In a surprisingly quiet voice, he addressed the dais but also turned his head to left and right as he spoke, as though asking everyone assembled for approval.

"Supreme Brother, things had become much more dangerous than any here had supposed. The reporter was much closer to us than had been believed."

"How could that be? Give me *details*, Brother."

Brother Jerome approached the dais and laid a small book upon it.

"This speaks more eloquently than I. Read of treachery, of betrayal, by one who is even now within this cavern — present at this meeting," he snarled.

Slowly, his eyes never leaving Brother Jerome's face, the Supreme Brother picked up the book. He broke eye contact in order to read; what he read made him roar with anger.

"You have done *well*, Jerome." Use of the ritual name not prefixed by 'Brother' was a rare compliment. "The reporter?"

"Dead — no suspicion may attach itself to me."

"There are no other copies of the information within this book?"

"There were three sets in all. One you hold; the second was in the memory banks of a computer.

Unfortunately, due to a disruption of the supply of electricity and the magnetic field which ensued, that information has been erased."

"You located the third copy?"

"Yes; the reporter was extremely anxious to tell me its location before he died. That copy, too, has been destroyed."

Although this was good news, the atmosphere within the chamber had become icy. The Brothers glanced at each other surreptitiously, knowing that this was not the end of the matter. The Supreme Brother motioned for Brother Jerome to resume his seat, which he did, still glaring zealously.

Supreme Brother glared slowly at the assembled Brothers, noting any who refused to meet his gaze. He could have used his occult powers to locate the traitor, yet did not feel that he would need to.

The tension built up. Each Brother — innocent though they were — breathed an inaudible sigh of relief when Supreme Brother's eyes moved on. But for one Brother, this relief was short-lived.

"Brother John," the Supreme Brother whispered, in a tone more menacing than any normal speech could have achieved. "In the book, provided so excellently by Brother Jerome, I find a list of the larger corporate companies which are controlled by our Brotherhood." The voice became harsh. "How is it that the reporter got hold of this list?"

Brother John stood. "Supreme Brother, you know that I have ultimate responsibility for that area of our labours. I must take partial blame for this treachery. But, Supreme Brother, I have never betrayed my trust or my Brothers — look into my mind and see that I speak only the truth."

"Then," said the Supreme Brother coldly, "we must look elsewhere. Brother John, who had access to this information besides yourself?"

"Only one, Supreme Brother." He turned and looked at a Brother sitting in the second circle. "Brother William — but I find it hard to believe that he betrayed us."

The Supreme Brother turned his gaze upon Brother William.

Under that compelling stare, Brother William stood. "I ask for no forgiveness, for no leniency. Supreme Brother, Brother John is blameless. I abused his trust. I am guilty of this treachery; I have betrayed my Brothers."

Supreme Brother listened with an inscrutable expression on his face. "Brother John is one of the most trustworthy of us all; his previous works on our behalf would be enough to forgive him a *hundred* errors of judgement. Do not fear for Brother John."

The look became appraising. "Tell me why you betrayed us."

"I needed money quickly — the reporter was blackmailing me. He had some compromising photographs..." Brother William kept his eyes averted as he made this confession.

"Did you never think of appealing to your immediate superior?" Then, in a voice approaching a roar, he demanded: "Did you never think to disclose this situation to *me*?" Shaking his head, the Supreme Brother continued more quietly, "Could we not give a Brother in need *every* assistance, to the point of destroying your antagonist? We would have helped you, whatever the difficulties; but to *betray* your Brothers — you understand the consequences of your actions?"

"I do, Supreme Brother," he said, blanching visibly.

"Brothers Simon and Mark will be your custodians until your ritual execution. Brother Paul, you may not act in this matter, as it is the result of an act of betrayal. The execution will not be for the gratification of either ourselves or our Patrons, and it does not involve an unbeliever."

Brother Paul nodded his understanding. His would be the next uninitiate to fall into the Cult's hands.

Simon and Mark, who had no business to relate to the Supreme Brother, took hold of Brother William. At that second, a flash seemed to erupt from the eyes of the Supreme Brother and Brother William fell, senseless, into their arms.

"He will cause you no problems. Go now, and keep him secure until our next meeting, when this matter will be resolved."

With an awkward bow in the Supreme Brother's direction, the two Brothers withdrew carrying their semi-comatose burden.

The meeting quickly returned to business. Brothers stood, made various reports, and were commended or censured. Brother Jerome was especially commended, the Supreme Brother even offering him a cold smile with his congratulations. He promised Jerome a reward, which was declined, zealously. Supreme Brother nodded his understanding of Jerome's reaction.

"Now, Brother Martin; you had a special mission. I wanted you to ensure that the American side of the Baron lineage has been terminated. Let us hear your report."

"Supreme Brother, and Brothers," he began, and, noticing the frown growing on Supreme Brother's face, he quickly continued: "I decided to take one assistant with me to the USA, and we were given every possible aid by our American Brothers.

"We," he said, indicating a Brother called Gregory, who sat within the second circle, "checked the records very carefully. A female descendant of Anton Baron was the cause of our problems. Whilst our predecessors concentrated on the male members of the Baron line, the females were neglected to an extent. A female

66

descendant of Anton Baron decided on a 'new life', whether through fear of us or not I cannot say, and she took ship for America.

"However, the ship was lost, and it was years before it was realised that a few survived — the woman in question amongst them. She married, and thus, an American line descending from Baron was formed.

"After painstaking researches and following various hypotheses, I have reached the following conclusion. Supreme Brother, the last of the American Barons died in July of 1943; that line of descent is extinct."

"SUPREME BROTHER," thundered a voice from the second circle. Despite his normal poise the Supreme Brother jumped at the unexpected noise, the echoes of which took moments to die away. He looked at the red-faced Brother who had stood and was glowering at Brother Martin. It took him a second to connect the name with the face; when he had done so, he spoke quietly. "Brother Gregory, calm yourself. Why do you interrupt your superior Brother in this way?"

Brother Gregory turned slightly to face the Supreme Brother. "I regret the nature of my interruption, Supreme Brother, but I *must* speak. I *cannot* agree with Brother Martin's contention, and have told him so. But he, as is his right, believes that I am merely trying to bring myself to your attention."

The Supreme Brother turned his face towards Brother Martin. "This angers me," he said quietly, his tone of voice seeming to freeze the air within the cavern. "The matter of our vengeance upon the Baron line is of paramount importance — our curse *MUST* be fulfilled. *Nothing* must be left to chance. If there is *one* possibility in a million — *in a hundred billion*, that the American line is *not* extinct, I want to know."

Brother Martin licked his lips nervously.

"Then, Supreme Brother," said Brother Martin, "under your criteria, I cannot with *absolute* certainty state that the American lineage is extinct."

The Supreme Brother gazed at Brother Martin with open contempt. "Perhaps I placed the wrong Brother in charge of this operation. I *will* hear Brother Gregory's contentions."

Eagerly, Brother Gregory approached the dais. He had come prepared and spread several papers upon the platform. Intrigued with what he was being shown and with the explanations which Brother Gregory was providing, the Supreme Brother nodded slowly.

Chapter Five: Observations

The two men stood looking at the couple sprawled upon the sofa for a minute or so, before the man who had opened the door and introduced himself as John broke the silence.

"That was a first-rate idea; they are dead to the world. Are you sure there is no possibility that we might wake them?"

"Certain," replied the other. "They will not wake. Young Mr. Baron has a much stronger will than I gave him credit for. That could be awkward, but not especially so."

Both men returned their attention to Tony and Margaret, who were totally oblivious to what was occurring around them.

"Do you want me to move them now, sir?"

"Yes, John, I think so."

"Erm, separate ah...rooms, I take it, sir?" he enquired, smiling slyly.

"Yes, John, separate rooms," agreed the other, smiling grimly. There was no trace of humour in the smile. He watched, still smiling, as John picked up Tony, and disappeared through the door carrying him in his arms with no apparent effort.

The second man gazed intently at Margaret. From his expression, it would have been impossible for anyone to comprehend what was passing through his mind. He stood staring at her in that same way until, some time later, John reappeared.

He picked up Margaret as easily as he had Tony. "My God, they are in for one hell of a surprise when they wake up," he said as he headed for the door.

"You can count on that," said the second man, with another of his humourless smiles.

Neither Tony nor Margaret had shown the least sign of wakefulness as John had picked them up. He would have been startled had they so much as sighed.

As he left the room carrying Margaret, the second man's gaze followed him. He ran a finger down the bridge of his nose, thinking deeply. Standing motionless, he pondered recent developments. He was certain that he had made the right decision and was *hoping*, with a vague uneasy feeling, that he would not have cause to regret his actions.

He was still pondering this when, fifteen minutes later, John returned.

"You know, John, when you're puzzled, you don't make any attempt to hide the fact."

"I don't understand. Who is the girl?"

"Mr. Baron's girlfriend, and she's complicated things, somewhat." After a pause he added: "Thanks, John, you can go now."

John smiled and left the room, closing the door behind him. The second man remained puzzling over these complications. It could destroy all that he had worked for — and he determined that he would not allow *that* to happen.

It irritated him more than he cared to admit that plans which he had laid so carefully had suddenly been disrupted; yet he tried to take this as philosophically as he could.

He wondered to what extent, if any, Tony knew of the danger that he was in. Of course, he must know, or at least have a very good idea. He had taken the bait, hadn't he? He was here, wasn't he?

More seriously, he thought of the months, or was it only weeks ahead? He believed he knew what the outcome would be, at least as far as he was concerned; but he did not fear death, he simply felt sad at the prospect.

He sat on the sofa which had formerly been occupied by Tony and Margaret, and wondered what their reactions would be when they woke up in the rooms that John had taken them to. The time for explanations would soon come. He didn't like the prospect of being quizzed, but it would have to be gone through sooner or later. He preferred sooner. Should he tell them about the state of his health, he wondered. They had to know, he decided. The difficult thing would be picking the right time to tell them.

He felt a twinge of pain across his chest. He frowned, his right hand moving to massage the area. He stood and strolled over to the piano. He opened the lid, raised it, rested it on its support strut, and then sat on the piano stool, gazing at the white and black keys.

After only a momentary hesitation, he placed his hands upon them and began to play. It always soothed him, playing; the notes of Grieg's piano concerto filled the room.

He wondered how far the relationship between his two guests had developed — emotionally as well as physically.

He stopped playing abruptly, in mid-cadence, as another twinge hit his chest. Standing, he closed the piano carefully, and left the room. As he walked through the maze of corridors and past the doors which constituted his home, he found himself a little unsure of how he should proceed now that his guests had arrived. Entering his study he went directly to the safe, dialled three separate combinations and having opened it, took out the contents.

Amongst them was a book, reputed to have been both written and used by Anton Baron, on that tragic night, long ago...

He smiled the mirthless smile which so often appeared upon his features and replaced the book within the confines of the safe. Perhaps later...

Settling himself into his chair which was situated behind a large desk, he studied the almost bare desktop. To his left lay a brown manila file, creased from constant study. He took hold of it, opened it and poured over the contents again. It was a dossier on Margaret Hunter. He sighed as he read the all-too-familiar story; two paragraphs further, he laid the file aside, a look of contempt crossing his features for the briefest instant. He looked up as a knock sounded on the study door.

"Come in, John," he said, sitting back in his chair.

John entered, carrying a tray. A glass of water and a small glass bottle rested innocently upon it. "I'm sorry, sir, but you should have taken these half an hour ago."

The other looked coldly at John, then his face softened. "I *do* employ you to make sure I take my medication on time, you know."

"I'm sorry," John replied calmly. "But with seeing to the erm, comforts of the guests, the time slipped my mind."

"Forget it, John, I'll take them now."

Having taken the tablets, he took the tray from John's hands and put it on the desk between them, saying, "Sit down, John."

As John sat, the other smiled at him. "You've got something on your mind."

John smiled back. "I can never hide my thoughts from you. Tomorrow, when I take the guests their breakfast, do I answer any questions?"

The other man smiled again. "Of course not. I've ensured that they'll sleep the day and night through. Towards dawn tomorrow, they'll be sleeping fairly lightly. For the rest of today you could parade a circus through their rooms and they'd be none the wiser."

John grinned back at his 'employer'. "But they'll want to know how they got into the rooms that they are in."

"Well, I think...yes, tell them that they fell asleep downstairs, and you were kind enough to put them to bed."

"The young lady might find *that* a little embarrassing; I followed your instructions to the letter: stripped them naked, put them in bed, and took their clothes away."

"Well, if she seems embarrassed, tell her you kept your eyes shut whilst you did it," he replied, and actually laughed.

"If that's what you want."

"At the moment, it is."

John nodded, picked up the tray and left the study, quietly closing the door behind him.

Alone once more, the man thought more seriously about Margaret. Had he gone *too* far in having her stripped before being put into bed? He decided that he had not. It would, at least, give her something to think about when she woke up. He chuckled, a deep bass sound, which reverberated from somewhere within his chest. '*Really*', he thought, '*you must take this more seriously.*'

Another thought answered the first: '*I've taken it seriously for over fifty years, and never had cause to laugh.*' Throughout these thoughts, he still chuckled. As his mirth evaporated he breathed deeply and became aware of the fact that he felt tired.

He felt *old*; more than that, he felt the exertions of the previous night — of this early morning, really — and decided that he would feel more human after some sleep. Accordingly, he heaved himself out of his chair, crossed to the door, left the study and went to his bedroom.

As with everything else in the mansion, his bedroom was huge. On one side it connected with an equally large bathroom. On the other was an ante-room, where some of his clothing was kept. An unusual feature of the bedroom was that it had no windows and was, therefore, dark unless artificially illuminated. Turning the lights on,

73

he undressed, absently put on a nightshirt, climbed into the four-poster bed, turned out the lights and tried to sleep.

At first, sleep eluded him. His mind began to race, touching on everything that he had thought about that day. This was a regular occurrence, and he expected it.

Thoughts of the resistance he had encountered when putting Tony to sleep made him smile. He was a true Baron, no doubt of it. Margaret had been asleep scarcely a second after he had begun to concentrate. Perhaps she had been more tired than Tony — but he marvelled at the ease with which she had welcomed oblivion.

Sleep. That was what he was supposed to be doing, he reminded himself. Mentally forcing his conscious mind blank and slowing his breathing at the same time, it took only a few seconds for him to pass into a relaxed, calm void.

His eyes snapped open the very instant that a soft, almost hesitant knock became audible. Sitting up, he turned on the lights, glanced around, and blinked a couple of times.

Without saying anything, as though the very fact that the lights had been turned on were in itself permission, John entered.

"It's just gone five O'clock; I thought you might want to check on our guests."

"Yes, John, I will do, but first I need a shower. I feel dead."

"Well, sir, you don't *look* dead, if that's any consolation."

He looked at John with raised eyebrows, unsure if he was attempting humour or not.

"Well, dead or not, I'd like lemon tea, please."

John smiled. "It'll be here when you finish showering."

The other nodded his appreciation. Discarding his nightshirt, he made his way to the bathroom as John disappeared.

Having showered he dressed and then made his way back to his study, sipping his lemon tea as he went.

He retrieved the contents of the safe and sat behind the desk. He glanced through the book which had descended to him, so he believed, from Anton Baron. It detailed many strange and obscure rituals and ceremonies: incredibly powerful incantations; however the *most* interesting feature was the fact that alongside each were *scribbled* notes, detailing the dangers inherent with the use of each particular ceremony or incantation.

Who had inserted these notes wasn't known. He had checked them, and found that they were accurate as far as they went. He brought a sheaf of papers which comprised the rest of the contents of the safe to his desk and, comparing the two, he located the passage corresponding to the one which he was studying in the book.

Smiling, as he reread his handwriting upon the sheaf, the thought crossed his mind that this was *one* manuscript which he would never have published; Anton Baron's book, but with his own notes and insights incorporated into it.

He became absorbed with what he was doing, making an entry here, an amendment there, made a note to research a point he wasn't sure of, and time passed.

He only became aware of how long he had been working when John quietly entered the room, bringing his medication. He sat back with a resigned sigh. He took the medication without comment, then realised that if this was his *second* of the day, then it must be later than he thought.

He checked his watch. It was *much* later than he had even suspected. He massaged his eyes, then looked up at John's face and saw the unspoken question there.

"Yes, John, you're right! I *should* have checked on our guests long ago, but I got rather *interested* in what I was doing and I lost track of time..." he broke off, noticing the smile which appeared on John's face. "Okay, what's so funny?"

"Well, I've heard that one so many times — it could be the *Hayter Family Motto*."

"Heard *what* one?"

"That 'got rather interested in what I was doing and lost track of time' speech. I've heard it every week for the past nine years. I *knew* you were going to say that."

George Hayter smiled. "Am I really that predictable, John?"

"Only when you've got carried away, and feel that you have to defend yourself."

Hayter laughed, "Remind me to put 'Impertinent' on your reference, John."

"If it's all the same to you, I'd rather not."

Hayter laughed again as John turned and left the room. Had John really been with him nine years? Good lord, it didn't seem that long. Amused, despite himself, George Hayter decided that it was time for him to check on the welfare of his guests. As a host, he had been somewhat lacking in manners, he thought. It caused a smile to crease his features again. He left his study and ambled toward the wing that housed Tony, and, further on, Margaret.

He made his way slowly to Tony's room. On entering, he turned on the lights and then, using a dimmer switch on the wall, he softened it until it was a dull glow, but still adequate to see by.

He approached the bed and gazed down upon the unconscious form of his only living relative. Tony lay, sleeping deeply, on his side. Thinking that they were the last two of the Baron line saddened him. There had once been an American offshoot of Anton Baron's descendants, but it had become extinct in 1943. He remembered Scott Hobard, although they had only met once. Scott had researched his lineage and somehow had found Hayter, whom he had visited one weekend. Only weeks later, he was dead.

Now, it was just Hayter and Tony against — he didn't even know the approximate numbers that comprised the Cult. He knew the Cult had grown alarmingly — the decrease (or decease) of his own family was a testament to that.

He smiled a bitter/sad smile at his relative, and then, turning, he retraced his steps, turning out the lights before closing the door.

As he made his way to Margaret's room, George thought briefly of Scott, remembered the familiar story Scott had told him about the death of his mother; a bus out of control, his mother never regaining consciousness.

He shook his head sadly as he stood outside Margaret's room. He entered, wondering if she would live out her normal lifespan or would the Cult, taking no chances, murder her as surely as it had murdered others of the Baron line.

He gazed at her face, not smooth in peaceful sleep, but frowning in anguish, and quickly became more alert. As he watched, she twisted in the bed, half uncovering herself in the process. She cried out unintelligibly. What she was having a nightmare about he wasn't sure, but he could guess. The point was that she should *not* be having any nightmares at all.

He could only explain this phenomenon to himself by assuming that she had been unnerved by the unpleasant occurrences which she experienced as the journey here neared completion. Nevertheless, he found that he couldn't stand there watching her have a nightmare — not when he had the power to help her.

He reached out, touched her forehead, then withdrew his hand. His eyes became distant as he concentrated, focusing his will. "Margaret, sleep calmly; you will not have nightmares whilst you remain within my mansion." As he spoke, Hayter made a gesture as if he was throwing a handful of air in the direction of her face. She became quiet immediately. He took hold of the bedclothes and drew them up, covering her. Suddenly, he smiled at her, surprising himself.

"Pleasant dreams, Margaret," he said, as he switched out the light and left the room.

He returned to his study, having made a detour to get a book on the Baron lineage from his library, and there he settled down to muse over his ancestry.

The lineage had been drawn back only as far as Anton Baron as he had been an orphan, parents unknown. The line descended through John Baron, illegitimate son of Anton. According to the list John Baron had fallen under a wagon and been crushed. He had left a son, Paul, who eventually sired three illegitimate children before he tripped and was impaled on a metal stake.

Hayter grinned despite the nature of the material that he was reading. It seemed very easy to carry out a curse back then; a convenient stake, or wagon.

The first child, a girl, died in infancy. Of the other two children, James and Henry, it was known that each had married and each produced a child. The statement that James had: 'accidentally decapitated himself' caused another grim smile to linger on Hayter's face. It was, after all, hardly a convincing report.

It appeared to Hayter that things began to get awkward for the Cult about the time that one of Anton's descendants left Britain for America.

He moved over the list, jumping from ancestor to ancestor, from murder to murder, although almost all causes of death were officially accidental.

Hayter finally reached his nephew. He sighed. The Cult had certainly made sure that day. Tony's parents had been mangled beyond recognition even though

Tony's mother was guilty of no other sin than bearing him, it had been enough to condemn her. It was a grim reminder of the guest he had recently visited.

His own father was on the list — a form of blood poisoning, it had been called. He suspected the truth, however. Officials, in their wisdom, had been unable to pinpoint the cause of the blood poisoning: cause unknown.

And what would be the manner of his own death, he caught himself wondering, discarding the lineage in favour of the book he was updating and revising.

Turning to the last pages of the copy which he had made, Hayter puzzled over the final few lines seemingly having nothing to do with the rest of the book, so far as he could tell. It had been scribbled in the original book by the same hand that had made notes against the rituals described. Having modernised it, it read almost as prophesy.

> 'When the flesh of my flesh again be united, then
> Shall my kin do battle with my eternal enemies;
> The days of the Brotherhood shall at last be
> Numbered — my offspring, even though it mean their
> Death, shall enable my victory.'

Hayter had puzzled over that one verse more than he had anything else in his lifetime. It seemed obvious to him — had done for a long time — that the only way the flesh of Anton's Baron's flesh could be united would be when he and Tony were united. Then, united in purpose and in blood, they could begin to fight back against the Cult.

But what then? The prophesy — if that was what it was — seemed to state that at least one of the last descendants of Anton Baron would come very close to death — if not die in the attempt to extirpate the Cult.

Annihilation of the Brotherhood was Hayter's goal. Anything less would not mean the removal — or rather the destruction — of the curse which had haunted his family for generations.

If he had to die then so be it, he was prepared for that possibility; but he would be damned before he would allow the Cult to exterminate the entire Baron line, as they undoubtedly would unless they were stopped, and they had to be stopped soon.

He glared at the page before him, bringing the verse back into focus. He did not know how much trust he could put into what was written. Anton Baron had not been known for prophesy, although a gut feeling told him that there was more to the verse than met the eye. He wanted to trust his intuition, but wasn't sure that he could ask Tony and Margaret to do the same. His instincts about the verse, he felt, were as fallible as anyone else's.

At one time he had had all his plans laid out — as far as anyone could lay plans when threatened by a curse of death. He had envisaged meeting Tony, explaining things, maybe even tutoring him in certain occult mysteries pertinent to the desperate situation in which they were embroiled.

Although that had been his original idea, the wide plan on which all other considerations had been based, he had never even thought that things might become more complicated by Tony becoming involved with a woman — even though the Baron line had more than its share of illegitimacy.

Knowing of Tony's interest in the occult — an interest which had seemed strangely non-existent in other Baron family members, as far as he knew —

Hayter had, perhaps naively, believed Tony's studies would overcome all other interests. Obviously, in Tony's case, he had inherited some of the more physical inclinations which were inherent in the attributes of the Baron family genes.

When he found out about Margaret, he had erupted into a fury which startled John into insisting that he take an extra dose of medication. After calming enough to think clearly, Hayter had the idea of preventing them from seeing each other, which he could have achieved fairly easily. However, two things stopped him.

The first thing was the adage that absence makes the heart grow fonder, which implied to him that he might defeat his own objective.

Secondly, he became convinced the more he thought about it, that he had no right to interfere. If this was an obstacle, he would overcome it, providing the obstacle was what it appeared and not an attempt at manipulation and murder by the Cult.

Accordingly, he had checked into Margaret's every move — he had her checked so thoroughly that he knew her better than she did herself. In less than three weeks he had found out all her secrets and more. It had taken Tony nearly eight months of effort to prise less information from her.

All this time, whilst waiting for the correct moment to make contact with Tony, he had resented her and the fact that she had thrown the proverbial spanner into his works. He was so methodical that *any* forced alteration to his plans annoyed him. As she had mixed herself up in the curse by dating Tony, Hayter had been forced to invite her here with him; and although that didn't exactly cause a crisis it would be a distraction — an unwelcomed one.

She would be an annoyance; and who would end up looking over his shoulder every five minutes to make sure that she was okay? He shook his head angrily. The verse hadn't mentioned Baron's relatives having to look after a girlfriend whilst they fought for their lives.

Musing over this he again felt angry and resentful. What right did she have to force him to alter his plans? Another part of his mind told him he was being unreasonable, that she hadn't understood — how could she?

But the part of his mind that wanted to feel aggrieved about all the effort that had to go into new plans and new ideas told him he was justified in feeling resentful. Her animosity to anybody who studied the occult was another reason for his rancour.

With a deep sigh, he settled back into his chair. Yes, Margaret was a new variable suddenly thrust into the equation. What effect that might have on the outcome — if any — was incalculable.

A smile threatened his face. He knew she had tried to stop Tony studying the occult, and that she could not have succeeded. When a descendant of Anton Baron took to studying occultism, no power on Earth could hinder or prevent that individual from striving to achieve their goal. Still, she had tried, and he found that fact hard to forgive. He expected to have a difficult time when he went to see her tomorrow — today, he amended, as he glanced at his watch.

He was certain that tempers would run high, and given his own present antipathy towards her, he knew he would not take much provocation. He simply would not stand for anything less than total cooperation from her. If she wouldn't give it, fine. She could be physically prevented from leaving, in the interests of her own safety. If, however, she was reasonable, and cooperated, then the time ahead might not be as daunting for him as it had at first appeared.

He thought of the nightmare which she had experienced and then of how he had neutralized it. That she had been victim to any bad dreams whilst in his mansion puzzled him slightly; and the sadistic affections to which her father had subjected her angered him. Yet paradoxically, it made him think of her in a new light — one which irritated him far less, despite the inconvenience which she had caused.

Taking into account his contradictory and paradoxical feelings concerning her, he frowned. It was a long time since any female had perplexed him to this extent.

Rubbing his eyes, he stood, made his way to his study door, not realising he had not replaced the material that he had been working on in the safe. There was, anyway, no likelihood of it being stolen.

He made his way to his bedroom, undressed, put on a clean nightshirt, and slowly eased himself between the sheets of his bed. As always, his mind began to revolve around the day's events and to force questions upon his consciousness. He dismissed such questions as what would Margaret's reaction be, what was he going to say to her and so on.

Refusing to let any more distractions prevent him, he slept.

Chapter Six: Contentions

The last echoes of Brother Gregory's voice died away within the cavern. The entire assembly sat, some holding their breath, knowing that if Brother Gregory had failed to justify his interruption to Supreme Brother's satisfaction a harsh punishment would ensue.

Brother Gregory stood gazing at Supreme Brother, trying to assess whether or not his reasoning had been followed and accepted. Try as he might, he could glean nothing from the face which stared impassively back at him.

Hesitantly, he reached for the papers which he had placed upon the dais and picked them up. Assuming that he had been dismissed, and hearing nothing to the contrary, he turned to retake his position within the second circle.

"Stay."

Just one word, uttered softly. Gregory stood dead in his tracks, felt his fear mounting, his heartbeat racing as he turned back to face Supreme Brother's cold glare. He had known the danger he was courting the moment he opened his mouth to attract the Supreme Brother's attention. Now he regretted his action. For interrupting in the way he had whilst the meeting was in progress and shouting down his immediate superior, the punishment could not be light.

"Brother Martin, are you *still* of the opinion that Brother Gregory is merely attempting to bring himself to my attention?"

Brother Martin stood. He did not believe Brother Gregory's contentions any more than Brother Gregory believed his, but there was no personal animosity between them. He answered as honestly as he could. Feeling the gaze of the Supreme Brother boring into him, he weighed his words carefully. "I *do* think so. But I think his desire was simply to let *you* judge the matter, rather than accept my judgement."

Brother Martin felt an immense relief as the penetrating gaze moved from him and settled onto Brother Gregory.

"Brother Gregory, I too believe that you wished to bring yourself to my notice."

Gregory hung his head. "Supreme Brother," he replied quietly, "I believed that what I had discovered was of importance, and since Brother Martin would not bring it to your attention I determined that I must do so. If I was wrong, I await my punishment — but I must say this," and he glared straight into the Supreme Brother's face. "I do *not* regret my action. If, another time, I am entrusted with a similar mission and feel I have important information to disclose, I will interrupt the Supreme Brother himself, if I must, to be heard. Having been heard, I am content."

An amazed whisper broke out among the three circles. Nobody ever dared speak that way to the Supreme Brother whilst in his direct presence. They waited for his roar of anger and each, within his own mind, pondered what punishment would be Brother Gregory's reward for his impertinence. The conservative amongst the gathering favoured the lash — whilst the more extreme pondered the slow removal of some fingers. All waited for Supreme Brother's reaction.

Slowly, the Supreme Brother's gaze travelled around the assembled Brothers. He smiled his cold, cruel smile.

"Brother Gregory, take your place."

An amazed gasp broke from those watching. It appeared that Gregory was to be excused what he had said, without even a stinging rebuke from the Supreme Brother.

Experienced Brothers eyed each other and the Supreme Brother warily, and were aware that something was about to happen.

As he reached the second of the three circles and was about to take his place a sudden command came from the dais: "No."

Startled, Brother Gregory stiffened. He knew that he had been treated incredibly lightly, but now realised that the Supreme Brother had been toying with him.

"You have gone to the wrong circle, Brother Gregory."

Everyone comprehended at the same instant. Brother Gregory had been demoted to the first circle — not a very severe punishment, but it was a beginning. All guessed that there was more to come.

As Brother Gregory, head down, approached the first circle, the voice spoke again. "You've gone to the wrong circle, Brother."

Gregory looked up at the Supreme Brother, confusion written all over his features. The Brothers looked at each other, trying to solve this riddle. None did, and when it was solved for them, none could believe what they heard.

"Brother Gregory, from this moment your place is within the third circle."

Gregory's eyes opened wide but he had the presence of mind not only to comprehend what he had heard but to hurry to the third circle and to sit in a vacant chair. Never had he believed that his information would be believed, but to receive promotion for it...

All eyes were on the Supreme Brother who was still smiling his frigid smile, pleased at having fooled the assembled Brothers so thoroughly. Glancing quickly at Brother Gregory, he addressed the assembly again: "Yes, Brothers. I have promoted Brother Gregory because he has pleased me. Do you know how he pleased me? Do you know the extent of my pleasure? Did any of you lift a finger to help your Brother when you thought him demoted? Did any, save Brother Martin, speak a word in his defence?"

The Supreme Brother glared at the assembly, anger making his eyes glint; they might almost have been ice.

"No: you were content to let your Brother suffer. You, each and every one of you, feared for yourselves. Am I surrounded by cowards with no convictions? Beware of me, my Brothers. *Beware my anger.*"

Panting with rage which he found difficult to bite down, the Supreme Brother took his time in looking at each and every member of the assembly. Each, in his turn, felt the icy chill of Supreme Brother's glare.

Moments later, when his rage was under some semblance of control, the Supreme Brother spoke again, in his more accustomed frigid tone.

"All of you have heavy responsibilities, who knows that better then I? But here we have a case whereupon all other matters pale into insignificance. Our vengeance upon the Baron line.

"Brothers, you know that our Brotherhood was very nearly exterminated by Anton Baron many years ago. The then Supreme Brother, despite being close to death, swore vengeance; that vengeance became a basic tenet of our Brotherhood. Throughout the years upon years that have followed, we have carefully brought about the deaths of most of the Baron lineage — but we have had to be cautious *and* meticulous.

"Earlier, you all heard Brother Gregory interrupt his immediate superior, Brother Martin. It seems that Brother Gregory is the more meticulous of the two. His contention is not supported by Brother Martin, but it doesn't need to be. I believe what Brother Gregory says. I *feel* that he is right and that the American lineage of Anton Baron is not, as yet, extinct.

"And Brother Gregory has produced to me indications that Scott Hobard, the so-called 'last' of the

American Barons, may have sired a child, although he must have been ignorant of it at the time of his death.

"Brother Gregory, have you traced the woman concerned? Have the American Barons again begun to thrive?"

Brother Gregory stood, feeling a little weird; events were moving so quickly. His rapid promotion and now the queries about the Baron bloodline made him feel unreal.

"Supreme Brother, as I told you, there are indications that the line continues. I was forbidden," said Brother Gregory, with a brief glance at Brother Martin, "from continuing my researches into this matter."

The Supreme Brother began to swing his stare towards Brother Martin, when Brother Gregory's voice caused it to return to *him*.

"I must admit that I deliberately ignored my superior's direct order. Upon my own authority I have instituted a search for any material which might lead us to the offspring of Scott Hobard, for I am *convinced* that there *was* a child."

"*Brother Gregory, you astound me*," whispered the Supreme Brother. "Having just shouted down your *former* superior, an offence few would dare, you now confess to me that you have deliberately disobeyed a direct order. Are you very clever, or a fool, Brother Gregory?"

"Neither, I hope, Supreme Brother. I am merely anxious to put my abilities, such as they are, unreservedly into the Brotherhood's service."

The Supreme Brother pondered this, all the while keeping his eyes carefully upon Brother Gregory. He was shrewd, clever, and resourceful. '*He could be very useful, in the right place*,' argued Supreme Brother to himself. "And, Brother Gregory, have your searches found any trace of Hobard's offspring?"

"Not as yet," replied Brother Gregory. "Although I am expecting news at any moment."

The Supreme Brother nodded briefly: "Your action in disobeying your superior I find deplorable — but excusable in this case. Do not make a habit of it, Brother."

"Of course not, Supreme Brother," Brother Gregory replied.

"This matter of our vengeance is of such importance that I suspend all other business which was to have been discussed. As I recall, two Brothers were detailed to keep a watch upon Robert and Tony Baron respectively. Brothers, make your report."

Brothers Alex and David glanced nervously at each other, neither of them looking forward to relating what they had to say. They took no comfort in the fact that Brother Gregory had somehow managed to turn adversity around — both feared that they would not be so lucky.

"Brothers? We are all waiting for your report; does your silence denote that you have nothing to say? Surely not." In a voice becoming cold and dangerous the Supreme Brother continued: "Then you fear what you have to say. Nevertheless," the Supreme Brother's voice became icy as he spat out each word slowly, with heavy emphasis, "*Give...your...report.*"

Both Brothers stood and after a quick look at each other, Brother David began. "Supreme Brother, I was assigned to keep watch on Tony Baron, Brother Alex upon Robert. Over the last two weeks we have been combining our efforts." Noticing the frown that appeared on Supreme Brother's face, David hurried to explain. "It appears that Tony Baron received a communication from his Great-Uncle. What it contained we don't know, but we can surmise that it included an invitation to his mansion. For the last two days we have been following his progress as he journeyed to meet Robert."

"And you made no attempt to stop him?" queried the Supreme Brother. "He travels alone?"

Another nervous glance. This time, Brother Alex took the initiative. "Supreme Brother, Tony Baron travelled with a companion — a girlfriend by the name of Margaret Hunter."

"There is more, I take it?"

"Yes, Supreme Brother. Brother David and I decided to try to part Tony Baron from the girl, in the hopes that we might be able to deal with him without any chance of a witness. We waited until they stopped for the night at a country inn. We felt that our incantations had worked, but I confess that we failed. Instead of Tony Baron leaving the inn alone the following morning, both he and his girlfriend rushed off before dawn.

"We thought it simply that our attempt at mind control had been unsuccessful and so, as they were travelling through winding country roads, we caused a local dense fog to manifest itself, a few trees to fall. We very nearly crushed them. But again, for no reason that we could understand, he managed to escape our trap.

"We intensified our efforts, but suddenly all the energy we had summoned seemed to...to drain away, as though a plug had been pulled in a wash basin. Again we created the fog, but the same thing happened. We tried a third time — but Supreme Brother, from then on any energy we expended on creating the fog was drained as fast as we could expend it. I cannot explain why, or what caused it."

The Supreme Brother sneered. "Then, Brothers, I shall explain," he whispered.

"In effect, Brothers, you pitted your talents against George Hayter — that is Robert Baron's pen name... I see the name is familiar to you, Brothers. You suddenly look frightened, and with *good* reason. I, myself, would think twice before battling Hayter alone.

"But more to the point, you realise that your precipitous action has revealed to them that we are watching? And that your failure to eliminate Tony Baron emphasises the extremes to which we will go. Your failure has told Hayter much, Brothers."

Brothers David and Alex again glanced at each other and failed to notice the hurried entrance of another Brother. He looked around, as if searching for someone, and, having spotted Brother Gregory, moved towards him.

"But I am not *dis*pleased," continued the Supreme Brother, much to the relief of Alex and David. "Because the end result is one that I wished brought about. That it has occurred *sooner* rather than *later* is of no consequence. The pressure is now on Hayter to act and we shall be ready for him, if he does.

"I find myself thinking that with Tony Baron's girlfriend in our hands, we would be in a position to exert a considerable leverage. Of course, kidnapping Miss Hunter would be no easy task — but it would be an option which we would be *foolish* to overlook. Continue your vigilance, Brothers."

Brothers Alex and David, stunned at having escaped the Supreme Brother's anger, both bowed and sat. "Brother Martin, do you think *you* could look into the feasibility of kidnapping Miss Hunter?"

Brother Martin knew that this was his reward for not going along with Brother Gregory's contentions — to be given an almost impossible mission. On one hand he would regain credibility if he managed to succeed, but on the other would almost certainly be demoted if he failed. Summoning all the conviction he could muster he said, "I will do my utmost to bring Miss Hunter into our protection."

"Yes, but take care you do not confront Tony Baron or his Great-Uncle; nor set foot on Hayter's land, or you may *not* live to regret it."

Brother Martin inclined his head, acknowledging he would abide by the restrictions imposed upon him.

The Supreme Brother was about to enlarge on his plans for dealing with Tony Baron and George Hayter when he noticed a movement from the corner of his eye. It was a Brother leaving the chamber hastily. As he looked questioningly at the assembly, Brother Gregory stood, drawing Supreme Brother's attention.

"Supreme Brother, I have important news to relate."

The Supreme Brother waited calmly. "Does this have to do with the matter under discussion?"

"Indeed, Supreme Brother. A moment ago, another Brother — James — arrived." The Supreme Brother nodded his recollection of the incident. "He has handed me the proof which was lacking when I discussed the matter of the American Barons earlier. Supreme Brother, there definitely *was* a child sired by Scott Hobard; a daughter."

"Brother Gregory, let me see this proof."

Gregory approached the dais for a second time and placed a piece of paper there. The Supreme Brother picked it up, scanned it and took a deep breath. Gregory returned to his seat.

Expelling the air from his lungs slowly, Supreme Brother asked, "And what are you doing to trace the rest?"

"Supreme Brother, Brother James is even now on his way to cross-check all public registers and a few private ones besides, which are held by those companies which we control. If Scott Hobard's bastard brought any more American Barons into the world, we shall know soon."

"Excellent, Gregory, *excellent*," the Supreme Brother enthused. Then, standing, he walked to the edge of the dais and descended from it. He approached the third circle and embraced Brother Gregory, an action which stunned the assembly.

"*BROTHERS,*" thundered the Supreme Brother, "I name Brother Gregory my successor and my immediate subordinate. Does any here contest my choice?"

The assembly were too surprised to register anything but amazement. Even if anyone had any strong objections to Brother Gregory as the *next* Supreme Brother, there was little they could have done about it. The Supreme Brother's choice was final, and once announced the successor was, to all intents and purposes, a law unto himself. He was subject only to the Supreme Brother with all other Brothers being subordinate to him. It demonstrated more fully than could anything else the regard in which the Supreme Brother held Gregory. Not surprisingly, there were no dissenters.

"Brother Gregory, and Brother Gregory alone may now refer to me as Paternal Brother, which befits his new status as my successor." To Gregory he added, "You have done *excellently*, beyond anything managed by your peers. You deserve your reward. *Savour* it, Gregory."

The Supreme Brother returned to his seat upon the dais, and motioned to his successor. "Bring a chair and sit with me, as your rank demands."

Brother Gregory, in a haze of disbelief, walked unsteadily to the nearest vacant chair, picked it up and placed it upon the dais next to the Supreme Brother. He sat down, feeling very unusual at sitting in this exalted position next to his leader. The fact that he was now the deputy leader of the Cult didn't completely penetrate his mind. Feeling totally bemused, he surveyed the gathering from upon the dais, the view seeming both unreal and daunting.

"Brother Gregory has given us the proof we need. Scott Hobard *did* sire a bastard; we have the mother's name, which is Catherine Kingley. However, she is dead. At this time we know very little more. This *confirms* my fears that the American Barons are not yet extinct. I trust that we shall have more information by the time our next meeting is convened?"

Gregory inclined his head in what he hoped was a suitable gesture of acknowledgement, and tried to emulate the Supreme Brother's poise.

"I feel certain, Supreme...er Paternal Brother, that when we next meet, Brother James will have gathered the information which we need to complete our vengeance."

The Supreme Brother smiled his bleak smile. "Then Brothers, I adjourn this meeting. Keep yourselves constantly alert, for either attack by Hayter or summons to our next meeting. We have the matter of a traitor to be ritually executed. We shall discuss those matters which were suspended then. If time allows, we may discuss our efforts to destroy Hayter, Baron, and any of the American line. Be evil, my Brothers."

The last sentence, delivered so casually, was always the Supreme Brother's way of terminating the meeting. The Brothers moved out of the cavern in groups, the robed figures exiting by a different route to change back into more normal apparel. The quiet talk and murmur of voices died away quickly and Brother Gregory felt awkward being alone in Supreme Brother's or rather, in Paternal Brother's presence.

"Wait here for me," Supreme Brother instructed, standing and making his way to the cave where he had changed over four hours ago.

Gregory began to take in the fact that he was, indeed, the Supreme Brother elect, and as such controlled the Brotherhood subject only to Supreme Brother. Try as he might, he found it impossible to think of Supreme Brother as Paternal Brother.

He had attended the meeting as an ordinary second-circle Brother, and now here he sat upon the dais, outranking all except one; and that was due to nothing more than his stubborn instinct which had told him that

94

every possibility must be explored. He had simply checked where Brother Martin had not and had received the reward.

Footsteps approached and Gregory stood, feeling somehow uneasy sitting in the presence of the Supreme Brother. He frowned as he caught sight of him. It was Supreme Brother who stood before him, yet his features were subtly different. If he had passed this man on the street, he would have thought that there was only a slight resemblance to his leader.

The Supreme Brother smiled a relatively warm smile compared with others which he was prone to when conducting meetings. He indicated a passage and they began walking. At first they walked in silence. Brother Gregory jumped when Supreme Brother's voice said, "I think we'll discuss things over coffee."

Brother Gregory carefully scrutinised the Supreme Brother as, guided by him, they reached the stone steps which led to his cellar. They climbed them, Supreme Brother indicating that Gregory should go first. Once at the top, Gregory noticed a lighter patch of grey for which he headed. Supreme Brother followed him closely, pressing the concealed spring as he did so, causing the wall of his cellar to pivot back into its normal place, concealing the steps behind it. Turning on the light, more for Gregory's benefit than his own, Supreme Brother led the way through his cellar and up the stairs to the exit, turning out the lights negligently as they left.

Once out of the cellar, Gregory found himself looking around in surprise. He had half expected the Paternal Brother to live in a house lit by dim candlelight, perhaps guarded by a couple of entities. In reality the house was well furnished, but nothing spectacular caught the eye. Gregory followed Supreme Brother up more stairs and into a room which looked, to Gregory, to be a study.

It was the same room the Supreme Brother had left hours before to attend the meeting. He waved Gregory to a chair, and then left the room.

Gregory took the opportunity to look around. Desk and chairs stood in one half of the room. Three easy chairs, one of which he occupied, filled the other half. A coffee table stood immediately in front of him.

Glancing at the wall facing him, Gregory noticed a painting — a classic nude. He raised his eyebrows more in surprise than anything else. He was just about to stand, to examine the painting a bit more closely, when a voice from the door behind him made him jump.

"Ah, I see you're admiring my Venus. It's not an original, I'm afraid, just a cheap print. I think Titian painted it, but art's hardly my strong point." He placed a tray upon a coffee table, and poured for them both. Indicating the tray, he nodded, "Add your own milk and sugar: — I take it black."

Brother Gregory carefully added milk and two sugars. Stirring the coffee thoughtfully, he wondered what was going to happen next. He raised his eyes from his coffee to Supreme Brother and noticed the Supreme Brother studying him.

"You're wondering why I brought you here?" he asked, face neutral.

"Well, Paternal Broth..."

"Look, when in a meeting, Paternal Brother is fine. But when we're alone, or amongst outsiders, you'd better use my name. Call me Paul. I'll call you Gregory — even though I know Gregory isn't your real name, it will do."

As Gregory nodded, Paul continued, "You are here quite simply because you need training. Yes, I elected you my successor but, without training, the constant strains of the job will destroy you. *I* didn't believe it when I was given the same speech by my predecessor, but now I am wiser than I was. Without the training that he gave me — and much of it I learned by being attentive to how he tackled problems, how he kept discipline — I would have been crushed by the weight of responsibility. Of course there was more to it than just observing him. He'd set me complex problems, place me in an imaginary scenario, and tell me to solve the problem without compromising our Society but at the same time to achieve a desired end. I found that my predecessor was a *very* devious man."

"Is that where *you* get it from?" asked Gregory, without thinking. The instant the words were out of his mouth, he jerked his eyes to Paul's, hoping his remark hadn't caused offence.

To his infinite relief, Paul actually laughed, which Gregory found a little incongruous.

"Gregory, you do me good. It's years since anyone spoke to me like that. But, to answer you; yes, I absorbed *some* deviousness from my tutor, but I am naturally so. What made you ask?"

"I don't know. I suppose It's nerves. I find what happened today completely unbelievable."

Another smile crossed Paul's features. "I remember the feeling," he remarked. "But let us discuss more important things. At our next gathering you, not I, will be the centre of attention. You must learn never, ever, to let your feelings or emotions show. You must be aloof, cold, withdrawn, and yet your mind must be constantly alert. Can you achieve this?"

"In time, I think so," Gregory murmured. "With your example to follow, it will be that much easier."

Paul smiled an easy smile, and he continued, "Of course, I'll help all I can; but don't expect me to abdicate my position."

Gregory stared at him.

"Just so we *both* know where you stand. Now, bring your coffee over here," said Paul, heading towards his desk. Gregory complied, and they sat on opposite sides of it. Paul indicated the book which he had been reading. "It's very good, very well written. Take a look."

Gregory took the book, glanced at the chapter headings and realised that it discussed the implications and ramifications of Ceremonial Magic. Opening it at random, he found himself reading about the summoning of elemental forces. As he read further he found himself thinking that it was so obvious, why had it seemed difficult when he first attempted controlling elementals? He glanced at the cover of the book. It was entitled: Ceremonial Magic in Theory and Practice' by George Hayter. Gregory looked up at Paul in surprise; the other gave a grim frown.

"You see what we could be up against? I've read every one of his books — he knows the subject inside out; but knowing the subject and knowing how to put that knowledge to use are two different things.

"As you know, I've had a watch kept on Hayter. Basically, my reports are that he keeps his mansion and grounds constantly surrounded by a form of barrier — not to keep people out, but to inform him if anyone enters. A side effect of this barrier is that any force which we might aim at the mansion rebounds off the barrier. What d'you make of that?"

"Rebounds *off* it? I've never heard of anything like that before. Have you any other evidence of Hayter actually practising?"

"No, not a thing. I have been able, on occasion, to see into his mansion; but that's more directed clairvoyance and it can't really be relied upon.

"Now do you begin to understand why we must act with caution? Do you see why I went to such pains to direct Martin to attempt the abduction of Tony Baron's girlfriend?"

"Do you *really* think Hayter could defeat us, once we are assembled?"

"No," answered Paul slowly. "But I do believe he would do considerable damage before we could overcome him. Tony Baron is an unknown quantity in this context. Therefore, I will try the subtle before risking anything in all out confrontation. Think what would be the result if we held Margaret Hunter."

Gregory frowned. "You are then gambling on Tony Baron's feelings for her being such that he will follow his instincts and attempt to rescue her?"

"Yes, but not so much of a gamble, really. Even if he didn't react in the way you suggest — although I think it likely — we could then utilise her in the confrontation with Hayter."

Gregory saw the light. "That's *superb* planning, Paul. I confess I'd not thought of it that way. You were right — you *are* naturally devious."

"There are other things to be considered, of course. If, for example, the abduction of Miss Hunter does not work, we might end up in a confrontation situation anyway — and I'm not sure that I altogether like the idea."

"But why not?"

"Just an instinct — but I've learned to trust my instincts." Paul made a gesture as if something else had come to mind.

"Another coffee?" he asked. "I've just thought, perhaps it would be an idea to make some *contingency* plans."

"Concerning what, exactly?"

"Well, we have an execution which must go ahead, and we must be prepared for whatever information Brother James might give us. We should attempt to anticipate his information and have our plans *clear* when he reports to us. Our Brothers must be given some idea of what to expect if matters come to a head. You and I must be clear in our own minds what we are going to do if Martin is successful. You *do* know what will be expected of you during the execution, I assume?"

"Yes, I attended the last one — six years ago, I think it was."

"Quite right: anyway, what about another coffee? And then we can discuss and consider these matters more fully."

"Why not?"

Chapter Seven: Conversations

Hayter woke, hearing the familiar light knock upon the door. Taking a deep breath and rubbing his eyes, he began to sit up in bed when the knock was repeated. With a muffled grunt he managed to call out, "Come in."

John entered, looking as neat and alert as always. "John, why is it that when I'm not sleeping heavily you come in without being asked, but when I take my time waking up you not only knock again, but wait for me to call out before you enter?"

"I don't know," he confessed. "Just one of my irritating habits, I suppose. Do you want breakfast in bed, or downstairs?"

"Do I look ill?" Hayter demanded.

"No, but..."

"And when was the last time I ate breakfast in bed?"

"Last week...erm yes, Tuesday, last week."

"I didn't..." began Hayter, his early morning irritability beginning to rise, when he remembered bringing a draft copy of his latest book to bed with him, to check for errata needing correction. The job had taken all night — it had seemed to him that there was more errata than text, and he had spent all night correcting the damn thing. By the time John arrived, with his customary speech about breakfast, he had been feeling exhausted and the idea of eating breakfast in bed and then getting some much-needed sleep had appealed to him; he had done so and forgotten about it.

"All right, John, you win: downstairs, okay?"

Suppressing a smile, which Hayter noticed, John turned and left, leaving Hayter alone.

He was in the middle of dressing when John reappeared. "When do you want me to take the guests their breakfasts?"

Hayter considered for a moment. "Are their doors locked?"

"Yes."

Hayter closed his eyes for a few seconds. "Margaret will wake in a moment or so, Tony in about an hour. Take Margaret her breakfast now, Tony's later. Don't forget to lock their doors after you."

John raised his eyebrows at the very idea, and realised this was Hayter's way of getting his own back on him for the barely suppressed smile. Without answering, he left the bedroom.

Hayter finished dressing and wandered downstairs to the dining room. In contrast to the rest of the mansion, which was in grand style, the dining room was a modest affair. Sitting at a table which could have sat six people, he inspected his breakfast. A choice confronted him. Toast, boiled eggs, cereal. '*If only all my problems were this easy to solve*,' he caught himself thinking as his thoughts turned to the forthcoming encounters with Margaret and Tony.

Having devoured the eggs and the toast, Hayter left the table and made his way to the room which had been the scene of his guests' unexpected slumber. He felt unaccountably nervous about the approaching discussions with his visitors — especially Margaret.

He replayed recent events in his mind — focussed upon Margaret's nightmare. Something at the back of his mind nagged at him. He remembered drawing the covers up over her breasts, wishing her pleasant dreams.

In an attempt to introduce some calm into his chaotic thoughts, Hayter sat at the piano, and a few seconds later, it burst into violent crescendo as he slammed into Chopin's 'revolutionary' study.

A moment later, he broke off, and stood up. It wasn't working. Taking a deep breath, he sat again and this time managed to lose himself by playing Rachmaninov. As the last strains of the prelude died away Hayter stood and headed out of the room, in the direction of Margaret's bedroom. His pace slowed noticeably as he neared her door. He hesitated briefly before he knocked.

***

On waking, Margaret's first conscious recollection was of the lovely melody which she had dreamed about, which had relaxed and calmed her. Later, she had begun to have the nightmare about her father, but it had been interrupted somehow — not that she minded, but she felt vaguely puzzled about it; it had *never* happened before.

She tried to hum the melody running through her mind, but the only sound she made was a croak. Swallowing, she became aware of how dry her mouth was. She stretched her body, luxuriating in the feel of muscles stretching, the way the sheets rubbed so smoothly over her naked body...

She opened her eyes in mid-stretch, all of her feelings giving way to ones of apprehension. She had been in the room with Tony, and that man — John, that was his name, had said Hayter wouldn't be long. She had sat down, said something to Tony, and couldn't remember anything else. Yes, she could remember having a couple of dreams, but damn it, how had she got *here*?

Who had stripped her? She blushed crimson at the thought.

Why hadn't she woken up when she was being undressed?

She sat up, feeling for a bedside lamp or a light switch; anything to give her some light. Her grasping fingers came into contact with a wall switch. She clicked the switch down, and a dim light appeared. She noticed the control next to the switch and, by degrees, gradually increased the light's intensity. Looking around she saw a bedside table, but more importantly, she felt, three doors. She hoped that one was a bathroom. That was her immediate need.

Grabbing the top cover from the bed, she draped it around herself, as she tried the door opposite the bed. It was first time lucky; she had found the bathroom.

She swallowed a palmful of water before she returned to the bedroom, relieved in one way but grasping the cover around her like a long shawl. She felt totally confused, her nudity having the effect of making her feel more apprehensive and vulnerable.

She tried the next door, which was to the right of where she had been lying in the bed. It opened onto a smaller room, which she immediately recognised as a dressing room. She searched eagerly through the chests of drawers and both wardrobes, but there were no clothes there — nothing.

Feeling frightened and irritated, she returned to the bedroom. She tried the third door, which was opposite the dressing room. She knew that this door would lead out into the rest of the mansion and she knew before she tried it that it would be locked.

She felt her anger burning up inside her. Whoever had done this had some nerve; what had they done to Tony? Was he all right? She began to feel cold, although it was quite warm within the bedroom. She slipped back into bed throwing the cover over it as she did so, not caring how it landed.

She tried to work out what was happening and why; but before she could fix upon any one aspect of her predicament the fact of her nudity reasserted itself, insisting that she resolve the problem. She was just stepping out of bed to re-examine the dressing room in the hopes that she had overlooked something, when she heard a knock upon the door.

She jumped back into bed, pulling the bedclothes up to her chin, and holding them there, the knuckles of her hands turning white, her heart speeding. The knock was repeated.

"Tony?" she asked in a hoarse voice.

The door opened, but she was sure she hadn't heard a key turn in the lock — come to think of it, there *was* no lock, so why....?

The thought ended abruptly as the man she recognised as John walked in smiling cheerfully, carrying a breakfast tray. "Good morning, Miss Hunter. I hope you slept well?" he enquired of her.

"Er, very well, but..." she said as he approached her and placed the tray on the bed, over her hips.

"That's good; nothing *like* a good sleep, is there?"

"But how did I get here? Who undressed me?" she blushed, but John chose not to notice. "And why was the door locked?"

John had been retreating towards the door but he turned and smiled at her, a warm, friendly smile. "Well, you fell asleep downstairs waiting for Mr. Hayter, and he told me to put you and Mr. Baron to bed."

"But why didn't I wake up?"

"Perhaps you were more tired than you realised...anyway, I undressed you. Don't feel embarrassed, I kept my eyes closed. The door doesn't have a lock on it, but it does get very stiff at times with not being used very often."

"Why were my clothes taken away?"

"I imagine Mr. Hayter will answer your questions shortly; enjoy your breakfast, Miss Hunter."

He disappeared before she had time to take in what he said. After a couple of moment's thought she moved the tray and got out of bed, shrouding herself with the cover which she had previously utilised for the same purpose, went to the door and tried it. It wouldn't budge, no matter how she tugged at it.

More confused than ever, she returned to the bed. Having replaced the tray, she glanced at its contents. Had she been drugged, this morning? No, she hadn't eaten or drank anything; however, Tony *did* have a drink...

She replaced the cover over her breakfast and moved it to one side. If Hayter expected to drug her that easily, he would be disappointed.

Glancing around, she noticed her cigarettes and lighter upon the bedside table. '*Had they been there before John had brought her breakfast,*' she wondered. She couldn't remember. She reached for the pack, drew one out and lit it, looking for an ashtray as she did so. There wasn't one. After a hesitation, she took the saucer from under the cup on the breakfast tray and decided that it would serve just as well.

Five minutes later, a heavy double-knock sounded upon the door. She jumped, realising — although she didn't know how — that she was about to meet Hayter. She felt her anger and resentment building up. She set her jaw. She wasn't going to be put off again. She wanted *answers*, *explanations*, and she was *determined* that she would get them.

***

Hayter stopped outside Margaret's door. His mind was vaguely troubled. He promised himself that he would try to keep his temper in check — although he always found that difficult when being interrogated. He knocked twice, deciding that he would simply have to do his best. The sound seemed too loud in the empty corridor. He waited for an invitation to enter, but it didn't come. He knocked again, and a voice said, "Come in."

Hayter entered the room, closed the door (which had caused him no problems) behind him and approached the bed being careful not to appear threatening in any way.

"Good morning Margaret. I hope you slept well?"

"Yes, but I want some answers, *Mr. Hayter.*"

Hayter smiled. "Yes, I thought you would; and so will Tony. That's one of the reasons I'm here — Margaret, do you mind if I sit? Standing is no fun for a man of my age."

Margaret immediately felt guilty in the face of this request and her anger diminished as a result of her confusion. He made it seem as though he was a guest in *her* room, rather than the other way round, and it disorientated her. "Of course," she replied without thinking. Her resolve to demand answers weakened. The man before her was about six feet tall, had a medium build and a wrinkled face. At that moment he was smiling benevolently, but she guessed that he had a great deal of determination built into his personality.

She put out her cigarette, feeling a little self-conscious about using the saucer as an ashtray. She placed it on the bedside table. "I see you haven't eaten," Hayter observed. "Why not? I assure you it isn't poisoned."

Hayter's remark, although intended lightly, caused some of Margaret's weakened resolve to return. Ignoring her breakfast she said, "Since you mention it, how did I manage to fall asleep — so deeply asleep that someone could not only carry me here but undress me as well without waking me up? You drugged me — and Tony too, for all I know, didn't you? Well?" Margaret's voice had risen in volume as her anger returned and the last word was almost a shout. Hayter looked at her calmly, and despite the certainty that she was right she began to feel foolish.

Hayter let the silence build before answering her. "Margaret, I'll answer your questions, but shouting won't do either of us any good. There are some questions that Tony will want answering, too — all of us will talk later. If I ask you to wait until then for *some* explanations, try to bear with me."

A sceptical look crossed her face. Hayter noticed it and continued, "First of all, I didn't have you drugged — although I admit I did help you to sleep. Next you'll want..."

"How? You don't make sense."

107

"Well, Tony would understand, I think. To put it crudely, I used a little magic, the point was..."

"Why? We were supposed to come here to meet you and the first thing you claim to have done was some...some..." as she spluttered to a halt, lost for words, Hayter shook his head. He stood, moved closer to her and sat down by her side. Taking hold of her hand, he smiled at her. "Calm down," he said softly. "At least give me a *chance* to get a word in — I don't remember managing to finish a sentence in the last few moments."

His grip on her hand was almost tentative, but reassuring. She glanced at him, and saw his face crinkle into a smile. She took a deep breath and smiled back at him.

"Margaret, can we take it one question at a time?"

She nodded. "Okay — why make us sleep? Although I'm not saying that I believe it."

Hayter sighed. He was getting nowhere fast. He decided to try a different approach. "Why not eat your breakfast as I explain?"

Margaret looked suspiciously at him, and Hayter couldn't stop himself laughing. "I'll join you — if it is drugged then I'll have to have words with John."

"No need, it's cold," she laughed back, delighted that the problem of having to eat the breakfast had now been resolved. She noticed Hayter's eyes upon her, then upon the breakfast tray. They seemed to go distant for a second and then he smiled triumphantly at her.

"It's hot now," he said, placing the tray across her hips. He took a piece of toast and bit into it.

Margaret gazed at the tray and then followed his example. Her appetite quickly asserted itself. She poured coffee into a cup, adding milk and sugar. Hayter nodded his approval. She suddenly realised what must have happened. She glanced at him questioningly. He nodded, "Yes — just a minor demonstration, of course."

She looked at him seriously for a moment and then, surprising herself, she said calmly, "Tell me why you went to such lengths to get us here — and then used your erm...*abilities* to make us sleep."

He took a deep breath. This was it. If she didn't believe what he had to say then there would be no way of convincing her. Thinking intently before he spoke, he began, "You might find what I have to say difficult to believe. I have documents downstairs which support what I'm going to tell you; I'll show them to both of you later. The reason I had to get you here was firstly to protect you. Secondly, I need Tony here — and by extension I need you here, too. If I hadn't taken the course of action that I did, you could easily be dead by now."

Margaret's eyes were intent upon his face as he continued: "Centuries ago, a man named Anton Baron attempted to..." but Hayter got no further, for Margaret interrupted, annoying him.

"But we heard that story at the inn — I wasn't sure if it was true or not. You mean that the curse exists, don't you? It's real, isn't it?"

Hayter's eyebrows lifted in surprise. He had been certain that he would have an impossible time trying to convince Margaret of the danger of a five hundred year old curse — and someone had already done all the hard work for him. It annoyed him, perversely, that he had worried about convincing her when he need not have done.

However, he didn't let his feelings show. He looked her straight in the eyes and nodded slowly. "Yes, it's true — but I thought I'd have difficulty convincing you. As you already know the story I hope that, for the present at least, you'll accept my other reasons on trust. I want to explain to both of you later."

Margaret nodded thoughtfully. "Right," she murmured, "but it doesn't explain why you made us sleep for a few hours — or why I'm not wearing anything."

Hayter smiled. Margaret agreeing to take his reasons on trust was more than he had dared to hope for. His good humour restored, he let go of her hand as she reached for a cigarette.

"It's quite straightforward," he said, lighting her cigarette for her. He raised an eyebrow as she brought the saucer from the bedside table to within reach upon the bed. "You both needed sleep, and I wanted to speak to each of you alone. It seemed obvious to link the two events.

"You had a couple of unpleasant experiences on your way up here, and I thought you needed time to recover — you've not slept a few hours, Margaret, you've slept a day and a night."

Margaret looked up at him with an intense gaze. "*That* long? Mr. Hayter, I don't think I needed that much sleep."

Hayter stared back at her. "Call me George. Believe me, you must have needed it; that was probably what caused your nightmare."

Although he said it casually, he was watching for Margaret's reaction. It wasn't long in coming. Eyes opening wide, her voice becoming defensive, she asked, "What d'you mean?"

With a casual wave of his hand he resumed, "When I looked in on you last night, you weren't exactly sleeping peacefully. It seemed to me that you were having a nightmare. So I ah...*ended* it, and made sure that it won't bother you again."

Margaret frowned in genuine disbelief. "It's true I had a nightmare — and it's true that it ended suddenly; do you know what I was dreaming about?"

"How could I?" Hayter smiled. "But if you want me to know, you'll tell me in your own time."

110

Margaret was relieved that Hayter seemed to have limitations — or was it just that he didn't want to probe? Or could it be that he didn't want to admit that he had? Whatever the reason, she felt comfortable with the end result. If it was true that Hayter had expunged the recurring nightmare about her father and that she would never be plagued by it again, she felt that, whatever else happened or would happen, maybe coming here with Tony hadn't been such a mistake after all.

Had Margaret *any* idea of what the future held for her, she would have been far less sanguine about matters — in fact, she would have taken her chances alone rather than face what fate had reserved for her.

With hopes that what Hayter said was true, and she had no reason to disbelieve him as yet, churning around inside her, it was a few seconds before she realised that she had only received half an answer. Feeling another blush on the way as she framed the question, she began, "Of course, I'm grateful if you have..." she got no further. Hayter interrupted her, misreading what she had been about to say.

"I know you're sceptical about my abilities — but you'll realise the truth of it eventually. There's no need for gratitude, just look on it as a present from an old man who would like to be your friend."

The sincerity in his eyes stirred a warm emotional response within her; the embarrassment caused by the question she wanted to ask was replaced with a feeling akin to affection, which caused her both pleasure and surprise. How could it be that she was meeting someone for the first time and already feeling affection for him? She relegated the question to the back of her mind, promising herself that she would think about it later. Steering the conversation back carefully, not now wanting to cause offence, she tried again. "I think I'd *like* to be your friend, George — but you still haven't told me why I'm not wearing anything."

Hayter's forehead creased in a frown not of anger, but as though he was trying to think of the best way to explain. Thinking she was being helpful, Margaret volunteered some information. "The man who brought my breakfast — John, I think his name is," Hayter nodded absently, "well, I asked him, but all he would say was that he'd undressed me and that I shouldn't feel embarrassed because he kept his eyes closed, and..."

A sudden guffaw made her jump. She stopped dead in mid-sentence and stared at Hayter as he sat upon the side of the bed, rocking to and fro as laughter convulsed him. She wondered what it was she had said which had caused such mirth, and when his laughter showed no signs of lessening, she suddenly found it contagious — despite her resolve and her predicament.

As their laughter died down, they eyed each other with a new interest. It had been a long time since Hayter had laughed like that with anyone. She realised she hadn't felt any embarrassment when telling Hayter of what John had said, which was surprising in itself — she almost felt that she could confide in him, tell him anything, and that he would understand her. Again she wondered why she should feel like this after such short acquaintance — and in such peculiar circumstances.

She was pondering these newly-awakened feelings when she became aware of Hayter's laboured breathing and the ashen complexion of his face. He fumbled in his pocket and took out a bottle of tablets. Having opened it, he took two and seized Margaret's cup to gulp down what was left of her coffee.

She felt anxious for him. She reached for his arm, clutched it, taking no heed of the bedclothes as they fell away from her breasts. "George, are you all right?" using his name came so naturally at that moment.

He managed a weak smile, the ashen complexion fading away slowly, a shade of his normal colouring returning. When he spoke, his voice was as strong as ever. "Yes, Margaret, I'm fine — I didn't intend you to learn of my illness just yet, but that can't be helped. It was worth it just for the laugh you gave me."

"But what illness is it?" Margaret asked, intrigued.

"Degenerative heart condition — I'm afraid I haven't got that long to live — but we can discuss that another time."

There was an awkward silence. Margaret resumed her former position, absently pulling the bedclothes back over herself. Again the realisation that she hadn't been embarrassed, didn't feel threatened by her nudity in Hayter's presence, came into her mind. She was used to her reactions being automatic, causing her to panic, her heart to race with fear. With Tony, if she (subconsciously or otherwise) felt threatened by his advances, she simple froze. She wondered about this, and whether or not it was a result of Hayter's intervention. These revelations disorientated her, and it was with difficulty that she dragged her attention back to him.

"What did you find so funny?" she asked, "you even had me laughing."

He smiled at her again. "It was what you said. John asked me what to say when he brought you breakfast, and, thinking he was joking, I suggested that answer. I never *dreamed* that he'd use it — I think I'll have to have words with him."

"You like him, don't you?" she said intuitively.

Hayter's piercing eyes searched her face. "What makes you say that?"

"The look on your face when you talk about him."

"I suppose he *is* rather like a son to me..." Hayter mused.

Feeling that her questions were becoming somewhat *too* personal, she returned to the unanswered question of why she was naked. Hayter seemed to jump back to the present, as though he had been pondering what he had revealed to her a few seconds ago. "Well, it was done on my orders, of course, but basically because I resented you."

Margaret frowned at him. "But why? You'd never even met me." She felt a sense of outrage that someone could form a judgement of her without actually knowing her.

"Well, I thought you might just deflect Tony from studying occultism. Oh, I know that you didn't, but you did try to make him stop. You implied that you would feel safer if he left the occult alone. It's called: 'emotional blackmail'." Margaret said nothing, knowing that what he said was true. "You tried to stop him coming here to meet me — which would probably have meant your deaths.

"As far as you were concerned I was, perhaps still am, the epitome of evil. Not only do I study the occult, but my books explain and simplify it, and that you fear. You resented *me* first, Margaret. I wanted you to know that I can be resentful, too. I wanted to give you something to think about.

"But now that we have met, I sense that perhaps I was wrong to take offence. What you did was done for motives that, at the time, you believed in. You didn't know the danger that threatens us — still do not, to a large degree, but you shall in time."

As Hayter lapsed into silence, Margaret knew that he had read her correctly — she didn't know how he had found out what she had or hadn't done or felt and it didn't seem that important. That he knew was the important thing.

"It seems that I was a bit of a fool," she murmured quietly.

"Aren't we all, at times?" Hayter asked. "We're still friends I take it? Plain speaking sometimes gets me into trouble."

She nodded, "I'd like to be," she said. She felt *elated* when Hayter's face crinkled into one of those smiles that she saw so rarely in the time that she knew him.

"Good." With that, Hayter stood and headed for the door. "I'll tell John to bring your luggage. When you're dressed, he'll take you down to the sitting room. Make yourself at home. I'll probably bring Tony down myself." Hayter left her bedroom, closing the door after him, leaving Margaret examining her many differing emotions.

She waited for the knock on the door and when it came she called out, "Yes?"

John entered and deposited her luggage at the foot of the bed. "After I've taken you to the sitting room. I'll come back and unpack the rest of your things, Miss Hunter."

"My name's Margaret."

John nodded and smiled at her. "I'll wait for you outside."

As soon as the door closed she got out of bed and went to the bathroom. She washed quickly, returned to the bedroom and opened the suitcases. She looked first for underwear and then for jeans, blouse, jumper. These located, she dressed and brushed her hair. Feeling more secure now that she had some clothes, she went to the door and felt a wry smile cross her face as it opened easily.

John grinned at her and, taking her at her word, said, "If you'll come this way, Margaret."

Her smile widened.

Chapter Eight: Explanations

As he walked through his mansion in the direction of Tony's bedroom, Hayter found that he was more optimistic than ever about the future. His new-found attitude towards Margaret was mainly responsible, coupled with the feeling that he didn't think she would be as much of a burden as he had at first believed. She was an easily likeable young woman. He smiled, wondering if she had yet realised the extent of his help — it *wasn't* just her nightmare which he had remedied...

He stopped walking suddenly and stood considering his mood. He felt calm, relaxed, despite all the worries upon his shoulders. It seemed that his encounter with Margaret had brightened his day — even though he had nearly laughed himself into his grave. The thought, morbid though it might have been, made him chuckle. Why did she have that effect on him, he wondered.

Baffled, he continued walking towards Tony's bedroom savouring the fact that he was, at long last, about to meet and talk with his Great-Nephew.

He approached the door, feeling a little apprehensive, but anxious to meet Tony. He knocked lightly upon the door, and heard a muffled call which he assumed was an invitation to enter.

He did so and immediately took in the fact that Tony had reacted to his being stripped and incarcerated here in a way that was almost diametrically opposed to Margaret's, in that he was casually sitting up in bed munching toast, drinking coffee, and reading a newspaper. He looked up as Hayter walked in, a smile brightening his face.

"Great-Uncle Robert, I presume?"

"Tony, call me George. That 'Great-Uncle' stuff makes me feel as though I'm eligible for my telegram.

You don't know how much I've looked forward to us meeting."

"Me too, Great...George, I mean. Why the occult reception and not allowing me my clothes?"

"Well, reasons dictated what I did, of course. You both needed sleep and I didn't want you wandering around until I'd had a chance to talk to you — and can you think of a better way to immobilize someone temporarily?"

Tony grinned: "True, I suppose. Bet Margaret wasn't too pleased about it?"

"Yes, but she understands, to a point."

"You mean she didn't try to strangle you?" Tony asked incredulously.

Hayter smiled at Tony's expression. "No. I think that we're going to be friends."

"You'll have to teach me that trick."

"Tony, there are more important things for you to learn, at the moment," said Hayter, gazing intently at him. "But we'll discuss that later. By the way, how did you get John to bring you that paper?"

Tony grinned again. "Easy, I told him I wanted one, pointing out that I *am* your guest."

Hayter laughed. "I'd have *loved* to have seen his face," he said, trying to imagine the imperturbable John's expression when confronted with this demand.

Moving closer to Tony, Hayter pulled up a chair and sat. "It didn't take you long to solve the puzzle," he observed.

Tony folded the newspaper and placed it on his tray. He shrugged his shoulders. "Why should it? It was obvious. I woke up naked in a strange bedroom. I remember that for some reason I slept like the dead — and unless the date on the paper's wrong, I've slept close on twenty-four hours. I never sleep that heavily or that long. Either I was drugged or sleep was induced. My

117

Great-Uncle's one of the greatest living authorities on the occult — it was obvious that it was you who was behind it. I knew I was in no danger — I would have sensed it if I was."

Hayter nodded, smiling. "Bravo. Correct on all counts, of course. So you decided to let events run their course?"

"Yes," Tony replied, "besides, it's ages since anyone's brought me breakfast in bed —+ it was worth the inconvenience just for that."

Becoming serious, Hayter asked, "Do you remember meeting me?"

Tony considered his answer. "I think I do, but I'm not sure. Didn't you have an argument with my parents?"

Hayter nodded. "More with Kevin than with Susan. It got a little too heated. Eventually I realised that I was flogging a dead horse, and I left."

"But what did you argue about?" Tony wanted to know.

"Occultism — Kevin didn't want to hear about the danger that threatens us; he hit the roof when I suggested that I be allowed to teach you all I knew of the subject. Eventually, as I say, I left."

Tony thought about it for a moment and then said, "But not before Dad had made you promise that you'd never contact me whilst either of them were still alive?"

Hayter looked at him shrewdly. "Your deductions are quite accurate — I can see I'm going to have to be careful what I reveal."

Tony flashed his grin at Hayter again. "Why send the cryptic messages?"

"Just to attract your interest and curiosity. The first letter was intended to make you think me unfeeling, make you angry at me. The second was calculated to arouse your curiosity."

"It succeeded. I'm glad that it did; so far it has been — interesting. There are so many things that I want to ask you, but I don't know where to start."

"Well, let me start. How much do you know about why you're here?"

Tony shook his head. "Only what we picked up from that bloody inn; and what I can deduce from the artificially created fog that damn near got us killed."

"How did you work out that it wasn't natural?" Hayter wanted to know.

"I didn't, not at the time," he confessed. "Since I woke up and began thinking about the problems we had getting here, it became more and more obvious that someone had tried to manipulate us. When that failed they managed to manipulate the weather, but they seemed to get into erm... difficulties."

Hayter acknowledged the implied compliment. "We'll talk about the Cult and their curse shortly, when Margaret is with us. You *do* realise that the curse extends to include her?"

Tony nodded. "I did half-expect it. Why else would you have made a point of inviting her here? How could the Cult know that I haven't... that we...?"

"Tony, you should hear yourself. I know what you mean; I know as much about her background as she does herself." Hayter paused as if to emphasise what he had said. "I did a lot of thorough digging and I can't say I liked what I found — no wonder she found it difficult to believe that all men aren't like her father, and I use the term loosely."

Tony hesitated, unsure whether or not he approved of Hayter's knowing all this; he concluded that Hayter had to know about it since the curse now extended to include Margaret, if he was to protect her.

"I know all about the attempt to kill you with the falling trees and the fog; but tell me about this inn."

Tony related what he could remember of what happened at the inn, although he was very vague on several points. He remembered the story of Anton Baron, but precious little after that.

As he listened, he marvelled at the way the two of them were talking — as though they had known each other for years instead of this being their first meeting. He was impressed with Tony's casual acceptance of the circumstances in which he found himself — and at Tony's insights into what had happened to him. Permitting himself a slight smile, Hayter wondered if that was a trait of the Barons. He smiled more widely when he realised it wasn't. If it was there might be more Barons alive than there actually were.

Hayter thought over what Tony had told him. "Yes, I know the place. It's nothing to do with the Cultists as far as I know, but what I know about them is limited. I don't think it had been divined that you would choose that particular inn; I think it was pure coincidence. It is much more likely that you had been followed from the time you set out to come here. They must have been keeping you under observation for some time. It's understandable, now that there are only the two of us. But I'm digressing — the end point is, Tony, that if you and I fail in what we have to do, our failure will have condemned Margaret to death. You do understand that, don't you?"

"Yes," he admitted reluctantly. "Yes, I know it but I'd have been happier if you hadn't put it into words."

"At least we aren't deluding ourselves about what will happen to her if we do fail."

"Just what have we got to do? Destroy the Cult?"

"More or less," Hayter admitted. "But there is one thing I want to ask you. Do you think Margaret should be made aware of what could happen to her if we fail?"

"I wish you'd stop talking about failing," Tony muttered, "it's making me nervous." Hayter didn't reply, just continued looking at him, waiting to hear what he had to say. "Yes, I think she should know. Really, we've no right to keep that information from her."

"I'm glad that we are both of the same opinion about this," said Hayter smoothly.

"Just out of curiosity, what would you have done if I'd been against telling her?" Tony demanded.

"I'd have told her just the same," Hayter grinned back.

Tony found the grin infectious. "I expected that," he said. They looked at each other, sharing the silence in comfortable companionship. "Why did you say that time was getting short in your second letter?"

Hayter sighed. "We are the last two Barons, Tony. The time is getting short because in the not very distant future, there will be only one Baron — you."

Tony frowned. "I don't follow you — what exactly are you telling me?"

"That I'm terminally ill: heart condition. I've not got that long — that's why I said time is short. I was going to tell you about it some other time." Hayter's face crinkled into its smile. "I didn't intend either of you to find out about this immediately. At least now you *both* know."

"How did Margaret find out?"

"You could say that she got me to see the funny side of things," he replied, an amused expression coming into his eyes as he took in Tony's expression. As he watched, the disbelief left Tony's face and one of concern or anxiety replaced it.

"Robert," said Tony — the only time he ever called Hayter by his true Christian name without prefix, "is there no chance? Four years ago my parents died; you're my only relative. I tried to find you — Christ did I try. Now that I finally meet you, you calmly tell me that you are dying and that we've no time left to get to know each other. It might sound strange to you, but knowing that hurts like hell. I just want some time with you, is that asking too much? It's so bloody unfair," he said softly, dejectedly.

"Yes, it is," Hayter said, tears coming into his eyes, "but that's the way it *has* to be, Tony," he said gently.

"But surely you could..."

"Yes, I could. But I won't. When we discuss things a little later, I'll show you the reason — and it isn't because I haven't been tempted, either."

They both lapsed into silence, Hayter trying to give Tony a chance to accept what he had heard. All the pleasure of meeting his young relative drained away from him as he saw the anguish that his statement had caused. He took a deep breath, wondering why he had ever thought that this interview was going to be easy; it had been the success he had when speaking to Margaret, he deduced.

"The knowledge does have its plus side, you know," Hayter murmured. "We know that we should make the most of what time is left to us — we can cram as much into the remaining time as possible — even *with* the Cult to worry about."

Tony lifted his head and looked straight into Hayter's eyes. "I suppose you're right, George. I am glad we've met, at long last."

Hayter stood, feeling that Tony needed some time alone. '*Perhaps it will take him longer to get used to the idea than I first thought,*' Hayter mused. It was strange, in one way, that the knowledge should hit him so hard. Ever since he had walked into this bedroom, they had talked like old friends. Hayter had never heard the view propounded that you had to know someone for a long time before you could feel empathy for them; perhaps they had a natural affinity.

"I'll leave you to think, Tony. John will bring your luggage, and tell you where to find me when you're ready."

Tony nodded, "Thanks, George. I won't be too long."

Hayter smiled at him and left the bedroom. All in all, it hadn't been a bad introduction. It had taken a turn for the worse when he had discussed his approaching death, but that was hardly surprising.

Hayter located John and passed on the necessary instructions. John knew from Hayter's face that something was on his mind but he didn't feel that now was the best time to talk to him about it. He simply acknowledged his instructions and executed them.

Hayter walked through his home and finally found himself outside the sitting room where he had told John to take Margaret. He entered, a smile upon his features which melted away again when he took in the fact that she wasn't there.

He went to the bar and poured himself a flat orange. *'Where has she got to?'* he thought to himself. He came to the conclusion she was either exploring the mansion or had gone to the bathroom. Well, no doubt she would find her way back eventually. He looked around the room; the fire burning, casting a subdued light; the way the light reflected off the piano, the...

He walked to the piano without knowing that he was doing it and mechanically opened the lid, put the support strut in place. After only a moment's thought, he put his fingers to the keys and Debussey's music filled the air.

He moved from piece to piece, from composer to composer. All his apprehensions, fears and worries gradually fled away from the onslaught of the music. He relaxed and began to enjoy himself. He stopped playing, plucked his glass of orange from the floor next to him and drank deeply. He replaced the glass and resumed playing.

***

Margaret had been escorted to the sitting room by John, who had assured her that she only had to call if there was anything that she wanted. He left her there, excusing himself on the grounds that he had work to do.

Margaret, finding herself alone in the room which she could only vaguely remember, looked around it taking in every detail. She wandered over to the piano. After only a momentary hesitation, she lifted the cover from the keys and pressed a couple of them. The resultant sound was discordant and she frowned. Suddenly, the melody that she had woken up with in her mind presented itself. She pulled out the piano stool, sat down and tried with one finger to reproduce the tune. She managed to string two or three notes together in the correct order, but then she would hit a wrong note and the melody in her mind would distort, causing her to have to clear her mind and concentrate again on how it began. After a few minutes, she gave up in disgust. She stood, looking at the black and white keys, wishing that she knew how to manipulate them and create the music that repeated itself in her mind. She shrugged, closed the cover over them and replaced the stool where it had been. She walked across the room, wondering just how long she might be left on her own.

Becoming bored, she decided to look around the mansion — she was sure that Hayter wouldn't mind, but equally, she made a point of not calling John to make sure that would be the case. She wandered out of the sitting room, down the corridor, turning left here, right there randomly, taking a peep into some of the rooms which she passed. Most were tastefully furnished, but tasteful furniture didn't impress her that much. One thing that she did notice was that there were rather a lot of pianos. She counted five, not counting the one in the sitting room. She wondered if that meant that George could play — perhaps he would know the tune going around in her mind. She stopped to admire a painting on a wall — a landscape. An autumn scene, hills, valleys, trees, their leaves adding a richness of colour to the sunny day. She stared at the picture, almost enthralled by it. There was some elusive quality about it that seemed to demand her attention, but what it was she couldn't comprehend. Eventually, she tore her gaze away and continued her exploration. She opened a door and found herself in a room which contained four chairs, a desk, a filing cabinet and little else. This was in such stark contrast to what she had seen elsewhere, that she had walked up to the desk before she had realised it. Upon it lay a brown folder, an old book, and a sheaf of papers.

Margaret ignored the folder — which seemed battered and uninteresting. Her opinion might have been different if she had looked inside and read all the information that Hayter had collected concerning her. She would have learned some things about herself of which she was not aware.

She picked up the book, opening it carefully. She squinted, trying to make out what the words said, but could only make out the odd word here and there. She closed it, replaced it upon the desk and turned her attention to the sheaf of papers. Immediately she realised that she held a translation — or transliteration — of the book which she had just looked at. It still didn't make much sense and she jumped from page to page. She frowned as she caught sight of a verse on the very last page. She read it slowly.

> 'When the flesh of my flesh again be united, then
> Shall my kin do battle with my eternal enemies;
> The days of the Brotherhood shall at last be
> Numbered — my offspring, even though it mean their
> Death, shall enable my victory.'

"Does Mr. Hayter know you're in here?" John demanded, making her jump.

In fact, when he spoke she jumped and lost her grip on what she was reading. Five pages fluttered to the ground around her. Before she could move he was picking up the offending sheets and placing them with the others in their correct position.

"I take it you didn't reply because you hadn't asked if you could take a look in Mr. Hayter's study?"

Margaret laughed but felt intimidated, guilty about being caught, and wondered whether she should have got permission first. "No, I didn't answer because you scared me to death. I wasn't told I couldn't look around."

"Of course you can," John said with a smile. "Forgive me for frightening you — it was so unusual to see *anyone* but Mr. Hayter in here that I didn't think before I spoke. But if you want to come in this particular room again, I'd check with Mr. Hayter first. Sometimes, I gather, it can be dangerous."

"Okay, John, I promise I'll get permission next time. Would *you* show me around?"

He smiled again. "I'd be happy to," he said, indicating the door. He followed her out of the study. "Well, Margaret," he said, "what do you want to see, the rest of the mansion or the gardens?"

"Both," she replied, smiling enthusiastically.

He shook his head. "I'm afraid I won't have time for that," he said. "I can manage a quick guided tour of one or the other."

She moved down the passage until she stood in front of the landscape again. "It's fascinating," she said to John, who had moved up to her side. "Do you know who painted it?"

"Oh, yes," he replied, laughing. "Although, *I* don't think it's that good."

126

She took in the amusement on his face and guessed the answer. "You painted it, didn't you?" she enthused. "I think it's fantastic — have you painted anything else?"

He seemed surprised at her enthusiasm. However, he smiled and said: "Yes, as a matter of fact, I have. There are one or two of mine dotted around the mansion, but I paint more for my own pleasure than anyone else's."

"Can I see some of your other paintings?" she asked impulsively.

He frowned. "Well, I'm sure that you'd find the mansion more interesting."

Margaret deduced that her praise and asking to see more of his paintings had, if not embarrassed him, certainly made him feel uncomfortable. She felt vaguely culpable, in that he might think she was trying to coerce him into showing her his paintings by abusing her position as Hayter's guest. She liked him instinctively, and couldn't allow him to think that.

"I'm sorry, John, I didn't think," she said.

"Pardon?" he looked bewildered.

"I shouldn't have asked to see your other paintings. I understand. I remember once when I wrote a story I felt so embarrassed when other people wanted to read it. It's almost as though it's a part of *you* that they're asking to be allowed to see; sometimes that part is *personal* and you don't feel that you want other people to evaluate or criticise it. Honestly, John, I'd like to see your other paintings, but if you don't want me to see them, I'll understand. I *do* love this one, though."

He looked steadily at her. "Yes, you're right, y'know? About the personal aspects that creep into art. Why do you like the landscape?"

"I don't know. There's something about it that tells me that I must keep looking at it until I understand what the painter — you — were trying to say."

"And what do you think I was trying to say?"

127

She studied the painting with a new intensity. In one part of her mind she felt the joy of watching the leaves fall, of seeing the myriad of colours, the beauties of nature.

Blinking, she came back to reality, glanced at him and said, with a certainty which surprised her: "You were trying to capture your own feelings about what you saw — you were trying to paint your own happiness within the context of what generated it." She paused, wondering where the intuitive knowledge had come from. She looked at him a little uncertainly.

He stared at her intently. It wasn't just an inquisitive glance, he *stared* at her as though he couldn't believe what she had just said. "I find it hard to believe I heard what I just heard. I *tried* to capture my happiness on canvas, it's true, but I thought I failed. I really *don't* think that much of it..." he trailed off, looking at her with a new interest in his eyes. "Would you really like to see some of my other paintings?" he asked, almost shyly.

"I'd love to, if you don't mind showing them to me," she said seriously.

"Then I'll have to show you around the mansion some other time," he said, beginning to walk towards the end of the passage. "I have a wing of the mansion to myself and I use the top floor as a studio," he informed her.

"What do you paint? Apart from landscapes?"

"You name it. It depends what mood I'm in. Fields, portraits, land and seascapes — anything and everything."

"Portraits? Does someone model for you?"

"Well, er...no," John confessed, looking a bit flustered. "I occasionally go into town for various supplies — most are delivered to some outbuildings just outside the perimeter of the grounds. I observe people, and if someone catches my eye, I try to keep them in memory and, unknown to them, they become my models. Most of my portraits are, therefore, part fiction, part reality."

"I see," Margaret murmured, as he led her towards the West wing of the mansion. "Don't you ever use friends or relatives?" she asked. He glanced at her a little sharply. "No," he said abruptly, offering nothing further in explanation.

Several minutes later, he indicated a door on the right, which they passed through. Inside, everything contrasted with the rest of the mansion. The room she found herself in was smaller than any other she had seen whilst exploring. The effect, however, was a cosy atmosphere which was missing from the rest of Hayter's domain.

The furnishings were less lavish, but comfortable, she noticed. Two easy chairs, an occasional table, a sideboard and a stereo unit. John went to a door directly opposite the one by which they had entered. Going through this, she wasn't surprised to find herself in another of the ubiquitous passages within the mansion, except that this passage was relatively short. It led off to the left; a few yards in front of her was a staircase. With John leading, they climbed it. At the top was a small hallway, with two doors leading off it, and another flight of stairs. She looked at him, wondering which way now. He grinned and nodded at the stairs. "Last flight, I promise. The studio's at the top."

As they climbed, she asked, "How long have you worked for George?"

He considered quickly. "Nine years or so. Funny you should ask, I only recently reminded Mr. Hayter of how long I've worked for him," and he chuckled.

"That's funny?" Margaret asked, puzzled.

"No," he replied, "you might say it's a private joke."

As he finished speaking they reached the top of the stairs. There was only one option this time, a door immediately ahead of them. John opened it, entered and flicked a switch on the wall. Margaret followed him into a room so large that it took her several moments to take it in. Easels stood in various positions, most of them holding canvas — although each canvas was covered. She noticed some stools and plain wooden chairs against one wall. In a corner, neatly stacked, stood several canvases. Next to these, against a wall, stood a table on which, neatly arranged, were various brushes, palettes, and other paraphernalia associated with painting.

"Coffee?" he asked, indicating a worktop to her right. She turned and saw the sink, worktop and electric kettle. Smiling, she said, "I'd love one."

As he made the coffee Margaret slowly walked over to the neatly stacked canvases. "Mind if I look?"

He glanced at her and came over to stand beside her. "I painted that lot some time ago," he told her. "I don't think you'll be bowled over by them. Go ahead, see what you think."

She needed no second urging. She moved the blank canvas which was at the front of the stack and knelt in front of them.

Behind the blank canvas was a painting of a boy against the bleak background of a coal pit. She caught herself wondering who it was. She tilted the picture in order to see the one behind. It was a seascape, two galleons engaging each other. She frowned, not liking the violent undercurrent which ran through it. The next was a landscape, although this one didn't affect Margaret as did the one which hung near Hayter's study. She pulled it forward, looking at the portrait behind it. She caught her breath, it was a nude.

"Coffee," said John, indicating the steaming mug. She reluctantly got up, replacing the stack as it had been. He pulled two stools from their resting place against the wall and they sat facing each other, trying to think of something to say.

"That painting the nude," Margaret said, "it almost seems out of place."

"Did it surprise you? Every artist has studied the human body at some time. I've only started painting portraits and nudes relatively recently."

"Yes, I was surprised, although I don't know why I should be. You don't strike me as the type of man who's interested in women."

He frowned and then looked at her with a quizzical expression on his face. "What do you mean?" he asked, finally. She replayed what she had just said in her mind and realised that she had come as close as possible to implying that John seemed, to her, to be gay.

Embarrassed, she replied, "No, I meant not interested in painting women — you seem happier with land and seascapes — anything like that where your own emotions become involved. That's what I think, anyway."

"I'll go along with that," he agreed pleasantly.

"Does George play?" Margaret asked, changing the subject.

"What? Oh, yes, you must have seen all our pianos — all twelve of them?"

"No, I've found six so far."

"Yes, Mr. Hayter is a very good pianist — let me know when you find the others."

"Why?"

"I can honestly say that — Mr. Hayter excepted — nobody has ever found the twelfth piano. Its whereabouts are a mystery even to me."

Margaret drained the last of her coffee and standing, looked towards the easels. "Can I look at them?"

John smiled, "I warn you, you might not like what you find."

"I'm willing to take the risk," she said.

"Okay, then," he said, moving to the closer of the easels. He lifted the cover in a dramatic gesture.

Margaret stared at the explosion of colours so bright that they hurt the eyes. "What *is* it supposed to be?" she asked.

"I call it '*When Suns Collide*' — or I will do when it's finished."

She looked at the painting again. "Sorry, it's too garish for my taste." She moved to another easel and lifted the cover. John replaced the cover over the colliding suns and followed her.

She stared at the painting — one of a wood lit by moonlight. "This is like your other one, the landscape — but it has a disturbing quality to it. It's haunting, in a way, but not really threatening."

"I disagree. It's terrifying. It's meant to convey the horrors of the night, how beauty may mask ugliness, that type of thing."

As Margaret moved towards the next painting, she asked, "Do you always have so many half completed at one time?"

He grinned. "Yes, I get bored easily and I like to have plenty of variety when I'm painting so I can carry on with whichever takes my fancy."

She looked at the next painting which she found was no more than an outline. She moved to the next and was about to lift the cover when John placed his hand upon her arm. "I'd rather you didn't, Margaret," he said.

"Why not?" she asked, looking at him curiously.

He blushed. "You remember I told you about observing people and using them for my portraits?"

"Yes," she replied, confused.

"The truth is, that painting is of *you*...I'm sorry, I didn't think to ask your permission but I never *dreamed* that you'd want to see what I painted."

Amazed, Margaret looked at him, and then her curiosity got the better of her. "Please, John, can I see it?"

"It's scarcely more than an outline at the moment," he protested, but seeing that she wanted a definite answer either way, he removed his hand from her arm and nodded.

She lifted the cover, half-fearing that she would see her own nude body looking back at her — and was surprised when she saw that John had transposed her into the period costume of the 1700's. The portrait was only in its rudimentary stages, but she could see a definite likeness. She slowly replaced the cover.

"I'm...*sorry* if I offended you," he apologised.

"I'm not offended, but I think you *might* be trying to make me look prettier than I really am."

"Oh, I wouldn't do *that*," he assured her.

They stood looking at each other, what *hadn't* been said seeming somehow more important than what had. After what seemed an age John broke the spell by looking at his watch.

"Gods, I've got work to do; and I'll bet Mr. Hayter is looking for you."

He made his way to the door with Margaret following. They quickly retraced their route to Hayter's study. "Know your way from here?" he asked.

"Yes," she replied as John turned hurriedly and began walking away from her. She stood watching him until he turned left and disappeared from view.

Margaret thought over what she had seen of John and how attractive she found him. It was a new situation for her. Tony attracted her on a very different level — one that she had always considered as 'safe'. She knew instinctively that an attraction to John was dangerous — but not because Tony was in the same building. How she knew this was a mystery. It was clear to her that, if she wasn't careful, John would change her whole life, her very outlook. She comprehended that she would never feel 'safe' again. She was amazed when a shudder of excitement tore through her at the very idea.

133

Music? She remembered what John had said about Hayter being a very good pianist. As she slowly drew closer to the sitting room the individual notes became distinct. She recognised the melody but couldn't put a name to it. She debated with herself whether or not she should enter and disturb Hayter (for who else could it be?), all the while listening to the melody coming from within the room. Finally, holding her breath, hoping she wouldn't make any noise which would cause him to stop, she turned the handle slowly and opened the door to the sitting room. She slipped quickly inside and closed the door softly behind her. She knew that if she left the door ajar, the slight change in the acoustics would inform Hayter that the door had been opened and that, therefore, someone had entered. She turned to face him, remembering from her own clumsy attempt to play the melody which she had dreamed of that he would be positioned with most of his back turned towards her. Silently, catlike, she came closer to the piano, being drawn like a fly into a spider's web, the music casting its spell around her. In the back of her mind, she heard a voice telling her that she was no better than a voyeur; that she should announce to him that she was there, listening, observing. The music continued and she began to feel her emotions stirring in response. She felt happy and sad at the same time, saw Hayter's hands moving unerringly on the piano's keys. With a final octave run down and then up the piano the music died away, the only sound being his slightly rapid breathing. His hands rested on his legs and Margaret was just about to try clearing her throat when he reached for the keys again and began the second movement of the concerto which he was playing. She moved her position to get a better view of his hands upon the keys. It was only when she had done this and could see the side of his face that she noticed the tears rolling steadily from his eyes, running along his jawbone, and finally dropping off his chin. It took some seconds for her to realise that he was crying because he thought himself alone and was therefore free to release the emotions which the music generated within him. The knowledge made her blush with shame — the voice at the back of her mind castigated her for intruding furtively upon Hayter's private moments, for violating and abusing his hospitality. All the time that this voice spoke to her the music worked its spell — a different spell from before, making her emotions whirl. Feelings of sorrow, desolation, utter despair pervaded her being with relentless ferocity. She became aware that she, too, was crying, tears rolling down her cheeks as the tempo of the music changed, bringing with it hope. She gulped, trying to comprehend that there *was* hope when all had seemed to deny it, all had been *despair*. The music continued wringing every last vestige of emotion out of her. She couldn't help herself. Overcome, her sobs became audible.

Silence descended. Margaret gradually became aware that Hayter had stopped in mid-crescendo and turned on the piano stool, regarding her with a mixture of surprise and anxiety. He pulled a handkerchief from his breast pocket and ran it over his face. He seemed to have recovered his composure, for, placing the handkerchief upon the piano, he said, "Margaret? What's wrong? How long have you been there?"

She was still attempting to gulp back her sobs, and not really succeeding. A sudden impulse, long repressed, burst within her, and she ran to him, flinging her arms around him instinctively, asking to be comforted. To her surprise, that was exactly his reaction. He guided her to the sofa, sat her down, murmured comforting phrases, stroked her hair, until at length, she quieted.

"Want to tell me what the problem is?" he gently asked her.

Margaret raised her head to look into his eyes. "It was the music that you were playing; it made me feel such despair, such hopelessness — I never knew that music could do that to you."

Hayter looked at her astutely. "Yes, music does have that power — but only if you are receptive to it and then usually only if you let it. I take it that you're saying that you couldn't stop what happened?"

"No, I couldn't," she replied.

"Where did you get to? When I came down here, I was looking forward to seeing you, but you'd disappeared."

"I went exploring. John told me off for going into your study. If I'd known it was your study I'd never have gone in. Anyway, I was interested in the landscape on the wall outside it and we ended up talking about painting. John took me to his studio to show me some of his other paintings."

Hayter's eyebrows shot up almost comically. "*John* took you to his studio to show you his paintings?" he echoed in disbelief. "That's a *rare* honour — he won't allow me anywhere *near* his studio, let alone *in* it."

"He showed me back to your study and I came here, heard you playing — I should have let you know I was listening. The music was so compelling that I didn't want it to stop — even though it made me feel so devastated I wanted to hear more."

Hayter nodded as Margaret dried her face on a handkerchief which she had pulled from her jeans pocket. She stood up, feeling awkward. "I feel that I was *wrong* to listen to you like that; it's as though I was *spying* on you."

Hayter laughed. "Not at all — if I had wanted to be undisturbed I would have chosen another piano, where nobody could find me."

Margaret remembered what John had said and, resuming her seat asked, "Where *is* the twelfth piano?"

Hayter laughed again. "You know, John's been asking me that same question for about five years. It annoys him that he can't find it. It makes him feel that he doesn't know this mansion as well as he thinks he does. The whereabouts of that piano is my secret."

Margaret nodded. "Will you play some more for me?" she asked.

Hayter looked her directly in the eyes as though considering whether or not he should accede to her request. In fact, he simply wanted to be sure that she really meant what she said and wasn't just humouring him. What he saw on her face convinced him, however, because he nodded slowly, a ghost of a smile hovering upon his features. He stood, walked back to the piano and replaced his handkerchief in his breast pocket as he sat down.

He turned his head towards Margaret, who was still sitting upon the sofa, and asked, "Is there anything particular that you'd like to hear? Any favourite composer?"

She considered. She knew the names of a few composers but the problem was that she couldn't remember which composer had written what. She wasn't even sure whether or not she liked the composers that she could name. Frowning, she stood and followed Hayter's path to the piano. He watched her with half concealed amusement, as though he understood her problem and had rather expected it.

"It might be better if I don't play the more emotionally draining pieces — another outbreak like the last one and we might flood the place."

She smiled at that, as a thought came to her. "Can you play a piece if I hum the tune?"

"Only if I know the tune," Hayter replied quietly. It annoyed him when anybody called a melody a tune, but he let it pass.

She began to hum a fragment of a piece of music that she had known for a long time, but had never been able to identify. Hayter began humming along with her after only a few notes but made no attempt to play the piece, as yet.

"Yes," he said a few seconds later, "the only thing is that it's from a symphony. It wasn't written for piano. I do know an arrangement of it, however." Hayter positioned his fingers above the keys and began to play. She hummed along quietly, again feeling the beauty and power of the music. She drifted along with each cadence and crescendo and felt a subtle outpouring of *something* within her which she couldn't readily define. With each diminuendo, the flow ebbed within her. As the adaptation drew to its close she had to ask, "What *is* that piece? It's gorgeous."

"Isn't it?" replied Hayter, not yet answering her question. "At times I think that it's too beautiful to have been written by man, yet it was, and I think that *that's* one of the eternal mysteries that lie within the music. The piece as a whole is exceptional, that melody being one of its most famous passages, and yet, not long after its first performance the composer was dead. Is there a moral there, I wonder?" Hayter turned to look at Margaret, but the expression that she wore told him that she hadn't been able to comprehend what he was getting at. With a rueful smile, he added, "It's Tchaikovsky's sixth symphony — commonly known as the *pathetique*."

"It's unbelievable. How much of *you* goes into what I hear?"

Hayter's head jerked up. "What do you mean?" he asked.

"Well, the piece has its own beauty — yes?"

He nodded.

"Well," she continued, "surely you have to interpret that beauty, otherwise it couldn't flow; your own emotions must add an element to what you play, so I wondered just how much of yourself goes into it?"

He stared at her for what seemed a very long time. It was obvious she had asked a question which he hadn't expected. He was surprised that she had been able to perceive his interaction with the music to that extent. He ran a finger down the bridge of his nose — a certain sign that he was considering what to say carefully, as John would have known. Margaret simply took it to be one of Hayter's eccentricities.

"An awful lot," he conceded. "When I'm playing, I don't know where I stop and the music starts. It's difficult to explain, but it soothes me when I need to think. If I let go, then I seem to become one with what I'm playing; it's almost like a fusion. I prefer to think that it's not me that brings the music to life but the music that brings *me* to life." He turned back to the piano abruptly, in a way that seemed, to Margaret, to imply that he already regretted his disclosure of a few seconds ago. His hands reached to the keyboard again, and he played a few half-hearted chords.

She suddenly remembered the melody which had relaxed her whilst she had been asleep, the echoes of which had remained with her when she woke. Partly through curiosity and partly as a means to stop the gulf which she sensed was opening between them widening any further, she spoke. As soon as she did, Hayter stopped playing the half-hearted broken chords and switched his attention back to her.

"George, do you know what this is?" and she whistled (admittedly in several different keys) the melody, as best she could. Before two seconds had passed he was smiling enthusiastically at her and nodding. Imperceptibly at first and then more strongly as he concentrated upon what he was doing, the strains of Grieg's piano concerto filled the room. Her off-key whistling died away. Hayter took it that she merely recognised what he was playing, but there was more to it than that.

She glanced from Hayter's face to his hands gliding over the keys. She frowned. She knew that she only remembered this from a dream, but she was sure that this was an exact representation of what she had heard in that dream. Every inflection, every slightly sustained note that she could remember Hayter faithfully reproduced as though he were seeing into her mind and carefully duplicating what he found there.

She moved to his right and still couldn't shrug off the feeling that this was the very essence of her dream. She stood enthralled as he continued playing, drawing the first movement to its conclusion. Before he replaced his hands above the keyboard to commence the second movement, Margaret interrupted. "Would everyone play it *exactly* like that?"

He twisted to face her, "I don't follow what you mean."

She waved her arms for emphasis. "Well, if someone else played it, would it sound the same to me?"

He laughed, "Of course not — everyone has their own style of playing, of interpreting what they play. You'd recognise it for the same piece, of course, but someone else would play some parts more quickly, other parts more slowly, with differing emphasis and so on. Why do you ask?"

"I know it sounds absurd but I could *swear* that I heard that piece last night in my sleep. From what I can remember of it, it could have been *you* playing it. Isn't that weird?"

Hayter looked at her intently. "Are you certain of what you say?" he asked.

She nodded, "Absolutely," she replied. "I don't think that I'd ever heard that piece before last night."

He frowned at that, and his gaze became distant as he tried to make sense out of what she had told him. The problem was that it didn't make sense, not unless she possessed some latent psychic ability which had been released in reaction to his inducing her sleep. Even so, Hayter felt that there was more to it than that, but what it might be he didn't realise until it was too late.

He opened his mouth to ask her exactly what she remembered but at that instant the door opened and Tony entered, looking rather pale. George's question died unasked and another formed instead. "Tony, how are you?"

He managed a weak smile. "Fine — it was just the shock of what you told me. I'm okay now."

Hayter nodded, dismissing what Margaret had told him to be pondered upon later. "Well, we may as well discuss the reason you're here." Hayter glanced at them both. "Sit down, Tony, there's something that I want you to see, and I think that John should be here as well."

With that, Hayter stood, made his way past Tony, and left the room.

They looked at each other, both trying to understand what the other was thinking. Almost timidly, they approached each other, as though meeting for the first time. Her arms encircled his neck, drawing his head towards her. Surprised, Tony guided his hands to Margaret's back, holding her close, as though he feared that she might pull away from him. They kissed.

Breaking their kiss by unspoken agreement they slowly sat upon the sofa, their eyes locked upon each other.

He whispered, "Margaret?" and she was again in his arms, lips kissing his face, his neck, his lips. He felt more than a little overwhelmed, but not so much so that he wasn't aroused by her urgency. He stroked her hair, held her close to him only to release her as Hayter and John appeared in the doorway, Hayter carrying the book and sheaf of papers which Margaret had already seen.

They disentangled themselves and sat attentively as Hayter and John settled themselves into the leather chairs opposite the sofa.

There was silence for a moment, then Hayter began.

"I take it we all know the important points about Anton Baron, the events which led up to his death, and how we are now threatened by the Cult which Anton opposed. Its revenge may seem slow from our point of view, but it is lethal. All of us are in danger. Tony and myself because we represent the last descendants from Anton; Margaret because of her relationship with Tony. The Cult fear her producing another Baron and will murder her, if they get a chance. If we fail, Margaret, it could well mean your death. John is in danger because..." Hayter glanced at him. "Would you rather I didn't mention it, John?"

John looked at Hayter, his face unreadable. "I don't mind them knowing," he said.

"John," resumed Hayter, "is in danger because he's tangled with the Cult before. We know that the Cult controls various companies, is involved in drug smuggling and so on. John's brother found out about one of these operations, somehow. He never managed to relate how. The official story is that he committed suicide — but *we*," and Hayter looked meaningfully at John, "know better. This all happened about nine years ago. John had begun to find out the truth of the matter when he came to my notice. You could say that I helped him out of an awkward situation, and he's been with me ever since."

Margaret and Tony stared at John, but he gave no indication that he was even aware of their stares. He sat, allowing no emotion to cross his face.

"So," Hayter continued, "we are all at risk. We know that if we do nothing, then our deaths are assured. At the same time, to engage the Cult in outright battle might equally destroy us. There are no guarantees of success, none whatsoever." He looked at Margaret as he spoke, trying to gauge what effect his words were having upon her.

"Why is it that they never kill children as soon as they are born?" Tony wanted to know.

"It's to do with the way the curse was phrased," Hayter answered. "They are bound by the wording not to attack any of the Baron line under twenty years of age. That's strange in itself, since there isn't really any symbolism associated with that number." He glanced at Margaret who nodded, although she was confused by the explanation.

"I am working upon these assumptions. First, that the Cult knows that both of you are here. It's almost certain after the way you were attacked before you arrived. I believe the leader of the Cult to be a devious man, but given to caution. Therefore, I expect him to observe us to the best of his ability and to prepare his followers for a surprise attack from us. That might just give us breathing space."

Tony cut in, "Then you have no real plan of action?"

Hayter smiled. "That is what I want the Cult to think. My plan of action is here, Tony," and Hayter indicated the book. "We'll discuss it shortly." Tony nodded, accepting what Hayter said even though it implied that John and Margaret had no part in the forthcoming discussion.

"What do you know about the Cult?" Margaret asked, desperate to find some facts that she could understand. It was starting to seem unreal to her again.

"Well, I don't know that I can be much help," Hayter demurred. "They are a group of people dedicated to the worship and fostering of — I will call it 'evil' for want of a better word; anything which can help them further that cause they embrace. No perversion exists that is too foul for them. It's a tightly controlled and highly secret organisation, run by one man who is considered to be

143

omnipotent during his reign and lifetime as leader. He cannot be deposed, for his occult power is backed and augmented by the Cult's Patron Demons. Which demons they might be, I haven't been able to discover."

"Satanists?" Margaret queried.

"Oh no, nothing so mundane. They exist to promote evil, but at the same time they hold each other in the highest esteem. If a member wishes to defile a child, one is procured for that member's gratification, but not for any occult purpose. Their personal preferences and their occult rituals are rarely mixed. They take their Society too seriously for that, under normal circumstances."

"Do you know who any of the members are?" asked Tony.

"Yes," Hayter answered, "but it doesn't help us much. We need to destroy the whole, not just clip off one or two individuals."

"How powerful are they?"

Hayter raised his eyebrows, "Isn't that one of the things that we're going to find out?"

Tony smiled back, "What else do you know about them?"

John cut in before Hayter could answer. "It's a Brotherhood. The leader is called the Supreme Brother and his word is law. They meet regularly so members can report upon their various activities. The body of the Brotherhood exists in three circles; the first consisting of those Brothers yet to prove their worth and new initiates. The second consists of those who have proven themselves and possess a fair occult ability. The third circle consists of the hierarchy, excellent occultists, from whom the Supreme Brother may choose a successor.

"If anything in this world can be totally depraved and bestial," John continued softly, "then the Cult is it." He fell silent, ignoring the surprised glances from the others in the room which his interruption had caused.

144

"Do you mean," Margaret asked Hayter, "that we just sit here until the Cult decides to attack us, or hope that they won't?"

Hayter nodded, "It might sound like that. Perhaps I didn't explain as well as I might have done. The Cult will observe us, but their Supreme Brother is cautious. He knows that this mansion and its grounds are protected by a field of energy — a barrier which deflects any incantation he might send against us. On occasion I allow the energy to deplete in order that the Supreme Brother may glimpse this mansion and what he sees confuses him.

"In fact, his caution may well work in our favour. Depending upon how fast Tony absorbs what I have here," said Hayter, again indicating the book, "I will negate the barrier, thus leaving us open to attack. Of course, the Cult will suspect a trap. The barrier works in two ways. I cannot pierce it with my will any more than the Supreme Brother can pierce it with his; so when it is noticed that the barrier no longer exists, it will be obvious that it is the prelude to an attack by us.

"Whether we or the Cult attacks first isn't important — the Supreme Brother's fear or indecision will prove to be a distraction to the rest of them; and we do need every bit of help that we can get."

Hayter glanced at Margaret again. "Do I make myself any clearer?" he asked. She nodded slowly, "I suppose it makes sense, as much as anything does."

"I know this must seem difficult to understand, Margaret," he said softly.

"It's not just that; a week ago, I wouldn't have believed that I could be hearing this — it's so completely unreal. I'd like to understand, but it sounds complicated."

Tony laughed, "You think this is complicated? You should try reading George's *Advanced Treatise on Demonology*; *that's* complicated."

145

Hayter smiled at him. "If you really want to attempt to gain some understanding of occultism, Margaret," he said, moving his eyes from Tony to her, "there are lots of books on the subject in my library — not all written by me, I hasten to add. I would explain everything to you myself, in other circumstances, but as things are, I don't have the time. I must make certain that Tony grasps the importance of this book. By all means browse through the library and if you have any specific questions about what you don't understand, I'll try to answer them."

Margaret made no comment as Tony asked, "What's so special about the book?"

"It appears to be the book which Anton Baron used when attacking the Cult — but I must admit that I was surprised to find a mistake in the final incantation in one of the rituals described, which I have rectified. As I say, we'll study it later, alone. It explains why I can't do what you were thinking of earlier," said Hayter cryptically.

"This barrier," Margaret asked, "whilst it's there we're safe, aren't we?"

"That's a relative term. Safe in that the Cult can't really get at us, but virtual prisoners." She was just about to ask why it was necessary to risk everyone by dissolving the barrier, when Hayter added, "But you know that I won't be here for that much longer, don't you?" And she understood that with Hayter dead, the barrier would cease to exist, leaving them quite vulnerable. The expression on her face left Hayter in no doubt that she comprehended the meaning of what he had said.

"Can I ask another question?" she asked.

Hayter nodded.

"What does that verse mean?"

He looked at her, frankly puzzled. "What verse do you mean?" he asked.

"The one about flesh of my flesh being united; something like that."

146

Hayter's eyes narrowed, his gaze became wary, calculating. His glance flicked quickly to John, who gave a barely perceptible nod, then swept on to Tony and finally came to rest on Margaret again, who was wishing that she hadn't asked.

"I wish I knew," he answered her softly. "It seems to be a cryptic message to the last descendants of Anton Baron, but as for what it means — I'm not sure. That's something which Tony and I have to discuss alone, since it concerns us two and no one else."

Margaret heard the mild rebuke in those words and felt her cheeks going red.

"Where do they meet?" Tony came to her rescue, bringing the subject back to the Cult, for which she was infinitely grateful. She squeezed his hand in thanks.

"The Cult? Various places, but never the same place twice in a row, and some gathering places are only used on special occasions. Most often the gatherings are held within seventy miles of here, I believe."

John glanced at his watch and Hayter noticed the movement. "Anyone feel like lunch?" he asked, "we can always talk again."

"Fine," John muttered, seeing Margaret and Tony nodding assent.

"I think, Tony, that we shall retire to my study. Believe me, there's a lot of information in here," Hayter said, waving the book, "for you to absorb."

Tony nodded, his face serious. "That's okay with me."

"That would seem to leave you at a loose end, Margaret. You can explore some more, or read, listen to music — or even keep John out of trouble."

John's head jerked up sharply at that and he looked at Hayter, a slight smile hovering on his lips.

The seriousness of the meeting died away as Hayter chuckled at John's expression. Both Tony and Margaret became aware of the lighter atmosphere at the same moment.

"Hungry?" John asked them.

"I'll have something later," Tony answered him.

"I'll take mine in my study. Coming, Tony?"

Tony glanced quickly at Hayter, nodded, turned to Margaret and kissed her. "See you later," he grinned, turning to follow Hayter's lead.

John looked at Margaret. "It seems that you're out of things for the moment."

"I know. Are you going to be busy, this afternoon?"

He pulled a wry face. "Yes and no. I'll go and prepare lunch and then I'll see what can be done to stop you becoming totally bored."

"Can't I help you?"

"Help me?" it was obvious John had no idea what she was talking about.

"With lunch — I don't mind."

"Well..." he hesitated, wrong-footed by her offer, "I suppose so."

They left the sitting room, John leading her down a flight of stairs on their right which took them to the kitchen.

Some fifteen minutes later John left the kitchen laden with a tray which held Hayter's lunch. Margaret poured coffee for them both. Taking two plates of sandwiches to the worktop, she pulled out a couple of stools conveniently placed under it, and sat.

She glanced around the white interior of the kitchen as John reappeared. He sat on the vacant stool next to her and attacked one of his sandwiches as though he was famished.

Sipping her coffee, Margaret asked, "Were you and your brother close?"

John swallowed the piece of sandwich which he had just bitten without chewing it. As his eyes focussed more strongly upon her, she knew from his expression that she was on thin ice. Before she could open her mouth to apologise for her curiosity, he spoke.

"Yes, very close. Closer than you could ever imagine." He picked up his plate and standing, walked over to the incinerator chute, opened it and threw the remaining sandwich in.

Margaret stood and walked over to him. "I always seem to manage to say the wrong thing at the wrong time."

John looked into her eyes, "No, I just lost my appetite — I don't care to think about my brother, it's something that I wish I could forget." His face had taken on a harsh expression which Margaret found disturbing.

Attempting to change the subject, she asked, "What are you going to do this afternoon?"

He looked at her as though startled back into the present. "Erm...I've got to go to the stores and get more petrol for the generator, and then I think I'll have a look at the land rover; it's started pulling to the right," he explained. "Then I *might* get some painting done. With a bit of luck, after I've prepared tonight's meal, I *should* have the evening to myself."

"Didn't you tell me that the stores were just outside the grounds?"

He nodded, "That's right."

"Can I come with you?"

He considered the request. "I'm not too sure that Mr. Hayter would approve of that," he said, finally.

"I'm not a *prisoner*, John; and anyway, it won't take long, will it?"

He shrugged, "About twenty minutes, altogether."

She smiled a winning smile at him, feeling that she had won this battle, at least.

"Okay," he laughed. He returned to where his now tepid coffee stood, drained it, and placed the cup in the sink. He gestured to the door and she left the kitchen with him close behind her. They retraced their route to the sitting room and from there, with John leading, made their way to the mansion's main door. She recollected the door opening and John standing there, questioning Tony, but seemingly paying her no attention at all.

He pulled back two bolts which made a mild grating noise. Taking a bunch of keys from an inside pocket, he unlocked the security deadlock. He hesitated before taking hold of the handle and pulling the door towards him. Margaret left the mansion, inhaling beautifully fragrant scents, taking in the cloudless blue sky, the sun high overhead. She glanced back to see John locking the door.

"Why all the security?" she asked. "Wouldn't the barrier tell George if anyone were near?"

John began walking, following the driveway around the mansion with Margaret close behind him. "It's a habit," he said with a grin. As they rounded the side of the mansion she noticed a garage had been built onto it. "Couldn't we have gone straight into the garage from inside?"

He smiled again, "Yes, but there are four doors locked and bolted, not to mention that they are covered by alarms which I'd have to switch off and then back on again. Believe me, it's quicker this way."

With that, he opened the garage door and disappeared inside. After a few seconds she heard the sound of an engine turning over. It was revved a couple of times, and then the land rover slowly rolled into view.

She ran to the passenger door and got in, as John got out and closed the garage door. He slid back into his seat and motioned to her, saying, "Seat belt."

She nodded and slid her seat belt into place. John manoeuvred the land rover onto the driveway and headed away from the mansion, but not in the direction from which she and Tony had arrived.

Although the drive only lasted minutes, Margaret drank in every detail her eyes could pick out. The fields that they passed; the trees, their leaves giving the eye so many shades of green it would have been impossible to count them. She was entranced by a brook bubbling its way through a field upon her left, reflecting the sunlight into her eyes, making its surface seem to be of silver.

A moment or two later the outbuildings which John had spoken of came into view. "This is the boundary of the grounds," he said, beginning to slow the land rover. About a hundred yards further on, he braked to a halt in front of the nearer of three outhouses. They were single-storey buildings made of stone it seemed, rather than brick. Margaret noticed that there were no windows visible. The structures implied age, to her, but further thought was halted as John swung himself out of the land rover and walked to the door. She caught up with him, noting that it was simply secured with a hasp, staple and padlock. It seemed a little incongruous compared with Hayter's security measures within the mansion.

Unlocking the padlock and opening the door, John disappeared inside. He reappeared carrying a large drum which he deposited with a grunt in the back of the land rover. As he repeated the process, Margaret peeped into the storeroom. It was dark, but she could make out several of the drums immediately inside to her right. She walked to the nearest, tried to lift it and was surprised when it didn't move. A sharp laugh from behind made her turn, panting with the effort she had expended.

"They are rather heavy, Margaret — there's twenty gallons to the drum. It might be an idea if you leave this to me — Mr. Hayter wouldn't be too pleased if I took you back with dislocated arms."

So she stood watching as he carefully carried and deposited three more drums. "How long will that last?" she asked, as he locked up the store again.

"A few weeks or so, depending on how much demand is put on the generator."

They climbed back into the land rover. John started the engine, turned the vehicle in a wide circle and began the brief journey back to the mansion. This time, Margaret found herself looking to the wood which was only about a hundred yards from the mansion at its nearest point. The fields and flowers now drew her attention only fleetingly; the wood claimed her, flooding her senses, seducing her with its mysteries.

She didn't realise that they had arrived back at the mansion until the land rover had actually stopped and John was struggling with the first of the containers.

She got out, watching him place all five drums upon the driveway. That accomplished, he unlocked the garage door, and tackling the nearest of the drums, he rolled it on its rim into the garage.

He told Margaret that the generator was actually located in a converted cellar under the mansion. As he moved the fifth drum she followed him. The garage was lit by fluorescent strip lights which cast an antiseptic glow which she associated with hospitals.

On her left she saw Tony's car. She surmised that John had parked it there and glanced at him as the thought crossed her mind, to see him loading the fifth drum into a recess at the back of the garage. He pressed a button and the drums slowly began to descend. Margaret guessed that the recess was in actuality the equivalent of a goods lift.

"It certainly beats carrying the bloody things down," John grunted, wiping his forehead. "I'd better get some overalls on before I get under the land rover."

They walked back to the mansion's entrance. John opened the door and allowed Margaret to enter first.

"What are you going to do?" he wanted to know.

She thought, frowning. She didn't fancy watching the land rover being repaired. "I'll do some more exploring, I think."

He nodded, assuming that she meant the mansion. "Okay then," he said, as he headed in the direction of his rooms.

As soon as he disappeared from view, Margaret left the mansion, taking advantage of the fact that John hadn't locked the door. Once again on the driveway, she looked around and then at the wood which still beckoned her.

Heading for its nearest point rather than following the track, she breathed the air, took in the green grass she trod underfoot and the brown trunks of the trees getting ever nearer. She wondered whether or not John might reappear outside the mansion before she could slip into the protective cover of the wood. She increased her pace — it wasn't *certain* that John would attempt to stop her, but she didn't want to try putting that to the test.

Until she had stepped out of the mansion with him, Margaret had felt no real urge to explore outside — but the glorious weather, the manifestations of nature around her, the wood itself, had all conspired against her. Her love of nature had taken over and she paused to take another look at the wood before walking in amongst the trees.

After a couple of moments she stopped walking, taking in her surroundings. Trees, obviously, lots of them. She saw one that seemed shaped like a deformed hunchback, and wandered up to it. She reached out and touched the cold bark, wondering whether the tree could possibly be aware of her.

Moving on, she was attracted by another tree which, in stark contrast to the last, had grown straight upwards. She placed her hand upon it, and gazing into its branches, tried to estimate how high it might be. Unsure, she moved around its trunk to get a better perspective, not looking where she was putting her feet. She let out a squeal of surprise as she put her foot down into a hole which seemed to have been filled with mud. She overbalanced and, arms swinging, fell heavily upon the ground, her bottom taking the full brunt of the fall, leaving it smarting as though it had been slapped.

She slowly got to her feet, glaring at the hole. She rubbed her buttocks with both hands until the stinging began to fade. She glanced at her foot and was annoyed to see that it was covered with dark brown mud.

She wished that she had made time to change her shoes earlier, but if she had then she knew it was more than likely John would have seen her before she could have reached the wood.

She walked on, her right foot making a *squelch*ing sound with every step she took. Her spirits were somewhat dampened by this experience, but slowly, as the pain from her bottom died away, her spirits recovered their former cheerfulness and she caught herself seeing the funny side of what had happened.

A twig breaking held her attention. There couldn't be anyone else here — could there? One part of her mind said, '*No, of course not*', but another warned that even Hayter was not infallible — he could make mistakes.

Further off, ahead and to her left, she saw a bush tremble, but it was not the wind making it do that — come to think of it, there was barely a breeze. Walking on, cautiously, she reached the bush and walked around it — nothing.

Feeling utterly stupid, she moved away from it and glanced around her. Some wild flowers caught her attention as they struggled for light against their more powerful neighbours. Wondering what they could possibly be she walked over to them, squatted down in front of the blooms and considered.

Deep blue petals, six of them, but arranged in an oval shape. Frowning, she shook her head, unable to name

154

what she was seeing. It was then, as she crouched unmoving and silent, that she heard the soft scraping noise behind her.

She turned her head slowly towards the sound.

As she caught sight of the author of the scraping, Margaret's face lit up in a smile. A grey squirrel less than fifteen feet away was examining the ground, searching for anything edible, she guessed. It seemed to hop a few more yards away from her and she followed, fascinated.

She tried to get closer to it and succeeded, until it suddenly stood up on its hind legs and regarded her with what seemed to be a grave stare. She knew that it was insane, but she was certain that the squirrel was saying, with its stare, '*I know you won't try to hurt me, but even so, come any closer and I'm off.*'

Then the squirrel went back to searching for food with Margaret still following it, but more discreetly now, until she became aware of the fact that for several minutes she had been hearing a sound which hadn't registered as such.

Water? She glanced in the direction from which the sound originated, wondering if it might be the source of the brook which she had seen from the land rover. She took a few steps forward and was rewarded by a grey blur as the squirrel, feeling threatened, ran for the nearest tree and quickly climbed it.

As it neared the first branch it stopped dead and looked directly at her. '*I told you,*' the squirrel seemed to be saying, '*I didn't think you'd try to hurt me, but now I'm not so sure.*' It made its escape into the tree's upper branches.

Margaret felt vexed with herself for frightening it. She looked up into the tree half-hoping that the squirrel would put in another appearance, but she was disappointed.

She turned her attention back to the sound of running water, and made her way towards it. It took her longer than she had expected to reach, because as she made her way directly forward toward the sound which the water made, she found her way barred by thick gorse. She received a couple of scratches by way of reward for attempting to force her way through it.

Finally, she found a point where the gorse thinned out, and there she managed to find a way through. She stood in a clearing in the wood where the brook not only meandered through, but had filled a natural depression, creating a small lake, or a large pool.

Her first thought was that she could at least attempt to clean some of the mud off her shoe. She pulled her handkerchief from her jeans pocket and approached the edge of the water which lapped gently at the bank. Dipping the handkerchief into the water, she rubbed at the mud on her shoe.

Eventually she managed to clean it to her satisfaction. She decided against trying to clean her sock or the leg of her jeans; both were heavily stained.

She looked over the expanse of the lake, heard the call of birds, saw the swaying of the tree tops in the light breeze — which seemed absent within the wood. The clear water looked inviting — she would have loved to swim in it; the problem was, of course, that she hadn't brought a costume with her. Reluctantly, she turned away from the lake, just as a small voice in the back of her mind whispered: '*Why not...?*'

She turned back to face the lake, considering. It was *very* unlikely that anyone would pass by here; she hadn't seen anybody whilst she had been walking — and she would *still* be inside Hayter's barrier, wouldn't she?

She took another look around the clearing and then pulled her jumper off, dropping it a few yards further away from the edge where water met bank. Sitting upon springy turf she undid her shoes, took them off and threw her socks after them. Still sitting, she undid the cuffs of her blouse and then the blouse itself. She glanced around the clearing again, feeling more than a little strange at stripping herself in the open air; it was something which she had never done before and she felt quite self-conscious about it. She shrugged her blouse off her shoulders. It fell to the ground, alongside her jumper. Standing, she undid the clasp of her jeans, pulled down the zip and eased the tight denim off her hips and down her thighs. She paused for a moment to prevent her panties being drawn down her legs by the clinging fabric.

She stepped out of her jeans and tossed them upon the collection of garments which she had shed. She felt the air upon her back, her legs, her chest. She felt exposed yet was enjoying the sensations pulsating through her. She checked the clearing again and seeing nothing out of the ordinary, she unhooked her bra, hesitated for a long moment and then allowed it to fall down her arms; it fell amongst the rest of her clothes. Finally, she slid her fingers into her panties and a couple of seconds later she stood naked in the clearing.

She stood for some time feeling the cool breeze upon her body, acutely conscious of her nudity yet luxuriating in the sensation of freedom which it seemed to bring out in her. She stared at the water and then ran into it, the sound of splashing shattering the comparative silence.

It was deeper than she had realised and she was out of her depth very quickly. She swam to the approximate centre of the lake and looked down to its base. The water was so clear that she could see the rocky bottom easily. She took a breath and swam down to it. Apart from the odd loose rock the base seemed uniform and uninteresting. She let her buoyancy carry her back to the surface. She swam from the centre of the lake to the bank as nearly opposite to the one where she had undressed as possible and back again. She thoroughly enjoyed every second. The water touching every part of her body as she swam, cool, yet not cold, was mildly erotic, especially against her nipples which had hardened in reaction to the relative temperature.

Time passed. She swam, floated and luxuriated in the lake. She had given up watching the banks for any sign of someone approaching, having become too absorbed in discovering the pleasures of nude swimming.

As she swam she was not aware of a pair of eyes, grey and hard, which watched her every movement.

From the bottom of the lake she swam for the surface as fast as she could, erupting half out of the water before gravity pulled her back.

She enjoyed this sensation and repeated the manoeuvre dozens of times, until she noticed someone sitting on the bank watching her, from the corner of her eye. She got no clear picture as her hair clung to her face, and the next second she plunged back underwater. She began to feel the exposed, self-conscious reaction which she had felt when getting undressed. She floated to the surface, turning her head to see who had been watching her, moving her hair out of her face. Whoever it was must have got a real eyeful — several real eyefuls — she thought, with an apprehensive shudder. The knowledge simply embarrassed her further.

Her eyes locked with John's. He was dressed in overalls, which were covered in grease and oil. His face was stained with it as well. She wondered whether or not he was getting a good view of her from where he sat and her mind made her squirm by providing the answer that as the water was so clear he must be seeing her in all her glory — or at least in all her nudity.

"Enjoying yourself?" he called out.

"Yes," she called back, unsure whether or not there had been anger in his tone.

"Well, this escapade's over. I have to take you back to the mansion."

"But why?"

"WHY?" he exploded. "We have been looking for you for the last three hours — and guess who had to search the wood?"

"What?" she asked, confused.

"I'll tell you about it as we go." He stood, waiting for her to emerge from the lake.

"Turn your back," she insisted. He gave an exaggerated sigh as he did so, glancing up at the sky in exasperation, and walked a few paces away. She made her way to the bank and then realised that she hadn't brought anything with which to dry herself.

Mentally cursing her own stupidity in giving in to the urge to swim naked in the first place, she pulled on her underwear; her panties immediately clung to her.

Her bra was easier, but her blouse seemed determined to fight for as long as possible. She finally managed to button it up and then tried putting on her jeans. The denim attempted to cling to her legs, but she pulled, and reluctantly the jeans settled into place.

"Okay," she said, pulling on her socks and shoes. John turned to face her and now she could *see* the anger smouldering in his dark blue eyes, making them appear more *black* than blue.

"Mr. Hayter asked where you were. I had assumed that you were in the mansion — but you weren't, were you? Made me seem a *complete* fool. Mr. Hayter thought that the Cult might just have managed to get their hands on you — and then he had the idea of trying to trace you through Tony. It worked, after a fashion. We found out that you were in the wood, somewhere, so here I am."

"Does that give you the right to sit ogling me whilst I didn't know you were there?" she snapped back at him, her own anger beginning to flare, fuelled by her embarrassment.

"If you don't *want* to be *ogled*, as you put it," John retorted viciously, "then *don't* parade yourself *naked*. And another thing, *don't* you appreciate the danger..."

"I wasn't in *any* danger," Margaret insisted, interrupting him.

He took a deep breath, apparently trying to gain control of his anger. He continued in a gentler tone. "Maybe not from the Cult," he conceded, "but it's dangerous enough around here," he swept his hand around, indicating the wood.

Margaret sighed heavily. '*Why was it,*' she wondered, '*that everyone seemed to know more than she*?' She felt that whatever she did she couldn't win. "I don't understand," she said quietly.

"There are ancient mine tunnels under this wood. If you don't know where they are you can find yourself falling a hundred feet or more — it's a hell of a way to find them. Luckily, you headed away from the general area which is riddled with them and ended up here. Margaret, this wood is ten miles square — do you think that the barrier covers it all? It doesn't. Another thing," he said crisply, as if to emphasise a point, "you tell me which direction the mansion is in."

She opened her mouth and then realised that since her fall she had lost track of direction. She had no idea which way to go. She was well and truly lost. Weakly, she pointed in the direction of a tall beech.

"Sorry," John shook his head. "That's just off west. We need to head north-east," and he took a compass from his pocket. "I do *hope* you had a *good* time, Margaret," he added sarcastically, "I enjoy *nothing* more than searching the wood for missing guests."

Margaret said nothing. The fact that she had been lost had shaken her, and the story about the old tunnels sounded gruesome. The wood took on a more sinister aspect, to her. She followed John meekly, eventually summoning the courage to say, "I didn't *mean* to worry anyone, John."

He turned quickly; his eyes burned into her. He took the step which separated them and his arms encircled her waist, drawing her close to him. It was so unexpected that she was, for a second, unable to register what he had done. As he turned his face to her she pulled away from him, a little frightened and intimidated.

"John, no. I like you, but that's as far as it goes. I'm Tony's girlfriend. I felt safe with you — I'd *never* have believed you'd try to do *anything* like this."

He looked at her, seemingly stunned by his own actions. "I can only say I'm sorry... I just didn't realise what...don't know what I was..." he stammered. "I was so *relieved* to find you, *worried* in case something had happened to you. Margaret, I...I'm..." he stopped speaking, at a loss for words.

His expression faded her sudden anger and she managed a laugh which broke the tension. "It's okay, John, no harm done."

They continued on their way, side by side.

"Was George angry?" she asked, changing the subject.

"Furious," John replied, "but he'll calm down. Next time you feel like a swim, let us know."

Eventually, after what seemed like hours, she spotted the mansion through the trees. Five minutes later John locked the main entrance behind them.

"We'd better let Mr. Hayter know that you're all right," he whispered, guiding her towards Hayter's study. On reaching the door they heard the murmur of voices. Margaret felt a little like a naughty schoolgirl being taken to the headmaster. John knocked and entered, Margaret followed him.

"...united in purpose, *perhaps*," she heard as she entered.

"Here's our runaway," John declared.

161

"Margaret, why didn't you tell anyone where you were going? What do you think..." Tony began in an annoyed tone, but Hayter interrupted him.

"Margaret, all I ask is that next time you have an idea like this, let us know. One of us, anyway." His eyes locked with hers for a moment, then his face crinkled into a smile which somehow made *everything* alright again. Margaret felt tears start to her eyes, and rubbed them to prevent the tears becoming obvious. Hayter smiled slightly, and then spoke again, drawing immediate attention away from her: "My dear, you look as though you could use a bath and some sleep," his voice was calm, relaxing.

"Yes, I think I will," she said, turning to leave when a thought occurred to her. "George, may I borrow a book from your library to read until I feel sleepy?"

He nodded, "Of course. John will show you where the library is."

They left the study, Margaret feeling very uncomfortable in her damp clothes. As the door closed the discussion resumed, although what they said was indistinct.

"The library is on the way to your room," John informed her.

He walked with her to the top of the stairs where she would have normally turned right. John opened a door upon her left. "This is it," he announced.

She entered and was immediately intimidated by the hundreds upon hundreds of books stacked from floor to ceiling.

"What type of thing do you want?" John asked.

"Anything on basic occultism that's easy to read."

He walked to a stack and after a slight hesitation pulled out a slim book which he handed to her. "Try this," he said.

She took the book and retreated from the library. "Thanks, John. I'm sorry if I've been a pain today."

He smiled at her, his eyes twinkling now in good humour. "Good night, Margaret," he said, and descended the stairs.

She proceeded to her bedroom. Once there, she placed the book which he had given her upon the bed and went into the bathroom. She shed her clothes into the laundry basket and ran herself a bath. Whilst it was filling she went into her dressing room and located a skirt, underskirt, blouse, jumper and socks. She placed them ready for tomorrow and, putting on her dressing gown, she went back to see how the bath was filling.

She stepped into it, having turned the taps off. She began soaping her body, impatient to feel clean again and to relax in bed.

Five minutes later, she towelled her body roughly, making the skin glow. Having put on her nightie, she drew the bedclothes back and swung herself into her bed with a sigh of contentment.

She picked up the book, was about to begin reading, when she heard a knock upon the door.

"Yes," she called.

John entered; he had washed and changed out of his overalls. He carried a tray which contained sandwiches and a glass of hot milk. "I took the liberty of making you a snack — if you're hungry?"

"I'm not yet, but no doubt I soon will be. *Thanks*, John."

He smiled nervously, and hesitated before depositing the tray upon the bed. He then returned to the door, reached outside, and brought in a rectangular bundle covered in brown paper. Blushing, he said, "I'm sorry about what happened in the wood. I like you too, Margaret, but more like the sister I never had. Anyway, I want you to have *this*." He placed the object at the foot of the bed and then he was gone, the door closed behind him. The flat rectangle lay where he had left it.

Baffled, Margaret reached for it, being careful not to jerk the tray. She pulled the brown paper from the rectangle and sat staring at the landscape which she had so admired.

"John, I just *don't* understand you," she whispered, gazing at the painting.

Chapter Nine: Solutions

A freezing-cold wind whistled around the bleak moorland, driving rain before it. As night grew darker, an observer might have been justified if, considering the scene, he had decided that God had neglected to watch over this particular moor, had deserted it for some reasons of His own, leaving other, less benign forces, to wreak whatever havoc they wished, unhindered.

Whether or not this was the case, the moor presented as bleak a picture as is possible to imagine. Mile upon mile of it existed as if for no other purpose than to exist; only the most resourceful of creatures survived here. Grasses struggled to grow, to force meagre shoots through the barren, rocky soil; the grass was, therefore, so weak and stringy in texture that it provided little nourishment for those few beasts brave enough to attempt eating it.

As far as the eye could see — were it light enough to do so — all that could be seen was the moor; no tree, bush, or man-made structure was visible except for the ruins of a long-abandoned building. Strangely, as one approached these ruins a feeling of revulsion would build up, preventing the wanderer approaching any more closely. Any brave enough to make the attempt would find that the revulsion turned into intense nausea, which would result in vomiting, and finally, paralysis.

But no man ventured near those ruins this night — not unless specifically invited to do so. The wind howled over the moors sounding like a demented creature of the damned — as it could well have been, and the driving rain deterred even the most determined and tenacious of moor-walkers had any been partial to walking the moors at night.

The bleak, almost unholy atmosphere which accompanied the stony moor seemed somehow enhanced by the foul weather, as had been intended. But, as those invited individuals knew, as one came closer to the ruins the howling wind died away completely, the rain ceased. Around and among the ruins the night was warm, but not uncomfortably so. Some found this change of weather disconcerting, but most accepted it calmly.

Thus, by various routes, leaving cars some distance away, most of the Brotherhood approached the ruins: although the meeting would not be held there tonight... not exactly.

On reaching them, each Brother knew exactly where the entrance stone to the catacombs beneath was located. To a casual glance, the stone might have been the same as many others embedded in the ground. However, a skilful touch in exactly the right place caused the counterweights beneath to operate, and thus the stone appeared to raise itself, displaying the steps carved into the very rock which was the ruin's foundation.

As a Brother placed his weight upon the last of the steps the counterweights operated again, closing the entrance smoothly. For this reason, it was not considered safe for more than five Brothers to enter at one time, as the closing entrance-stone could crush the unfortunate who entered sixth.

The passage in which the Brothers emerged led downward, with occasional passages leading off to both sides. The main passage itself curved to the right, giving the feeling of walking in a large circle. After a walk of perhaps five minutes one reached the chamber where tonight's meeting was to be conducted.

It was a large chamber, with a dais at the far end. Interestingly, there were two chairs upon the dais rather than one. Chairs had been set out in three circles, facing it, but leaving a space between them and the dais of about fifteen feet. Sand had been spread over this area; above it, ominously, hanging from a pulley set in the rock ceiling, dangled a metal hook. The rope to which it was attached passed over the pulley and angled down to the wall of the cavern where it was secured by means of two metal spikes set into the wall, around which the rope had been wrapped in a figure '8'. Immediately below the hook, secured into the rock floor, were two large metal staples, set about a metre apart.

As the Brothers arrived, each took in the hook, and its import. The usual subdued murmur and discussion died away as each thought upon what they would soon witness. Those of the third circle, whilst changing into their ceremonial robes in the chamber allocated to them, couldn't help but think of Brother Richard. Not only was he a qualified doctor and surgeon, but his would be the role of torturing Brother William and then executing him.

In another smaller chamber, off from the main passage which led to the cavern and the dais, the Supreme Brother sat facing Brother Gregory — now to be known as Brother Fidelis, the traditional name of the Supreme Brother's successor. His whole being radiated an aura of calm, as though this could be any meeting rather than one where a Brother was about to be executed.

Brother Fidelis shifted in his chair, hearing footsteps approaching and then fading, as Brothers made their way to the cavern where the meeting would take place. "You seem nervous, Gregory."

Brother Fidelis turned his face to the Supreme Brother. "Yes, I am," he admitted. "Not of the execution, but of taking your place in the meeting afterwards. I don't want to make any mistakes."

The bleak smile rested upon Supreme Brother's face. "Remember what I told you; make no hasty decisions, refuse to be rushed, take everything in your stride. I'll be right next to you."

167

Gregory nodded and tried to look reassured; it had been Supreme Brother's idea to let Gregory 'chair' this meeting, and if all went well he could then be left in charge of other meetings if the need arose. Primarily, the Supreme Brother was curious to see how Brother Fidelis reacted to this pressure.

"You have familiarised yourself with the form the execution takes?"

"Yes," Gregory replied simply. "Statement from me, the lash from Brother Graham and then Bother Richard will perform the erm..."

"Torture?" interrupted the Supreme Brother. As Gregory gave him a bland glance, he continued, "It is the correct word. Brother William broke his vows — the punishment for which is torture and death; it always has been."

"I know," Gregory conceded. "And I accept that — but before my promotion I had never been responsible for giving an order which would result in a Brother's death. It's a strange feeling, knowing that soon I will give just such an order, and that a man's life will end because of it. Did *you* ever get used to it?" he asked, looking directly into Supreme Brother's eyes.

"No," the Supreme Brother admitted, smiling his frigid smile.

Gregory sighed, wishing that the waiting were over, the meeting finished. He knew Supreme Brother would be watching his every move, and the knowledge daunted him.

They sat in silence, the waiting serving to stretch Gregory's nerves until he thought he would scream. He took a deep breath to calm himself, and at the same moment heard footsteps approaching. Hesitantly, a young Brother who looked to be in his early twenties but whom Gregory couldn't name, entered. He looked first to the Supreme Brother, opened his mouth to speak, thought better of it and turned to Brother Fidelis.

168

Flustered, and obviously not knowing which of them to address, the Brother decided to play safe.

"Supreme Brother, Brother Fidelis, all are assembled, all is prepared," he glanced from one to the other, as though to make sure he had done the right thing.

"Unless otherwise directed, Brother erm..."

"Alan," interrupted the Brother eagerly, to be silenced by Brother Fidelis' cold glare.

"Unless otherwise directed Brother *Alan*, you will address yourself to *me* and if necessary, *I* will decide whether what you have to say is of importance to Supreme Brother. And *never...*"

"Of course, Brother Gregory," interrupted Brother Alan. He turned to go, only to hear Brother Fidelis snarl, "Stay."

Alan turned to see Gregory glaring at him, cold eyes full of fury. "I was about to tell you, Brother Alan, never to interrupt me again when you did. My name is Brother Fidelis; I think you need help to remember that fact," said Fidelis slowly. "After this meeting, you will report immediately to Brother Graham, and tell him that it is my command that you receive sixty strokes of the lash — then perhaps you will learn not to interrupt me and to remember my name. Now you may go."

Visibly swallowing the lump which had risen in his throat, Brother Alan hastily inclined his head to both Brother Fidelis and Supreme Brother, turned quickly and disappeared into the passage beyond. After a few seconds Gregory looked at the Supreme Brother.

"Feeling better now that you've flexed your claws?"

"But..."

"You were feeling the strain of this meeting, and needed someone to release it upon. Brother Alan happened to be there."

"I suppose so," Gregory admitted. He hesitated and then added, "Do you think I should cancel his punishment?"

The Supreme Brother smiled. "No: it was a little severe, perhaps, given the nature of his crime and that it was unintentional, but you had to underline your authority. I agreed with your action in ordering him lashed, it was your motives which I felt were suspect. It isn't surprising, under the circumstances. Come, let's get this over with."

Gregory looked at him, surprised at what he had heard, but he nodded. Together, they made their way to the cavern where the Brothers were assembled waiting, impatient, much as Brother Gregory had been. They all stood as Supreme Brother and Brother Fidelis entered. They made their way around the cavern, following the curve of the wall, until they reached two steps behind the dais, climbed them and then stood before the chairs facing the assembly. Brother Fidelis felt his heart hammering in his chest, knowing that this was it. The meeting was about to begin.

They sat, and at this signal, the assembled Brothers followed their lead and sat silently, waiting for the first move to be made by the Supreme Brother. The silence which followed stretched painfully long; so long that each Brother began to suspect that something was amiss.

Supreme Brother watched Gregory from the corner of his eye. He was reassured to see that he showed no signs of being frozen by the enormity of the task before him; on the contrary he seemed to be, with the exception of the Supreme Brother himself, the most relaxed person within the chamber.

In one smooth, almost liquid motion, Brother Fidelis stood. Deliberately and slowly, he swept his gaze around the assembled throng. The silence seemed to deepen, to intensify were that possible, and Brother Fidelis realised for the first time exactly how much power he now wielded.

He inclined his head to the Supreme Brother. "Paternal Brother; Brothers," he began, turning to face his audience. "The reports of your various endeavours will be heard later — for the present, all of you know of the treachery practised by Brother William. Supreme Brother sees no reason for leniency, and neither do I. Any Brother who betrays the vows made to our Patron Demons and to his fellow Brothers has no excuse. The punishment for such is clear and has not varied except in the form of torture inflicted, for over five hundred years," Fidelis paused, pleased with the effect which he was achieving.

"And so," he continued, "I order the ritual execution of Brother William. I exhort our Patron Demons to draw near and to feast upon his sufferings. By name I summon D—; by name I summon G—; watch over us during this meeting and accept the blood of one who would have betrayed us."

He fell silent. A slight chill in the air, an almost imperceptible thickening of the atmosphere informed all that the summons had been answered and that the Brotherhood's principal Demons were now scrutinising proceedings.

Fidelis imperceptibly let out a sigh of relief. If the Patron Demons had failed to act upon his summons it could have been interpreted by all present that the Demons were displeased with Supreme Brother's choice. That they had arrived reinforced his standing as successor. The summons which Fidelis had used was more of a polite invitation which could be declined or accepted, rather than a summons which had to be obeyed. The latter form, being rather dangerous, was only used in extreme circumstances.

He ran his tongue around his lips which were dry, he suddenly realised, and then resumed, "Are Brothers Simon and Mark here?"

After the traditional moment of silence, Brother Jerome stood and glowered at Brother Fidelis. His eyes, as always, burned with zeal. "They await your command

171

regarding Brother William, Brother Fidelis," he said in his quiet tone.

"Tell them to bring in Brother William," he replied savagely.

Brother Jerome left the chamber and, the message delivered, returned to his place. All the Brothers turned to watch as Brother William, still in his semicomatose state, wearing the green robe of a disgraced Brother, was guided to the sanded area beneath the hook, facing the dais.

The Supreme Brother stood and directed his gaze upon Brother William. As previously, a flash of light seemed to erupt from Supreme Brother's eyes, this time restoring William to full consciousness. That accomplished, he sat, leaving control of the execution in Fidelis' hands.

Brother William glanced around, unsure at first of where he was. He took in the green robe, the memory of the last meeting, and knew what had been done to him. He was just as certain that this meeting would be the last which he would ever attend; these faces, the last he would ever see. He considered tearing free and running, but he knew Supreme Brother could paralyse him before he had managed to turn a half circle. He knew that there was no escape.

"Brother William," said Fidelis calmly, "I have ordered your execution — yet you have the right to speak if you will. Have you anything you wish to say?"

He shrugged his shoulders then shook his head.

Brother Fidelis nodded, and Brother Graham stepped forward, bringing with him four lengths of rope. With these, he bound William's wrists together tightly. He secured his ankles, binding one to each of the metal staples set into the rock floor.

He looked to the wall where the rope attached to the hook was secured around the metal stakes, saw a Brother there, ready to assist. He nodded; the Brother undid the rope and lowered the hook until Brother Graham could place it under the rope which bound William's wrists, but between them so the hook lifted Brother William's arms as it was raised.

As William's body became taut, ankles straining against the rope binding them to the staples, the result of his hands and arms being stretched upwards, Brother Graham nodded again. The Brother assisting him fastened the rope to the stakes set within the wall, thereby securing William in that position; arms and back stretched, ankles savagely secured.

Brother Graham looked to the dais, to Brother Fidelis, waiting for the command which he knew must come.

Brother Fidelis, still standing, hesitated before saying, "Begin the execution, Brother Graham. Two hundred strokes."

Brother Graham inclined his head solemnly, and then moved to a briefcase which he had placed beside his chair. Opening it, he took out the first of the four rawhide whips which resided inside. He would change whips after each set of fifty strokes, as after that amount the whip would become clogged with blood and flesh and would therefore become less and less effective.

Whilst he was doing this, Brothers Simon and Mark pulled the robe off William. As it was sleeveless, the shoulders seams only being held together by four buttons, this was easily achieved. Brother William hung naked, anticipating his forthcoming torture. Their duties completed, Simon and Mark took their places among the assembled Brothers.

Brother Graham took up a position somewhat behind and to the left of Brother William. Seconds later the *wush* of the whip flying through the air and the *thwack* of it landing upon Brother William's back was audible.

Most of the assembly watched impassively, as the sounds of the flogging filled the cavern. The spasming of

Brother William's body as each stroke landed testified to the amount of pain being inflicted; but, perhaps stubbornly, he made no sound and suffered in silence.

There was one Brother amongst the gathering who found himself trembling and flinching involuntarily at each stroke. Brother Alan imagined himself in a similar position to William, and could almost feel the lash landing upon his own flesh. He watched as Brother Graham changed whips and saw an exact replay of what had just been inflicted, except that William's spasming became more pronounced, as though the whip was biting more deeply than previously. Almost in a trance, Brother Alan watched as the whip was changed for the second time.

He had become a full Brother only six months ago — his mistake in calling Brother Fidelis Brother Gregory was his first infringement of the Cult's strict code of decorum. He feared telling Brother Graham to practise his art upon him, but feared not doing so even more. Never having been on the receiving end of the lash before he could only surmise how painful it would be and, judging by the spasms affecting Brother William's body as the lash continued its song, it would be worse than he had believed it could be.

Blood flowed freely down Brother William's back and the rest of his body to be absorbed by the sand. Brother Graham changed whips for the last time. William's head had fallen forwards onto his chest, as though he didn't have the strength to lift it anymore. The coppery smell of blood tinged the air; Brother Graham began the last fifty strokes.

As the flogging ended Brother Graham turned to the dais panting slightly from his exertions, and slowly bowed his head to Brother Fidelis, indicating that his order had been carried out. Then, collecting the three whips which he had dropped to the floor one after the other when they needed replacing, he coiled them and placed them in the briefcase. He closed it and calmly returned to his seat within the third circle as though what he had done was the most natural thing in the world, which as far as the Cult were concerned, it was.

Brother William hung from the hook, still making no sound, apart from his heavy, rasping, laboured breathing.

Brother Fidelis waited a full minute after Graham had sat before speaking, giving all a chance to view his expertise. William's back — from shoulders to calves — was a raw, blood-covered mass. The occasional weal was visible where flesh could be seen, but the running blood stained what was left of the flesh upon his back, making the flogging appear as severe as it had been.

"Brother Richard, are you ready?" Brother Fidelis asked, in a voice which surprised him — he sounded much more relaxed than he felt.

A tall, slim Brother arose from the third circle and approached the dais before he answered, "I am ready, Brother Fidelis."

"Then begin," he ordered.

Without acknowledging Brother Fidelis' command, Brother Richard turned on his heel and approached Brother William. He felt the pulse in his neck, lifted his head and raised his eyelids.

"Brother Fidelis, I assume you wish Brother William to face his Brothers for the last time — it is, after all, their right to *watch* his execution."

Fidelis stared at Richard, his first feeling one of anger that Richard was attempting to ridicule him. He realised, a second later, that he had made a mistake and Richard was offering him a way out without causing him any embarrassment. He should have ordered William's ankles unbound, his body turned and his ankles retied so that he faced the Brothers whom he had attempted to betray, whilst he was tortured.

"Of course that is my wish, Brother Richard," he said smoothly with a glance at Richard which thanked him

175

for his thoughtfulness. "Brothers Graham and Simon, would you attend to that?" It was phrased as a question, but all knew that it was not.

Whilst William was being turned to face the assembly, Brother Fidelis noticed Richard frown, leave the chamber for a moment, and return with his doctor's bag. Brother Stephen brought a small table, which had been stored behind the dais, to Richard's side. He grunted his thanks as Stephen, along with Graham and Simon, returned to their respective places.

He took several instruments out of the bag and laid them upon the table. Placing his bag upon the floor — in an area not turned brown by blood — he approached Brother William and repeated his original examination.

Shaking his head, he returned to the table and lifted his bag from the floor. After a second, he took out a syringe and began to fill it from a vial.

"Brother Richard, what *are* you doing?" demanded Fidelis, frowning.

Richard paused as he filled the syringe. "Brother William is half unconscious — he will be comatose by the time I am finished. This drug is being experimented with by the Psychiatry department of the hospital where I lecture. It will not only revive him, but it will enhance certain of his senses. The sense of touch — or rather of pain, is among these. It will keep him conscious long enough for our purposes."

"You are certain?"

"Positive, Brother Fidelis," he replied, resenting the implied doubt of his competence.

"Proceed, Brother. I acknowledge your expertise, and did not mean to imply otherwise."

Accepting the apology, Richard finished filling the syringe and approached Brother William again. The needle slid into his arm apparently without his being aware of it; having depressed the plunger, Brother

Richard placed the empty syringe next to the vial upon the table.

For several seconds nothing seemed to happen; and then William began to groan. He lifted his head, shook it from side to side; his eyes cleared and his face mirrored the pain and discomfort he was enduring as the drug began to take full effect.

Brother Richard smiled. "Welcome back to consciousness, Brother. We decided it would be an insult to our Patron Demons to deny them your screams of agony; believe me, Brother, only death will release you."

Brother William opened his mouth to protest or to make some reply, but Richard had been hoping for that reaction; as William's lower jaw opened, he grabbed his chin in one hand and pulled sharply downwards.

There was a crunching, splintering sound as William's lower jaw dislocated. A scream of agony erupted from his throat, filling the cavern and echoing throughout the connecting passages. Richard took hold of what looked like a pair of long pincers, but were in reality arterial clamps, along with a scalpel and, having closed the clamp upon William's tongue and drawn it out, he cut through the root of the tongue with the scalpel.

A half-strangled ululation filled the cavern, but it was cut off by a gurgling noise as the blood filling Brother William's mouth threatened to choke him. The removal of the tongue had been accomplished so rapidly, most of the watching Brothers only realised what had happened when Richard casually dropped the bloody red object upon the sand.

Richard stood back, regarding William's body as he pulled uselessly against his bonds. Picking up the scalpel again, Richard approached William, his gaze fixed upon his eyes.

William, still in agony from his dislocated jaw and the removal of his tongue guessed what was coming next and shook his head violently, closing his eyelids.

Brother Richard smiled. He grabbed a handful of William's hair, and pulled his head back in a vice-like grip. He knew that he couldn't remove William's eyes whilst he shook his head, and knowing that he wouldn't be obliging enough to open his eyes, he sliced around William's eyelids which he threw to the ground. Then carefully, still holding William's head in that grip of steel though the body convulsed, he sliced around the eyes, gently removing them from their sockets and severed the connection to the optic nerve. He let the eyeballs roll to the floor, where they glared redly at the assembly.

Throughout, William had managed to shriek out his torment; his screams sounding unearthly now that his tongue had been removed. A bubbling, gurgling sound escaped at times, when the blood trickled down his throat. Eventually his screams and ululations died away, by degrees, and were at length replaced by a babbling wail of continual torment.

Brother Richard approached William for the last time. In his hand he held a long, wickedly sharp knife. Although William couldn't see him, he sensed his presence; his body stiffened, expecting some new assault.

It was not long in coming. Richard held William's penis and scrotum in one hand and paused as William's sightless eyes seemed to turn upon him, begging him to kill him now, before inflicting *that* indignity. With one swift motion, drawing the knife upwards, Richard emasculated him. His body threshed and convulsed sickeningly. Gouts of thick blood poured from between his legs; his mouth opened wide in a soundless roar of agony.

178

Brother Richard glanced casually towards the dais, waiting.

"Complete the execution," ordered Brother Fidelis.

Brother Richard turned back to William and casually placed the knife to the side of his throat; then pulling the knife to the right, savagely, almost severed William's head from his body.

Blood erupted from William's neck, splashing Brother Richard who hadn't managed to move back quickly enough, and fell in a crimson fountain upon the sand which slowly turned a rusty brown colour. Brother William's body continued its twitching and spasming in reaction to the manner of his death.

The blood ceased its rapid eruption, by degrees, and the body hung still.

Brother Fidelis stood, "Thank you, Brother Richard," he said, as that Brother headed out of the cavern, presumably to attempt to clean some of the blood from his robe.

"Now, Brothers, do we give all honour and worship to our Patron Demons. I, Brother Fidelis, thank them for honouring us with their presence at this execution. But now, having feasted upon the blood and agony of the renegade, by name I call upon D—, and upon G—, and ask them to depart to their natural realm and ever to watch over us in our evil."

Brother Fidelis concentrated and the atmosphere became less oppressive as the Cult's Patron Demons withdrew.

Slowly, Fidelis relaxed his concentration and returned his awareness to the Brothers facing him, to the corpse of the former Brother. "Brother Adrian, have all preparations for the disposal of the corpse been made?"

A Brother within the second circle stood. "Yes, Brother Fidelis. I have made the usual arrangements."

"Very good, Brother. I suspend this meeting for thirty minutes. Brother Adrian will remove the corpse. All

Brothers are at his disposal should he require *any* help. Inform me when the cavern is ready."

"I will do so, Brother Fidelis," Adrian replied.

Fidelis nodded, and turned as Supreme Brother rose from his seat. He led their descent from the dais and their exit from the cavern, with Brother Fidelis following closely. Meanwhile, Brother Adrian set about cutting the body down and cleaning up the cavern so that the meeting could proceed onto more important matters.

Brother Fidelis entered the chamber from which he had emerged nearly two hours earlier. He felt as though he had aged in those two hours; and the meeting wasn't over yet.

"Not too bad," the Supreme Brother murmured, "so far, that is. Although you *did* put yourself in an awkward position when you forgot to have William turned to face our Brothers before you called on Brother Richard."

"I know — and yet Richard went out of his way not to embarrass me when he could easily have done so. I know it was my fault — I don't deserve to be let off so lightly."

"I agree," the Supreme Brother added drily, "you *don't* deserve it; and when Brother Richard wants a favour in return, you might do well not to make an enemy of him. No, Gregory," he said, raising a warning finger, "I both like and respect Richard — yet *you* plainly insulted him. Whether or not he accepted your apology isn't the issue. It would have been better not to insult him *at all*. That was what I meant about making no hasty decisions, refusing to be rushed. Brother Richard helped you out of an awkward situation — *don't* be surprised if he expects you to show your gratitude."

Brother Fidelis nodded, "I will learn from the experience," he promised.

The bleak smile appeared upon Supreme Brother's face, "Good," he said.

The two of them sat looking at each other, the features of each inscrutable. At length the Supreme Brother stirred and asked, "Is there any news from Brother James?"

"Yes," said Gregory. "He phoned me last night; he refused to say anything over an open line, but he implied that he had good news and would be here for the meeting."

"I didn't see him," Supreme Brother muttered.

"No doubt he has been delayed; I'll be very surprised if he doesn't manage to get here in time."

"And I'll be rather annoyed," Supreme Brother said in an ominous tone. He was about to continue when Brother Adrian entered the chamber. He smiled at the Supreme Brother almost insolently, and then addressed Brother Fidelis. "The chamber has been cleared of the remains — and of the mess. We can continue when you are ready."

"Thank you, Brother Adrian," Brother Fidelis replied. He stared as Adrian bowed his head, turned and left them.

"Why did you allow that?" Fidelis demanded.

"Allow what?"

"That impertinent smile he threw at you."

"It's a long story; basically, only four people know exactly how we dispose of the occasional corpses we end up with. Adrian was — and is — the brains behind it. His idea was *so* good that I immediately offered to promote him."

"I wondered why it was being dealt with by a second-circle Brother. Why does he not take his place within the third?"

"Because he refused the promotion. There was no way I could *make* him accept it — we had a furious row about it. At first he said that he didn't like the uniform," and as he saw the shock register in Fidelis' eyes, he continued, "and *then* he said that he wasn't going to

181

dress up like a reject from a Benedictine Monastery for *anyone*."

Brother Fidelis opened his mouth, only to find himself speechless. The Supreme Brother chuckled.

"That was my own reaction at the time," he laughed. "His insolence shocked and angered me, until I stopped to think."

"And?" asked Brother Fidelis, who was warming to the story.

"Adrian's one of the few Brothers who remembers my predecessor. Indeed, he held Adrian in very high esteem; so rather than react angrily, which was my first instinct, I questioned him more closely and he finally told me the reason why he wouldn't accept the promotion."

"Are you trying to keep me in suspense?" Gregory asked.

"No, just thinking back. Brother Adrian is *terrified* of responsibility. He wouldn't accept promotion because he was frightened that he couldn't live up to it. He would rather remain within the ranks of the second circle and perform tasks more suited to a member of the third. As he put it: 'If I make a pig's ear of it, I won't be demoted to the first circle; and if I do it well, I'll be a valued member of the second.'

"So, you see, I allow him to remain where he feels comfortable and in private he reminds me of how he insulted the third circle Brothers and got away with it. That's why I allow it, it's a private joke between us. I treat him in *all* ways as a member of the third circle and allow him the privileges which they enjoy. Do you understand?"

Gregory nodded: "Best not ever tell that story to the third circle; he'd be lynched."

"That's for sure. I think that it's time we called this meeting back to order again — we've indulged in enough levity to last for months."

The slightly warmer glow that had begun to suffuse the Supreme Brother's face as he laughed over Brother Adrian and which had made him seem mildly human, disappeared abruptly. They stood; with Supreme Brother leading they returned to the cavern and to their position upon the dais.

Apart from the staples set into the floor, and the pulley set into the cavern roof, all signs of the recent execution had been obliterated. The hook had been removed, the sand gathered up into plastic bags and removed from the chamber. By a minor act of occultism the air within the chamber had been purified, removing the bloody odour. The corpse had been taken away under Brother Adrian's personal direction. Only he and the Supreme Brother knew the exact whereabouts of the body at that time.

As soon as Supreme Brother had seated himself, Brother Fidelis spoke: "I call this meeting back to order. We have matters of extreme importance before us. Any Brother wishing to report anything except matters pertaining to our vengeance on the Baron line may do so now."

Brother John stood. "All goes well with my area of responsibility — security has not been breached."

"Very well, Brother John."

As Brother John sat, Brother Richard — who had managed to sponge the blood off his robe — stood.

"I was asked to look into the feasibility of removing organs from fresh corpses, for sale to various interested parties — for example those organisations specialising in transplants. The results of my...researches are encouraging."

"I know the Supreme Brother will wish to speak privately to you concerning this matter. He will, no doubt, arrange a time and place," said Brother Fidelis, noticing the Supreme Brother inclining his head in agreement.

Brother Richard resumed his seat and when no other rose to report, Brother Fidelis continued, "Well, let us move on. Brother Alex, what do you have to report?"

Brother Alex stood, "Hayter rarely leaves his mansion. I cannot pierce the barrier; I have not seen him since I was given this assignment and regret that I can report nothing."

"Who is watching now?" asked Brother Fidelis.

"Brother Francis."

Brother Fidelis nodded as Brother Alex sat. After a few seconds he called "Brother David, make your report."

Brother David stood, "My report is similar to Brother Alex's. Since his arrival at Hayter's mansion, Tony Baron hasn't set foot outside. I decided to keep a physical watch upon the mansion, whilst not intruding into the area covered by the barrier. One unusual thing *did* occur, however..." he hesitated.

"Proceed, Brother," said Brother Fidelis.

"I don't wish to presume upon the information which will be produced by the Brother it concerns," he said, glancing at Brother Martin, who smiled at David's courtesy.

"Very well. Thank you, Brother David. Now, Brother Martin, will you impart this information to us? And tell us of the feasibility of kidnapping Miss Hunter."

Brother Martin stood, a slight smile hovering over his features. His mission had appeared impossible, but it might not be as difficult as he had at first feared.

"Brother Fidelis, my report, as Brother David hinted, I feel to be important so far as my mission is concerned. I was ordered to ascertain whether or not it would be possible to kidnap Miss Hunter. I kept the mansion under observation — adopting the same tactics as Brother David. I was amazed to see, shortly after noon, Hayter's servant John Brandon, whom we have had dealings with before," he paused, allowing the echo of

184

his words to die away. He saw both Brother Fidelis and Supreme Brother nodding their remembrance of the event and he continued, "leave the mansion. That in itself isn't unusual; we resolved not to antagonise Hayter by further attacks upon Brandon, until our vengeance upon the Barons be completed. But, Brother Fidelis, Brandon did not visit the mansion's storehouses alone; he was accompanied by Miss Hunter." He stopped as both Brother Fidelis and the Supreme Brother turned sharp glances upon him.

"Brother, this becomes more and more interesting; continue."

"John Brandon took her to the storehouses and after a few minutes, she took a look inside one of them. Brandon loaded the land rover with petrol drums and they drove back to the mansion."

"This is welcomed news, Brother."

"But there is yet *more*," Martin continued eagerly. "Having returned to the mansion, Brandon went inside; but Miss Hunter apparently decided that she wanted to visit the wood."

"Alone — you mean she went there *alone*?" Fidelis demanded.

"Exactly that, and she wandered out of the area protected by the barrier. She stripped herself and swam in a lake."

"For how long?" queried Brother Fidelis.

"About three hours. Brandon searched the wood for her and took her back to the mansion. I *could* have kidnapped her then, but I might have had problems dealing with both her *and* Brandon. I therefore decided to be cautious, to report, and ask for the aid of another Brother."

Caught wrong-footed, Brother Fidelis glanced at the Supreme Brother, who nodded and then stood. Brother Fidelis sat.

"Brother Martin," the Supreme Brother said slowly, calculatingly, "you have done far better than I expected. Perhaps it is merely fate being kind to you, random events playing into your hands; however, if you are *again* presented with an opportunity to kidnap Miss Hunter, take it. Brother Richard will help you. But I still constrain you not to enter Hayter's barrier under *any* circumstances."

"I understand, Supreme Brother."

The Supreme Brother resumed his seat and Brother Fidelis stood. "Has any other Brother anything to add?" he asked. When no Brother rose to answer, Brother Fidelis looked intently around the assembly hoping he would be rewarded by the sight of Brother James' face; but he was disappointed.

"Brothers, hold yourselves ready to answer a summons at a moment's notice. Hayter may attack us, or the Supreme Brother may order us to attack. It seems certain that our final vengeance is near. I adjourn this meeting; be evil, my Brothers."

The usual subdued murmur began as Brothers started to leave their places. Suddenly, a shout was heard.

"BROTHER FIDELIS."

The noise from the Brothers subsided as they turned to locate the person from whom the shout had originated.

Brother James' face was white, his clothes dishevelled; he approached the dais limping, his face echoing the pain he was obviously feeling.

"Brother James, what does this mean?" demanded Brother Fidelis, heading towards James and wondering what to do in this situation.

He noticed the Supreme Brother glancing at him. Feeling pressured he said, "James, what happened?"

Brother James stared intently at him. "I must speak to you and the Supreme Brother in private," he said. There was a sudden muttering from the assembled Brothers at what they saw as insolence.

"Brother, it is *urgent*!" Brother James exclaimed.

Brother Fidelis straightened himself and addressed the whole assembly. "I call this meeting back to order. We will interview Brother James in private. Let all Brothers remain here until the meeting is adjourned. Brother Tony, help Brother James to Supreme Brother's chamber."

Supreme Brother stood and led the way back to the chamber which they both used, for the second time. They entered to find Brother James sitting in the Supreme Brother's chair. Brother Tony was told to wait in the passage outside in case he was needed further.

The Supreme Brother took one look at James sitting in his chair and turned to Gregory, one eyebrow raised. He sat in Gregory's chair, a cynical smile upon his face.

"Brother Fidelis," said Supreme Brother, "this had better be more than important. To reconvene a meeting after it has just been adjourned is almost unheard of." And turning his attention to Brother James, he asked, "What happened to you?"

"Car crash," Brother James said shakily. "A woman rammed me — I don't think she even saw my car. Anyway, I had to give the police a statement, then they wanted me to go to hospital; I got out of that by telling them I intended to see my doctor."

"And who is he?" Fidelis enquired.

Brother James managed a grin. "Brother Richard," he replied.

"Well, what do you have to tell us that is of such *urgency*?"

"I have found some interesting information concerning Margaret Hunter," Brother James stated, reaching inside his jacket and drawing out a piece of paper. He hesitated and then passed the note to Brother Fidelis.

He perused the paper without comment, then passed it to the Supreme Brother.

187

His eyes devoured the paper avidly and then raised to lock with Brother Fidelis. "You *realise* what this means?" he asked.

"I think so, but hadn't we better talk to Brother Paul?"

The Supreme Brother glared at him. "Well, let me explain, as it seems you *don't* understand," he said.

***

Shortly afterwards, Brother Tony was ordered to inform Brother Paul that his presence was required immediately by both Brother Fidelis and the Supreme Brother.

Whilst they were waiting, Supreme Brother turned his bleak gaze upon Brother James, who looked as though he was on the verge of collapse.

"I think Brother Richard should check you over," Supreme Brother murmured. "You have *well* proved yourself, Brother, *and* justified Brother Fidelis's confidence in you." The thin frozen smile appeared. "The next time I consider promotions, I will keep you in mind — in the meantime, Brother, think upon a suitable reward."

A few seconds later Brother Paul arrived, accompanied by Brother Tony.

"Brother Tony, assist Brother James to Brother Richard. Say I ask that he take care of him."

Brother Tony nodded, and supporting Brother James, left the chamber. The Supreme Brother motioned Brother Fidelis to the now vacant chair. Knowing that the Supreme Brother wanted to handle this interview, Brother Fidelis, wisely, remained silent.

Supreme Brother's eyes bored into Paul's, as though he would examine every secret hidden behind them. Eventually, the Supreme Brother spoke. "You did well, I recall, in increasing the rate of our drug smuggling — so much so that I rewarded you with the torture or defilement of the next outsider to fall into our hands."

188

"That is so, Supreme Brother," Brother Paul replied, puzzled.

"Have you *anything* to tell me?" the Supreme Brother demanded.

"I'm afraid that I don't understand where this is leading."

"Do you remember our last meeting when Brother Alex told us all that Tony Baron travelled with a companion — a girlfriend by the name of Margaret Hunter? And that Scott Hobard's bastard was brought into the world by a woman named Catherine Kingley?"

Brother Paul hesitated: "Yes, I remember that, but I *thought* it was coincidence...You mean...?" he trailed off, the question unasked.

The Supreme Brother nodded, "It appears that your daughter, Margaret Hunter, will be the next outsider to fall into our hands. It would normally fall to *you* to extract certain information from her — unless you would prefer someone *else* to take your place?"

Brother Paul looked steadily at the Supreme Brother, his eyes glittering. "Supreme Brother, I do *not* wish to relinquish my place. Whatever information you require, I will be more than happy to extract it from my *bitch* of a daughter."

His eyes glared malevolently and dangerously. Slowly, the Supreme Brother nodded. "Very well," he said. "Now tell me all about your relationship with her, her mother, and any other relevant facts."

"There isn't much to tell, really."

"Tell me anyway; and tell me why you did *not* think to question this *remarkable* coincidence," the Supreme Brother said, in a voice approaching a whisper.

After a little thought, Brother Paul nodded and began: "Well, Supreme Brother, it was like this..."

Half an hour later they returned to the cavern. Brother Paul, having been told to say nothing of what he had spoken about, resumed his place, whilst the Supreme Brother and Brother Fidelis stood upon the dais.

"Brother Martin," the Supreme Brother said crisply, "your orders are amended. You, along with Brother Richard, will kidnap Miss Hunter at the earliest opportunity when she next leaves the mansion — even if it means having to enter the area covered by the barrier; in that eventuality, cloak yourselves in darkness, that Hayter may find it more difficult to locate you."

Standing, Brother Martin asked, "May I know the reason for my change of orders?"

The Supreme Brother's eyes turned several shades darker as his anger mounted. "No," he rasped, "apart from that fact that it is because *I* wish it so; and Brother, fail me in this and I promise you a slow and painful death that will make William's demise seem *merciful* by comparison."

It was only by a great effort of willpower that Brother Martin stopped himself shaking at the result of his audacity. Attempting to cover the sudden trembling which he felt in the pit of his stomach, he asked, "And if Brandon accompanies her again?"

The ice-cold eyes bored right into him as the Supreme Brother replied. "He is of no consequence. Incapacitate him: if that is not possible, then *kill* him."

There was a sudden stiffening of the Brothers within the chamber; for the Supreme Brother to authorise a killing in this way displayed how eager he was to have Margaret Hunter in his hands, and emphasised the fact that he no longer cared whether he antagonised George Hayter or not.

"Do you wish her brought here?"

"No, I have a *more* comfortable place for her; I will give you your instructions later."

Dismissing Brother Martin, the Supreme Brother turned his gaze upon Brother Richard. "How is Brother James?" he asked.

Standing, Brother Richard replied, "He'll be fine; just delayed shock. I gave him something to calm him."

"Where is he now?"

"Resting in a cavern allotted to some of the third circle. Do you wish me to bring him to you?"

The Supreme Brother considered. "Is it advisable to question him?"

Brother Richard nodded, "Oh yes, I only gave him something to settle his nerves — he's up to being questioned."

"Good: tell him that Brother Fidelis and I will need to question him about where his information came from, and will come to him shortly." The Supreme Brother looked around the gathering. "This meeting is adjourned; be evil, Brothers."

Chapter Ten: Consequences

Very slowly, by long, drawn-out degrees Margaret began to wake up. She wondered vaguely whether or not to open her eyes just now, or whether to try to go back to sleep — she was sure that she had woken absurdly early today. Eyes still closed, she rolled over in bed, trying to find a new position that would offer her an added inducement to sleep again. It didn't. Her pillow seemed to have decided that it preferred being flat; irritated, she turned it over and the sudden coolness drew her a few more degrees into full wakefulness, but she refused to be drawn all the way. Gradually, breathing evenly, she managed to retrace her steps back down the road towards sleep. Even so, she didn't manage to complete the journey but simply lay dozing, one moment heading for sleep, the next for waking. She couldn't decide how long this had been occurring, (although in reality it was less than twenty minutes) when, almost involuntarily, she opened her eyes. She frowned at having lost her private battle not to open them, but smiled as she realised she hadn't even understood that she was viewing it as a battle. The bedside table came into focus, which, for some reason that she couldn't bring to mind, didn't make sense. Closing her eyes again, she tried to understand what it was about the table that wasn't quite right, but the knowledge, obstinately, refused to come and make sense of what she had seen. Frowning again, she glanced at it, her eyes adjusting to the light and in that second the answer came to her. She remembered the first time she woke in this room, when she had pawed for a light switch and had found it with a dimmer control next to it. The light was already on — more correctly, it had not been switched off the night before. She remembered reading the book which John had suggested to her and eating the sandwiches which he had prepared as she read. She remembered that she had placed the tray by the side of the bed; by levering herself up and glancing at the floor, she saw that it still lay there. Next to it, open, was the book. Her mind suddenly seemed to decide to begin functioning again. The book, she recalled, had explained some aspects of occultism very clearly and simply — but she knew that it only covered a very limited amount. When the author gave a brief summary of the ancient myths from various cultures she had become quite interested — so interested that she hadn't realised just how tired she actually was and had fallen asleep reading. Yawning, she stretched herself, wondering what time it was and whether or not anyone was already up. She rubbed her eyelids, the pressure on them feeling good. She hoped today wouldn't be as eventful as yesterday had been — with John having to search the wood for her. Her mind returned to the lake and the swim she had so enjoyed until his appearance, when the pleasure had turned to embarrassment — which hadn't been as intense as it should have been, she realised. In fact, ever since her arrival she had comprehended a sense of inner freedom: things that would have embarrassed her days ago, like John giving her the landscape, didn't have that effect any more. Even thinking about John's quip in the wood that if she didn't want to be ogled she shouldn't flaunt herself naked didn't embarrass her as it once would have done. Admittedly, at the time, the quip had brought a slight blush to her face, but now the embarrassment she had felt paled into insignificance and if John brought the subject up she knew that she would be able to discuss it with him without feeling at all uncomfortable or uneasy. Why this change of attitude had come about she didn't know, couldn't understand. Lying there pondering upon these things, her mind suddenly jumped to Hayter's claim that he had cured the nightmare which afflicted her from time to time — and again, intuitively, she knew that

193

he had told her the truth. There seemed to be more to it, a connection to be made, but at that moment she sat up in bed, scattering the thoughts and unmade connections by wondering what she would do today.

Thinking that getting out of bed would be a good start, she did so and walked to the bathroom. She noticed a clean towel and wondered how it had got there — she didn't remember it from yesterday — or did she? Shrugging her shoulders, she turned the shower on. She slipped her nightie over her head, dropped it into the laundry basket and climbed into the bath under the shower, turning her head up into the spray. She turned the hot tap slightly and stood luxuriating in the spray cascading down into her face, the water running down her body. Humming a melody which she only half recognised even though Hayter had played it for her after she had whistled it (in several different keys), she began to wash her hair. Ten minutes later she stepped out of the bath, reached for the towel, and began drying herself taking care around her arms where the gorse bushes had left their mark. Nevertheless, she felt invigorated and thoroughly *alive* thanks to the shower. Quickly, almost impatiently, she went to the wash basin and brushed her teeth. Then, still humming fragments of the melody, she re-entered her bedroom and paused to glance at the book lying next to the tray where it had fallen after she had succumbed to sleep. Smiling to herself, she went through to the dressing room and proceeded to get dressed. She pulled on the clothes which she had put ready the night before; when she got to her socks she half stifled a giggle. Why she had placed them ready for today she couldn't think. She replaced them in their drawer her question still echoing in her mind, even though it received no answer. Buttoning up her blouse, she turned and regarded her reflection in the full length mirror set into the wall. Frowning, she returned to the drawers which contained her clothes and after a couple of wrong guesses, managed to locate some of her sweaters. She selected a pale blue one which she knew emphasised her eyes, which were several shades darker, and pulled it on. Absently, she picked up a brush from the dresser, and returned to the mirror. She brushed her hair slowly, her gaze never leaving her reflection. She appraised her appearance; from her legs — what could be seen of them — up to her face. Keeping her gaze on the reflection of her face she wondered if she was attractive — why had John kissed her in the wood? Was she attractive to men other than Tony? Her breathing increased as she realised she would never have asked herself that type of question before she came within Hayter's sphere of influence. She ran her hands down the front of her body, smoothing the clothes out, feeling a mild thrill as her hands passed along the sides of her breasts. The feeling, though pleasurable, confused her; '*What had been happening to her the last couple of days*?' she caught herself wondering. She was not able — or willing — to supply the answer, although she had come so close to making the connection earlier; she blinked, bringing herself abruptly back to the present, to reality. Margaret returned to her bedroom, thought about taking the tray back down to the kitchen where it belonged and then thought that John might misinterpret the gesture, might think that she was trying to attract him. Not wanting to complicate things after yesterday, she decided to leave it where it was for the time being. She glanced at the painting lying on a chair where she had placed it the night before, still half-covered by its brown paper wrapping. It confused her. Apart from Tony, it was a new experience for her to receive gifts from men and she didn't understand why John had given it to her. Shaking her head, as though to clear it of all these things which seemed to have no explanation, she picked up the book from the floor and found the place she had read to before sleep had claimed her. She left the bedroom, walking slowly, not really paying any attention to where she was going until she realised that she was standing outside the door to the library which John had shown her the night before. She opened it and entered; this time the stacks of books didn't intimidate her. She looked slowly around the library, attempting to take in its vastness, until she saw the desk.

Standing as she was in the doorway, it was situated obliquely away to her left. From its position it commanded a view of more or less the whole library. Not bothering to close the door, she approached the desk, saw the wooden chair drawn up behind it and then noticed, on top of the left side of it, sheets of paper, a pen and a pencil laid neatly parallel. So perfectly parallel that they seemed almost to have been laid with military precision; at least, that was the impression that they gave to her. With the sudden flash of intuitive knowledge which seemed to be functioning within her more and more frequently and with a greater certainty each time, she knew that this had to be John's doing. Coming up to the desk, she ran her fingers along the smooth wood. It felt softer than she would have ever believed. She moved around it, drew the chair out and sat, placing the book in front of her. Opening it, she turned to the final chapter which dealt with occultism and beliefs of different cultures — in a very simplified way, she knew, but she found it interesting. As she read the final pages she caught herself wishing that the book had gone into greater depth; equally, she wondered whether she could possibly hope to understand a book on this subject which went much deeper than the one which she had just read. Standing, she walked to the stack nearest her and checked the authors. Finding herself looking at authors beginning with 'L', she moved to the next stack moving anticlockwise around the room. At length she came to what she was looking for, a stack devoted to the works of George Hayter. She looked at the titles. 'Beliefs of the

Druids', 'Ceremonial and Ritual Magic', 'Witchcraft in Ancient Europe', 'Occultism and its Applications', 'Talismanic Magic'. It seemed to Margaret that the stack she was looking at was filled with nothing but Hayter's occult output. Volume after volume filled shelf after shelf. The titles all seemed to fade into one big blur with the same theme at the centre: occultism. Then again, she hadn't expected anything else so she wasn't very surprised; the thing that *did* surprise her however, was the sheer *number* of books that he seemed to have written. How was it, she wondered, that he had *ever* managed to find the time to write all this? How had he done the necessary research? She puzzled over that for a few moments and then turned to go back to the desk, the idea of actually *reading* one of Hayter's books having receded in her mind. There had been simply too much choice — just looking at the titles had made her feel lost in a world which she felt she could never understand.

As she turned, however, a title caught her eye, registering only after she had completed that manoeuvre. Turning back, she re-located the book in question. It was entitled, 'An Advanced Treatise on Demonology'. Margaret thought back to Tony's laughter, and his statement: "You think this is complicated? You should try reading George's 'Advanced Treatise on Demonology'; *that's* complicated." She reached out and pulled the volume from the shelf. She turned again, and reaching the desk she sat and began reading. Although Hayter had a reputation for explaining things easily and clearly, Margaret found herself going back over a paragraph again and again until she felt sure that she had comprehended it. Perhaps an hour or two later, she laid the book down having struggled through the first chapter. She yawned. At least she had managed, or so she believed, to absorb the points which Hayter had been trying to get across about Demons and Demonology. Thinking about what she had just read, and about Hayter, her eyes were drawn to the stationary that John had placed so neatly upon her right. She placed a piece of paper in front of herself, moving Hayter's book more to the centre of the desk next to the one which John had picked out for her. She glanced at the paper and almost automatically picked up the pencil. Frowning, she tapped it against her teeth. She thought of how she already felt 'at home' in this oversized house, how she had felt relaxed and calm, no matter how many times it had been stated that danger and death lurked outside. Absently, her mind upon Hayter and John and the interaction between them, she began to draw. Without thinking about what she was drawing her mind continued to ponder, thinking of the vast difference there seemed to be between Hayter and his Great-Nephew and between him and John. Suddenly, she realised that she had finished her sketch and all that was missing was a legend to go at the bottom. She tapped the pencil against her teeth again and an image of the landscape that John had given to her arose in her mind. Almost at the same instant the caption that she wanted jumped into focus; she wrote it in block capitals at the foot of her sketch. It was only then that she turned her attention seriously to what she had been doing and took in the end product. She gasped aloud in amazement at her own audacity; but then a part of the Margaret Hunter that had lain hidden for so many years, a humorous part which had been forced into hiding long ago by repeated beatings and chastisement, suddenly crept out of its confinement cautiously, until it realised that its re-emergence wasn't going to result in physical pain. She found herself laughing from somewhere deep inside herself. She rocked back and forth, surprising herself at the intensity of her mirth, that humorous part of her taking over. Quietly she laughed, spasms convulsing her. As the fit subsided her eyes were pulled back to what she had drawn and her laughter erupted again as if from an extinct volcano which had suddenly burst into activity. This time, however, her convulsions were less violent but still strong enough to cause her sides to hurt. Wiping tears from her eyes she turned the paper face down, just in case that humorous side of her — now released from its long confinement — wished to flex its new-found freedom again. Feeling good to be alive, she had just begun wondering whether to attempt reading chapter two of Hayter's treatise or whether to go downstairs to the sitting room, when she heard a noise; a muffled sort of *thud*. Her first idea that it might be a burglar was dismissed even before it had fully formed. She stood, listening more intently, heard the noise again, a little louder this time, and thought that she detected a footstep. Hoping that it was Tony, she left the library to investigate. Reaching the foot of the stairs she caught sight of John heading in the direction of the kitchen. She ran after him, attempting to catch him up but he disappeared down the flight of stairs which led there. By the time Margaret managed to reach the top of the flight, he had already made his way inside. She walked down the stairs slowly, and finding the door open she peeped inside and saw John standing with his back to her. He put down a cup as she entered and she realised he was watching the microwave, its contents going round and round. She opened her mouth to speak, taking a step further into the room as he turned quickly, seeming surprised to see her.

"Good morning, John," she said, startled.

He grinned at her. "Morning. I thought you were still asleep."

Moving to one of the stools and sitting, she said, "No, I woke early, and I went to read in the library."

He nodded acceptance of what she said. "Was the book okay?"

"Yes, I finished it, so I picked out something else."

He turned as the microwave's bell sounded, taking a tray from its side.

"Coffee?" he asked her.

"Please," she replied. "Is that George's breakfast?" she asked, indicating the now-dark interior of the microwave.

"No, Tony's; Mr. Hayter would have a *fit* if I offered him anything as heavy as bacon, sausages, tomatoes, mushrooms and fried bread for breakfast. In fact, I don't understand how anyone can eat like this first thing of a morning." He poured her coffee and brought it over to her.

"Did Tony say that was what he wanted?"

"Yes — as long as it wasn't any trouble," John smiled.

"And was it?" she asked, grinning mischievously, taking a sip from her coffee.

"Not nearly as much trouble as searching the wood, and then being accused of being a professional voyeur," he retorted, an equally mischievous glint in his eyes.

Margaret grimaced, her eyes full of amusement. "I supposed I asked for that; how long *were* you watching me, anyway?"

His expression was one of pure innocence as he replied, "About five seconds before you noticed."

"I don't believe you," she said, realising that she wasn't in the least embarrassed about the subject. "Well, I hope you got a *good* look; I don't intend to let you get *another* opportunity."

His face lost its humorous, innocent expression. "You sound as though you're angry at me."

She laughed at him. "No, not *angry*, just a bit irritated that I didn't realise I was being watched sooner. John, I *don't* really have any objections to someone taking a look at me when I'm not wearing anything — so long as *I* have *some* say who that person is."

John turned to the microwave, taking out the plate which contained Tony's breakfast. He added a pot of coffee, a cup, saucer, milk jug and sugar bowl almost negligently.

"Can I take it to him?"

John looked at her, surprised. "You know where his bedroom is?"

She shook her head, "No, but I'm sure you'll tell me."

John smiled as he supplied the necessary information. Margaret stood and, taking the tray, headed for the door.

"Are you ready for breakfast and what would you like?" John enquired.

"Yes, anything hot, I don't mind," she called back.

Carrying the tray carefully and slowing her pace accordingly, she climbed the flight of stairs from the kitchen, passed the sitting room and then climbed the stairs which led to the library. From there she followed John's directions, heading away from her own bedroom, until she stood outside what she believed was Tony's bedroom door.

She knocked twice and receiving no answer reached out to open the door; the tray tilted alarmingly and for an instant she envisaged everything sliding off, but managed to grab its edge before the downward angle became critical. She caught herself wondering if John ever had that trouble — he seemed to make everything look *absurdly* easy.

She placed the tray upon the ground, opened the door, and half stifled a giggle. Unless Hayter had put Tony up in a broom cupboard she had located the wrong room. Mentally recounting the number of doors she had passed, she realised that Tony's room should be the next one along. She repeated her knock upon the next door, and again received no answer. Placing the tray on the floor she opened the door ready to encounter another cupboard of some description.

But this time, she had the right room. It wasn't dark inside, as for some reason Tony had left the light on although it was dimmed. She picked up the tray and entered, closing the door behind her with her foot. She carried the tray to the bedside table and put it down, before turning to look at the room itself.

She didn't get much of an opportunity to make comparisons, apart from noticing that it was similar to her bedroom; the furnishings were almost the same. What drew her attention, however, was Tony. He had obviously had a restless night; the sheets and quilt lay twisted around his feet and upon the floor. He himself lay upon the bed naked, more upon his stomach than on his side, the back of his body exposed to her gaze.

Her eyebrows raised, she decided, after a brief hesitation, to drape the covers over him. She caught herself hoping that he would turn over before she succeeded in her task; the idea brought a mild blush to her cheeks.

She realised that her physical closeness to Tony and his nakedness were attracting her; as she covered his body with the sheets she fantasised about taking her own clothes off, and joining him in bed...

Bewildered by her sudden yearning, the urge to listen to the demands that her body was making of her, she simply stood by the side of the bed attempting to clear her thoughts. Her sexual response had thrust itself upon her so quickly that she just hadn't had time to adjust, she realised. That understanding formed the basis of her decision. She accepted the way she felt, but needed a little breathing space. The urge to join Tony receded, and the smell of the coffee made her remember why she was here.

She reached out to shake his shoulder; but her deep sense of fun, only recently released, pressed her into playing a more dangerous game. Sitting upon the side of the bed, she leaned over and gently kissed his neck. He murmured and turned over, uncovering his chest as he did so. Covering him up again, she kissed his lips several times, until at last his eyes blinked open.

He obviously thought that he was still asleep and dreaming, as he made no attempt to return her kisses. It was not until he blinked his eyes a few times and was thus reassured that this was no dream, that Margaret *was* here in his bedroom, that she *was* kissing him, that he responded. His arms reached out from under the bedclothes, embracing her. Their kisses became more intense, more demanding.

He broke away from her, a slight frown upon his face. "I could get addicted to being woken up like this," he assured her.

"I've brought your breakfast," Margaret informed him.

He glanced at the tray on the bedside table and then pushed himself up the bed, yawning. "Right now, I can think of other things I'd prefer to breakfast," he said.

To demonstrate his meaning his hand gently pulled her head towards him again, and the kiss that followed was delicate and protracted. She found her response automatic, felt her heart pounding; she felt the fingers of Tony's right hand moving up under her sweater, undoing the buttons of her blouse, moving the obstacle her bra presented and his hand cupping the breast it had uncovered.

Startled, she began to break from his kiss, but abruptly the arousal which his fondling of her breast generated within her took over; exciting and disturbing sensations pulsated through her. The urge to undress and get into bed with him reasserted itself, and she could feel herself succumbing to it.

Using all her will power she managed to drag her lips from his, removed his hand from her breast and stood, pulling her bra back into place and then rebuttoning her blouse.

Tony grinned at her. "How about trying that again?" he asked. "You see, I was asleep first time around..." he left the sentence hanging.

Margaret smiled sweetly at him. "Your breakfast would get cold," she informed him quietly, indicating the tray with a wave of her hand, "and so would mine," she added.

She lifted the tray from the table as Tony pulled himself up into a sitting position and placed it over his knees. He pulled a wry face and Margaret laughed. "There'll be other times," she promised.

Tony smiled back at her, his eyes piercing. After a moment he took hold of her hand and asked, "Do you regret telling me about your past?"

Margaret considered. "No, I don't think so," she admitted, "although it seems as though it happened a long time ago; it almost seems unimportant, now."

He looked curiously at her, trying to account for this sudden change of attitude. She smiled at him again, kissed him quickly, then turned and headed for the door.

"See you downstairs," she called over her shoulder. When she received no reply, she turned to look at him again. He was increasing the intensity of the lighting, and having achieved the desired brightness, he turned his attention back to her.

"Yes," he agreed, "if I don't fall asleep — George kept me up half the night, and I don't really feel as though I've slept."

She nodded, opened the door and left him to his breakfast. On her way back to the kitchen she tried to comprehend *why* it was that the sight of Tony's body had had such a profound effect upon her — and why her response had been so intense.

The more she thought about it, the more certain she became that there was a perfectly logical and simple explanation — although it seemed to take a perverse delight in hiding from her. Mentally shrugging and deciding not to allow it to worry her, she dismissed it until such a time as the answer decided to jump unbidden into her awareness.

Reaching the kitchen she found toast, two boiled eggs and a bowl of cereal waiting for her. She wondered where John had disappeared to as she cut the top off an egg and began eating. Soon after, he reappeared. He placed a stool next to her and sat.

"Where d'you get to?" she asked, around a piece of toast soaked in egg yolk.

"Oh, just something I needed to check. I'll have to go back to the stores today or tomorrow."

Margaret registered the information silently.

"Margaret," John began, and then stopped, as though struggling for words.

"What?" she asked, spooning the last of her egg into her mouth.

"Well...nothing," he replied, his face beginning to go red.

She looked squarely at him, "John — *what*?"

"Will you model for me, sometime?"

Margaret stared at him. "I told you earlier, I'm *not* giving you another chance to..."

"No," he interrupted, "I *don't* mean nude. I'm having problems with the painting I'm doing of you — the one in period costume."

She looked thoughtful. "I don't know — I'll *think* about it," she promised him.

He nodded, apparently content with that answer. Having finished her breakfast, she stood and asked, "Is George up yet?"

John smiled at that. "I should think so; try the sitting room," he said.

She left the kitchen, climbed the flight of stairs, all the time expecting to hear the sound of the piano. It was conspicuous by its absence. By the time she reached the sitting room door, she had convinced herself that Hayter was elsewhere; however, when she entered she saw he was sitting upon the sofa pouring intently over a massive tome. He looked up at her, and his warm smile crinkled his face into the mass of lines that she remembered from their talk in her bedroom: it would *always* be her abiding memory of him.

"Ah, Margaret, did you sleep well?" he asked.

"Very well, George; you?" she said, advancing into the room, closing the door behind her and sitting down next to him. He closed the tome he had been perusing and placed it upon the floor.

"Oh, I slept well, the little that I do actually sleep, these days," he replied, a smile hovering on his lips.

"I'm sorry if I had you worried yesterday when I went to the wood, but I just *didn't* think that you might become anxious about me. I lost track of time, *and* my sense of direction. If John hadn't come for me, I don't know *what* I'd have done."

Hayter smiled again, "It wasn't so much of a worry, more disconcerting than anything. You can bet the Cult would like to get their hands on you; you're safe enough inside the barrier — that's *not* said by way of encouraging you to take chances, by the way. I gather from John that you actually left the area that is protected by it. He mentioned that he found you swimming." Hayter's face remained perfectly straight as he added, "He said that he *liked* your breaststroke."

She focussed her eyes sharply upon Hayter's face, but she could find no trace of humour or cynicism there and he continued blandly, "At least, I *think* that's what he said..."

George laughed at Margaret's discomfiture: "I'm sorry, Margaret, I *shouldn't* tease you like that; it's just my perverse sense of humour."

"Exactly what *did* John say?" Margaret asked.

"Nothing you could have taken exception to," Hayter answered her.

Margaret knew that no matter how hard she tried, she would get no more than that out of him; accepting defeat gracefully, she decided not to belabour the point.

"What were you reading?" she asked, changing the subject and nodding towards the tome which lay upon the floor.

"It's an account of a discussion which took place about six hundred years ago debating the question of whether or not witches could fly. Most of it is a waste of time, but there are the occasional flashes of insight into the way the occult was comprehended in those days."

"And can they?" Margaret pressed.

Hayter frowned, not following her train of thought. "And can *whom* what?" he queried, his perplexity obvious.

"Fly," Margaret said. "You said they were discussing whether or not witches could fly — can they?" Her smile was slightly mocking.

Hayter laughed, his laughter filling the room. "I don't believe so," he said, after his laughter had subsided. "Can you imagine the headlines? 'C.A.A. ORDERS INVESTIGATION AFTER BOEING 747 COLLIDES WITH FLYING OCCULTIST.' Levitation is possible, and to some extent movement; and there is a phenomenon known as relocation. As for occultists flying through the air in feats defying gravity, no, I doubt it."

Margaret couldn't stop a squeal of laughter escaping her.

Hayter joined in, his deep, throaty chuckle intensifying Margaret's own. As they subsided, she noticed Hayter looking at her with a more piercing gaze as though shrewdly looking *beyond* what was visible at surface level.

"Did you play last night — or rather this morning?" she asked, attempting to stop his frank appraisal of her. She succeeded, as his gaze became less piercing.

"Yes, actually I did. Why?"

"I dreamed that tune again — I thought I must have heard you in my sleep, like last time."

His frown reappeared. "That just doesn't hold water, Margaret. The piano isn't audible from your bedroom, even with the door open. The bedrooms are pretty well insulated against sound, anyway."

Margaret frowned. "Then why do I keep dreaming about that bloody tune?"

Hayter winced at the use of the word 'tune' as opposed to 'melody', but said nothing about it. "I don't know," he answered. "It's almost as though you dream about it when I play it, but that's too far-fetched to believe. I think it's just the circumstances that led up to your arrival here; you heard that tune — er melody I mean, somewhere, dreamed about it and then you were with me when I played it. It was probably all churning about inside you whilst you were asleep."

She was about to debate the point when the door opened; John and Tony entered. Hayter's attention was immediately attracted.

"Tony, no rest for the wicked, you know — we've still got a fair way to go through that grimoire, for want of a better word."

"How far did you get yesterday?" Margaret asked, intrigued. Immediately, both Hayter and Tony looked at her as though she had said something obscene. "Sorry," she muttered, a vague reminder of her previous feelings of being off balance returning to her.

Hayter's laugh broke the sudden silence. "It's not quite that easy, Margaret," he informed her softly. "In a book like this, you might get to the last page in an hour, and then spend the rest of your life just unravelling that one page. However, I *have* studied that book most of my life," he added drily, "and so am in a position to guide Tony — although I don't know *all* the answers myself. We got further than I expected to," he said, acknowledging Tony's frown. "We wouldn't normally discuss this in front of you," he continued, "but I can understand your curiosity. We got bogged down in one section, one that I believe deals with the very situation we are in. Tony follows my reasoning, but doesn't agree with my conclusions. As we don't have the luxury of time to spend deciding what the passage *may* mean, we are going to suspend judgement upon it for the time being and try to get through the rest of the grimoire."

"Is that altogether wise?" Margaret cut in, caught up in the conspiratorial tone of Hayter's quiet revelations.

Immediately, his gaze sharpened and he focussed his unerring glare upon her. It was the first time Margaret saw the steely side of Hayter's personality. She instantly regretted questioning his decision.

"Margaret," he snapped at her, in the coldest tone she had yet heard him use, "I will not tolerate *you* — or *anyone* else here — questioning my judgement or any decisions I may make where the occult is concerned. Is that clear?" he demanded, his face going several shades redder.

She opened her mouth to make some reply, but found that no words would come. A sense of outrage, of pure naked anger, coursed through her. Tears of rage filled her eyes as she slowly stood and walked to the door. She opened it and realised that she had to say *something*. Voice shaking with barely suppressed anger, she said, "I wasn't questioning your *judgement*, George, I was asking your *opinion*. I would remind you that I *don't* have to stay here, and I *don't* have to sit and be yelled at. I'm just *happy* that you're not *my* Great-Uncle or *my* employer," and she left the sitting room, slamming the door behind her.

Once outside, she bolted for her room, tears of anger and frustration pouring down her face. Reaching it, she ran through to the bathroom and quickly washed her face. By force of will she regained control of her rage, although only just; making a decision, she marched, face set, back into her bedroom.

She closed the door which she had left open in her frenzied haste. Grabbing a suitcase which stood neatly against its companions and taking it into the dressing room, she began to pull clothes from their drawers, throwing them into it. Dresses and skirts were pulled from their hangers and thrown into the case without any thought being given to how creased they would be when taken out again.

She was in the middle of this when she became aware of someone knocking upon the bedroom door. She stopped her reckless assault upon her clothing and hesitated, unsure in that one instant what to do.

She re-entered her bedroom, and after a second's hesitation opened the door. Hayter stood outside, his face unreadable, his gaze steady upon her, appraising her mood.

"May I come in?" he asked, in a tone of voice that gave away the fact that he was unused to making requests inside his own home.

Margaret stood away from the door, and indicated the room with her hand, "It's your house," she replied in a dull, flat tone.

He entered, advancing upon a chair which stood unobtrusively against a wall. Sitting upon it, he let out a deep sigh. Margaret sat upon the edge of her bed, saying nothing, simply waiting.

"I went too far, Margaret, I admit it. I didn't think, I just *reacted* to what you said — all I can do is ask your forgiveness."

She sat, strangely embarrassed by Hayter's frankness, and the sincerity his words conveyed.

"I'm afraid I can't let you leave my protection," he said sadly. "The risk is much too great, believe me. I know, other people have told me I'm arrogant, stubborn and a misogynist," he paused as Margaret's look became surprised. "Yes," he assured her, "I don't like women — never have, never met one that I could like or love," he hesitated. "Until a few days ago, that is," he said softly, so softly she only just heard him.

Margaret stood. "Can't you speak plainly?"

Hayter smiled. "Not really. I'm sorry I snapped at you, and I do want you to stay here freely as my guest. I care about you, Margaret, and I care what happens to you. *Please* stay."

Her mind was whirling with his words, but she knew that he was not weaving any spell about her; that any spell being woven was that of the truth being spoken and nothing more.

She walked over to the old man who seemed to have aged since he had entered her bedroom, her anger still within her but muted, somehow, seeming now vague and impotent against Hayter's softly spoken words.

"Of *course* I'll stay," she said, tears starting into her eyes again. "I don't care if you *are* stubborn *and* arrogant *and* a misogynist *and* dictatorial *and* overbearing *and* despotic *and*...

"Margaret," he interrupted, "you don't *have* to list all my faults to me, you know," he looked horrified at the very idea.

"It seems to me," Margaret added slyly, "that under that cold front that you put up, you're a *lovable* old rogue."

Hayter's head jerked up abruptly, and he looked at her, aghast.

"Don't worry, I won't tell the others — it can be our secret," she smiled at him in triumph and he looked at her in dismay.

"Don't *ever* tell anyone that," he pleaded in a half-strangled voice; the tone he used was so unusual — especially coming from whom it did — that she felt that humorous part of her nature trying to assert itself. She struggled to stifle a giggle, bringing home to her the fact that her anger and outrage had evaporated without her even being aware of it, as Hayter continued: "Apart from anything else I've got a mutiny on my hands." He glanced sideways at her, "I wanted to come after you and make peace, but I was blackmailed into doing it anyway."

"Blackmailed how?" she demanded.

"Well, Tony refuses to study further until I apologise — stupid attitude under the circumstances — and John offered his notice; *and* he informed me that whilst he was working his notice I could look forward to soggy toast and sweet tea. I'm only human — there are some things that no man can face, and John happens to know what mine are," he sighed the sigh of a man who felt totally defeated.

"What were you doing when I knocked?" he asked suddenly, catching her off guard.

"Nothing, really."

"You took a long time doing nothing," he answered. "I can tell when you want to evade my questions — you don't look me in the eyes."

"I started packing," she admitted, feeling absurdly guilty about it.

Hayter's eyes started from their sockets as though he were in the grip of apoplexy. "For God's sake don't tell John — I'll never hear the end of it. Would you unpack, Margaret, in the interests of keeping the peace?"

"I did the packing, I may as well do the unpacking — but some of my dresses will need pressing."

Hayter rolled his eyes heavenwards. "I'm not sure that John will be too happy about that," he mused. "Would you mind telling everyone that we're friends again?"

She smiled at him.

Hayter returned the smile, "I knew I hadn't misjudged you," he murmured softly, standing slowly.

"How do you mean?" she asked, curious.

"Well, I thought, logically enough as it turns out, that if I cared so much for you, you couldn't *help* but reciprocate the feeling. Don't worry, I can understand it," he continued, despite Margaret's open-mouthed look of protest.

"You conceited, egotistical..." she trailed off, speechless, until she realised by the glint in his eyes that he was laughing at her. It was his sense of humour as well as his sensitivity which attracted her to him. It was a *strange* attraction, she thought; completely unlike the way Tony attracted her, or the way John stimulated her; she found it difficult to comprehend.

Stepping closer, she threw her arms around him, feeling strangely comforted as she did so. "I was right," she muttered.

"About what?" Hayter enquired, breaking her embrace.

"You *are* an old rogue."

He looked at her, his eyes reflecting her amusement. "Of course I am, it's a Baron family trait. *All* the Barons have been rogues."

"How do you mean?" Margaret asked, thinking vaguely of Tony.

Hayter laughed. "You should see the family tree — there are more illegitimate Barons in our ancestry than legitimate ones. It does imply a certain predilection towards lust rather than marriage in the Baron males."

"Are you implying something?" she asked.

"No, of course not — I was simply stating a fact that the family tree makes interesting — and disturbing — reading."

"Why do you say that? Oh, I'm being dense, aren't I? The family tree lists how they died, and they all died unusual deaths?"

"Some did," he admitted, "some simply died from illnesses which would not have been thought serious enough to account for their deaths. One or two even died natural deaths — and *that's* a rarity. The Cult's hallmark seems to be that we Barons should die slowly and painfully; you might have been told that Tony's parents were trapped inside the wreckage of their car for hours, yet died just a few minutes before they could be reached." He shook his head. "If I ever think I'm taking this curse too lightly, I just read through the family tree, and I know that it's true." Hayter suddenly realised he was talking about things he normally considered too personal to be spoken about — especially to a *woman*, but she, at least, was different, he thought to himself. He smiled wryly at her, raised his right hand slowly and ran his forefinger down her cheek affectionately.

"I'd better go back to the others — they'll wonder what I'm doing to you." His smile turned into a parody of itself.

With unconscious ease, without it seeming in the least unnatural, Margaret embraced him again and kissed his cheek. "We'll both go down," she murmured.

Her assurance that Hayter had apologised and they were now back on the best of terms was greeted with relief by John and a broad smile by Tony. The mansion's smooth running quickly returned.

Hayter retired with Tony to his study. John disappeared, which left Margaret to her own devices. She was, in a way, glad to be on her own; such a lot seemed to have happened since she had woken up that morning, but she felt that, at least, she understood Hayter a little better than previously.

She wondered what she should do now — the thought that she wouldn't mind another swim crossed her mind, but this time, she thought that she should check with someone.

She felt a little hesitant about disturbing Hayter in his study, so she decided it might be better to ask John. The drawback, which jumped into her mind, was the fact that he might well insist on accompanying her and that she didn't have a swimming costume. She thought it just possible that he might have a costume hiding somewhere that she could borrow which caused her to seek him out to ask. She wandered slowly through the mansion, hearing the drone of voices as she passed Hayter's study, and then silence after she had passed it. She made her way to John's wing of the mansion.

She came to the door on her right which she knew from her previous visit to this part of the mansion led into his private rooms. She knocked at the door, not liking the idea of walking uninvited into his domain. Her knock brought no immediate reply, and she tried knocking harder, but still to no avail.

She tried the door and it opened smoothly; she felt dubious about entering, but the decision was taken away from her as she heard footsteps and John appeared framed in the doorway, wearing an overall which was smeared with various shades of blue paint.

"I thought I heard someone knock," he said, ignoring the fact that his door had been opened by Margaret and that she must, therefore, have been thinking of entering regardless. "Believe me, it's rare for me to get visitors." He stood, apparently waiting for something. Margaret was suddenly aware of the fact that John hadn't invited her in.

"Can I come in?" she asked, knowing from what Hayter said that John regarded his wing of the mansion as the one place he could seclude himself without fear of interruption.

He seemed to think that over for a second before answering, "Yes, come up to the studio."

He moved away from the door. Closing it behind her, she followed him as he led her towards the studio, following the route he had previously taken.

Entering it, Margaret immediately noticed the painting upon which he had been working; it was the one of her in period costume. It had been much worked on since her last visit — was it really only yesterday? But the finer features of her face, shoulders and arms had not yet been attended to.

He followed her gaze with a smile: "What d'you think of it so far?" he asked quietly.

"I like it," she replied. "When do you think it will be finished?"

"Not too long — did you come here to offer to model for it?" he enquired with a brief smile.

"Not really; after what happened yesterday, I thought I'd ask if it would be all right for me to take another swim — if you know where there is a costume that I could borrow, that is," she added hastily as John's eyebrows lifted.

He frowned and considered. "I'm afraid not," he said. "On both counts. It might seem that I can produce rabbits out of hats, but I can't; that's more George's province than mine. I doubt if you'd find a bathing costume if you scoured the mansion; the main problem is that the place you were swimming in is outside the barrier, and I *know* Mr. Hayter doesn't want you running about outside on your own. *You* are a guest here, but I have to work and I haven't the time to come and nursemaid you; much as I find the idea of watching your swimming acrobatics — minus a costume — attractive. That *was* what you were suggesting, wasn't it?" he asked, looking at her appraisingly.

Caught off guard, she felt the colour mounting to her cheeks. She looked away, wondering how she could blush so furiously when she felt only mildly embarrassed.

"No, it wasn't exactly," she replied crisply. "It was a case of *if* you had to come with me and could have lent me a costume, fine. If I could have gone alone, fine. Have you always had voyeuristic tendencies where women are concerned, or is it that you just like ogling *me*? And does that quip about my swimming acrobatics mean that you *were* watching me for longer than you said? It never crossed my mind that you might be a voyeur *and* a liar — until *now*, that is."

His eyes opened wide under her sudden diatribe; for a second he stood speechless, taken aback by the accusatory frankness of her attack.

"You...think...*me*...?" he stammered, his eyes *darkening* with anger.

Margaret grinned. "No, I don't actually, but *you* seem to think that *I* want you to gawk at me when I'm half-dressed or undressed — the fact is I don't. And I'm getting tired of you talking about it *every* time we meet. It seems as though you expect *me* to put up with it, but when I turn the tables on you and say something *you* don't like, then you're free to become angry about it. Don't you think that's a rather *unacceptable* double-standard?"

She stood, eyes glittering with triumph at how well she thought she had made her point. John continued looking at her, but the anger reflecting from his eyes was now fading, as he considered what she said.

"*Perhaps* you're right," he admitted grudgingly. "But can you *blame* me, when I see so *much* of you?" he asked, sighing and turning towards a chair which hadn't been there the last time she had. He sat and ran his hands over his face.

"What do you mean?" she asked, puzzled and unsure how to interpret what he had just said. "I've not tried deliberately to flaunt myself in front of you."

He laughed at that; he laughed so hard tears appeared in his eyes. "Just *what* do you think you have to *do*?" he managed to gasp out. "You're a woman, good-looking with it, and you suddenly turn up out of nowhere and end up living here..." he took a deep breath and continued: "Have you any idea how long it is since I last had a conversation — or *anything* else for that matter — with a woman?"

Fascinated at the insight which he was beginning to give her, she shook her head.

"Just about eleven years. That was when the Cult murdered my brother. It took nearly two years of careful searching and investigation to track them down before they realised what I was doing. At that time my thoughts were on nothing but finding my brother's murderers, but I bit off more than I could handle; and, as George said, he got me out of a very *nasty* situation. I've lived here ever since."

"But there was nothing to stop you..."

"Really? Tell me, if *anything* had happened to me, who would have looked after Mr. Hayter?"

"Tony would..." she began, but was cut off sharply.

"Mr. Hayter had given his *word* not to contact Tony whilst his parents were still alive. He *never* breaks his word. No, I owe George a lot *more* than my life and the lack of female companionship seemed a relatively *small* price to pay. Apart from which, he has very definite views on women, generally. I couldn't bring any woman here, it would have made George *very* uneasy and I wouldn't take the chance that the Cult might take advantage of my absence.

"Everything was *fine* until you arrived; you *attract* me," he said simply, "and as for watching you swim, do you *blame* me?"

She hesitated, seeing things in a new light, trying to understand what she had just heard. Realising that John was still waiting patiently for an answer, she took a deep breath. Letting it out slowly, she replied, "No, I don't *blame* you; as far as I'm concerned you just did what *most* men would have done, given the same opportunity." He seemed about to protest, but she hurried on before he could articulate his objection. "But that *doesn't* give you the right to refer to it ever time we talk — or is it simply that you enjoy embarrassing me?

218

Does embarrassing me appeal to some part of your masculinity that I don't understand?"

John's eyes locked with hers, but a troubled frown creased his brow. "Does it *really* embarrass you?" he asked, his tone making it clear that this idea was totally new to him.

"Yes, it *does*," she replied, her gaze still holding his, until he broke the contact by wrenching his gaze down towards his feet.

After a few seconds, his gaze moved from the floor back to lock with her. "I'm sorry, Margaret," he said, "it never occurred to me that I might..." he trailed off quietly, the sentence unfinished.

"Now you know, can I at least look forward to being able to talk to you without having to worry about whether or not you're trying to embarrass me?" she wanted to know.

"Yes, of course — I'd never have mentioned it if I'd realised it made you feel *that* uncomfortable."

They stood facing each other, the silence stretching out, each trying to reappraise the other in the light of what they had confessed. It was Margaret who broke the lengthening quiet.

"Did you have a girlfriend before...?"

John nodded. "Yes, but we were never close — to be honest, we weren't really compatible. We had similar interests, but different outlooks and attitudes. We irritated each other more than anything. After my brother died we kind of drifted apart."

He looked at his watch. "Christ," he exclaimed, making her jump. She was certain that it was the first time she had heard any strong language from him. "Mr. Hayter's medication — and lunch — I didn't realise it was getting so late."

Saying no more, he pulled his overall off, and with Margaret trailing close behind him, he hurried from the studio and into his domain. Leaving her at the foot of the stairs he disappeared through a door and reappeared combing his hair a few seconds later.

Quickly, he guided her out and as she was being led she smiled inwardly at the vision of the man — normally so imperturbable — showing suddenly just how ruffled he could become — and over such a small thing as losing track of time.

He paused only to close the door leading to his rooms, before hurrying in the general direction of the kitchen, leaving Margaret to try to catch him up or not, as she thought best.

Refusing to run through the mansion, she slowed to a walk but still managed to catch up with him; as she approached Hayter's study, he exited from it. He seemed to have recovered his normal poise and smiled at her, giving no hint that he even remembered the confidences that they had shared.

"Lunch in ten or fifteen minutes," he informed her as he started off again at a brisk pace towards the kitchen.

She hesitated, wondering what Tony and Hayter were discussing. She shrugged her shoulders in annoyance, knowing that she probably wouldn't understand it, even if they told her.

She made her way to the sitting room, and over to the piano. Lifting the lid from the keys she placed a finger on one of them and slowly depressed it. She sighed, again wishing that she knew how to manipulate the keys and make the sounds that Hayter made look so easy. Closing the piano lid, she crossed to the bar. Her eyes passed over the alcohol without interest, but paused as they lit upon a bottle of lemonade. Taking a half pint glass, she poured herself a generous amount and was disappointed when she realised that there was no ice. She sipped her drink and her thoughts turned again to John and what he had told her.

She'd no idea that he had been forced to isolate himself from women '*how could she have*?' she asked herself — for so long. His intense reaction to her presence suddenly became clear, obvious — even *restrained*. She thought about him telling her he considered her good-looking; whether it was true or not the memory brought a pleasant blush to her cheeks.

She realised that she was starting to feel sorry for him and intuited that she must not do so. She sensed, with that inner clarity, that he would resent it.

Her thoughts still very much on him, Margaret walked to the kitchen. As she entered, he was approaching the doorway, tray in hands.

"That could have been nasty," he observed wryly.

Stepping out of his way, Margaret noticed two steaming bowls of soup. She walked over to them, placed her glass of lemonade on the worktop and drew one of the bowls closer to her.

She could tell from the amount of steam coming from it that it was scalding hot. She ate carefully, being careful not to burn her mouth. She repeated the procedure mechanically, scarcely tasting the flavour, her mind still twisting and turning upon what John had told her.

He returned and silently drew up a stool next to her. He didn't seem to heed the soup's temperature and seemed to be thinking as intently as she herself had been.

They ate in silence, except for the spoons scraping against the bowls.

As she finished, she realised how warm she was now feeling. She turned on the stool and pulled her sweater off, feeling the relatively cool air upon her blouse as she did so.

"I think you'll find Tony and Mr. Hayter in the sitting room," John informed her, "I'll be along shortly."

She stood, feeling mildly as though she had been dismissed or asked to leave, but John was smiling at her, his face negating any overtones his words might have conveyed.

Leaving the kitchen and carrying her sweater, she wondered whether John would begin acting more formerly with her now that she had discussed her feelings towards his (harmless?) teasing. She hoped not; she liked him, wanted his friendship. Perhaps, she thought, she had been wrong to tell him how uncomfortable his teasing made her.

Pondering this, she entered the sitting room and heard the piano being played quietly. She didn't recognise the piece, but was sharply aware that whoever was playing, it was not George Hayter.

She took in Tony, sitting at the piano and Hayter standing by his side grinning. The melody died away as they became aware of her presence.

"Margaret," Tony exclaimed enthusiastically, jumping up from the piano stool to approach and embrace her. He gently kissed her, his lips brushing hers.

As his embrace relaxed, Margaret looked him squarely in the eyes. "You never told me you could play," she said.

Tony laughed, "I can't — not really; that was something I learned to play at school years ago. I can't even read music."

As she gazed into his eyes, Margaret felt an unfamiliar warmth run through her. Her arms went around him and she pressed her lips to his, unconsciously dropping her sweater as pleasurable sensations coursed through her body.

A sudden cough brought them back to reality. Breaking their kiss, Margaret covered her confusion by picking up her sweater. They turned to Hayter, whose brow was raised in amusement. "In *my* day, such things were done more privately," he observed. "Obviously, being born when I was, I have missed out on a lot."

At first they couldn't believe what they had heard. It was Tony who broke the silence by laughing. "George, are you telling me that if you'd been born into our generation we might have caught *you* in a similar position?"

Hayter frowned, "God forbid," he muttered fervently, to Tony's delighted laughter. "I'm quite happy with John."

"*Great-Uncle Robert*!" Tony exclaimed in a shocked voice, "I can't believe it."

Caught out, Hayter glared at Tony. "I find your impertinence nauseating."

Tony shook his head apologetically, "You know it was only said in fun," he said defensively.

Hayter managed a grin, "I wonder if arrogance and impertinence are Baron family trademarks?" he mused.

Margaret sat upon the sofa, Tony joining her a few seconds later. Hayter remained standing. The door opened and John entered, looking thoughtful. He sat in one of the leather chairs directly opposite Hayter.

"Margaret, how did you manage with the book John gave you last night?" Hayter asked without preamble, as though John's presence was all that he had been waiting for — as though the previous few minutes had been forgotten.

"Fine," she replied, "I found it a bit simplistic in parts, but mostly I enjoyed it especially when it discussed differing cultures and how those cultures affect their perceptions of the occult and its applications."

Tony looked from her to Hayter, his expression one of amazement at what she had said. To be fair, he had hardly ever heard Margaret utter a sentence concerning the occult without qualifying it with a derogatory comment, so her speech took him totally by surprise.

Hayter seemed quite relaxed with what he had heard; he was about to ask her whether or not she wanted to read further upon the subject when she spoke again, for the moment distracting his train of thought.

"George, remember you said that I could ask you questions on anything I didn't understand?"

"Yes, Margaret," interrupted Tony, before Hayter could get a word in. Hayter looked at him, eyebrows raised.

"Well, there are two things that have occurred to me, so I thought I'd ask." She directed her gaze at Hayter, but it was Tony who answered, "Go on."

Margaret cast a glance at Tony, unsure whether to address herself to him or Hayter. Hayter waved a hand in Tony's direction, as though resigning himself to taking second place.

She turned her gaze fully upon Tony and after a moment's hesitation in which she saw the mild amusement he felt reflected in his eyes, she blurted, "Just how far can an occultist very the geometric accuracy of the Kabbalistic symbols associated with any given ritual? And can the incantations within the ritual be altered to cater for the changes made to the Kabbalistic signs?"

Tony looked at her blankly, for a second, before he furrowed his brow in thought; the amusement faded from his eyes. She glanced quickly at Hayter and caught him attempting to smother a grin, although he couldn't quite manage it. The corners of his mouth kept twitching, no matter how hard he struggled to prevent them.

"I don't think the actual symbols can be varied — accuracy is essential: but changing the incantations to take in any inaccuracies — that sounds rather dangerous. I suppose it *could* be done, but I wouldn't like to be the one to try it. I suppose you'd better ask the expert," he said, looking at Hayter and catching a reflection of his mirth. "All right," Tony said, "it's not *that* funny."

Hayter allowed himself a chuckle. "It amused me to see that there are *some* things you don't know," he commented drily. "Yes, Margaret, what you say *can* be done, but as Tony said, it's highly dangerous; even if you happen to be a powerful and experienced occultist, there can still be problems. Symbols can be — and indeed have been — altered in the way you suggest, and the incantations may be amended. I have done something of the sort myself; I take it you were referring to how certain rituals have been amended and incorporated into yet other rituals, the incantations and symbols varied so the end result is totally different from the purpose of the original ritual?"

"Yes," she answered simply. "It was mentioned in the book John gave me."

Hayter smiled, "And a very subtle question it was, too. Does my answer make things any clearer? — of course there is a *lot* more to it than that."

"I can believe it," she smiled. "Yes, that does make it a bit clearer. I *think* I understand."

"Good," Hayter said, moving to the second leather chair and sitting in it. "Any other questions?"

"Yes, just one," she replied. She glanced at Tony, but he didn't seem to be at all eager to try and answer whatever question that she had thought up, but he flashed a grin at her. "It has to do with demons," she began, and saw Hayter's eyes narrow. He glanced at Tony, then at John. His gaze returned to her, but it was calculating now; he waited silently for her to ask her question.

"In your book, you said that knowing a demon's name gives you power over that demon, or words to that effect. Later on, you state that a demon might have several names or even a *secret* one as well. If a demon were known by seven or eight different names, and yet none of those names were its real one, its *secret* one, would that give you less power over it, or none at all? If you don't know its *true* name, I don't see how you can have *any* power over it."

As she stopped speaking, Margaret became aware of the utter silence within the sitting room. All three of them looked at her; Hayter still calculatingly; Tony with a look of astonishment; John with open admiration. As abruptly as she became aware of it, the silence was broken by Hayter's voice.

"What do you mean, Margaret?" She was so taken by surprise that she couldn't answer, let alone comprehend what he had said to her. Her confusion must have been evident, for he explained his meaning. "You said, 'In your book', does that mean you have tried reading one of my works?"

"Yes," she replied, "I finished the one John gave me, so I got one of yours off the shelf in the library. I read the first chapter this morning — although it was a little difficult to understand in places, but I kept rereading it until I felt I'd grasped your meaning."

"I see," said Hayter with a half-smile. "I did say that you could read anything on the occult, and I meant it. Which book was it that you picked out, by the way?"

Margaret glanced at Tony, almost guiltily, before she said, "It was called, 'An Advanced Treatise on Demonology'."

She heard Tony's gasp of surprise and saw Hayter's eyebrows rise questioningly. He glanced at John, who nodded, stood and quietly left the room.

"Did you understand it?" Hayter asked quietly; whether or not the question was addressed to her or to himself, Margaret didn't know. "Rather interesting, wouldn't you say, Tony?"

"I'd say unbelievable," Tony murmured. "The first chapter's just full of theory; it's *very* heavy going." Hayter nodded his agreement. "I find it hard to believe myself," he admitted, "but Margaret's question does bear out what she says."

He looked at her: "I'm sorry if I seem sceptical," he announced, "your question surprised me. If a demon is

226

known by a name, that gives you an amount of control over it. The more *personal* the name, the *greater* the control. Therefore, knowing a demon's *secret* name gives you immense control or power, and equally the demons *guard* their secret names *very* closely. Demonology is perhaps the *most* dangerous of occult fields as they can be unpredictable, are invariably *malicious* and possess an amount of cunning it's difficult to comprehend."

Margaret chewed her lip. "That makes sense," she said finally, as John returned to the sitting room, books held under his right arm, his left hand behind his back. Without a word, he handed the two books to Hayter, who glanced at them and nodded. He placed the books upon the floor.

"What puzzles me, Margaret, is that I aimed this book at people who already had a fair understanding of occultism — I don't understand how you got through chapter one so easily."

She shrugged, this discussion was beginning to bore her. John must have realised it, because there was another matter which he wished, in his own perversity, to bring to Hayter's attention.

"There is one more thing, sir," he said, stiffly formal. "Those two books weren't the only things occupying the desk," he said mysteriously.

Hayter frowned at him. "Well, don't keep me in suspense, John, what else did you find?"

"This," he replied gravely, handing Hayter a piece of paper.

Hayter frowned at John, then turned his eyes casually upon the paper which he was holding. As soon as he realised what it was he was looking at his eyes widened in disbelief. He opened his mouth to speak, but no words came. His expression went a shade redder as he turned his gaze upon John. "Is this your idea of a joke?" he snapped at him.

"Not *my* idea," John replied, absolutely straight faced: "I don't draw caricatures —especially not on paper."

"This is an *outrage*," Hayter snapped.

"Personally, I think it's rather good," John added, and received another sharp glance from Hayter. He looked from John to Margaret and Tony.

"Well?" he asked.

Tony reached out for the paper, took it by one corner and turned it the right way round, studying it. Suddenly, there was a strangled choking sound as he collapsed into convulsive laughter.

"It's no laughing matter," Hayter stormed, making to retrieve the paper from Tony. He, avoiding Hayter's grasping fingers, passed it to Margaret, who was intrigued to know what all the fuss was about. The second she looked at it, she remembered her doodling in the library, and how funny she had found the end result — which she now held. She remembered that she had simply left the paper on the desk, rather than throwing it away, or at least putting it somewhere where it was less likely to be found. She felt the blood drain from her face as she gazed at what she had drawn. It was of a man — John — standing at an easel, painting; another much older man — Hayter in grotesque parody — stood at the doorway, glaring at the painter. At the bottom of the page ran the legend, 'WHEN I SAID I WANTED YOU TO DO SOME PAINTING JOHN, THIS WASN'T *EXACTLY* WHAT I HAD IN MIND'.

By degrees, Tony regained his composure, but Hayter sat glowering darkly. "Now that you've recovered yourself, would the budding artist care to own up?" he demanded, his eyes locked upon Tony.

"I'm afraid…" Margaret began, "I'm afraid that it was *me*."

Hayter's gaze swung to her in amazement. "*You?*" he squeaked in a voice so unlike his normal one, it brought smiles from Tony and John. "And do you *really* see me as a grim dwarf with an oversized head?"

"Of *course* not, George, I was just doodling after reading your book — it wasn't meant to be insulting, honestly." She smiled at him uncertainly.

He considered what she said, and finally a slow smile lit his features. He gestured for her to pass the paper to him, which she did. He looked at it again but this time he allowed himself a chuckle. "You know, John, you're right, it *is* good. But I'd appreciate it if you'd find another subject," he added.

John moved to the chair which he had previously occupied and sat down.

Grinning at Hayter's sudden change of attitude, Tony brought the conversation back to what he felt were more serious matters. "George, do *you* understand how Margaret could have got through that chapter so quickly? I remember studying it for a fortnight before I felt I could follow it, and you know I'm no novice; before she came here, Margaret hadn't ever read *anything* about the occult — she went out of her way to avoid it."

Hayter placed the paper on top of the two books which John had passed to him. "To be quite honest, Tony, I've no idea. I would have thought that for anyone to take in chapter one at one reading — even if they *did* reread several sections, would be impossible. Mind you," he added slyly, glancing at Margaret, "we *do* know that it would be in keeping with her character."

"What d'you mean?" she demanded.

Lazily, Hayter indicated the caricature. "It's obvious, just from looking at the drawing, that she's a bit of an imp, so reading about demons *might* come naturally," he smiled as he saw the flash of anger in her eyes.

"At least I can take a joke," she replied sulkily.

Hayter inclined his head graciously. He thought briefly about Margaret's dream of hearing him playing...perhaps there was more to her than met the eye, and he determined to understand what it might be, before too long.

"You don't seem to be taking this very seriously, sir," John's voice was quiet, but carried a quality that he thought it might be.

"Oh, I am, John, believe me," Hayter assured him, "but I have more important things on my mind than why someone can read an advanced book on demonology without having done any background reading."

His veiled reference to the Cult reminded them all of the forthcoming confrontation.

"George," Margaret asked hesitantly, "exactly *how* powerful an occultist are you?"

Tony's mouth dropped open in sheer disbelief at what he had heard. "Margaret," he protested, "that's a question you *never* ask an occultist. It's the height of impudence."

"Well," Hayter demurred, seeming to take no notice of what Tony said. "I could levitate myself, or I could relocate, I..."

"You are not even to *think* of doing such a thing," John interrupted sharply, angrily. "I don't believe that I just heard you boasting about your abilities...or could there be an *unusual* reason for that?"

Hayter's eyes grew steely and smouldered with anger as he turned them upon John. He returned the stare defiantly. After what seemed an age, Hayter dropped his eyes and nodded. "You are right, John, as usual," he admitted. John stood and walked over to him, placing a comforting hand upon his shoulder.

"Time we got back to work, eh, Tony?" Hayter asked in a different tone of voice, standing.

Tony nodded assent and wordlessly the two of them left the room. John sighed aloud.

"What was all that about?" Margaret wanted to know.

"That was George making a fool of himself for your benefit."

"For me?"

"He loves you, Margaret. He probably won't *ever* tell you so, but his boasts about what he can do were to impress you."

"But that's crazy. Nothing could impress me about George more than the man himself."

John nodded. "I know that and you know that, but George is totally at sea where women are concerned. He doesn't understand that you might be drawn to him by his being what he is."

She frowned and bit her lip.

"Well, I'm going to do some painting; d'you feel like modelling for your portrait?"

"All right," she said.

Later, as she was undressing before getting into bed, she caught herself reflecting upon the things that had happened that day; a long day it had been. She had spent what seemed like hours standing, whilst John carefully painted her image onto that of her portrait. At length, when she had felt sure that she would have permanent back pains if she wasn't allowed to sit and she begged John to let her move, he had forbidden her even to speak, and then relented; she had been free to stretch and rub her back in an attempt to unknot all the kinks which seemed to have developed.

After a coffee, and the luxury of sitting, the torture had begun again, but it didn't last so long. Finishing off, John had refused to show her the portrait until he had added 'a few final touches', as he put it. Content with that, she had left him cleaning up and returned to the sitting room. She had proceeded to retrieve the books — and the caricature — which she took to her bedroom.

She ended up back in the library, returning the book which she had read to its place. She had decided to carry on reading Hayter's book and had sat and read undisturbed until John came looking for her, asking what she wanted to eat.

It had been later than she had realised — and she was over half way through the book — but she cheerfully accompanied John to the kitchen, ate ravenously through the meal piled high on her plate, and through the fruit and custard which followed.

She had done more reading, this time in the sitting room. It was only when she looked up and glanced at her watch that she realised it was past midnight.

She had brought the book to bed with her, thinking *vaguely* of reading some more before she went to sleep, but her eyes were feeling tired, and she didn't *really* feel like trying to finish it. She glanced at the bookmark, realising that she had read over three quarters of what both Tony and George considered very difficult material; the knowledge made her smile. She knew she would finish it tomorrow.

She finished undressing, showered, put on a nightie and climbed into bed, yawning. She noticed John's landscape still lying where she had placed it. She would remember to ask him to put it up for her tomorrow. For tonight, she was tired. Dimming the light very low she turned on her side, closed her eyes and was asleep in moments.

But tomorrow was not going to be as smooth a day as Margaret expected it to be. Random events would conspire to throw *everything* into confusion. Margaret, secure within Hayter's mansion, had gone to sleep with no inkling that by this time tomorrow she would be enmeshed in a web of nightmare and abject terror.

Chapter Eleven: Disclosures

Brother Gregory lit a cigarette whilst waiting for the kettle to boil. He felt parched; he thought over the night's events. After the meeting had been adjourned by the Supreme Brother and the assembly had begun to disperse, they had walked in silence to the cavern where Brother James was resting. The other members of the third circle allotted to that cavern moved as far away as possible unobtrusively, to allow their leader as much privacy as they could. Without having to ask, chairs were provided for them, and they sat, one on either side of Brother James, who seemed to be more than half asleep. Gently, the Supreme Brother touched his shoulder. Immediately, his eyes opened and he started, seeming bemused for a few seconds. Finally, realising where he was, and who was sitting next to him, he made to stand, but Supreme Brother restrained him with a shake of his head.

"I said earlier that you have done *well*, James, and I meant it," he informed him. "But I am intrigued by something: just *how* did you manage to obtain *this* information?" and the Supreme Brother took the paper which Brother James had given to him from inside his robe.

Brother James looked at the piece of paper, squinting at it until he finally sighed. "Supreme Brother, it's a very long story; I don't know what Brother Richard gave me, but I can't focus too well on that," he said, waving vaguely at the paper. "Although I well know what it contains. I can't seem to get my thoughts in order; I'm so tired," he added sleepily, his eyelids beginning to droop.

Supreme Brother looked around irritably. The cavern was now almost deserted save for Brother Richard

233

himself, dressed in more orthodox clothing. He approached at Supreme Brother's signal.

"Brother, I thought you said we could question him — but he can hardly focus and says he can't get his thoughts in order; not to mention the fact that he's nearly asleep."

Brother Richard took Brother James' pulse. "Hmm," he muttered. "He's probably just very susceptible to the drug I gave him. A couple of hours' sleep and he'll be fine. I wouldn't advise giving him another injection to counter the first," he cautioned, guessing the Supreme Brother's question before it was asked.

Standing, Supreme Brother gazed at the now sleeping form of Brother James. "Very well, thank you, Brother." As Brother Richard nodded and withdrew from the cavern, Supreme Brother turned and looked at Gregory.

"It seems, then, that we will have to spend some time with Brother James to hear this story. But I can think of a better place to do so. Let's get changed; we'll take Brother James somewhere more comfortable."

"Agreed," Brother Fidelis said, although it seemed weird agreeing with Supreme Brother when his word was law.

They made their way back to the cavern where they had changed, the same one where Brother Alan had made his mistake, and where James had given his information. As they were changing into more casual clothes, Gregory broke the silence by asking, "Paul, did you *really* expect what Brother James found?"

The bleak smile with which he could praise or condemn appeared on his features. "Oh *yes*, I expected it — I *always* expect the unexpected; that is why *I* am the Supreme Brother."

As they finished dressing and placed their robes into a suitcase which Gregory had brought with him, he asked, "Where are we taking him?"

"To a flat I know of," Supreme Brother smiled. "It's owned by a certain corporation which we control, but I use it when the need arises." What he considered to constitute 'need' and what other uses he might put the flat to he didn't elaborate upon.

They returned to the cavern where Brother James sat, snoring softly. "Can't say I feel like carrying him," Gregory said.

Supreme Brother nodded his agreement. "It would not be in keeping with our standing within our community," he added wryly. He frowned and appeared to make a decision. "You know my car?" he queried.

"Yes," Gregory said, wondering what was on Supreme Brother's mind.

"Clear your mind of *everything*: concentrate upon it, and *nothing* else."

Gregory pictured the car, concentrated on it in minute detail. He closed his eyes to make his vision of it clearer, became vaguely aware of Supreme Brother whispering. He felt a sense of dislocation for a moment, of being in two places at once. Momentarily the feeling threw him and his concentration slipped, but then he caught it and concentrated upon Supreme Brother's car as hard as he could. He became aware of wind and rain upon his hands and face; opening his eyes, he realised that they were no longer under the ruined church but several miles away, standing by Supreme Brother's car. It had been backed off the road behind a row of trees which camouflaged it.

Gregory *stared* at Supreme Brother; this was the first time he had given him any indication of how advanced an occultist he was. To relocate not just himself but *two* others...it staggered Gregory's imagination to realise that Supreme Brother didn't seem at all drained by the effort which he must have expended, he just looked slightly pale. He was supporting Brother James with one hand and fumbling with his keys with another. Gregory quickly relieved him of Brother James, who was still asleep despite the rain in his face. A distant peal of thunder sounded as the Supreme Brother got the car door open. He entered, scrambling over to the driver's seat and then he helped Gregory to deposit Brother James in the back of the car. Gregory sat in the passenger seat and ran a hand through his wet hair.

Five minutes later, they were travelling along a well-lit road, heading presumably for Supreme Brother's retreat.

It was a dreary drive; Supreme Brother seemed in no mood to talk, and Gregory found his efforts at conversation received only grunts in reply, so he gave up trying. Brother James seemed to be sleeping deeply.

At last they drove through a built-up area which didn't look too prosperous. Litter and graffiti abounded. Supreme Brother pulled up in the car park of a block of flats that looked even more dilapidated than others they had passed, and Gregory hadn't thought that possible. They got out, Gregory pulling Brother James after him; this time, however, he breathed deeply and opened his eyes. After blinking a couple of times he stood and nodded, as though confirming that he could manage. Supreme Brother locked the car, murmured a few words.

They turned and approached the main door of the block. Gregory was rather surprised that the door was locked; inserting a key, Supreme Brother opened it, and they followed him into a nondescript hall. There were two lift doors facing them. Supreme Brother walked to them and pressed the call button. Seconds later, one of the lifts opened its doors. Motioning them inside, the Supreme Brother entered last.

"Which floor?"

"The tenth," he grinned.

Gregory's hand went to stab the relevant button, but it wasn't there. As far as the lift was concerned, there were only nine floors. Supreme Brother inserted a key into the panel, turned it, and then hit both the nine and one buttons simultaneously. The lift rose smoothly up to the eighth floor, hesitated at the ninth but only opened its doors when it reached the non-existent tenth.

Without seeming to notice the confusion evident upon their faces, Supreme Brother removed his key and led them to the only door off a small hallway which they had stepped into.

Opening this, he indicated that they should enter, turning on the lights as he did so. He closed the door behind them, motioning them to three armchairs which were set in a rough half circle about a gas fire. Further away, set against the walls were bookcases, bureaux, and a sofa.

He lit the fire, and pulled a coffee table so that it stood near to hand.

"Sit, Brother," he said to Brother James, who was hesitating about the protocol involved in sitting before the Supreme Brother. Turning to Gregory, he said, "The kitchen is through there. Would you mind brewing us all coffee, Gregory?"

Surprised, Gregory had said no, and now stood impatiently waiting for the kettle to boil; he was as anxious to hear this story as Supreme Brother appeared to be. The kettle finally boiled. Gregory brewed the coffee and took in their drinks.

Placing the mugs upon the coffee table, Gregory took his seat and waited for the story to be told.

"Brother James," the Supreme Brother rasped, "are you *now* able to tell us how you got hold of this information?" he indicated the paper which he had drawn from his pocket.

"Yes, Supreme Brother," James replied. "Before, I couldn't think straight, but now I can tell you *everything*; although I must warn you it is a long and in some places a twisted and convoluted story."

With a sigh as bleak as his countenance the Supreme Brother settled back into his armchair, as though

237

savouring in advance the pleasure which this story would afford him. He glanced at Gregory questioningly.

"I'm as intrigued as you, I think; James, give us your account of how you ferreted out this information."

James took a sip of his coffee, frowning, collecting his thoughts. Gregory noticed an ashtray upon the fire, and picking it up, he balanced it upon his knee.

"Well, what you see on that piece of paper wasn't really hard to find — but may I begin from my researches when I was convinced — as Greg...er Brother Fidelis was — that Hobard *did* sire a child?"

The Supreme Brother raised his eyebrows slightly and glanced at Gregory.

"I haven't heard the story myself," he admitted. "When James gave me the information that there *was* offspring, we didn't have time to discuss how he'd managed to find it out."

Supreme Brother nodded. "By all means, tell us, James," he said, quietly.

"Brother Gregory wouldn't go along with Brother Martin's contentions; he ordered me to use our American Brothers to try and trace any relative of Scott Hobard. The same thing had, at your instigation, Supreme Brother, been tried twice before but to no avail.

"I decided that the best way to go about such a private matter would be to make it as public as possible."

"Explain that!" exclaimed the Supreme Brother, coldly.

Brother James nodded, seeming unaffected by the change in Supreme Brother's tone. "In America, the more quietly you attempt to uncover information, the more likely it is that someone snooping for some magazine or other will get hold of it and try to follow the trail. But if the information is a matter of public record, people are more likely to ignore it."

The Supreme Brother nodded his agreement: "Continue, Brother, and be sure that I will *not* interrupt again until your story is told."

"Our American Brothers control many companies — as we do — but on a different scale entirely. Our Brothers decided that the most obvious way to find a descendant of Scott Hobard would be to advertise. All we needed was something to make the advertising credible.

"We finally decided to use a firm of lawyers owned by one of the Brothers. Their advertisement stated that the firm, Robinson, Franks and Co., were the executors of Hobard's Estate. We summarised Hobard's life and in legal double-talk explained that Hobard's Estate would devolve to charities, unless there was an actual heir under the stipulations of his Will — even though he died over forty years ago. We offered a reward to *anyone* who helped us trace that heir. The lawyers explained it better than I ever could — so well, it almost had me fooled.

"It was then simply a case of sitting back and waiting. The usual cranks appeared and were followed up to the inevitable dead ends. But eventually, we received a letter which wasn't obviously an attempt at getting the reward, but seemed, from the way it was written, as though the author, a Mr. Simon Meyes, had actually known Hobard. It was the first — and only letter or phone call — which proved to be genuine." Brother James paused to take another sip from his mug of coffee. Gregory had lit another cigarette and sat quietly, his whole attention upon James.

"So," he continued, "we invited him to come and talk to one of the lawyers representing Hobard's Estate. I was present at this meeting, ostensibly taking notes, but in reality just to hear what was said.

"Simon Meyes is a tall, thickset man. He fought alongside Hobard, but wasn't officially in his unit — which I suppose is why he was never traced before. The

239

two became firm friends. Meyes was eventually wounded and invalided out of the army.

"But they kept in touch with each other by letter, and it was this which provided the breakthrough we had been looking for. Mr. Meyes brought a Xerox of the last letter Hobard had written to him. It made fascinating reading. It was dated just three days before Hobard died — and he told Meyes of how he had managed to trace a distant relative and had spent a weekend with him."

At this, Supreme Brother's gaze sharpened and his lip curled, but he said nothing.

"But the most interesting part was when he told Meyes that he was in love with an English woman, and she with him; that they had discussed marriage, and had decided not to marry before the war was over. Hobard apparently had a premonition that he would not survive the war, and told Meyes of it. From what he wrote, it seemed that Hobard slept with this woman on a regular basis; but more importantly, he disclosed her name and the area where she lived. That name was Catherine Kingley.

"As soon as the meeting broke up, I caught the next flight back here. I checked the public records for a Catherine Kingley in the area Hobard had indicated. There was only one; eight months after Hobard's death, she had a child. Hobard's child, a girl. It was when my researches had reached this point that I rushed to give this information to Greg...er Brother Fidelis, just after his promotion, and left the meeting immediately afterwards to conclude my researches. The result of them, verified by much cross-checking, is what you see upon that piece of paper."

The Supreme Brother sat without saying anything for a moment and then he reached out and plucked the single sheet of paper from his lap, where earlier, he had placed it. Although he had memorised it, he explored the few lines again.

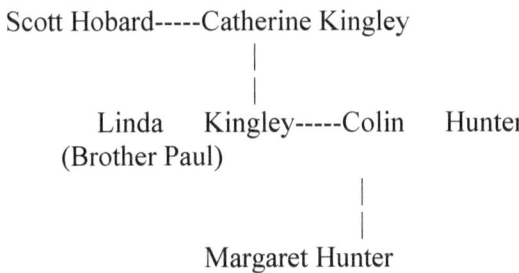

Scott Hobard-----Catherine Kingley

Linda   Kingley-----Colin   Hunter
(Brother Paul)

Margaret Hunter

The information seemed so obvious, trivial, in fact; and yet it had eluded Supreme Brother's best efforts until now. He exhaled slowly, thinking intently.

Rousing himself he said, "Brother, I sense that there are *many* gaps in what you have said."

"Yes, Supreme Brother, I wished to inform you of all the most important facts and then fill in any details that you wish to know."

"You said that Meyes wasn't officially with Hobard's unit — why was he there?"

"It was a temporary secondment but no records were ever kept of it, or if they were then they were lost; apart from others in the unit — and not many of them survived the war — I wouldn't think his secondment would be remembered."

"I remember we advertised for anyone who knew Scott Hobard to get in touch with us two years ago and got nowhere. I wonder why Meyes chose *now* to come forward?"

"Supreme Brother, the answer to that is simple. He didn't respond to your advertisement because he probably didn't see it. He lives in Italy, and was only in the States visiting his son. It was pure luck that he was there at the right time. As soon as he saw our advertisement, he called his wife to photocopy the letter and send it to him urgently."

"But dealing with matters both personal and pertaining to a dead friend, I don't understand why it was that he was so *willing* to let you read it."

"Did I give that impression?" Brother James asked rhetorically. "It was quite the reverse, actually. At first he was sceptical and suspicious. It was only after we showed him the Will — a fake, of course — and explained how desperate we were to follow *any* lead that might help us find whether or not Hobard *did* have an heir, that he became more reasonable.

"He tried to track Catherine Kingley down himself after the war, but didn't get anywhere, so he told us. I think that *any* search he made was half-hearted at best. After all, he didn't know the woman, and certainly didn't know that she had had Hobard's *bastard*.

"It was only then he admitted that he had remained in contact with Hobard after being invalided out of the army, and that he *still* had his letters. He didn't like showing us Hobard's last letter, as parts of it *were* so personal, but he decided it was essential that we see what Hobard had said."

"Is there any possibility that he might become suspicious or inquisitive?"

Brother James grinned. "None: he was assured that we, that is, Robinson, Franks and Co., would inform him of the results of our search — of course, we will inform him that there was no heir, and that the Estate has devolved to the charities named in the Will, and that will be that."

"But weren't you gambling that Hobard hadn't made a Will whilst in the army? And that Meyes didn't know about it?"

"No, Supreme Brother, such things had been checked into most carefully before we decided to run our advertisement. I pride myself on my methodical approach to problems of this sort — I wouldn't have made such an *obvious* mistake."

Silence descended in the room, punctuated only by the sound of Gregory crushing out a cigarette in the ashtray.

"At *last*," the Supreme Brother hissed, indicating the lineage upon the paper. "I *knew* it. It was *too easy* to believe that Hayter and Baron were the last! But the knowledge brings with it a feeling of disquiet, an uneasiness which *gnaws* within me."

"But why?" Gregory asked, incredulous. "You wanted to know whether Hobard continued the Baron line, and now you know where it leads; even more, Margaret Hunter is *here* — that makes our task easier, surely?"

The Supreme Brother glared at Gregory, his bleak face becoming even *stonier*, if that were possible, as he replied, "That is the *very* thing which causes my anxiety. You would imagine that, given the circuitous route which the Baron line has taken, Hobard's offspring would be a very long way *distant* from Hayter and Baron; and yet what do we in fact find?" He rasped an answer to his own question. "We find that Hunter is not only Baron's girlfriend, but that she was *sired* by one of our *own* assembly. I'm sure that the *irony* isn't lost upon you."

"Can you be sure that it's not just a *massive* coincidence?" Gregory inquired cautiously.

"There is no such thing!" Supreme Brother snapped back irritably. "Somehow, I sense that there has been some force at work manipulating events towards this end, but I don't understand what it might be. Perhaps," he mused, "I am simply being paranoid; I want our curse fulfilled before my death — it has taken five hundred years already — and yet I sense *danger* in confronting Hayter in outright battle. We are circumscribed too by our laws to bring the deaths of the Baron line about by utilising the occult, *not* by physical assault upon them. Everything within my being *screams* at me to be cautious; and yet, now that Hayter and Baron are together the threat they pose becomes too great to tolerate and logic dictates that we attack them. I have deferred making the decision because I cannot decide what my resolution should be. *That* is why I ordered Margaret Hunter kidnapped whether Brother Martin has to enter the area covered by Hayter's *infernal* barrier or not! With her in our hands, the odds may well tip so much in our favour that my reluctance to attack is overcome.

"And it is interesting, to my mind, to ponder whether or not Hayter realises that she is *related* to him. I don't *think* he knows," he murmured. "He would *never* have allowed her outside the barrier if he did. Soon, she will find herself in our complete control — so long as Brother Martin values his life."

"How do you know that she will leave the mansion again? Hayter might have forbidden it," Gregory observed.

"Because Hayter thinks that Brandon can protect her. If she wants to explore the area I expect Hayter to allow it, and Brandon will accompany her — but he will *not* be able to protect her *or* to stop Brother Martin. If Hayter will *not* allow it, I have at my disposal at *least* one way to *force* her to leave the mansion, although I'd rather *not* use it unless all else fails. Do not worry, Gregory, shortly she *will* be in our hands. I am looking *forward* to making her acquaintance," he stated in a voice so cold, bleak and *menacing* that Brother Gregory recoiled as from a blast of freezing air.

Later that day, Margaret asked John about borrowing a costume so she could go swimming again. It was only a combination of his not having a costume to hand and the fact that he couldn't nursemaid her which saved Margaret from Brother Martin's efforts at kidnapping.

The three sat in silence, each turning Supreme Brother's words over in his mind. For Brother James, it was quite a revelation since he had never heard him speak so freely before. He became aware of Supreme Brother's eyes upon him and he turned his head to meet that disturbing, piercing gaze.

"Of course, Brother, you are *not* to repeat anything that you have heard or may hear us say," Supreme Brother warned him.

Brother James nodded. "I understand, Supreme Brother; you can trust me."

Supreme Brother glanced at Gregory, who nodded, adding, "I know James well; you may, indeed, trust him."

Supreme Brother grunted acceptance of Gregory's assurance.

"What did you make of what Brother Paul told us about his wife and...?" Gregory began to ask, but was interrupted.

"We will speak of *that* only privately," replied Supreme Brother pointedly. "However, I understand *why* he acted as he did — his explanation *does* make sense of a sort. It does explain why he is so *eager* to take up his option on the torture of our next victim. He is taking my exhortation to be evil quite literally. I find it rather refreshing; I'm sure he'll *relish* the situation when his daughter is within his grasp once more."

"Didn't you say that according to our laws we couldn't use physical violence upon members of the Baron line?" asked Gregory.

The Supreme Brother smiled his bleak smile triumphantly. "That is so, but we are only debarred from *killing* through physical violence; that doesn't mean we can't *torture*, or sacrifice as part of a ritual. It means that she must *not* die under torture — I have told Brother Paul that the torture he employs must in *no way* endanger her life."

Glancing at his watch, Gregory realised that the day was upon them. Supreme Brother noticed the gesture,

245

and copied it. "Is there anything else that we need to discuss?"

"Where will she be kept?" Gregory enquired.

"That might appear to be a problem; originally, I told Martin *not* to take her to the crypt, but that might well be the *best* place for her — after all, it *does* contain all the features that might be needed," he smiled. "So, I have told Brother Martin that he should first transport her to a place of safety and then, at night, to bring her to the crypt."

He closed his eyes, running events of the past few days through his mind. A calculating smile appeared upon his features, distorting it into a grimace of evil.

"Well, Brothers, I think we should return to our respective homes and await developments. Remember, Brother James, *think* upon what reward you deserve for your labours. Can I give you a lift?" he enquired.

Both nodded assent. Supreme Brother stood and turned the fire off. They followed him to the door, switching off the lights as they went.

***

Some distance away from the block of flats with the non-existent tenth floor two men sat talking quietly, exchanging platitudes whilst trying to keep warm. They were some distance from Hayter's mansion but were outside the barrier which would have alerted him to their presence. They waited for dawn, yawning; every few seconds one or the other would put a pair of binoculars to his eyes to keep the mansion under observation. Both sensed that this was going to be a dreary day, and neither looked forward to it. Immediately after Supreme Brother had given Brother Martin his instructions he had left to arrive here, to keep a close watch in case — although he knew it wouldn't happen — Margaret Hunter left in the night, or in what was left of it. Not long afterwards, Brother Richard had arrived to share his vigil, although he didn't seem too concerned about the prospect. The sky to the East slowly became much lighter and brighter, at least seeming to promise that they wouldn't get soaked. This close to the barrier, they were both very hesitant about using their powers — formidable though their powers were — in case Hayter were to learn of it and become more suspicious than he must surely be already. They were positioned somewhat to the south-east of the mansion, on a rise in the ground. The wood blotted out the view of the area approaching the mansion and partly concealed the mansion itself. But, by utilising an old gnarled tree and climbing to its lower branches, they were able to keep watch quite satisfactorily, if, at times, uncomfortably. Richard muttered to Martin to keep watch whilst he scrambled down the tree, cursing when he slipped a few yards, which made Martin smile. He had never really *liked* Richard — probably because he was held in such high esteem and always officiated at ritual executions, where his medical knowledge was invaluable.

The minutes crawled by and the day grew brighter yet, as the sun's rim appeared upon the horizon. Richard returned, telling Martin to come down. He complied, taking the mug of hot soup which Richard proffered. It was just another example, he thought as Richard resumed his perch amongst the leaves, of *why* he dislike him. He hadn't thought to bring any sustenance with him; Richard had shown him the boot of his car which contained not just a spare wheel, but a sack full of assorted cans, a small primus stove, a couple of dented pans and some mugs secured within a wooden box. Richard had grinned at the expression upon Martin's face and explained that when, a few years ago, he'd broken down miles from anywhere, the *worst* thing had been sitting waiting for help, and being hungry. The cold he had been able to combat but he had promised himself not to be caught the same way again, hence the supplies. Martin drained the mug, and placed it at the foot of the tree. The sun had risen, fighting its way through the slight mist which rose from the vicinity of the wood. Martin climbed up to a branch on the same level as Richard. He raised his binoculars and trained them upon the mansion. He saw the door clearly, saw everything clearly, and sighed heavily. He had a feeling that it was going to be a very long and boring day. He looked around. Not far from their position he could see the roofs of the storehouses which Hayter utilised. Supplies were delivered there by unknown traders who had keys to the various padlocks. At one point, Martin had considered ambushing one of the deliveries but had reluctantly abandoned the idea as being too likely to draw attention to them, and by extension, to the Cult.

He listened to the silence, broken only by the call of birds, off towards the woods proper. He shifted position cautiously. His behind felt numb; Richard grinned at him, seemingly not bothered by such petty irritations. Above, the sky promised a lovely day, only the odd cloud could be seen; the mist had vanished and now that the sun's rays fell more directly upon him, Martin began to feel the chill easing off. He thought about the girl they would have to kidnap for him to regain his standing within the Cult — he felt sorry for her in one way — but vindictive that she was causing him so much inconvenience. He remembered the Supreme Brother's warning about what would happen to him should he fail and felt the icy coldness return, even though he was being warmed by the sun. He didn't think about failure — couldn't even contemplate what Supreme Brother might dream up for him if he should fail. He knew he would succeed, he must. Musing upon this, his eyes closed and he entered a nether world of his own fantasies and illusions of success. He came back to reality as, with a warning yelp, Richard lurched towards him as he overbalanced and fell off the branch which he had been perched upon. Richard's alertness paid off, as he managed to grab Martin's arm just as his balance failed. Gritting his teeth against the sudden wrench which his shoulder received, Richard began pulling Martin upwards. Martin, shaken witless, at least had the presence of mind to grab the branch with his free hand and, swinging his leg up, managed to hook it over the branch and scramble back to his former position. Richard glared at him, rubbing his shoulder.

"If you're *that* tired, go and sleep in your car," he snapped. "When you've rested, you can take over for me."

"Sorry, Richard," he replied, "but this is my third day without sleep — I'm completely exhausted."

"You mean you didn't bring someone else with you to take over? That you've been watching all that time alone?" Richard asked, incredulously. "Martin, I don't wonder you dropped off — sorry, no pun intended," he grinned weakly. "You go and catch up on that sleep you've missed. Don't worry," he cautioned, patting Martin's shoulder, "I'll let you know if *anything* happens. After you've slept, we'll change places. No argument, *I'm* the doctor, remember?"

Martin nodded and slowly, making sure that he didn't lose his grip, he made his way down the tree and then to his car which was parked only a hundred yards away. He unlocked the door and got into the rear of the vehicle. He tried lying on the back seat, and although it wasn't very comfortable he didn't notice, and was asleep very soon after. His last conscious thought was that Richard wasn't such a bad chap after all.

When he opened his eyes he knew that he had slept a long time. The car was in shadows and as his eyes adjusted to the light, he realised that the sun had set. '*What was Richard playing at?*' he thought angrily. He jumped up and out of the car, and made his way to their observation post. Richard was still there, blending in to the leaves. He took a quick look at the mansion through his glasses and then let them drop to his chest, where they hung secured by the strap around his neck. He turned as Martin approached, even though no noise had given his approach away.

"Feeling better?"

"Yes, but why let me sleep so long?"

"You needed it, and nothing's been happening over there." He indicated the mansion with a jerk of his thumb.

"Time for me to take over, I think," said Martin.

"Sure," Richard assented, stretching. "It's bloody boring, this job. I hope this bitch doesn't keep us waiting indefinitely." He climbed down the tree with remarkable agility and stood stretching his back. "Fancy something to eat?" he asked, as Martin climbed up.

"Please, Richard," Martin replied, and then, "I don't think she will keep us waiting too long — Supreme Brother mentioned that he had at least one means of forcing her to leave the mansion, but he'll only use it as a last resort. It depends on how impatient he is to capture her."

"I think he's pretty impatient already," Richard answered, heading for his car which was parked ten yards from Martin's.

Twenty minutes later they perched companionably upon a branch having eaten and slaked their thirst with coffee; still nothing moved about the Hayter mansion.

"Looks like it's going to be a cold night," Martin observed.

"Aye," Richard agreed distantly, "perhaps we'll have better luck tomorrow."

"I hope so. I think it's your turn to catch up on some sleep — I'll call you at dawn."

"Earlier if anything happens," Richard put in.

"Of course."

The sun had long disappeared when Richard lay down in the back of his car. He thought about this venture and felt vaguely uneasy, but why he couldn't understand. He pondered what tortures would be in store for this young woman, and made a mental note to discuss his thoughts with the Supreme Brother. Being a doctor, he knew better than most the areas on the female body most susceptible to pain. He smiled at the thought of the stereotypical doctor alleviating pain; nevertheless, when he slept he dreamed as pleasantly and as sweetly as an innocent child.

Martin sat upon the branch keeping a lonely vigil, knowing in his mind that there was no chance that Margaret would appear at this late hour but that a watch had to be kept just upon the off-chance. He pondered whether or not he should have done as Richard implied and brought a subordinate Brother with him to watch through the night. The only thing against that was Martin's own penchant for doing things himself.

It was, he realised, his failure to do the research into the Baron lineage himself that had placed him in this insidious position. That was why, he told himself, he was watching the mansion. Well, it was one way to while away the evening — but he could think of better. Joanna, for one...a sudden gust of wind buffeted against him, making him grab the tree for support. The wind subsided and he found himself frowning angrily. After all this bloody effort, Margaret Hunter's screams had better be worth it!

He spent the night uncomfortably, watching the mansion, seeing the same monotonous *nothing* in front of him. Time seemed to slow and stop, each minute seeming to take an eternity. He lost count of the number of times he had glanced at his watch — once putting it to his ear to make sure it was still working. The hours passed and eventually Martin was treated to a rerun of the dawn as he had seen it presented for the last three days. He had become sick of seeing it, it held no pleasure for him whatsoever.

As the light grew stronger he checked his watch. Another half hour and he would call Richard.

"Morning."

Martin jumped and almost lost his balance. He glared down at Richard who stood grinning up at him inanely. "Sorry, Martin. When you've been on call as many times as I have you learn to wake up at whatever time you choose."

Martin nodded, still frowning. Richard joined him upon the tree, carefully choosing a different branch to Martin's. "Anything happening?" he asked.

"Not a bloody thing. If I didn't know better, I'd swear that the place was deserted."

Richard nodded, thinking that if nothing happened today he might just go and seek out the Supreme Brother to see about the possibility of him using whatever means he had at his disposal to lure Hunter out of the mansion. Richard was not looking forward to another day — no matter how fine the weather — stuck up a tree looking like a fool.

The sun rose and made its slow ascent above them; they sat without speaking, each feeling the *tedium* of their allotted task. Martin nudged Richard's shoulder, indicating to their right. A hedgehog hurried across their vision, seemingly making for the wood.

Martin climbed to the ground, announcing that he had to stretch his legs. Richard nodded his understanding. Martin returned minutes later declaring he felt much better.

"Can you think of *anything* more boring?" Martin asked some time later, glancing again at the mansion.

"No," Richard replied. "The monotony gets to me, I find." He glanced at his watch.

"What time is it?"

"A quarter past one. Want a drink?"

"Well, I wouldn't say no."

Richard climbed down to the ground and made his way to his car. He had just ignited the primus stove and was in the process of pouring water into one of the dented pans when he heard a low, half articulated cry. He looked up quickly to see Martin running towards him as fast as he could.

"It's Brandon and Hunter. They're heading towards the storehouses; we can *just* get there before them."

Richard killed the flame issuing from the little stove, and dropped it to the ground. He paused only to retrieve a small leather pouch which he rammed into his pocket. "Well, don't just stand there," he hissed.

They set off at a fast run towards the storehouses. Richard suddenly felt *exhilarated* after so much inactivity. He glanced at Martin, keeping pace next to him. "This is *it*," he gasped. Martin grinned and nodded.

Chapter Twelve: Casualties

Margaret opened her eyes, taking in the darkness. She had turned the lights off last night, but her night's slumber hadn't left her feeling bright and refreshed — quite the reverse. She'd had a restless night, half waking a few times thinking that the room was stuffy and wishing that there was a window which she could open. A strange claustrophobic atmosphere had pervaded her dreams, and at one point she had half-considered going for a walk. Then she remembered the locked door, John opening the locks with security keys, and the information that to leave through the garage would entail more locked doors and alarm systems. It seemed, in her semi-conscious state, as though she was locked up inside this overgrown mansion whether she liked it or not. She had slept again but not deeply, had been restless all night, turning first this way and then that, unable to shake the murky undercurrent stalking her dreams. She lay awake thinking about her night's sleep, or the lack of it. She reached out, turning on the light. Its intensity hurt her eyes but she endured it. Becoming more conscious of herself and her surroundings, she suddenly realised that the bedclothes were damp against her legs. In fact, her nightie was damp against her. She had been more restless than she had thought. The sheets and blankets were tangled around each other both upon the floor and the bed, giving the impression they had been wrestling whilst she had been asleep, but had submitted when she had decided to wake up. She sighed, and running her hand through her hair, she sat up and reached for her cigarettes. She smiled at the ashtray, one that she had 'borrowed' from the sitting room when John wasn't looking. She inhaled deeply, placed the cigarette in the ashtray, rubbed her eyes, and decided that she wouldn't be content with a shower this morning — she felt so sleepy and uncomfortable — she would settle for a soak in the bath and nothing less.

She noticed John's landscape and remembered that she had decided to ask him to put it up for her. It was simply a matter of hammering a nail into the wall, she thought — or would John smile at her and then show her how it *should* be done, with his usual modest expertise? She giggled, despite feeling lousy. She finished the cigarette and slowly got out of bed, stretching. She took off her nightie and, walking into the bathroom, laid her bathrobe near to hand. She placed the plug in the plughole and turned the hot tap on full. Whilst the bath was filling she walked through to the dressing room and dropped her nightie into the laundry basket. She took out clean briefs, faded jeans, which she knew were tighter than tight, a clean bra, pale blue blouse, and a pale green sweater. Having arranged these things, she returned to the bathroom just in time to stop the bath overflowing. Vexed with herself, she pulled the plug out until the water drained to a more acceptable level. She added cold water until the water attained the desired temperature and then immersed herself in the bath, closing her eyes, trying to clear some of the cobwebs out of her mind. She wondered what she would do today; probably get bored again. She caught herself wishing that she could go out for a walk or for a swim, or *anything* as long as she got out of this mansion for a while. She would *even* put up with John ogling her, if that were necessary, so that she could get a few hours of fresh air and a break from the enforced monotony which her stay in the mansion had occasioned. She grinned at the thought of John accompanying her to the lake, expecting her to strip off; if *only* there was some way that she could get her hands on a costume. She imagined John's face as she took her clothes off at the lake, only to be wearing a swimming costume beneath. She would have given *anything*, at that moment, to have a costume to hand. As it was, if she wanted the swim she would have to pay the price. Her smile fading, she wondered about just going for a walk — but it would only be sanctioned if John was with her. It was *bloody* unfair, she thought; and then she *remembered* John talking to her — didn't he mention, yesterday, that he had to go to the stores today? The thought galvanised her; she finished her bath as quickly as she could, dried herself, dressed and ran out of her room hunting for him.

It seemed, however, that her luck had run out. She tried the kitchen, sitting room and library in rapid succession only to meet with the same cold, impersonal silence each time. The only evidence of John's actual presence was a pot of hot coffee in the kitchen. Where he might be was anyone's guess. Unless...

As soon as the thought formed she began running towards the wing of the mansion which John inhabited, wondering why it was that she had not tried there first. Her main fear, which surfaced in her mind whilst rushing towards his room, was that he would not be there; that he had *already* left to go to the stores.

The claustrophobic undercurrent which had been present in her dreams had pursued her, at a subliminal level, into wakefulness. The feeling that she had to go out was adamant within her; but if asked, she would not have been able to articulate *why* she needed to go out so badly. The fact that John *was* going out — admittedly not very far but far enough — was sufficient to play upon that murky undercurrent and result in an intensification of the desire for open space and fresh air.

She reached the door which gave access to his rooms and pounded upon it, remembering the problems that she had the last time, when it had seemingly taken him ages to hear her. She stood impatiently, hopping from foot to foot in anxiety, but no sound of movement indicated that the door was about to open. She tried it but it was locked; whether it was locked as a result of her opening it the last time she had been there, she had no idea. It struck her as odd, however, that John should lock his door when on the other two occasions that she had visited the studio, it had been *unlocked*.

Finally deciding that John wasn't about to answer the door, that he must already have left for the stores, she made her way back to the sitting room feeling more despondent and depressed by that realisation than she would have believed possible. Finding her way back there without looking where she was going, she didn't notice John suddenly appear in front of her until she was almost upon him. She started and he grinned at her in perverse appreciation.

"*John*!" she blurted, in such an excited voice that his eyebrows rose, "I've been looking for you."

"I *see* — you've decided that Tony is a poor catch compared with *me*, and you want to *seduce* me, so *then* we can run away together?"

"Will you be *serious*?" she asked, although she was smiling; her despondency and depression had disappeared the second he came into view.

He let out an exaggerated sigh of disappointment: "I can fantasise, can't I?" At the look which she gave him, he smiled a resigned smile.

"Right, you found me — what can I do for you?"

"Well, remember yesterday, you said that you had to go to the stores for something?"

"Yes, funnily enough, I just mentioned it to Mr. Hayter."

"So that's where you were? I looked all over," she exaggerated.

"Yes, with one thing and another, Mr. Hayter and I have not had *many* opportunities to discuss things over the last few days."

"What things?" she wanted to know.

"Oh, *various* matters," he replied, evading her inquisitiveness. "But yes, I am going to the stores later on. Why? Is there something specific that you need?"

"Oh, no, nothing — I just want to go *with* you."

He frowned down at her. "I'm *not* sure that's such a *good* idea, you know..."

"I know that I *can't* stay locked up indoors much longer without getting some air — without seeing the outside, if only for a few minutes. *Please* John, I...I *have* to come with you; being stuck inside is so *monotonous* — that was why I slipped away into the wood. I *have* to come with you," she repeated lamely, her voice trailing off.

He stood, considering her. "I *do* know what you mean," he said, finally. He thought for a moment whilst Margaret hopped from foot to foot in anxiety as he made his decision: "I'll call you when I'm ready to go."

The smile that she flashed at him was dazzling in its intensity, causing him to break into a returning grin. "Do you *always* smile like that when you've got your own way?" he asked.

"No, only when I'm *grateful* as well."

"I'm afraid that I've got to leave you to your own devices again," he said. "Mr. Hayter, with his usual sense of the absurd, has found a dripping tap which he wants me to fix."

As he turned to go, Margaret caught hold of his arm. "Oh, *another* thing, John."

"No, I'm *not* letting you drive," he announced.

"No, the landscape which you gave me — will you put it up in my room for me?"

He smiled again. "Yes, it won't take a minute — it just needs a nail hammering into the wall..." he broke off, surprised, as she burst into laughter.

"Well, if you're going to be so busy, I'll get my own breakfast," she gasped out between giggles. John nodded and headed away from her, shaking his head in confusion.

After eating some cereal which she found in the kitchen and drinking some now-tepid coffee, she decided to while away the time by reading more of Hayter's opus on demonology.

She retrieved the book from her bedroom and retired to the sitting room, the place where she felt *most* comfortable. It seemed to her that this room still vibrated with the music which Hayter played, and for some intangible reason the aura within the room served to relax her agitated nerves.

She took a glass from the bar and filled it with orange. She then settled down upon the sofa, placing the glass upon the table in front of her, Hayter's book opened up at chapter twelve. Even though this room had a relaxing aura, she found her concentration slipping before she had finished the second paragraph.

She flipped a couple of pages further into the book, and read the first paragraph; it concerned the nature of demons as opposed to elementals. She jumped another few paragraphs and now Hayter was explaining the malevolent nature inherent in demons, the difficulties control presented...

She reached out and drank deeply, replacing the glass upon the table. She frowned; reading the book like this just couldn't be done, she realised. What she was reading, being taken out of context, made no sense at all.

With a new determination she began the chapter again, but this time her concentration seemed equal to the task, and she was pleasantly surprised when she reached the end of chapter twelve without having to reread any paragraphs. She had grasped Hayter's explanations at the first attempt.

She took another drink, and after a second's thought, drained the glass. She had never realised that reading about the occult could be such thirsty work. She had

259

begun chapter thirteen, which at first seemed a little out of place. It had to do with levitation and lifting objects just by focussing the will. Later, it went on to tie in at a *much* deeper level with demonology and she realised that the chapter as a whole wasn't out of place at all — but it made *very* heavy reading.

She sat back, trying to digest what Hayter had been saying. She eventually concluded that he was implying if you knew just *how* to focus your will, then levitating an object became a *very* real possibility. She smiled at the idea but then her smile faded as she remembered just how quickly she had fallen asleep in this very room when Hayter had willed it to happen. Without thinking about it, she closed the book, placing it on the sofa beside her.

She thought about what Hayter had said and suddenly knew *exactly* what he meant. Levitating something was *easy* — it just took an awfully long time to learn *how* to focus your will. Her gaze fell upon the empty glass and the impish side of her nature goaded her into trying to levitate it.

She closed her eyes, concentrating upon the glass, attempting to focus her mind and *will* upon it. After a couple of minutes, when it had showed that it had no inclination to defy gravity, she opened her eyes just to make sure, and let out a heavy breath which she hadn't realised she had been holding.

Irritated, she glared at the glass, deliberately regulating her breathing, and began to concentrate again. She closed her eyes more naturally this time and perhaps helped by the surge of irritation she had felt, she suddenly felt her thoughts, her *will* coalesce — there was no other word for it; it felt as though her intangible will suddenly became a tangible thing. Holding on to the feeling she slowly visualised the room, the table in front of her, the glass upon it. A feeling of unreality *pulsed* through her. Fearing that like a badly constructed house of cards all her thoughts would suddenly collapse, her will return to its intangibility, her vision of the room falter, she tried to negate the feeling. She realised that allowing *any* extraneous thoughts or emotions to distract her would result in the very reaction she feared, and she determined *not* to allow that to happen.

Hesitantly, she focussed more strongly upon the glass, began to visualise it rising up into the air. She felt an almost immediate resistance which she struggled against. The effort to overcome it sapped her strength, but she resisted the temptation to breathe more rapidly. At length, just as she decided that it was too much for her, she *saw* the glass move slightly, in her mind's eye. The resistance seemed to fade a little — but it was enough to rally her determination.

She tried focussing her whole attention upon the glass rising into the air. The resistance disappeared completely, bringing a gasp of surprise from her. More importantly, she felt her *will* reach out, surround the glass gently and lift it into the air. She was vaguely certain that she had succeeded. She opened her eyes slowly, expecting to find that she had indulged in nothing more than an exercise in self-delusion. The sight which greeted her took *seconds* before it registered. The glass floated about three inches above the table top, quite steadily. The thrill of knowing that she had succeeded coursed through her and the glass swayed alarmingly. She gathered her concentration again and the glass became more stable — if that term applied to a floating object.

The door opened unexpectedly. "Margaret, are you in here?" called John's voice. The sudden distraction caused her to jump and glance in the direction of the door. She cried out as she heard a *smash* and turned her head back to the table to see the glass in fragments upon it, shattered. She took a deep breath.

"What was that?" John asked, entering.

"Oh, John," she hesitated. She *couldn't* bring herself to tell him what she had managed to do. She found it difficult enough to believe it herself. He would tell Hayter, she thought, Tony would find out, and they would *demand* a demonstration. She knew she would feel foolish if she failed; consequently, she said *nothing* about the levitating glass to him. She didn't realise that what she had just achieved was, under normal circumstances, considered to be virtually impossible and that Hayter would have been *intensely* fascinated by it. "I... er... you startled me, and the glass slipped out of my hand."

"You've not cut yourself?"

"No, I'm fine."

He made his way to the table, and started picking up and dropping the shards of glass into what remained of the glass itself. "I just came to let you know that Mr. Hayter and Tony have gone directly to the study. It appears they have a new insight into Anton Baron's grimoire — whatever that may mean. It won't surprise me if they *don't* appear again today." He finished picking tiny shards from the table. He left, presumably to dispose of the broken glass, and returned a few moments later.

"Believe it or not, the tap just wanted a new washer," he said, forcing Margaret to drag her thoughts away from floating glasses. "Oh," was all she could think of to say.

"I *liked* you caricature," John began hesitantly. "Have you ever thought of trying oil painting?"

She laughed. "Well, yes. Actually I have, but the furthest I got was painting by numbers."

John's face screwed up as she made the confession.

"I've never thought of trying oil painting *seriously*; I know that I would make a mess of it. I'm not a painter, I know my limitations."

"But, the caricature..." he protested.

Exasperated by his insistence she stood and marched out of the sitting room, telling him not to go away. She returned with a couple of pieces of paper and a pencil. She told him to move more towards the door and then sat upon the floor, resting one sheet in front of her upon the table. Glancing at him, she started to draw, breaking off only to upbraid him for moving. She ordered him not to move or talk, with a sly smile of revenge on her face.

About fifteen minutes later she laid the pencil down upon the table and gazed at the end product; a sketch of John against the background of the door frame.

Standing, she walked over to him and thrust the sheet of paper into his hand, and then she returned to sit upon the sofa where she had laid Hayter's book.

John advanced towards her, his attention not moving from the sketch. "That's *amazing*," he declared. "It seems so detailed, yet I can see that it's just really *clever* shading. Have you always been able to do that?"

She smiled self-consciously. "I was about fourteen when I realised that I *could* sketch almost anything I wanted to — but I could *never* paint. I don't sketch things that often — I need to be in the mood; it's not something that I've *ever* taken seriously."

"But surely you *should*," he protested, frowning. I'm sure that you could sell them — or illustrate books, *especially* children's books."

"Yes, I suppose so," she answered absently, "but the problem is that I don't feel that I could churn them out to order like that. It would take all the fun out of it."

He regarded her for a moment not speaking but assessing what she had said. "I suppose that's *one* way of looking at it," he admitted. "How far have you got with the treatise?" he asked, changing the subject.

"Chapter thirteen. It's not exactly light reading, you know."

"I know, I read the first three drafts of it."

263

He glanced at his watch, raised his eyebrows and asked, "Do you want lunch before or after we go to the stores?"

"What time is it?" she asked, curious. "It only seems like an hour ago you said Tony and George went straight to the study."

"Yes, but it was old news by the time I got around to telling you — it took me over an hour to find a washer for that tap that was the correct size; Tony and Mr. Hayter were shut up in the study before I started on it — about half an hour before I first spoke to you, it would have been. It's just past one."

"I can wait for lunch, but I *can't* wait to get out of here. You'll have to drive to the stores slowly, John, to make it last longer. I know I'm going to enjoy every *second* of it," she smiled.

"We'll see," he grinned back at her. "By the way, may I keep the sketch?"

"Sure," she said, although it had not left his hands.

"Right. I'll go and put it safe, then we'll go and get the oil and whatever else is on the list." Suiting action to word he left the room. '*He'll probably hide the sketch somewhere in his studio*', she caught herself thinking.

Minutes passed. Becoming impatient she went to his rooms, knocked and entered, surprised that the door was now unlocked. John almost collided with her as she did so. "I know you're eager, but you don't have to kill the driver," he informed her.

Together, they made their way down to the main door of the mansion. It was ten minutes past one.

He reached into his pocket and then swore. "Sorry, Margaret, I got changed when I did that tap — and I've not got the right set of keys. Back in a minute." He hurried back in the direction of his rooms, leaving her biting her lip in frustration.

It seemed ages before he returned, waving the offending key wallet. He began unlocking the door. The time was sixteen minutes past one.

Outside, he carefully locked the door behind them, and laughed at Margaret taking deep breaths. She felt the breeze, the warm sunshine, the tranquillity. They were *completely* unaware that their emergence from the mansion had nearly caused Brother Martin to fall from his perch for the second time.

She waited whilst he brought the land rover around, entranced with being outside again. Why she had felt so enclosed within the mansion, she couldn't think, and simply put it down to a poor night's sleep.

The roar of the land rover cut into her thoughts as John drew to a halt in front of her. Like a little girl excited by an excursion, she ran around it and climbed in, remembering, this time, to fasten her seatbelt.

He accelerated slowly, not knowing, never suspecting the trap he was heading into, yet ever afterwards blaming himself unmercifully for everything which occurred as a result of his falling into it.

Margaret remarked on how lovely the fields looked, how beautiful the shades of green were, not suspecting that the beauty shielded menacing evil.

She looked at the lake rushing through a field, remembered the first time she had seen it — she had been with John. She thought briefly of her swimming in it — and John had been there too. And the third time — here he was again.

Closer and closer they drew to the storehouses; closer and closer to the place where two Brothers of the third circle watched and waited. Two Brothers who knew what their leader demanded, and who were determined to deliver it to him.

John braked gently to a halt outside the furthest of the storehouses. Most of what he needed was inside — but something made him look twice at it. He killed the engine, absently pocketing the keys. He got out and headed towards the storehouse.

Margaret was too engrossed in taking in the scene which surrounded her to notice anything amiss — assuming that there *was* something to notice, which there was not. She felt calm, relaxed; she watched a butterfly make its lazy way across the field to her right. She felt a thrill of exhilaration surge through her. Nature had always fascinated her and watching something so simple, yet the product of such a complex metamorphosis, was enough to bring her love of nature surging through her other emotions.

She noticed that John had got out and was heading towards the storehouse; it crossed her mind that he seemed a little more hesitant than usual, but she dismissed the thought.

She got out of the land rover and was about to follow him, about to head closer towards the two who waited in hiding, those whom, if they managed to get their hands upon her, would cheerfully help in hurting and abusing and humiliating her, when something caught her eye off to her left: a movement.

She walked slowly towards it wondering what it could be; an animal of some description, obviously. As she came closer she realised that it was a bird; occasionally it threshed its body trying to flap its wings, but unsuccessfully. She could see now that one wing, the right one, lay twisted unnaturally under its body, obviously broken. At her approach, it threshed even more wildly in fear, a thin weak *keen* coming from its beak.

"Oh, you *poor* thing," she murmured sadly, slowly backing away. "John, there's a bird here with a broken wing, d'you think we can help it?"

John couldn't say for certain what seemed unusual about the storehouse. He heard Margaret get out of the land rover, and noticed her heading away from him. He knew now that he was becoming paranoid — '*It must be a side-effect of working for Hayter*,' he thought to himself with a grin. It was then that he heard Margaret's voice.

"John, there's a bird here with a broken wing, d'you think we can help it?"

He turned to regard her, took a step in her direction, saw her face distort in sudden fear, a warning shout forming upon her lips. He began to turn, as a fist slammed into his head, catching him off balance and causing him to fall to the ground. Out of the corner of his eye he saw Margaret begin to run towards him and he *immediately* realised what was happening.

"For *Christ's* sake, Margaret, *get away*," he yelled, as he rolled out of reach of the man who had hit him. The shout brought Margaret to a stop; John's tone of voice, the evident violence of the two men who had suddenly appeared made her hesitate — and yet she didn't want to desert him; but she knew he already understood that. She ran back to the land rover whilst John regained his feet and faced his assailants. Damn! He had the keys. She got out and began running down the road back towards the mansion, dreading hearing the sound of pursuit.

John picked his man, lunged at him, brought him to the ground, balanced on top of him. He landed a couple of vicious punches to the man's body, kneed his groin, ignored the punishment which the second man subjected *him* to. As his temper exploded into a murderous rage, his hands reached around the throat of the struggling man beneath him, gripping tighter and tighter. He realised, dimly, that the second man had stopped raining blows upon his head and body, and hoped that he had *not* gone after Margaret.

A few seconds more, and John would have succeeded in killing Brother Martin. Richard, however, having realised that his blows were ineffectual, picked up a fair-sized rock with both hands and smashed it down onto John's cranium with all his strength.

A heavy sigh escaped John as he fell forward, unconscious, blood flowing liberally from his badly gashed head. Martin breathed deeply, and wriggled out from under him.

"Thanks," he croaked, "where is she?"

"There!" exclaimed Richard, pointing to Margaret who could be seen running, about three hundred yards from them. "It looks like we've got a chase on our hands — and that means entering the barrier; remember to cloak yourself in darkness. I have no wish to tangle with Hayter. I value my life."

"*So do I,*" replied Martin, rubbing his neck, and landing a *vicious* kick to John's body.

They set off at a fast run, Richard slightly in the lead, Martin keeping up despite his laboured breathing.

The distance between them and their quarry closed steadily. It closed even more drastically when, as Margaret glanced anxiously back over her shoulder, she lost her footing and fell heavily. Richard glanced at Martin, a grin creasing his features; he knew that there was *no* escape for her. Barring intervention from Hayter, they had her.

Margaret pushed herself to her feet and continued running, her breath rasping and burning in her chest, leaving her unable to shout for help even if there had been anyone to hear, but the roads and fields were deserted. Her heart beating furiously, her legs aching with the sudden exertion, she knew it was only a matter of time before they caught her. She had looked back twice, the first time seeing John apparently on top of one of the men who now pursued her, the second time seeing them looking in her direction as she slipped and fell. She risked a second glance back down the road and saw them running furiously but silently after her, about a hundred and fifty yards away.

'*The barrier*', she thought. If she could only reach the barrier, then, when her pursuers entered it, Hayter would at least know that *something* was wrong; perhaps, just perhaps, she might be able to escape with his help.

She realised that she had slowed slightly, and forced her now-screaming leg muscles to work harder, increasing her speed. The difference was only marginal, however, and slowly but inexorably they gained, eating away the distance that separated them. The next time that she dared to look around they were less than a hundred yards away. The crazy thought that she had told John that she would enjoy *every minute* of this outing crossed her mind. She wondered what had happened to him? Was he still unconscious on the ground, as she had glimpsed him before she fell, or was his injury more serious? Surely he couldn't be...? She erased the thought before it fully formed, tears of fear and dread for him mixing with the tears of anxiety at her own predicament. '*She must now be within the sanctuary of the barrier*', she thought. The men still pursued, gaining more quickly now, it seemed. Didn't they *fear* the barrier? Dots seemed to dance at the periphery of her vision, which came in and out of focus.

She realised that she could hear them, their feet pounding upon the road, thought she could even hear their laboured breathing above the gasping of her own. She *had* to know how close they were; by some perverse law of nature she would rather *know* how much they had gained than *imagine* how much they *were* gaining. Again she risked a look behind her and jumped, almost losing her balance but regaining it before it could affect her futile attempt to elude capture. They were less than twenty yards behind her, strong-looking, one with black hair, one with light-brown. As she turned to look ahead again, coming up to where the lake meandered through the field, one thing struck her about her pursuers. Despite having fought John, despite this protracted chase, both of them were *grinning*. She thought of a fox-hunt, with the hounds closing in for the kill — it was the anticipation of having her completely at their mercy and the anticipation of running her to earth that caused their grimaces of pleasure.

She realised the utter hopelessness of trying to escape; she despaired then, wondering what they would do to her and fearing the things that her mind, rather cruelly, suggested.

One of them launched himself at her in a parody of a rugby tackle. She felt his hands make contact with her back and right foot a second later. It was this second contact which was Margaret's literal downfall. The contact upon her back had forced her off balance and as she tried to correct it the hand grasping desperately at her foot caused her to overcompensate. Her legs seemed to forget which was left and which was right as they tangled together and she fell with a dull *thud* full-length upon the road, sobbing, gasping for breath, making no effort to get up and carry on running. At that moment, whilst she was shaking with the shock and the effort she had exerted, she surrendered. She no longer cared *what* they did to her, as long as they got it over with quickly. Time seemed to stretch out as she lay there, gasping, indifferent to her fate.

She wondered why they hadn't done anything to her. Had they given up and gone away now that they had succeeded in reducing her to this state, she wondered.

Her question was answered in the same instant as someone leapt upon her, forced her right arm painfully up her back and grabbed a handful of hair, keeping her head twisted away from him.

She tried to struggle, but had already accepted that she was caught. However, he jerked her arm further up her back.

"Don't struggle and we won't hurt you," his voice hissed.

Margaret guessed that they were going to rape her here in the open, within Hayter's barrier. How could this happen? Still trying to regain control of her breathing and her heartbeat — although she was too frightened to do too much about either — she wondered whether she should simply let them strip her, or fight them *every* step of the way. Instinct dictated that she fight them — even if it cost her her life. She heard the second man approach, saw his shoes — black ones — and his trouser legs. The feet carried the legs out of her vision and she felt herself being appraised by this second.

"Pull her head back."

Her hair was yanked back savagely, raising her head. Instantly, a wad of some kind was clamped against her nose and mouth. She had no choice but to breathe the foul-smelling odour into her lungs. Almost immediately, she began to feel hazy. Thirty seconds later, she was unconscious.

Richard quickly felt for a pulse and nodded at Martin. "Fine, she's out. Give me a hand, I don't want to spend *any* more time here than I *have* to."

Martin nodded, and between them, half carrying and half dragging her, they headed back towards their lookout post and their cars by a more direct route than that which the road afforded them.

"I'm supposed to take her somewhere *safe* until tonight, when we move her again," said Martin.

"You can use my private clinic," Richard offered, somewhat generously. He felt that he could *afford* to be generous as, having helped capture Hunter, he could virtually *name* his reward, and he *already knew* what he would ask for...

"Thanks, I'll do that. By the way, did you *kill* him?"

"Brandon? No, but I wouldn't be surprised if he *does* die. It was as Supreme Brother said, he got in the way and I incapacitated him."

"Quite," returned Martin. "Shouldn't we bear more to the left?"

"In a second — the ground isn't too firm coming from this direction, and I want to avoid it if possible."

It took less than twenty minutes for them to reach their cars. "Richard, shall I put her in the boot or the back?"

"She *won't* wake up, if that's what you mean. I *don't* think we'd be very popular if she suffocated in the boot of your car."

"True: the back of the car it is."

"I'll give her an injection when we get to the clinic, just to make *sure* there's no possibility of her coming around too soon," Richard decided.

They got into their cars, carefully manoeuvred onto the road and then accelerated away from Hayter's domain.

Not far from the storehouses where John and Margaret had been ambushed by two third circle members of the Cult, a bird with a broken wing threshed once more, a pathetic *keen* came from its beak; it shuddered, and died.

***

Blackness. Greyness. Whirring. Rotor blades? Stone. Grey. Lighter. Light.

Noise. Pounding waves. Regular. Bang! BANG!

Vision. Vision? Burning... Hurts. Go Back... Greyness. Blackness.

Who?

What?

Where?

***

John opened his eyes, the sound of waves pounding threatening to deafen him, or so he thought. He saw where he was only dimly; his vision not just blurred, but filtered somehow, as though somewhere between his eyes and his brain there was a signals failure and only a

272

fraction of what his eyes actually saw completed the journey.

He lay upon the grass, fighting the spasms which his stomach generated. He lost the battle and vomited weakly. Tentatively, he put a hand to his head. An intense jolt of pain told him that he was in a bad way. His hand came into view darkly covered with blood. He knew somehow that something important had happened, something he had to tell to...to whom?

Groaning, he stood, feeling his stomach lurch alarmingly. He looked around, the effort making his head throb all the more. Through the grey haze he made out the storehouses, the one that he had meant to visit; the fields seemingly colourless to his vision. And then he saw the land rover. He staggered in its direction knowing that he had only to follow this road to reach help — but from whom he wasn't sure.

His legs buckled as he reached it, and he managed to save himself from falling only by throwing his arm over the wound-down window in the door. He closed his eyes and took a deep breath. Opening them again, he opened the land rover's door and managed to swing himself into the driver's seat at the first attempt. He gazed stupidly at the ignition for several moments before he decided that the keys weren't there. He ran his eyes over the dashboard before he thought of trying his own pockets, which yielded the key.

He managed, with a little difficulty, to fit the key and start the engine, but coordinating his hand and feet movements was impossible. As a result his driving was not just erratic, but *almost* demonic.

The vehicle lurched and swerved over the road as though driven by one demented. It was only a matter of time before he swerved off the road and the land rover ended up on its side in a ditch.

He climbed out and began walking in the direction which he felt certain was the way to a refuge; his walk

273

was hardly that, more of a drunken progress, painfully slow. He felt the evening breeze upon his skin, judged that the light must now be fading, but he could only guess at that. His own vision seemed to be failing, things becoming more difficult to make out, losing what little clarity they had.

At last the mansion came into his vision, hazy, out of focus, but *there*. Something pulled at his mind. He had been with someone *else*, someone very dear to him. Where *was* she? What had happened? The mansion acted on him like a magnet and he began walking directly towards it, his course not now varying. Did he live here? Did he know the occupier? Who *was* he?

He came to the door, fell, and spent anxious moments trying to get the strength together to get to his feet. He eventually managed it and leaned against the door, his breath coming in harsh, ragged bursts. His vision, apparently deciding that it wasn't needed any more, faded away and he realised with despair that he was blind.

He searched for a doorbell, or some other way to make his presence known. It was *then* his questing hand came in contact with the bellpull. Summoning the last of his strength, he took hold of it and pulled, and pulled, and passed out.

***

"...and there's no doubt in my mind that when this is all over — that is assuming that the Cult is wiped out; I know that sounds like a bit of a big assumption to make, but I'm sure that then you'll be able to look back on all this and think that everything was so obvious, and ask yourself why we didn't see the solutions immediately?

"Of course, some of the solutions may be so simple that we never even think of them, or we may be placed in positions where we have to make a decision which will hurt one who means a *lot* to us. If, for example, you had to decide between saving me and say, continuing an

274

attack upon the Cult which we'd both begun, I would *expect* you to continue the attack. No buts, Tony, because if the position were reversed, that would be *my* decision, much as I would castigate myself for it afterwards.

"It's either the Baron line that dies, or it's the Cult. If both die, well, so be it; it would still be a victory of *sorts*, to my way of thinking — although the Cult *would* have fulfilled their curse."

Tony nodded slowly. "I understand what you're saying, George, and in the cold light of day I can agree with it because I can think of the long term results of what we've got to do. But if it actually came to it...I *can't* say for certain that I'd be able to carry on attacking the Cult when I might be able to save you from *dying*."

Hayter sighed: "Tony, *I'm dying already*. We all are, to a lesser or greater degree; what is death that people fear it so? It is a natural conclusion which nobody can avoid."

"But it can be delayed," Tony argued stubbornly.

"And who are *you* to decide it is better to extend life than to allow it to terminate? You simply cannot know before events demonstrate, whether you were either right or wrong. And further, even if you consider that you *were* right, your perception may be imperfect so in *fact* you are wrong."

Tony sighed heavily. "I've read similar twisted reasoning in your occult works. I suppose I have to go along with you — but can you answer me this: if I were to allow anyone to die before they should, knowing that I could have helped them, how do I live with myself afterwards?" he asked, gesturing for emphasis.

Hayter's brow furrowed. "Yes, you would feel guilty about it, it's a natural reaction. I think that the answer lies in accepting the feelings that arise and whilst recognising that you feel responsible for the death of whoever, you have to recognise and believe that the decision you made was the correct one — the only one you could have made under the circumstances. You must *never* doubt that, since the knowledge at least helps to justify your action and hence alleviate some of the burden which you might feel."

Biting his thumb, Tony replied, "Where do you dredge all these answers from? Is there anything you *haven't* got an answer for?"

Hayter grinned at him. "As a matter of fact, I'm not too sure how to annihilate a certain Cult that's been a thorn for far too long." Although he said it jokingly, a hardness entered his eyes. "And that's just about where this discussion started."

"Not quite; we started with Anton's prophesy."

"We don't even know if it *is* prophesy," Hayter protested.

"*I* know," Tony said slowly. "Don't ask me how, but I just know it was written for us, specifically."

"All right, I'm a reasonable sort of man, convince me," Hayter said simply.

"George, I'm not sure that I can! *I* know that it was written by Anton the night before he was killed, but I just can't offer you any proof of *how* I know it. It's the same thing knowing it was intended for us; more for you than for me, although it concerns me more than it does you."

"Say that *again*," Hayter said incredulously.

Tony took a deep breath. "I just know, a gut feeling if you like, that the verse is genuine. It's intended for you more than me, but it's about *me* rather than you. It might contain anything, some warning which you can pass on to me that will be of value sometime, perhaps."

"So, Anton *knew* that he would die *before* he attempted the ritual, is what you are saying," Hayter murmured, and then, suddenly, growing enthusiastic, he declared, "Of *course* he did. He *deliberately* used a ritual with a *defective* ending. I remember correcting it and wondering why he hadn't noticed the fundamental error. But he *must* have known about it."

"That makes no sense at all," Tony concluded.

"Not upon the face of it, no. But what if Anton Baron was a lot *more* of a genius than we give him credit for being? Eh, Tony, what then? But I can see that you don't follow me. Perhaps, for the present that is for the best."

"Now you're talking in riddles," Tony complained.

Hayter smiled. "Am I?" he queried, looking directly into Tony's eyes. "An idea has just occurred to me which I've *never* considered before. I'd like to toss it about in my mind before I propound it to you, because if I am right, then the implications are *staggering*."

Tony thought this over, running what they had said through his mind. His mental recapitulation yielded nothing which, so far as he could tell, explained what Hayter might have thought of. He sat further back in his chair frowning.

"And how long do you expect it will be before you consider letting me in on this secret?"

Hayter laughed, "It's no secret, Tony, just an idea. I'll need to check up in some grimoires that I haven't read in years, literally. I don't see any sense in us sitting here discussing an idea which might turn out to be a mad flight of fancy on my part."

He nodded, "You're right, as usual," he conceded. "I suppose that the inactivity and wanting to be free of the threat that the Cult pose are making me jumpy."

True to his words, he jumped up as a bell jangled loudly somewhere outside Hayter's study. Before the echoes died away the bell rang again and again, and then fell silent, the sound echoing and then dying away. Tony looked at Hayter intently, as he jumped from his seat and headed for the study door.

"Jesus! What was that?" he asked as Hayter headed out of the study, Tony in close pursuit.

"It's the doorbell," Hayter answered suspiciously. "It isn't that which worries me, however. If anyone approaches this mansion, then *I* should be the first one to know about it. The closer they come, the more I am aware of them. But I don't feel *any* such warning."

"Couldn't it be John or Margaret?"

"John, yes, but Margaret..." he trailed off, seemingly confused. "John has the keys to the door, he wouldn't use the bell."

"Well, it must be Margaret."

"Whom I will *not* allow outside on her own? No: I think not."

They arrived at the door and Tony realised suddenly that Hayter didn't have a key to unlock it, but that didn't present a problem. He glared at the door for a second, his gaze abstracted, and Tony heard a *click* as the door unlocked. Hayter pulled the door open, and stood transfixed by the sight which greeted him.

John lay a foot or so away from the door, breathing barely perceptibly.

Tony lurched forward and without having to be asked, gently lifted John in his arms and carried him into the mansion. Hayter closed and locked the door and came hurrying after him.

"Take him to my bedroom," he snapped. Tony caught the anxiety in the old man's voice and began to worry that this might prove too much for him.

"Where is it?"

"This way," and Hayter took the lead, showing the way.

Once there, Tony half lay John upon the bed whilst Hayter commenced stripping him. Tony helped and they gently eased him under the covers.

"What happened?" Tony demanded finally.

"It seems our friends have decided to let us know that they are not to be forgotten," Hayter said drily. "We can discuss it later. There's a first aid box in the bathroom. Would you get it, and bring some water."

"What in?" Tony wanted to know.

"Anything; find a bucket or a bowl or something, anything."

Tony hurried out, and Hayter sat next to his private secretary / servant / friend / mentor. "John," he whispered, placing his hand on John's shoulder, "don't you *dare* die on me. You can't get away from me that easily. Fight, John, fight. You've *got* to live — I've never told you this, John, but I couldn't have got this far without you, your help, your strength, your reassurance when things didn't seem to be going as they should; and that infuriating sense of humour of yours. I couldn't love you any more if you were my own son, John, so you *can't* die — I won't let you."

He fell silent, appraising John's pale face, turning his head to see the extent of the wound there. At that moment Tony reappeared carrying a bowl which Hayter had never seen before, the first aid box pinned under his arm.

Hayter relieved him of it and opened it. He took out various articles and placed them within reach on the bedside table, pushing books out of the way impatiently.

"Have we got a pair of scissors in there?" he asked.

Tony looked. "Yes, here," he replied, passing them over.

He motioned to Tony to lift John's head and Hayter began cutting away the hair surrounding the gash, placing the clippings carefully upon the bedside table. He worked quickly and calmly, cutting as close to the scalp as possible yet never once touching the wound.

At length, Hayter gave a grunt of approval, and set the scissors back into the first aid box. "At least I can see what I'm doing now," he muttered, taking a small bottle from the table and adding a few drops to the bowl of water. He took a wad of lint and soaked it in the water,

279

gently dabbed along the angry red line of the gash along the white scalp. He half expected John to come around, but was disappointed.

"Really, this should be stitched; for the present, I think we can make do with sutures." He tore open a packet of sterile sutures and first drying the area with a fresh piece of lint, he gently affixed the adhesive plasters. He completed his ministrations by placing a third piece of lint over the gash. Taking a bandage and breaking the seal, and with Tony's help he bandaged the wound tightly enough to keep the lint in position, but loosely enough to avoid putting pressure upon it.

"At least the bleeding has stopped," Tony attempted to comfort Hayter with the observation.

"I expected it to start again when I bathed it. Looks like he's lost a lot of blood, Tony. Will you take the bowl and throw the lint and these packets away? There's a disposal chute in the kitchen that leads to the incinerator."

Tony nodded and picking the objects up, left carrying them. Hayter sat again looking at the pale face of his friend. His gaze became abstracted, as he concentrated his will upon John.

He was still in the same position when Tony returned, thoughtfully carrying two steaming mugs. He placed them upon the bedside table, Hayter acknowledging the gesture with a nod.

"How serious would you say it is?"

"I don't know. At least there's no sign of a fracture, that's something."

"How do you know?"

Hayter flashed a look at him and Tony understood. "Why didn't I think of that?" he mused, frowning at the recumbent form lying upon the bed breathing rapidly.

Hayter took John's pulse and frowned. "One hundred and thirty. Shock, no doubt. All we can do for the present is to wait. I see no real advantage in waking him."

"Where's Margaret?" Tony cut in, suddenly realising that she was conspicuous by her absence. His voice had an edge to it as though he realised that all was not well with her.

Hayter blew out a long breath. He brought a chair to the bedside where he could watch John with no effort and motioned for Tony to do likewise.

"She's not in the mansion," he declared seriously. "Nor is she within the area protected by the barrier."

Tony began to feel a cold fear gripping him; a dread which began deep within him and slowly spread throughout his being, numbing him, and yet stretching his nerves ever more taut. "What else?" he whispered, afraid that if he used his voice, he wouldn't be able to speak through the quiver within it.

"Yesterday, Margaret wanted to go and swim; John, for one reason or another, refused to accompany her. Today, he went to the stores. Neither you nor I realised that he hadn't come in to enquire about lunch — we were too wrapped up in what we were discussing. I think, Tony," Hayter murmured, "that the Cult have managed to kidnap her."

"But you said..."

"The stores themselves are just outside the barrier. Why that is, is a long story that I haven't time to tell now. Either Margaret has been kidnapped or she's out in the woods again — and frankly, I don't think that she is. Earlier, I became vaguely aware of a minor disturbance at the extremity of the barrier. Such anomalies are not unusual. I dismissed it almost as soon as I became aware of it. But I fear now that I have made a serious mistake," he finished lamely.

"But you're not certain?"

"There are *lots* of things I'm not certain about, Tony. Margaret is *one* of them — but in more ways than I care to mention, until things clarify a little."

"You could use me to locate her, as you did last time."

"I could, but I fear it would be useless."

"Why?" the question snapped out of him.

"Because *if* the Cult kidnapped Margaret, they cloaked themselves. *If* they have her, she will be cloaked, too. But *why* did they go to such extremes to accomplish it? *That's* the question that we should be addressing ourselves to, Tony, not to where she is, but *why* she was kidnapped. Under normal circumstances no member of the Cult would *dare* to approach my barrier. So *why* was Margaret such an inducement for them? That they dared not only my barrier and *me*, but did *that* to John probably because he got in the way."

"Try it anyway."

Hayter nodded wearily, but a groan from John froze them both. As they gazed at him he opened his eyes and raised a hand to his head.

"Easy, John," Hayter soothed him, moving his hand away from his head. "Can you hear me?" Hayter inquired gently.

John nodded his head and grimaced.

"John, we *have* to know, what happened? Where's Margaret?" Tony broke in.

"Margaret?" John croaked, as though the name meant nothing.

"Marga...ret," he frowned, obviously trying to remember. "*Margaret!*" he exclaimed, trying to sit up and instantly regretting the attempt which made his head throb as if it would burst. He sank back upon the pillows, his croaking fading to a whisper as he managed to say: "Stores...two men...don't know who. Told her to run...nearly strangled *one* of the bastards. Something hit me...came around...tried to get back...*crashed* the land rover. Sorry about losing the no-claims bonus."

Hayter and Tony exchanged disbelieving glances. Hayter held his hand in front of John's face, two fingers showing. "John, how many fingers do you see?"

John peered intently at the hand in front of his face. "I would guess at two," he said, to Hayter's relief — a relief which was shattered as John continued, "But I *don't* actually see any. *I'm completely blind.*"

With that stunning piece of intelligence his eyes closed and he passed into a more natural sleep than previously within seconds. It was almost as though he had willed himself awake just to provide the answers to their questions.

Hayter felt his pulse again and nodded his approval. "Down to one hundred," he muttered quietly. "I think one of us should be here in case he wakes again," he said with a resigned sigh. "And we've got things to discuss."

Tony nodded mutely. "But what can we do? Where do we begin?"

"First things first," Hayter rebuked him mildly. "I can guess that you're screaming for action, deep inside you; but that's no excuse for us to attempt anything until we've decided where we stand and what, if anything, can be done to remedy the situation. We can't just go charging in — you can bet that's *just* what their leader wants us to do."

"But you yourself said that they went to a lot of trouble and danger to get hold of her: why?"

"Several reason. To throw us into disarray; to use her as a lever against us; even as a form of blackmail. That is obvious, but there is a *lot* more to it than that."

"Such as?" Tony demanded.

Hayter's face betrayed the culpability which he felt. "Well, Tony, I had enough clues to work it out sooner, but I dismissed it as impossible. That doesn't *excuse* me, of course."

"What *are* you talking about? Margaret's in danger whilst we sit here calmly discussing things as though she's out at a picnic."

"It's no picnic, I'm afraid, Tony. There is only one explanation which fits the facts as we know them: Margaret Hunter is a member of the Baron line and the Cult knows it."

Tony leapt from his chair as though it were on fire. He turned his eyes upon Hayter, glaring at him, not believing what he had just heard. "That is *insane*," he declared loudly. Hayter held up a warning hand as John stirred and groaned. In a lower tone, but no less fiercely he continued, "When did you dream this up? I don't believe it."

"I've had the pieces in my hands for days, but I didn't recognise them for what they were — not until ten minutes ago, that is..."

"Get to the point," Tony said impatiently.

"On two separate occasions, Margaret dreamed of me playing a particular piece — *but when I was playing it*. No, there's more. I don't base what I said upon dreams. Earlier, when John rang the bell, you said that it could be John or Margaret at the door. I said that it *could* be John — and then it struck me."

"*What* struck you?"

"It could have been John at the door because he's sympathetic to the barrier — he helps keep it in place. I am not aware of him as he makes his way through it; I was not aware of any intrusion upon the barrier when the bell rang. Equally, I would not be aware of *you*, being of the Baron line, unless I specifically tried to locate you. The point is that *no one* can come as close to the mansion as Margaret did without my being aware of it. Tony, *I was never aware of Margaret whilst she was within the barrier*. There is only one explanation. She is of the Baron lineage."

"But how? You said that we two are the last of the Barons — and that the last of the American Barons died out in the 1940's."

Hayter sighed and spread his hands. "I don't know. I thought I knew *everything* about the family tree. Obviously, I don't."

Tony paced the room; Hayter stood and went to his dressing room, returning seconds later with a framed photograph. "Apart from you and your parents, this was the last of the Barons, as far as I knew, that is. I met him during the war. He actually managed to trace me, and you know that's not entirely easy."

Tony glanced at the photograph Hayter carried, frowning, his face a mask of worry. As he caught sight of it, however, he stopped pacing, and his face turned white. "Oh, my God," he said, as he ran out of the room.

Hayter stared after him incredulously, shaking his head. He glanced at John and then sat, gazing at the faded photo. He wondered where Margaret was and what would be done to her. He blamed himself for her capture, and for whatever treatment she received. He tried to view things dispassionately, but his emotions for John and Margaret overcame his resolve, and when Tony returned, clutching a photograph wallet, he found Hayter with his hands to his face, sobbing.

It took Tony minutes before he felt able to put his arms around him, and in that moment they became closer than they ever otherwise could have. They sobbed onto each other's shoulders their fears and frustrations.

Hayter regained control of himself, and Tony felt he had to do the same. To cover his attempts, he indicated the wallet.

"Look through this, and tell me if any face looks familiar."

Hayter looked at him, surprised, but opened the wallet nevertheless. He glanced over various photographs of people he had never seen before, turning the pages over to be confronted by yet more people. It was in the centre of the wallet he stopped, where two photographs stood out by their obvious age. One was of a young woman, clearly, by her features, Margaret's mother. The second was of two other people. The woman Hayter didn't recognise, but as his eyes looked at the face of the man he felt a stab of recognition. He brought the photo he still carried of Scott Hobard and held it next to the wallet. There could be no doubt that it was the same person.

Hayter's eyes found Tony's. "Yes, those are her grandparents," was all he said.

They said nothing. It seemed that there was nothing to be said. Each was suffering from the after-effects of their own revelations. Tony felt a helplessness build up within him but he knew that Hayter, taking advantage of the silence, was already forming a plan of action. He managed to contain his impatience, and maintain the silence, but only just.

The silence was eventually broken by John waking again and complaining that he was hungry. Tony, glad of something to do, offered to make some sandwiches.

John tried to tell him everything that had happened, and blamed himself mercilessly for her abduction, swearing that he deserved worse than blindness for having allowed it to happen. No matter how Hayter tried to ameliorate John's part in what had happened, he refused to be comforted and continued to berate himself until Hayter lost patience and told him firmly to stop.

He still muttered to himself, darkly, until Tony returned with the sandwiches and cold drinks. John tried to apologise to him, but Tony cut him short with a sensitivity Hayter hadn't believed he possessed.

"Look, John, I don't believe for a *second* you wanted her to be kidnapped — you did *all* you could, but you were outnumbered and attacked from behind. What you've got to do is get well enough to help us get her back."

"If a *blind* man can help," John cut in.

They ate in silence, casting furtive glances in his direction even though he couldn't see them. Hayter returned the photograph of Hobard to its place in his dressing room, returning with a tablet in his hand which he passed to John.

"You need sleep, John, this'll help. Tony and I have things to discuss. If you need anything, ring the buzzer."

Surprisingly, John made no fuss about taking the tablet and they left him prostrate upon the bed, carrying their plates and glasses with them as they went.

Once they had left the room, John retrieved the tablet from under his tongue and tried to decide what he must do.

In the study, Hayter sat and looked sleepily at Tony. "What a mess," he said.

"But what do we do about it?" Tony asked, a note of despair in his voice.

"Well, we can't call the police without sounding like crackpots and if we try attacking the Cult — they'll be waiting for us. Frankly, it seems like our hands are tied, if Margaret's life is important. Then again, she *is* a Baron, so she won't be permitted to live for long; but long enough for them to complete whatever they have in mind for her — and it's obvious that they'll want to use her to keep us guessing. We've got two options open to us, Tony. Attack, and we're in effect killing Margaret, or sit and wait for them to make the first move and maybe lose her without lifting a finger to help."

"Well, you can sit there doing nothing if you want," Tony began vehemently, standing, "but don't expect me to do the same."

"Don't you understand yet, Tony? That's *just* the reaction their leader is hoping you'll give in to and make it easy for him to kill you. What good will that do Margaret?"

Tony hesitated and then sat. "Besides," Hayter continued slowly, "we won't be doing nothing — in fact they'll wonder just what we *are* doing, so we *might* just be able to turn this situation around."

"At the expense of Margaret's life?" Tony snapped viciously.

"If necessary," Hayter thundered back at him, his temper finally fraying. Taking a deep breath, he bit back what else he was going to say. The silence stretched until Hayter broke it, his voice now considerably softer. "There is more *yet* that you don't understand, Tony."

He glared at Hayter resentfully. "More secrets?"

Hayter threw his eyes heavenwards in a '*give me strength*' gesture. "If you insist on it, yes. Earlier, I was reluctant to tell you of the idea that I had regarding Anton Baron. Well, here it is, and *listen* to it. Why would Anton Baron deliberately kill himself? He knew, so you imply, that his ceremony would fail, wrote that bloody verse the night before it. *Why* would he do that, *deliberately* use a flawed ritual when he *knew* that the end result would be his *death*?"

Tony shrugged. "I don't know," he answered. "Is this leading somewhere?"

"Tony, what if Anton *knew* that he couldn't eradicate the Cult in *that* time? How if he used a *different* magic which demanded his *death* as payment; *then* does his death begin to make sense?"

"It might," Tony grudgingly admitted, "but what 'other magic' could it be?"

"That's what you and I must discover, and I pray that we be successful."

"And Margaret?" Tony asked, his voice muted.

"I think that this is the only way we can help her. If I am wrong, Tony, I will die with her death upon my conscience. We have to be united in this. Are you with me?"

Tony thought harder than he had ever thought in his life. To stay here trying to help Hayter chase the ghost of a Baron long past seemed something of a betrayal of Margaret, especially when his whole being cried out in utter fury at thoughts of what might be happening to her. He shook his head, trying not to let his emotionalism cloud his judgement.

The door opened and John entered unsteadily. He stood, his head tilted as if listening. "Tony?" he asked.

Tony walked over to him and took his arm. John's arm, however, had other ideas. It followed Tony's arm until his hand rested upon his shoulder; the other hand copied the motion. His sightless eyes locked with Tony's. "You know, deep down, that George is right," he whispered. "Fight the Cult upon your own terms, Tony, not upon theirs; I hurt for her as much as you, but I can see more clearly blinded than you can with your eyes wide open. Your place is next to George. It always *has* been, and you've *always* known it."

"John!" Hayter snapped.

"All right, I'm going. And before you ask, *yes* I *was* listening at the door. Thank you Tony," he added as Tony took his arm and led him back to Hayter's bedroom, leaving Hayter momentarily speechless.

Whether or not anything more passed between them that early morning as Tony took him back to bed, no one ever said; but when Tony returned to the study, it was with a new sense of determination.

"You're right, George," he declared, "and as far as Margaret's concerned, I wouldn't even know where to start looking. At least let me in on your thinking, so I have the illusion that I'm actually helping you."

Hayter stared at him. "Is that you speaking, or John?" he asked, finally.

"It's me. God knows I'm frightened for Margaret. I've never been more scared in my life; but if there's any way of saving her, I know you'll come up with it. I doubt that I'll be much help, imagining what's happened to her, but I'll do my best. And, if the worst comes to the worst," he swallowed, "I won't mourn her alone."

Hayter stood for a second, and then nodded his head slowly. "Let's get to work, then."

"But where do we start?" Tony wanted to know.

"Where we've started so many times before, but this time we begin with a subtle edge. In the light of what we've just learned, what do you think this means?"

And Hayter read aloud:

> "When the flesh of my flesh again be united, then
> Shall my kin do battle with my eternal enemies;
> The days of the Brotherhood shall at last be
> Numbered — my offspring, even though it mean their
> Death, shall enable my victory."

Tony and Hayter locked eyes, the same thought occurring to both of them at the same time. "Are you thinking what I'm thinking?" Hayter asked, softly.

"It almost seems to be saying that our battle can only take place when we are reunited — and that means that they *can't* kill Margaret."

"No, Tony, you go too fast. It only *hints* that we shall be united, but how?"

"United in love?" Tony speculated.

"But what could *that* have to do with Anton Baron killing himself in a flawed ritual nearly five hundred years ago? That's the real question. I suggest we have a look at those grimoires that I mentioned earlier."

"But what do you expect to find?"

"That's it *precisely*, I don't!" And with that idiotic message, Hayter led the way out of his study and into the library.

There, for long hours, they read tome after tome of occult lore, Hayter saying only that he wanted information on relocation and bilocation.

Tony read until the print — and in many cases handwriting — blurred before his eyes. The repeated shocks that he had been subjected to took their toll in exhaustion. At long last he succumbed to sleep, his head dropping gently into an exploration of the myths of witches.

Hayter observed this with a wry smile, but he himself carried on searching for one piece of information. He remembered that he had read it here in this very room years ago. What he couldn't remember was what treatise it was in, and in what context it had been rendered.

His thoughts turned to Margaret, a bitter pang of regret stabbing through him. If only he had realised sooner: it *all* seemed so obvious now. Hayter thought that he had said words very similar to that to Tony earlier, before John had returned and acquainted them with the fact that Margaret had been kidnapped. Nothing seemed to be happening as it should, he thought. Things had stopped going smoothly for the Barons one cold, wild night, nearly five hundred years ago.

Grimly, he returned to the massive books and manuscripts, attempting to instil his reading with urgency. But that wouldn't happen. He could never hurry his reading, never skim though it in case he missed something important. But his concentration did waver several times as his pouring was interrupted by vivid thoughts of Margaret, tears running down her face as she listened to him playing. Her look of terror when she realised that Tony was looking at *her* caricature of him;

291

laughing at him when she deduced that underneath the surface he was a *lovable* old rogue.

A brief smile touched his face at that memory, and he clung on to it, savouring the pleasure that it brought him for long moments. It was a bitter-sweet memory for him, for even as the memory floated in his mind, he *knew*, deep down, that he would *never* hear Margaret Hunter say anything more to him, ever, in his life.

A single tear glistened upon his lower eyelash and made its way down his face. Hayter sat, indifferent to it, accepting what his instincts told him. Hopelessly, he returned to his search.

Breaking only to go and take his medication, when he remembered it, he continued to burrow through his library, with a feeling akin to looking for a needle in a haystack. He realised that even *with* Tony's help this could take months. He rubbed his eyes, becoming aware that he was feeling tired and irritable. Returning his gaze to the volume in front of him he tried to force his eyes to focus upon the fine print, but it seemed to be jumping and jerking in a *deliberate* attempt to prevent his reading it. He decided to take a break, and realised that he was hungry. It was a relatively surprising experience for him, since for the past nine years or so John had looked after him so well that he had almost forgotten what it felt like to be this famished. He smiled to himself as he quietly made his way out of the library and wandered down to the kitchen. The actual thought of cooking himself a meal made his appetite recede a little; he had never been a good cook — John had once said that if it were possible, Hayter would burn water. He filled the kettle, put instant coffee in the pot, got some cups, placed them upon a large tray, and then opened the refrigerator to see what he could purloin in the way of food.

He felt a vague sense of guilt; John guarded the contents of his fridge jealously, and Hayter began to feel like a small child raiding the larder. He smiled at the thought, his gaze running over eggs, milk, bacon, cheese....*cheese*! Hayter felt his mouth water as his eyes took in the large block — about two pounds of it. Of *all* the things which he had been forbidden to eat since his heart trouble was diagnosed, cheese was the one which he missed the most. John was rather unsympathetic about it and only *very* occasionally allowed him a *small* quantity which only tended to whet his appetite for more; and *here*, sitting in front of him was a golden opportunity for him to take advantage of John's incapacitation. With a sly smile, he removed the block, placed it reverently upon a large plate and, after some moment's hunting, piled two boxes of crackers next to the plate upon the tray. He rubbed his hands together gleefully. He added a dish of butter — *another* forbidden luxury — almost absently, followed by a cheese knife and a butter knife. He brewed the coffee and, somewhat surprised at the weight of the tray, carried his burden back to the library and placed it quietly upon the book-strewn desk, taking care not to disturb Tony.

There, he absently took a cracker from the packet which he had just opened, buttered it, cut a piece of cheese off the block and taking a bite, savoured the explosion of taste which resulted with half-closed eyelids. He poured a coffee for himself, glancing at Tony who was still dead to all around him. He frowned, and standing, made his way to his bedroom. He peeped in, to see John asleep — or so it seemed. Nodding his approval he returned to the library in a brighter frame of mind, even though Margaret's abduction still weighed heavily upon him. He sat and sipped his coffee, made another cheese cracker, and realised that Anton Baron's verse was running around and around in his head. It taunted him, challenged him to understand it, to reveal its solution. He sighed. It was obvious that someone was going to die in the forthcoming battle — it could even mean that they would *all* die; the only hopeful note

293

seeming to be the statement that the three of them, Tony, Margaret, and himself, would somehow enable Anton Baron's victory. How the three of them were to manage that was uncertain. Again, Hayter considered attacking the Cult, but knew that he could not do so. No matter how important the curse, he knew that he couldn't initiate an attack which he *knew* would result in Margaret's being murdered — were she still alive. He had grown attached to her before he ever realised that they were related; more attached than he would ever have believed possible. He thought of his words to Tony, that if he, Hayter, should fall seriously wounded, he would expect Tony to continue the attack — even if it meant his — Hayter's — death. Grand words, indeed, but Hayter had to accuse himself of being hypocritical in shying away from attacking the Cult in order to spare Margaret for as long as possible.

He believed in the maxim that where there is life, there is hope. He considered the possibility of using his abilities to try to get some idea of what state she was in — if it were possible. No doubt the Cult had both her and her whereabouts heavily cloaked. He could, no doubt, use the bloodline, but was afraid of alerting them. Any probing, he considered, which he indulged in, must of necessity be *very* gently and delicately handled.

He relaxed in the chair, considering how best to go about it. The idea came to him almost unbidden; he remembered how he had 'cured' Margaret's dream — it would be a relatively simple matter to attempt to find her by locating occult vibrations similar to or sympathetic to his own. He would have to punch a small hole in the barrier first, but that didn't create a problem.

Less than ten minutes later, his awareness encompassed miles. He stretched it further, examining every vibration that was in any way sympathetic to his own. He reached his limit and hesitated, wondering if there were any point in trying to extend himself further.

Narrowing his search, he continued pushing away from the mansion.

It was then that he felt a faint echo of a vibration so much in sympathy with him that he knew it *had* to be Margaret. He pushed his consciousness further, trying to get closer to her, but there was nothing more. She was blanketed too effectively. He tried willing her to become aware of him, tried to imbue his will with reassurance that he hardly felt. He received no response and, fearing that if he prolonged his search others might become aware of it, he drew his awareness back to himself. After a couple of seconds he opened his eyes and took a deep breath.

At least he knew that she was still alive. Absently, he sipped his coffee and glared at the tome open upon the table, next to the tray. It irked him that the information which he required was somewhere within this room, yet he couldn't retrieve it quickly. He took another cracker, and cutting another piece of cheese, he turned grimly back to the volume to continue his search.

It was some time later when Tony, trying to find a more comfortable position, turned his head from right to left, expecting it to come into contact with a soft pillow when it in fact hit a solid, unyielding desk, woke up. He stared around sleepily, yawning, trying to understand what he was doing here, when everything came flooding back to him. He was supposed to be helping Hayter, yet had slept most of the day away. He sat back in his chair wishing that he could feel more *alert* just after he woke, but knowing that it was a rarity for that to happen.

Hayter looked up from the book he was devouring. "Ah, welcome back, Tony. I've just brewed a pot of coffee — a second pot — I'm afraid that I drank the first myself. John would go *spare* if he found out."

Tony nodded, pouring himself a cup. "Found anything?"

"Not the passage I'm looking for, no."

"I seem to remember you said that you didn't expect to find anything?"

"I won't. Not if Anton Baron was as much of a genius as I suspect."

He nodded wearily. Hayter would explain things when he was ready and not before.

"Oh, Tony," Hayter said quietly, "Margaret is still alive. I sensed her earlier; they've cloaked her very well — at least, I couldn't get through to her without drawing a *lot* of attention to myself."

"How is she?"

"Alive: that's all I know."

Tony massaged his temples in frustration.

"How's John?" he asked, at length.

"Still asleep, last time I checked. Can't be a bad thing. It must have been a fair crack he took. He's very resilient; all his vital signs are normal."

"But what about his sight?"

"Can I do anything, you mean? It's possible, but I want to be sure he's fit again before I even think about that — assuming John agrees, of course."

Tony nodded, "Can you manage without me? I'd like to see if he's all right."

Hayter's glance sharpened at the implication that Tony didn't believe him, but he realised immediately that it wasn't meant that way. He nodded, as Tony stood, stretched, and made for the door. "Remind me not to drop off in a chair again. I feel as though my spine's warped," he said as he left.

Hayter returned his attention to the next volume. He discarded it almost before he had finished reading the title. He knew for a fact that what he wanted wasn't in it.

Anger and fatigue made him throw the book back on the table. It slid along, colliding with the book which Tony had fallen asleep reading, knocking it off the desk to land with a dull *thud* upon the floor. He sighed as he stood and moved around the desk to retrieve the fallen book. He glanced at the title, '*The Myths of The Witches*', and suddenly he *knew*, with an inner certainty, that *this* was the book which he had been searching for all along.

He raised his hand to his brow. Of *all* the books for Tony to fall asleep upon. It summed up just how their luck had been running all along. He sat in the chair which Tony had previously occupied, and began reading.

As he read the myths about relocation he tried to force the information into a scenario which made sense. He came to the section for which he had been searching; it told of witches and warlocks who had relocated spatially, and of one who had managed a minor temporal relocation. The myths then took off at a tangent, leaving Hayter biting his lips in irritation. He was *certain* that he was on the verge of something important, but then his mind went blank and the feeling of serendipity dissipated.

The door opened and Tony entered, closely followed by John. "Now tell me what is on the tray, please, Tony," he said, his face turned towards Hayter. Tony looked at Hayter as he looked guiltily at what was left of the block of cheese — a somewhat smaller block weighing about six ounces resided upon the plate. Hayter made a strangled noise and shook his head, then motioned frantically for Tony not to answer, drawing his finger across his neck several times, putting his finger to his lips to denote silence and then waving his hands as though to ward off the words which Tony spoke.

"There's a tray, a pot of coffee, milk, sugar, two packets of crackers, one empty, one a quarter full, some butter and a plate with a piece of cheese on it."

John's face remained impassive. "How much cheese?"

"About a quarter — maybe a bit more."

"I *see*," John said slowly.

"Did you *have* to tell him?" Hayter demanded.

Tony smiled. "Yes," he said. "John asked what you were eating, and he told me that you have a *passion* for foods that you aren't *supposed* to eat. He just wanted to know what you've been up to."

"And," John broke in, "I want a promise that there will be no more of it. You know what you can't eat and it won't do Margaret or any of us any good if you're incapacitated with a heart attack."

Hayter sighed. "I've had this argument with you before. I lost it then, and I know I'll lose it now. You have my word, John."

"Good," John said, sounding more like his old self.

"You should be in bed," Hayter insisted.

"No, George, I feel fine, considering. If I needed to be in bed, you *know* that I would still be there."

Hayter pondered this for a moment before accepting it with a nod.

"Tony, I found what I was looking for!" exclaimed Hayter, changing the subject.

"You did? Where was it?"

"You were sleeping on it," he said, handing the volume over. Tony read it quickly.

"But what does it mean?"

"That, I fear," said Hayter, "is what we have to work out between the two of us."

"Three," put in John. "You don't happen to have a quick guide to braille knocking about, do you?"

"I'm afraid not, John. We'll read it to you, so we can get the benefit of *your* thoughts."

"Right," John agreed.

Together, as night drew on, they cogitated upon what Hayter's unorthodox information might mean.

Chapter Thirteen: Dispositions

They sat facing each other in Richard's office, drinking in celebration of their achievement. He had phoned his clinic and arranged to stop off there, ostensibly to collect a few files. He had pulled up outside his private entrance, security waving him through their checkpoint and acknowledging his signal to let Martin's car through as well. A stony-faced male nurse waited at the door, wheelchair at the ready. They transferred Margaret to it and the nurse wheeled her away.

"Where's he taking her?" Martin asked as they reached Richard's consulting rooms.

"Just for some checks and then she'll be brought back here."

Martin nodded his approval, a smile playing on the edge of his lips. "I can't wait to tell our leader."

"Yes, he'll be *very* appreciative. Drink?" Richard asked.

"Only if it's alcoholic."

"Do you want to pass the good news along, or shall I?" asked Richard.

"You: after the fiasco about the lineage, I'm not really in favour."

"You will be when he hears this."

Richard picked up a phone upon his desk and, sitting on the desk's edge, dialled. When the ringing at the other end of the phone line was answered he said simply, "I appear to have the wrong number. I am phoning my brother, Richard." He waited, and seconds later his tone became more formal as he was connected with the Supreme Brother. "Your instructions have been successfully executed. Yes, one minor problem as foreseen but it didn't incapacitate us; quite the reverse. We are in a safe place and will see you tonight — I see," he raised his eyebrows at Martin. "We'll leave shortly," he said, and hung up.

"Trouble?" Martin asked, frowning.

"No, just the opposite. He's so excited at having Hunter in his grasp that he doesn't want to wait until tonight to meet her. He wants us to take her to the ruins now."

"I don't like it," Martin protested. "In broad daylight? It's remote, but there's always a chance that..."

"I know, I know," Richard replied calmly. "But the weather in that area is apparently going to become somewhat inclement, deterring sightseers."

Martin nodded gloomily. Just then a knock sounded upon the door. Richard called out: "Come in," and the male nurse entered, pushing Margaret's unconscious form in the wheelchair.

"The vital signs are all normal, Doctor."

"Thank you. I'll take care of her now." The nurse nodded and left, closing the door behind him. Richard walked to another door, unlocked it and entered. Martin saw him unlock a cabinet and take some small bottles from it. Re-locking the cabinet, he returned to Martin locking the door behind him.

He placed all the bottles in his doctor's bag except for the last which he placed near to hand. Breaking a disposable syringe from its packaging, he filled it to the desired level and then placed the last bottle with the others inside his bag. Taking the loaded syringe to Margaret, who had slumped to her right in the wheelchair, he took hold of an arm and nonchalantly swabbed it before injecting her. He glanced at Martin as he swabbed her arm again. "It's not a very large dose, but enough to keep her under. I've got something that'll bring her around, should it be needed.

"Well, we'd better get moving — it's about two hours from here — shall we use your car? If you can give me a lift later, that is."

"Sure," Martin agreed.

Less than ten minutes later they were on their way, Martin driving. Richard sat in the back, next to Margaret, giving the impression to anyone who passed them that she had fallen asleep on his shoulder.

The sun continued to shine; Martin wondered when the disturbance in the weather would hit. Probably only within a few miles of the ruin, he decided. He stifled a yawn, glancing at the occupants of the back seat in the rear-view mirror. Richard smiled at him.

The drone of the car's engine became monotonous. They passed fewer and fewer cars as they began to leave civilisation behind and head for the moors. It was then that Martin noticed the clouds thickening, hiding the sun, and almost at the same time the rain came sheeting down.

"How close do you think we should go?" he asked.

Richard considered, "I think you should park about a mile away. We shouldn't have any trouble walking through this, Supreme Brother will have thought of that."

He proved to be right. They parked and, having manoeuvred Margaret out of the car, saw a path leading in the direction of the ruin upon which the rain and wind seemed to have no effect. Without ceremony, Richard lifted Margaret over his shoulder and began walking the last mile with Martin following closely.

It took nearly thirty minutes to reach the ruins, Martin moving ahead to release the counterweights. Moments later they reached one of the numerous caves off from the main passage used for Brothers of the third circle to change in, or for general orgies, or whatever. Chairs were stacked against a wall. Martin took three from the stack. They sat a moment, Richard regaining his breath.

The atmosphere seemed to chill slightly and both glanced at the same instant to the arched doorway. The

Supreme Brother stood there, Brother Fidelis upon his right just behind him.

Supreme Brother's eyes glittered darkly with triumph, for once betraying his emotions. He glared at Margaret; Martin and Richard glanced at each other surreptitiously, each glad that *he* was not the recipient of that glare.

"Brothers," the Supreme Brother rasped, in his warmest frigid tone, "you do better than I could ever dream. Martin, you retain your standing within the third circle — and more. You both should think upon suitable rewards. I suspect that I know what *yours* will be, Richard."

Richard smiled and nodded.

"Fidelis, when Brothers Paul and Graham arrive, please bring them here."

Gregory nodded, "I will, Paternal Brother," he said, but made no move to leave. Instead, he plucked two more chairs from the stack and arranged them facing Margaret and her captors. They sat, the Supreme Brother almost smiling.

"And now, Brothers, tell me how you secured this pretty, *delicate*, *delectable* creature." His eyes hardened as he added in a tone to freeze the blood, "We must take *excellent* care of her."

Between them, Richard and Martin told of the circumstances which led to Margaret's capture and abduction, and of how they left Brandon unconscious.

"Dead?" Brother Fidelis enquired eagerly.

"If he didn't get back to the mansion, I'd say so," Richard said. "Otherwise, he won't be feeling too good for the next few days."

Fidelis stood abruptly and left the cave. He returned moments later with Brothers Paul and Graham.

"Ah, Brothers. You will be pleased to hear — and see — that Martin and Richard have been successful — especially *you*, Brother Paul."

302

Brother Paul stood staring *intently* at Margaret, a number of emotions flashing across his features — none of them pleasant. It seemed that he had to restrain himself from attacking her immediately.

"Remember, she *must* not die — and I would prefer no bloodshed. I don't expect Hayter to interfere but I would rather not leave him an easy trail to follow, as her blood would be. The small cells under the main cavern are ideal for our purposes. I want her tied hands behind her back, wrists to ankles, until she wakes to savour her predicament." He glanced at Richard who frowned, calculatingly.

"About three hours or so," he said finally.

"Long enough for her muscles to cramp?"

Richard frowned again. "Considering the cold and damp down there, I'd say yes. By the time she wakes she will be extremely uncomfortable, and when untied it will be about ten to twenty minutes before she can move her limbs properly. If you want to take advantage of the cramped muscles, the first ten minutes would be the most effective."

"Good!" Supreme Brother exclaimed, in a voice as bleak and cruel as it could be possible to imagine. "Paul, you will conduct the torture, whether alone or observed by us we will determine later. For the time being I do not wish her to know who you are. Therefore, I wish all who come into contact with her to be robed and masked. But you, Paul, are only to speak to her in a whisper. It will make you appear sinister to her and terrorise her the more. Graham, I wish you to lend Paul your expertise whenever he needs it. Feel free to make suggestions to Paul, Fidelis and to me. Richard, I think we might need your medical skills," he trailed off, looking at the only Brother who had not been named. "You appear to be redundant, Martin; you may leave."

"May I stay?" he inquired. "I would like to watch what occurs — I do not mind helping in *any* way."

303

Supreme Brother hesitated and then nodded. "Very well, Martin. Help Graham to take our dear Miss Hunter to her room and tie her up, *tightly*. I take it she brought no luggage?"

A general laugh greeted the remark. Again the Supreme Brother almost smiled. "Now, let us move on," he continued, as Graham and Martin carried Margaret out of the cave. "Richard, have you any more of the drug which you gave to Brother William?"

"Yes, I have brought a full vial."

Supreme Brother nodded.

"Fidelis," he said, turning his attention to him, "I want you to act a little. Give her the impression that she may have found an ally in you. Be kind to her within reason. Make it appear that what we do nauseates you but that you fear to protest. Let her hope that she can trust you.

"She might be naive enough to be fooled by that ploy. If she is and tells you what I want to know, it may save us time.

"Otherwise, Brother Paul will have to extract the information from her in a more painful and protracted way — *not* that I think he would object," Supreme Brother observed wryly, "but if you *do* succeed then Paul would be free to attend to her torture at his leisure."

Gregory nodded slowly.

"I want to know exactly what the situation is within the mansion; about Hayter and Baron," said Supreme Brother, moving his gaze from Fidelis to encompass Paul and then all of them. "With that understood, the methods of persuasion used upon her may be as severe as you wish. Some psychological torture might be appropriate, too.

"When we — any of us — are in her presence, I do *not* want *any* discussion of what is or is not planned for her. Obvious though it might sound I want it understood

304

that I wish to keep her as apprehensive as possible regarding what might be done with her.

"If you require extreme temperatures, Paul, Graham, use occultism to achieve them. None of us wants these passages smoked out with braziers." Another laugh greeted the remark. Supreme Brother glanced at them, his gaze showing that levity was the *last* effect he had been attempting to achieve.

"Are there any specific questions which you want answering?" Brother Paul asked after a momentary silence.

"Just what I outlined; if you want to extend your questioning to satisfy your own curiosity, you may. But I want my questions about Hayter and Baron answering first.

"I would suggest that you begin with relatively mild tortures and increase the severity if she proves stubborn; of course, this is more Graham's province than mine and I suggest that you accept his guidance. Remember however, she *must not* die — yet."

At that moment Martin and Graham returned. "All is as it should be," Graham informed the Supreme Brother. "I have taken the liberty of bringing some implements with me which may be needed."

They all nodded their approval of this statement. "Brother Graham, have you any *initial* advice from which we all might benefit? After all, you *are* a master in this area — much more so than we."

Graham inclined his head, accepting the compliment. "She must be kept mentally off balance at all times. I think it is important to remember that the strongest human instinct is that of survival. She will have been influenced by Hayter and it may take a considerable amount of persuasion to induce her to betray him. She will probably guess that she is not going to be allowed to live — that may well strengthen her resolve not to talk. We need to *degrade* and *hurt* and *humiliate* her to the point where she no longer cares about whether or not she talks, and will tell us *anything* we want to know to stop the pain."

"Thank you, Graham," Supreme Brother replied. "Now, let us prepare to welcome the last of the American Barons in an *appropriate* manner."

Chapter Fourteen: Humiliations

She felt cold, groggy, sick. As she fought against the drugs she slowly became aware of several things; the churning of her stomach threatening to evacuate itself at any moment, a thick, clogging, evil taste in her mouth, pain from her limbs, *especially* her legs. She groaned, a small sound echoing in the stillness. As she came closer to consciousness and her senses began functioning again, realisation began to edge into her mind. She shook her head, attempting to clear away the last barriers which the drug produced to come to full awareness, gulping air in the process. She managed to exercise enough will-power to open her eyes and the room she was in — what she could see of it — swam and distorted before them. She tried to rub her eyelids but her hands, or more correctly her wrists, suddenly seemed to be on *fire* as she attempted it. Her legs and ankles especially, hurt to a degree which she found difficult to comprehend. As coherent thought became possible she realised that she had been tied; not just as a means of restraint, but tied in such a way as to maximise the discomfort with a minimum of effort. She tried, tentatively, to test her bonds to ascertain just how tightly they had been secured. They didn't budge; frustrated, she forced her attention to what she could deduce about her surroundings.

She lay upon cold stone on her stomach, her wrists tied somehow to her ankles, stretching her arms, pulling her shoulders back and at the same time bending and stretching her legs. Pain seemed to run from her shoulders down to her arms and from her ankles to her thighs. Every time she breathed in, the pain in her arms seemed to intensify slightly. She couldn't see any walls from where she had been deposited, but she guessed that the room, or chamber, or whatever it was, was not really very large. At last, as full consciousness decided to return to her, memory returned with it. She suddenly remembered the bird, the fight, the chase — John upon the ground — what had happened to him? — her capture, the darkness closing around her; and now here she was tied up almost like a gift. '*A gift to the Cult*,' she thought bitterly, as yet *another* pain shot through her shoulder. Although her mind was now functioning, allowing coherent thoughts to be strung together, she still felt groggy. A new pain brought itself to her attention — the small of her back. She thought that so many aches and pains from so many diverse locations would tear the heaviness away from her eyes, but it didn't seem to work that way. Even though she *knew* she had been drugged, Margaret found it difficult to understand why it was that the drugs' effects seemed to take so long to dissipate from her system. As the thought went through her mind she became aware of another ache, but this one differed in that it was a more *natural* pain, a dull pressure informing her that she needed to urinate.

She groaned, straining against her bonds again, wincing as the cords cut into her wrists. The pain in her back intensified. By careful manipulation of her wrists and arms she was able, to a limited degree, to massage the affected area; it was only a temporary relief, but it was better than nothing. She twisted her head, trying to see *more* of the place of her confinement. Grey light filtered in, from where she could not see, but it was weak and did little to dissipate the almost total darkness. She could discern only the same things which she had already noted. Fear began to manifest itself within her as her mind, with its quixotic sense of humour, taunted her with questions about what her captors would do to her. When being chased, she had been *certain* that she would be caught and raped. Apparently they had gone to the trouble of bringing her *here*, instead. That seemed to argue that they had a use for her; but what that use might

308

be, or what they might want of her, she had no inkling. She knew that if she concentrated hard enough, she would soon have some insights, but she wasn't sure that she wanted them. She thought instead of Tony and George — they would be doing everything that they could to find her, of that she was sure. Would it be enough, though? Try as she might, she couldn't help thinking that maybe that was *exactly* what the Cult wanted; maybe it was all an elaborate trap to ensnare Hayter — and if that happened it would leave Tony alone against their might. Was he anywhere near ready for that? She doubted it. Surely Hayter would be aware that it might be a trap and act accordingly? She knew that would be the case — and so, could she expect Hayter to appear with all guns blazing? Despite the pain now coursing through her limbs and back, she managed a smile at the mental picture which she had drawn. No, there would be no quick attempt at rescue. If she knew nothing else, she had achieved an understanding of how Hayter's mind worked and she knew he would act with all caution. He would instil that course of action upon Tony, too.

Her train of thought came to a halt, the hard cold stone beneath her impinging upon her awareness. The chill filtering through her sweater and blouse seemed colder upon her stomach, making her need to relieve herself intensify. She wondered how long her captors would leave her tied in this painful way, before they showed themselves and gave her some indication of what they intended with her. Her mind began suggesting lurid scenarios and she clamped down on her thoughts, banishing them from her consciousness. They had their effect, however, and heart now beating faster with fear, her calm facade deserted her, forcing her to realise and accept that she was terrified. She heard a noise and started, pulling on her bonds. A *sickly* stab of pain erupted from her wrists. She listened more intently, paradoxically both dreading and hoping that her captors would appear, but the cell remained totally silent. She was hearing things, she concluded. It didn't surprise her; she was past the point of being surprised. She cried out as her left leg jerked in the grip of cramp. It felt as though someone had taken hold of the muscle and was slowly forcing it to fold in upon itself. She gritted her teeth, a whimper of pain escaping her as she exhaled. It seemed that it would go on forever, the incredible pain in her leg, her gritting her teeth; but finally the spasms began to subside, leaving a dull ache in addition to her other pains. She was very careful not to try moving her arms or rolling her shoulders in case the cramp returned, but that quickly intensified the pain which came from those areas.

She took a shaky breath, realising that those who had tied her in this way had done so deliberately; she suddenly made the connection which intensified her fears about what would be done with her. It was intended that she suffer these pains as a *preliminary* to whatever else the Cult wanted to do to her. It seemed obvious that *any* attempt to escape or not to do as they wished would be rewarded in a similar way — that she would suffer for it. She shook, partly through the cold now seeping through her bones, so it seemed to her, and partly through the fear which intensified when she considered — after a struggle not to — what kinds of things she might be subjected to. It was obvious that they didn't mind hurting her — that they had taken a little thought about how best to turn her confinement into a near torture. Her right leg cramped, causing her to yell out loud and pull on her bonds. As though it had been waiting for the signal, her left leg joined in, and racking pains shot up both, causing her to break out in a sweat, even though it was quite cold within the confines of the cell.

310

An eternity later, when the pain became manageable, she became aware of the tears upon her cheeks, themselves a minor irritation but one that she could not easily dispose of. In the end, she had to rub them as gently as she could upon the stone floor. Her clothes felt damp, making her feel even more miserable and uncomfortable than she had been. Feeling more despondent than ever, anxious about herself, about John, about Tony, but especially about Hayter, she began to cry, finally allowing all the pent-up emotions which had accumulated escape from inside her. When her weeping subsided, she felt able to face whatever was in store for her with at least a modicum of self-assurance. She realised that the last effects of the drug seemed to have worn off *without* her being aware of it. She grimaced, half in pain from a spasm in her shoulder, half in amusement that she had wanted it to wear off and that she could now feel her discomfort more keenly as a result. She began to shiver, the cold manifesting itself all over her body — especially the front of it. She sneezed, jerking her bonds as a result, and suffered repeated stabbing pains from her wrists.

She had realised soon after coming to consciousness that she couldn't feel her hands, wasn't able to move her fingers. She tried the experiment with her feet and toes but they seemed just as dead as her hands and feet. She let out a deep breath slowly, irrationally angry with herself for ending up in this insidious position. The thought that there wasn't much that she could have done about it, given that she had more or less *insisted* on accompanying John to the stores, didn't give her any comfort. Cold and shivering, she forced herself to wait patiently, trying to cut out all the messages of pain which her brain was receiving; although it was far from easy. A groan escaped her as her bladder reminded her that it needed to be emptied. Tied as she was, the only thing she could do would be to soak herself, and Margaret refused to do that until she had *absolutely* no choice. Cursing mentally, she tried to think of things that would take her mind off her bodily needs. She thought of the lake and immediately regretted it as her bladder demanded release. It was then that she heard a noise, a definite sound of footsteps approaching her. Her heartbeat began to pound; fear induced her bladder to renew its call to be emptied, but all Margaret focussed upon was the fact that someone — several people — were coming in her direction. After enduring so much pain and seemingly being secluded for so long, she was almost looking forward to seeing her captors.

The footsteps sounded louder and louder, came closer and closer; she could hear no voices, only the rhythmic noise of several pairs of feet now so close that they must be right outside. She tried to turn her head in the direction that the noise came from, but couldn't manage to do so. The reason was simple. When she had been deposited here, by whomever, they had placed her so her knees pointed towards the door, her head away from it. The advantage for the Cult was that they could approach her without her having any idea of what was intended; from Margaret's point of view the disadvantage was that she wouldn't be able to see who entered the cell when somebody did so. Not knowing what they were about to do, not being able to *see* them and being, in effect, deprived of her sense of vision all intensified her fear. There was no doubt in her mind that her positioning had been carefully considered. The noise of people approaching became even louder. It was *almost* a torture in itself waiting for them to arrive. Then there was an abrupt silence.

The silence stretched out until Margaret let out the breath she had taken with an explosive sound, and only *then* did she realise she hadn't been aware that she had been holding it. The silence was so complete she was almost certain that, out of a desperation borne of fear, she had hallucinated those sounds, and was simply terrified that she might be *left* here to die. Abruptly, all such thoughts were shattered by the sound of a key turning a lock, and the light within the cell suddenly intensified to an extent which forced her to clamp her eyelids shut, and even *then* it caused her acute discomfort. The door slammed shut, the key turned again. Her eyes began to adjust to the brightness, and she opened them a fraction. She glimpsed the far wall and swallowed as she took in the manacles and shackles built into it, their purpose of restraint and the overtones of torture obvious. It was grey. Grey wall, grey floor, no furnishings of any kind. Stark was *too* kind a word for it. As her eyes became fully attuned to the light now flooding into the cell, she realised that she was no longer alone, that people were watching her. She knew that they found her predicament amusing. Still no sound betrayed their presence, but they were *there*. She could *feel* their presence, their malevolence. All her fears exploded within her and her heart began beating as though it would burst. She could feel them appraising her; the tension she felt built up until she thought that she would scream.

Suddenly, surprising and confusing her at the same time, a hand took hold of her bonds and seemed to jerk them twice; the pain caused her to cry out deep inside herself, but she refused to give the cry utterance. It was *then* she realised that her bonds had been cut, and that her arms and legs had attained more natural positions. However, grateful as she was for her freedom — temporary though that freedom might be — the pain which now wracked her limbs caused her to moan in exquisite agony, her first resolve not to cry out forgotten as her cramped limbs complained at the treatment which they had received. Cautiously, she attempted to bring some feeling back into her hands, although she was sorry the instant that it returned. All the time she was aware of the dark menacing promise of more treatment like this to be inflicted by the people who stood behind her. Clumsily, muscles protesting at *every* movement, she managed to turn herself onto her back and thus got her first real look at her jailors.

There were six of them, each one wearing a robe that covered him from his shoulders to his feet. Each wore a mask covering his face, leaving only the lower jaw uncovered. Her gaze moved from one to another as she attempted, but didn't manage, to massage her legs. The man who stood on the extreme right turned his head and nodded, smiling a smile which made Margaret shake with fear. The man who wore that frozen smile was totally *evil*, she could sense, and more, he didn't even make any attempt to hide his evil under a facade. At the nod another of the robed figures took a pace forward, menacing her by his very stance. He reminded her vaguely of things that ought to be nice but weren't. Where this piece of intelligence came from, she was at a loss to know. She put it down to that intuitive part of her which had surfaced since she had met Hayter.

"*Strip*," the one who had stepped forward hissed at her, in a whisper which sounded utterly savage. Margaret wondered whether that was his normal mode of speech, before the full import of what he had said hit her. She lay upon the ground staring at him as though he was demented. He, in turn, nodded to another of the robed figures who advanced on her as though intent upon tearing her limb from limb. Much too late, she tried to crawl backwards away from him but her limbs refused to cooperate and then he was upon her. In one rough motion he pulled her to her feet, her legs threatened to buckle under her, feeling as though hundreds of red-hot knives were being stuck into them. He twisted her arms up behind her back. The sudden motion after they had been confined in one position for so long made her certain that her arms were being twisted out of their

314

sockets. Her legs refusing fully to support her weight, it was only by his extreme hold upon her that she stayed upright. Suddenly, he shoved her roughly and she slammed into the rock wall, the breath forced from her body.

She fell to the floor gasping, badly shaken. Obviously, these people weren't inclined to be gentle.

"*Miss Hunter*," the whisper rasped, "*you have a choice. You can either strip as I have told you to, or Graham will assist you. Unfortunately, he has a regrettable tendency to enjoy hurting people — especially* women; *the choice is yours*."

The silence returned, broken only by Margaret gulping in air. Intimidated by the treatment which she had received, and by the implied threat in what had been said, she managed to struggle to her feet.

"What are you going to do to me?" she demanded in what she hoped was a voice free from fear, attempting to buy time.

They simply stood looking at her, making no reply, seeming almost as though they had not heard her question. She glanced quickly at the figure who had been named as Graham. He was well built and thickset. He *radiated* violence. Their demand frightened her and she wondered what she had to lose by making him strip her forcibly. She had nothing to lose, she decided, except her pride. Self-consciously, she rubbed her ribs where the contact with the wall had bruised them. She was *certain* that being undressed by Graham would be a painful — and *humiliating* — experience: '*What place did pride have here?*' she asked herself angrily. Almost unconsciously, so much so that she was startled when she realised what she was doing, her hands slowly raised her sweater, pulled it over her head and dropped it to the floor. Her breathing laboured; she fought back the tears which threatened to pour down her cheeks as she became aware of how extreme was the debasement of being

315

forced to expose herself before these faceless, evil, inhuman bastards.

Numbly, slowly, her face deathly pale, she began to undo her blouse, whilst the six robed figures watched in impassive silence. She skipped the button that held her blouse closed between her breasts, moving on to the next. Time seemed to warp, to fragment, the whole experience suddenly seeming so unreal. She undid the last button but her blouse did not fall open. She realised that it was still fastened by the button which she had *not* undone. Trembling, her fingers returned to it, but no matter how she forced herself they refused to obey her brain's command.

She panicked, glancing suddenly at Graham as he moved slightly. She forced her hands to her jeans instead and tried to make her hands unbutton them. They shook and continued to rebel. Her arms fell to her sides. Graham stepped forward, a smile evident below his mask. One look at his eyes convinced her that this was an occasion where discretion was better than valour. Her hands fumbled at the button on her blouse and a few seconds later it lay upon the floor by her feet. Graham moved back to his original position, the stiffness of his movements indicating that he was not amused.

In the few seconds that her blouse had taken to reach the floor, she had been agonising about what to take off next. Her shoes, obviously. The problem was the jeans which she was wearing; they were so absurdly tight that if she tried taking them off, she knew that her panties would be drawn with them, exposing her to the cold glare of the six men assembled. She sensed that Graham would be upon her the *instant* that she tried to prevent it happening. The alternative, of course, was to take her bra off, exposing her breasts to them. Her nipples, she knew, had hardened, the cell being so cold. The fact that their shape was visible through the fabric of her bra was yet another source of embarrassment.

316

She decided that to expose her breasts was the lesser of the evils which she would have to endure, knowing that seconds later her efforts to keep her nether region covered for as long as possible would be rendered ineffectual. She would be forced to remove the rest of her clothes, and would only have delayed the inevitable for a few brief moments. She was actually reaching for the clasp of her bra, when a new voice cut in, much to her surprise.

"I *don't* see the point in this — at least allow her *some* covering."

Margaret stopped dead, her gaze jumping to the man who had spoken. He eyed her compassionately, seemed aloof to the malignant glances directed at him by his peers. At last, one of them, the one with the frosty smile, who struck Margaret as being totally *evil* smiled grimly.

"Gregory, as always you are too compassionate and you allow it to affect your judgement." He shook his head sadly. "Perhaps experience will be your tutor. However, for the present, let her keep her underclothes. But if she is not fully compliant you realise that your compassionate gesture will have to be paid for?"

"I do, Supreme Brother," he replied, holding the other's eyes for a second, and then turning his gaze to Margaret. "Your shoes and jeans, I'm afraid," he prompted her, gently.

A snort of anger erupted from Graham, but at a glance from Gregory, the silence became complete again.

In a total daze, Margaret kicked off her shoes and carefully undid the button of her jeans before sliding the zip down. She eased them off her hips, down her legs, taking care not to allow her panties to follow. The cold air assaulted her body, but at least her embarrassment was limited. Did this Cultist have a modicum of humanity, she wondered.

317

She looked timidly at him, the aches and pains in her body seeming to have faded into the background. His appeal had saved her from the degradation of having to stand here naked. True, she wasn't much better off, but at least she had *some* covering. "Thank you, Gregory," she whispered and noticed his smile of acknowledgement.

"Please, Miss Hunter," he said seriously, "thank me by answering whatever they might ask. My safety *depends* upon you."

She didn't entirely believe him but when she noticed the way that the one called the Supreme Brother glared at him she wasn't so sure. He had done her a favour and she owed him not only her gratitude, she believed, but her best endeavours to do as he asked, by answering any questions which were put to her. Even so, he was a member of the Cult and she had no wish to be cooperative with them. Her clothes were taken out of the cell by a man whom she thought familiar. He was one of the ones who had captured her, she decided. He returned seconds later, locking the cell door behind him.

"*Miss Hunter,*" whispered the first voice, "*what is your relationship to Tony Baron?*"

She considered; it was obvious that they must already know the answer. "I'm his girlfriend," she replied quietly. There was a pause whilst this was contemplated. Her answer must have been acceptable because her interrogator — Brother Paul — put another question to her.

"*Tell us all you know of George Hayter,*" he whispered.

So this was it; she looked pleadingly at Gregory, tried to appeal to him for help. "I can't answer that," she replied anxiously. "Please don't make me."

"*Tell us all about Tony Baron's involvement with Hayter. Where does Brandon fit in?*" the whisper demanded.

318

"No!" she yelled back.

"*Answer*," demanded the whisper.

"Go to hell," she raged back at him, her embarrassment and anger at being manoeuvred into this position precipitating her caustic reply. She shivered with fear. The silence was complete.

The figure with the bleak smile, visible beneath his mask, peered at Gregory. "Has time been your tutor, Gregory?"

Gregory glanced at her, his disappointment obvious. "I'm sorry," he said as he turned and stepped closer to the door.

"*Remove your underwear*," her tormentor whispered, jubilantly.

"Are you cold, Miss Hunter?" the frigid voice enquired: "Paul will be *happy* to warm you. You see, *we* can be considerate, too."

The fear she felt intensified slowly towards panic. She knew that any pretence was over, and the next phase in her torment was about to begin. She rebelled inwardly at the thought of exposing herself to them, but before the resolve could strengthen she heard a whispered voice proclaim, "*Graham, if she is not naked in ten seconds, you may help her.*"

She cast a despairing glance in Gregory's direction, but he stood near the door, his eyes downcast. Despairing, she glanced at Graham who was already clenching his fists. Her resolve crumbled to nothing and with the numb feeling which she had experienced earlier returning, she unclasped her bra, let it fall to the ground. In almost the same motion she dropped her panties and stepped out of them. She moved an arm to cover her breasts, the other hand between her legs.

Savagely, she glared at them, her anger and rage overcoming the embarrassment and humiliation which she felt. It gave her the necessary sense of outrage to make eye contact with each of them, leaving them in no doubt that although she might be frightened and embarrassed she was *far* from being broken.

Graham retrieved her underwear and left the cell, leaving the others standing there staring impassively at her, as though waiting.

The waiting became almost painful. Margaret's bladder reminded her that she had to relieve herself; as the silence stretched out her fear and embarrassment slowly ate into her sense of outrage, until it was non-existent. The ordeal of standing naked before these fiends, of being fairly sure — but not *certain* — that another form of torture was imminent combined to curb any further tendency to rebel. She found their gaze overpowering — especially that of the Supreme Brother, which seemed to freeze the very air through which it passed. She shivered more violently both with the cold and the ever-increasing sense of menace which manifested itself by their presence, and the way that they stared at her without saying a word. She could feel a scream of anguish building up inside her.

"Whatever you're going to do, just *do it*," she

shrieked.

Exactly on cue, Graham returned, carrying what looked like a velvet cloth. She stared at it, trying to ascertain its purpose. At the same instant two of the robed Brothers who had not yet had their names revealed — one of whom she was sure had been one of the two who captured her — approached her quickly. She managed to take a clumsy step back before each grabbed one of her arms and twisted them up behind her back; not so far that it hurt, but far enough to threaten her should she struggle. She saw Graham casually walk behind her and she twisted her head to try and see what he was going to do. She felt absolutely *terrified* in that moment, and was only dimly aware that she was now

320

fully exposed to the piercing gaze of the other Cultists. She knew that Graham was very close behind her, and let out a muffled squeal of fear as he brought the hood down over her head, covering it, and drawing a cord snugly, but not tightly, around her neck. He tied it, and she sensed him moving away from her.

She heard a vague buzz of conversation, an indistinguishable murmur that she couldn't convert into coherent speech. She guessed that the hood was to deprive her of her vision, and to some extent, to prevent her from hearing any clues about what was going to happen.

The pressure upon her arms relaxed somewhat but, almost paradoxically, now that she had been effectively blindfolded and couldn't *see* her tormentors, she felt *more* naked than she had done immediately after exposing herself.

It seemed that she was turned around by the men holding her several times. Whether this was to give them a good view of her body or just to disorientate her she couldn't decide. She could *feel* their eyes devouring every centimetre of her body. Because she could only *imagine* them looking at her, and imagination always tends to make things look darker, to intensify them, her embarrassment deepened. She found herself blushing furiously — something which she hadn't allowed the Cult to make her do whilst her face was uncovered. Whether it was a consequence of this, or whether it was fear, or simply the close confines of the hood, her face was soon damp with sweat. The hood seemed to retain all the heat which her skin radiated and reflected it back at her.

She could see nothing. Inky blackness seemed to be the only thing that registered. She remembered reading somewhere that when deprived of one of the senses the brain tended to compensate for it by intensifying one or more of the others, frequently that of hearing. But to a large extent she had been deprived of *that* sense as well. A feeling of disorientation flooded through her. She felt her arms being positioned above and to the sides of her head, a cold band was secured around each wrist. It was only a second later that her right leg was moved somewhat to her right and another cold band encircled her ankle. She shook her head, as if trying to force it to enlighten her as to what this portended. Her shoulders, arms and legs reminded her that they were still feeling somewhat the worse for wear by sending intense messages of pain, demanding that they be placed in more comfortable positions. She felt a hand take hold of her left leg and reposition it. Another cold band secured it in place. How far her leg had been moved she couldn't decide. The result of this repositioning of her legs was that her frame was only partially supported by them, the rest of her weight was borne by her arms.

Slowly, or so it seemed, her brain, almost reluctantly, gave her the information which she repeatedly demanded. She had been restrained by some kind of metal bonds, four of them, which stretched her limbs slightly, making it difficult for her to move in any direction. She felt incredibly vulnerable when the realisation that her legs were *widely* open forced itself into her awareness. The confusion which the hood had caused Margaret whilst she was being restrained had prevented her from taking in the full implications of her legs being moved. It had been done so quickly. With sudden clarity she realised that she must have been fastened to the manacles and shackles which were set within the wall — and yet she *couldn't* feel the wall in front of or behind her.

Her humiliation was *complete*, she thought, bound naked, legs spread apart. Again she became *aware* of their eyes upon her body, but not in any covert *sexual* way. If anything the glances which she felt were more *casual*, as though watching someone tortured was, for them, a regular occurrence. She *never* fully realised how close to the truth she came, with that thought.

Again time seemed to warp, to become an incalculable thing. It was *stifling* inside the hood and she had to remember to keep her breathing regular or she began to feel light-headed. It was no easy task being certain, as she was, that some form of pain was imminent. She remembered her outburst earlier, telling them to hurry up and do what they intended to do. It had not had any effect; they were obviously proceeding at their own pace, allowing her to savour the anticipation and ponder what was about to happen. For some absurd reason her mind jumped back to her childhood; her father had used similar tactics.

She heard another murmur but couldn't make sense of it. The waiting, the distortion of time, the actual thought that maybe she was already *experiencing* the torture crossed her mind — perhaps they were merely trying to alarm her. The trepidation and anguish that all this engendered within her forced her to struggle, albeit belatedly, against the cold bands restraining her. She recognised that it was a futile gesture but it was one which she felt she had to make.

She heard a dull *crack*, and in the instant before realisation dawned, she wondered what it was that she had heard. As the question formed within her mind, a sudden rush of stinging *agony* from her shoulder-blades answered her. The shock and pain caused her to flinch within her bonds. A scream built up inside her, but she clamped it down, determined that she would *not* give these sadists the pleasure of hearing it. She tensed her body, expecting and anticipating a second stroke, but it took a long time in coming. She could not hear the lash flying through the air, the hood prevented it. Apart from the dull sound which filtered through to her as the whip connected and the agony it inflicted, she had no idea or indication when or where the next blow would land.

After what seemed like minutes, a third stroke landed upon the small of her back. She had deduced by now that the lash which was being utilised was three stranded, and that the thongs tended to land within a few inches of each other. Curiously, a detached part of her mind took in the fact that she could feel exactly where each strand had caressed her by the intense smarting which it left behind, and that she could equally distinctly feel the few inches of skin between welts by their very *lack* of pain.

Another stroke landed upon her shoulder-blades, criss-crossing the area already stinging. She jerked her body in nervous reaction to the sudden intensification of the pain, an involuntary whimper escaping her. It was made worse by the fact that her breathing rate had increased dramatically. She struggled to regain control of it, but to no avail. Two more strokes landed within five seconds of each other, catching her completely unprepared, since it had seemed that minutes had elapsed between each of the previous blows. Her buttocks registered the pain first, and then her left leg. The agony of that one stroke upon her leg seemed to make the other strokes' intensity fade by comparison. It forced another whimper through her tightly clenched teeth.

She tried to relax her muscles, but they didn't seem to want to comply. Margaret could remember that the resultant discomfort from a beating tended to be worse when the muscles had been tensed, almost as though they bruised more easily that way.

She had deduced that she must be facing the rock wall although she couldn't feel it in front of her. As she attempted to relax her back and leg muscles the next stroke connected, each strand of the whip landing cruelly across her breasts.

The excruciating agony caused by that one stroke — *especially* by the strand which caught her nipples — was too much for her to hold in. She screamed a high, frenzied ululation of pure unadulterated agony.

324

Things began to blur after that, as though her mind was trying to protect her from the worst effects of the remainder of the flogging. The detached part of her mind seemed to begin to absorb her consciousness. She was aware of the strokes landing, however, and that she was *screaming* as each blow struck. Some landed upon the back of her body, some upon the front. They were so irregularly timed that she could never prepare herself for the next one.

Stroke after stroke landed, ensuring that she continued to scream out her misery, especially when the strokes landed upon the more sensitive parts of her body: her breasts, her stomach, her back, the back of her legs.

She even managed to keep a count. That detached part of her mind calmly informed her that she had received forty-five strokes on the back of her body and thirty upon the front, when she became aware of her bonds being removed, of falling limply to the floor, the pain in her back flaring into red-hot *agony* as her weight fell upon it. The hood was removed, the air was cold upon her face. She lay, pain flooding into her brain from all over her body, gasping breath. Tears which she refused to shed in front of them filled her eyes. She tried to see what she had been fastened to, but could see *nothing*. It was a mystery which she was never to solve.

One of them walked up to her and she felt the air around her drop in temperature as he turned his gaze upon her. After what had been done to her she was terrified of looking at him, but managed a glance full of hatred before his gaze overcame her own.

"Miss Hunter, we will leave you for a while to think upon things. I hope that Paul has warmed you up sufficiently — if not we can always *repeat* the exercise another time and increase its severity, of course. I hope that you decide to answer our questions when we return, otherwise I will have to let Paul attempt to persuade you *again* — and believe *me*, Miss Hunter, he has *never* failed me yet."

The Supreme Brother turned and, followed by the others, left the cell. The door closed behind them. She heard the click of the lock as it snapped into place. The light began to dim — she wondered how that was done, there didn't seem to be any obvious light fittings. It could simply be an occult manifestation, she supposed.

Her bladder had been increasing its demands and, now that she was alone she *had* to urinate. She chose a corner of the cell which seemed to slope slightly away from the door. Squatting painfully from her recent flogging, she relieved herself, securing ease from one of the many pains which laid claim to her attention. At least it seemed that her bladder was now content. Apart from the odd twinge, the dull ache which had been demanding her attention faded. She moved slowly back into the centre of the cell and there, alone and in darkness, she allowed the tears which had filled her eyes to roll down her cheeks.

That action released the dam which had been holding back a deluge of emotions: despair, terror, anguish. They all fought for release inside her and she found herself sobbing harder than she ever had in her life — except, perhaps, for when she was a child in her father's power. It wasn't that she was sobbing over the treatment which she had received, it was more a case of her feeling such an extreme amount of despair that the emotions simply *couldn't* stay inside her. The beating which she had just endured provided an easier release than she otherwise would have had. The choking sobs tearing themselves from deep within her continued, although her tears dried up. Eventually, her crying subsided to the extent where she was simply taking convulsive gasps. It was at about this time that the detached part of her mind began to recede, allowing her to regain full control of her consciousness. Parts of the beating seemed somewhat blurred in her memory but the pain which had been inflicted and the intense burning and smarting which had been left behind as a result now began to claim her attention.

Her breathing became more even and regular now that her emotions had been released, and her painful situation enforced itself more and more keenly upon her senses. It was virtually *impossible*, she found, to sit or lie in any position other than upon her side. This was simply because the rocky floor was so uncomfortable to begin with in conjunction with the fact that whenever she put her weight upon any of the parts of her body which had received Paul's attention, then the pain in that area increased radically to a red-hot eruption of *pure* agony. Lying upon her side was uncomfortable but it seemed that her sides had escaped the worst of the beating; she managed to put up with the uneven floor digging into her. The discomfort that it afforded was much less severe than that which she would have otherwise experienced. So, lying miserably upon the floor, she began to try and make some sense of this whole situation. She had already decided that Hayter would rescue her if he could, but would *not* endanger either himself or Tony in the attempt. It seemed pointless to rely upon him, she decided. That left, as far as she could see, only two options. Either she lay back and waited for the next time she was questioned and her refusal brought more torture down upon her, or she could attempt to escape.

Escape! The word conjured up a new meaning, which had always been there, but one of which she had never *really* been aware. To get away; to be *free*. Her hopes rose only to be dashed cruelly when she thought about what she was up against. She was presumably underground in one of the Cult's strongholds, locked in a cell, guarded by trusted members of that organisation, and who knew what else? She wouldn't be able to pass

327

herself off as one of them, and even if she *did* manage to get out of here she had no idea where she was. She hardly thought that outside the entrance to whatever this place was, she would find herself in a centre of activity from which the Cult would be *unable* to extract her. It was much more likely that she would find herself in a lonely, secluded spot — and how long could it *possibly* be before they realised that she had managed to escape? Not long, surely; she already knew that she couldn't outrun them and she wasn't at all sure that she could out-think them. They seemed to have anticipated every possibility and taken measures accordingly. Glumly, she had to allow the idea of escaping to take on an impossible aspect.

A sharp stab of pain from her leg made her wince. Her whole body felt as though it was slowly burning. She conceded to herself that Paul had done a *very* good job of whipping her. '*What kind of tortures would they have waiting for her the next time they came here?*' she wondered, shivering at the thought. If what she had just experienced was only the first step on the road to *forcing* her to answer their questions, they must have more painful methods at their disposal. Her shivers intensified to a trembling as the thought went through her mind. This one had been more painful than she could *ever* have believed. Gently, she massaged the leg which seemed to throb more than anywhere else. The motion helped in that it eased the pain, but hurt because it stretched the surrounding skin which had been lashed, causing an intensification of the smarting.

She began wondering again how long they would leave her to 'Think things over', as their Supreme Brother had put it. Probably only long enough for her pain to subside, so they could inflict more. Nevertheless, she had resolved *not* to answer their questions for as long as she could hold out.

Her thoughts were interrupted by a noise. She started up, causing pain to flood from several areas of her body. Her heart began palpitating as she thought that they were returning to continue the task of tormenting her.

She heard the lock click and then the door open. It closed and the door was locked again. She heard a cautious step and then silence. Was this another form of weird torture that she had never heard of? Her nerves stretched taut, she whispered, "Who's there?"

There was a slight cough, and the cell began to illuminate. It didn't get as bright as it had previously, but it was enough to see by. Near the door stood the man who had tried to prevent them stripping her naked. She tried to bring his name to mind, but it eluded her.

"*You!*" she exclaimed, trying to piece together what this might mean, why he had come to see her alone. "Don't tell me; you've come to make sure there's nowhere Paul missed," she snapped at him angrily, indicating the numerous bright red weals and welts that covered most of her body. She felt that her anger was justified — after all, he was a part of the set-up which had inflicted this upon her.

He stiffened, and winced as he did so. His eyes met hers, and he slowly limped towards her. "I'm sorry that I couldn't stop them harming you, Miss Hunter," he said. "I did try. I wanted to stop the senseless humiliations they were forcing you to endure. But my voice carries little weight with the Supreme Brother."

"Nice words," Margaret sneered back at him. "How many times did you rehearse them? You think I'm a fool? You are trying to make me trust you so you can use that trust against me. You can forget it...*Gregory*, you don't fool *me*." she said, as his name suddenly jumped into mind.

He gave her a sideways glance. "I don't blame you for not trusting me. *I* wouldn't, in your position." He turned and headed for the door, limping heavily.

She remembered that when she had first noticed him, he had no limp. It was obviously put on for her benefit.

"You haven't convinced me, and a *fake* limp doesn't really cut any ice; so, Gregory, hobble back to your friends and tell them you've failed."

He turned quickly as he reached the door, wincing again. "I don't limp, normally, Miss Hunter. You really do know how to be ungrateful, don't you? Tell me, do you always react like this when someone has done their best to help you? I was wrong to do it. The next time I feel pity for someone I'll remember paying for my compassion and think *twice*." He stood for a moment glaring at her in fury and then turned towards the door again, slowly shaking his head.

"What do you mean, '*Paying for your compassion*'?" Margaret demanded.

"Are you sure you want to know?" Gregory sneered back at her, moving away from the door and back towards her. She nodded mutely. *Something* in his bearing told her that she had made a mistake about him and it confused her. Slowly, his eyes never leaving her face, he undid six buttons on the robe, three at each collarbone. He let the robe fall to his waist. At first her eyes refused to believe what they saw; he turned so that his back faced her and she felt her stomach *retch*.

It was obvious that Gregory had been beaten *severely* — so severely that she felt her own torment must have been a playful exercise by comparison. Flesh hung in tatters from his back. Blood *oozed* from his wounds — his robe had been soaking it up. His chest was in a similar condition. If her welts were numerous, then his lacerations and contusions were *extensive*. She retched *again* and Gregory replaced his robe as it had been, slowly fastening the buttons.

"Jesus, who did *that* to you? Paul?"

"Oh, no," Gregory managed a chuckle at the idea. "Graham, actually. My intervention wasn't welcomed by

330

either the Supreme Brother, or by Graham. He got a chance to demonstrate to me *just* how he felt, and he took it. That's all."

She sat upon the floor, legs drawn up, trying to *ignore* the fact that he was getting a good view of her breasts — for God's sake they'd *all* seen them. She thought about what he had said, what she had just seen; was it *possible* that he might help her out of here? She dismissed that notion instantly — but he had already tried helping her once knowing what the consequences might be. She became aware of him looking at her with a quizzical expression.

"But *why* did you help me? I don't understand that."

"Perhaps I'm too compassionate by nature — my Brothers seem to think so."

"Then what *are* you doing here? How did you get mixed up with them?"

He frowned, "I can't tell you that," he said. "Cigarette?"

She looked at him in astonishment. He grinned, and sitting down opposite her, slowly, grimacing, he turned up the bottom of his robe revealing a small pocket fastened with a zip. "My own invention," he muttered modestly as he unzipped the pocket and drew out a battered packet. "We'll have to use the packet as an ashtray; if they find out I've been here or let you smoke, I'm in *real* trouble."

"What *more* could they do to you?" Margaret asked in disbelief.

He shook his head. "Physical pain is *nothing* to what can be done within an occult context," he answered slowly. "Anyway, I'm ready to take the risk — letting you smoke won't count for much once they find out that I've been here. It's just sensible to take precautions."

She nodded and hesitated before taking the cigarette. He produced a lighter; Margaret felt the cigarette calm her agitated nerves. She studied Gregory, as he carefully dropped ash into the packet.

"Is he always as *savage* with people?" she asked.

"Who?" he replied.

"That man you call '*Supreme Brother*'," she replied.

"Oh no. He can be a *barrel* of laughs at times," Gregory replied grimly.

"So why did you become a member in the first place?"

Gregory stared at her. "Let's just say that I have some '*peculiarities of character*' which blend in here more than anywhere else, and leave it at that."

In the silence which followed, whilst she tried to digest this piece of information, she regarded the many red weals crossing her body. This whole situation was unreal — here she was, naked, sitting and chatting with a member of the Cult which had promised to *murder* Hayter and Tony.

"Well, Gregory," she said, drawing on her cigarette, "if you are so concerned about what happens to me, tell me what they plan to do to me."

Gregory looked at her and smiled a sad half-smile. "I'm afraid I don't know," he said. "Only the Supreme Brother, Graham and Paul could answer that. The rest of us are here to do any work required of us. You might realise that secrecy is a way of life for us."

"So there is nothing you can tell me?"

"I can only advise you, Miss Hunter. I *don't* want to have to watch them torture you further; they will *force* you to tell them what they want to know and they have some *excruciating* methods of doing it, too."

"Such as?" Margaret demanded, wondering if he might let slip some indications of what might be in store for her.

"Well, there is the removal of toes or fingers or of internal organs without anaesthetic, of course, just for starters, and then..."

"But surely — if they did *that* they would kill their victim," Margaret said, both incredulous and nauseated.

Gregory shook his head, smiling. "There's *no* chance of that. One of the Brothers — one of the ones who caught *you*, as a matter of fact — is a *very* eminent surgeon, *highly* respected..."

Margaret was aghast. "You mean he uses his skills to...to *butcher* people?"

He returned her stare evenly. "I'm not *quite* sure that he'd see it that way, but yes, that's about right."

"And you go along with it — you *agree* with what he does?"

Gregory's gaze sharpened slightly. "Whether or not I condone it isn't the point. The point is that *that's* the way things are done — the way they've *always* been done, to a greater or lesser degree. I am *powerless* to alter things. Within our society only the Supreme Brother or his successor Brother Fidelis can do that; needless to say, neither of them pay *me* any heed."

"But you stand and watch people being tortured — you watched *me* being whipped — how can you sit there and accept what's happening? Or do you *enjoy* it? Is that one of the '*Peculiarities of character*' that you mentioned?"

Gregory winced; whether through pain or because what she had said had hit a mark, she couldn't tell. He stubbed out his cigarette carefully. She realised that he was about to leave and she didn't want to be left alone again. She tried to keep him talking, but he brushed her question aside.

"How long have you been a Cultist?" she asked as he stood, slowly and painfully.

"Longer than I care to think about," he answered obliquely, his mind obviously upon something else. "Miss Hunter, don't let the others know that I was here, *please*," he begged, emphasising the last word. "This time, my safety really *is* in your hands." He unlocked the door quickly, opened it and left, locking it again after him.

The illumination began to fade quickly, leaving her thoughts in turmoil. Could she trust him? Should she do as he suggested? What were Tony and Hayter doing? How was John? She took a last puff of her cigarette and realised that she should have put it out in Gregory's substitute ashtray, but it was too late for that now. She tossed the stub into the corner where she had urinated and hoped that it wouldn't be noticed when the Cultists returned.

The last of the illumination died away leaving her in inky darkness again, permeated only by the faint shaft of grey light. Now that she no longer had the distraction of Gregory to talk to and to accuse, Margaret's hurts began to impinge themselves back into her consciousness. She had managed to force the aches and pains into the back of her mind whilst he had been there but now that she was alone the irritating, burning sensations reasserted themselves. At least they seemed to have dulled to an extent where the pain was bearable — just.

She squirmed uncomfortably upon the rock floor trying to find a position where her discomfort was minimised. She failed. Standing, she walked slowly, arms held in front of her, to the walls and eventually located the door by touch. It seemed solid enough and closed flush with the rock. She located the keyhole but could find no handle by which the door might be pulled open, were it unlocked. She clenched her fists in frustration and pounded futilely upon it. More to keep her mind off her pains and occupied than in the belief that she would find a way out, she continued the exploration of the walls until she came to the manacles set at various heights in them. She remembered the cool feeling of them around her wrists and ankles. The memory brought the information to mind that it couldn't be long before her captors returned; the thought made

334

her feel queasy. She recoiled towards the centre of the cell and sank down to the floor, waiting hopelessly. She felt tired but knew that she wouldn't be able to sleep, not in this environment. She shivered, feeling the cold air upon her body.

She closed her eyes, attempting to remember how she had felt when she had last woken up, remembered the way she had rushed around the mansion looking for John. It seemed, to her, to be aeons ago, in another world, that another Margaret Hunter had done that; perhaps, in that other world, she was still free...

Something else claimed her attention then — for a *fleeting* moment she thought that she had heard her name being called. But before she had time to analyse who it could be, to focus her attention upon it, it was gone. For some reason, she felt more dejected than ever when she found that the call wasn't repeated. Was she imagining things, or had someone been trying to find her? If so, who else could it have been but Tony or Hayter? It was obvious, though, even to her, that if they had tried to find her, they had failed.

Her feelings a mixture of bitter helplessness and total despair, she realised that her resolve not to say anything to the Cultists was weakening — she considered what Gregory had said. Would Hayter be unable to forgive her if she saved herself from the torture to come by telling what little she knew? Would it even make any difference to the outcome if she answered their questions? Would they believe that she didn't *know* anything? That she doubted, somehow.

***

"Well?" Supreme Brother demanded, upon seeing Gregory.

"She doesn't trust me yet. I've given her something to think about. She was nauseated by the state of my chest and back — it's almost a pity that she doesn't realise it was just an illusion. I gave her a cigarette and

335

was careful to leave it behind — you could use *that* as a starting point."

"Do you think we'll need to use more extreme torture?"

"Almost certainly. I pointed out that Richard is a very capable surgeon and can perform amputations without anaesthetic. She considered that he was nothing more than a butcher." He raised his eyebrows in amusement at the expression which appeared upon Richard's face.

"You think, then, that she will be in a state of heightened anxiety concerning what we might do to her?"

"Oh, yes. She tried to find out what might be in store for her, but I didn't give anything away. It might be an idea to continue treating me as though I actually *was* on her side. Whether or not she trusts me, she will feel guilty about letting you know that I went to see her — I *sense* it. I might use her guilt to gain her confidence."

Supreme Brother nodded agreement. "Very well, Fidelis. I think we shall give her about an hour before we return and make a second attempt at getting the information from her."

***

She drowsed despite her surroundings, despite the fear and terror she felt at the prospect of the Cultists' return, as the events of the last hours finally took their toll. The throbbing from all over her body formed an unpleasant background to her sleepiness, a gnawing constant which pervaded her thoughts and was present within the dreams which she had as she approached sleep. It was a journey which she never quite managed to complete. Her nerves were stretched to too great an extent to allow her release from her fears that easily.

Visions of tortures scampered through her sluggish consciousness and she struggled to dismiss them. She dreamed of nature run rampant but perverted. Putrescent vegetation choked itself as it struggled to grow; animals

336

turning upon each other in fury for no better reason than bloodlust; all the innate beauty in nature turned in upon itself reflecting a negative mirror image of decay and hopelessness.

The approaching footsteps, therefore, merged into her dream, somehow sounding like the ticking of a gigantic clock gone wrong. It was only as the door opened and the Cultists were in the act of walking through it that she jerked fully out of her half-sleep. She regarded them in terror, not registering the fact that she hadn't, this time, been subjected to the mental torture of hearing their protracted approach. The cell illuminated as before. She gazed from one to another as they formed a semicircle around her. She located Gregory upon the extreme left, although his head was bowed and he seemed to be keeping his eyes fixed to the floor. She wondered, briefly, what his face might look like.

The one they called the Supreme Brother gestured to the floor; fetters appeared before her, seemingly embedded into the rock; four of them, strategically placed. She knew that illusions were amongst the easiest of occult manifestations to create, but somehow, she didn't think that this was an illusion.

"Miss Hunter, have you thought better of your stubborn instincts? Will you now answer our questions?"

She opened her mouth to reply, but whatever she was going to say wouldn't come. Her mouth was dry, and she suddenly realised that she was parched. Swallowing the lump which arose in her throat, she shook her head. The Supreme Brother sighed heavily.

"In that case, Paul, will you *again* attempt to make Miss Hunter see reason?"

"*I will be happy to, Supreme Brother*," he whispered, his eyes glittering. Although he answered eagerly he made no attempt to approach Margaret but stood calmly appraising her, whilst her apprehensions intensified, became almost unbearable. At last he turned his gaze

337

away, paced to the wall and back again. He repeated the motion, glancing at her from time to time. "Graham..." he began and then stopped, his gaze attracted by something which he realised was incongruous within this setting.

He sidestepped, picked up the cigarette butt and took it to Supreme Brother for inspection.

Supreme Brother's gaze swept the attendant Cultists. "Who came here without my express permission?" he rasped. When no answer was forthcoming, he glanced at Margaret. In two strides he was towering over her, his gaze radiating his anger so powerfully that she could *feel* herself being pushed back. "Who came here?" he demanded of her.

Margaret didn't reply, but her eyes betrayed her. She glanced involuntarily at Gregory; the Supreme Brother followed the movement and rounded upon him. "You came here. You broke my orders in doing so. Leave us, and await me in my private chamber — what you have done is little short of betrayal. I will have justice, Gregory, even if it costs you your *life*," he hesitated, discerning that Paul had something which he wished to say.

"*But Gregory has supplied the answer to the question which I have been wrestling with*," he said and he indicated the cigarette end. The Supreme Brother nodded his understanding.

"It seems that your meddling has achieved something, Gregory," he said. "Perhaps I was a little hasty, but your breach of discipline is inexcusable." He glanced at Margaret disdainfully. "If you wanted to *have* her, you know that you only had to *ask*."

Margaret felt the blood rush to her cheeks. The casual remark stung her, as it had been calculated to do.

"Thank you, Miss Hunter, for telling me exactly whom I should mistrust." He turned away from her. Gregory, with one last glance of reproach towards her, left the cell followed closely by Paul. A short time later Paul reappeared, a pack of cigarettes and a lighter in his hand. He muttered a few words to Richard and Graham and then stood apart from them.

They approached her slowly, but Margaret was ready for them. She launched herself at Richard, only to find herself repulsed as though she had hit a thick polyurethane sheet. She fell to the floor. They took advantage of her predicament by taking hold of her legs and fastening her ankles into the fetters which the Supreme Brother had provided; her hands they fastened to the ground in a similar manner. She lay upon her back only able to raise her head a few inches, her arms stretched out on either side of her, her ankles secured next to each other. Richard whispered a comment to Paul and left the cell, returning a few minutes later with a swab and a syringe half full of a colourless liquid. Kneeling by her he carefully injected the liquid at various points upon her feet.

"I find what you say hard to believe," cut in the Supreme Brother, his voice breaking the silence.

"Watch," answered Richard. He began tickling the soles of her feet. She tried to stifle a giggle, but failed. It was only then that she understood that she couldn't move her feet or toes.

"It's a muscular anaesthetic," Richard informed them all triumphantly, "but it doesn't affect the senses as such."

"*Excellent*," whispered Paul. He took out a cigarette and lit it, gazing at her all the while. "*Now, Miss Hunter*," he hissed, "*tell us what we want to know — beginning with Tony Baron and ending with George Hayter*."

"Go to hell," she managed to spit back at him, her fury masking the true terror which she was feeling.

He took another long draw upon the cigarette, flicked the ash onto the floor and then knelt by her feet. "*Your last chance, Miss Hunter. Why not save yourself the agony — and us the pain of listening to your screams? Tell us what we want to know."*

She shook her head, trying *not* to think about what he was obviously going to do to her. He was going to burn the soles of her feet with the lighted end of the cigarette. She screwed her eyes shut and prepared for the excruciating pain which she knew was to come.

But it didn't. She felt two toes being prised apart and something being placed between them. She opened her eyes and squinted down at her feet. The cigarette rested between her toes, the lighted end pointing away from her so she couldn't see how much it had to burn down before it would begin to burn the delicate skin between and around them. Paul sadistically placed an elastic band around the top of the two toes concerned, ensuring that as the cigarette smouldered it would burn as much skin as possible. He was using the natural tendency of the toes to spring back together to hold the cigarette in place — the elastic band was just to make sure it was as painful an experience as possible.

She took in a deep breath and attempted to move her feet, to wiggle her toes to dislodge it, but Richard's injections had done their job. Her feet resisted the impulses which her brain sent, the muscles unable to comply. She glared at Paul with all the *hatred* which she could muster, but he simply returned the glare implacably.

"Tell us about Hayter. What is the situation inside the mansion? How advanced an occultist is Tony Baron?" he whispered, menacingly. *"Tell us, and save yourself all this discomfort."*

She tried to shut him out of her consciousness, but it was nearly impossible with the knowledge that at any second she would be subjected to a viciously simple form of torture. She thought that she could feel the heat radiating from the cigarette as it burned lower, closer to the sensitive skin between her toes.

The Cultists stood impassively, watching and waiting, and all the while Paul whispered his questions, demanding that she answer them. She felt like screaming at him to leave her to her torture but knew that she would be wasting her breath.

She took another deep breath, but this time she could definitely feel the heat increasing and knew that it wouldn't be long now. She felt herself break out into a sweat, even though the rest of her body was so cool. Her toes were beginning to feel hot and she clenched her fists in reaction.

It seemed to Margaret that time somehow managed to reverse itself. It had seemed to take ages before she could actually *feel* the heat from the cigarette, but now, with waves of burning hammering into her brain, time seemed to slow down. It was as though, perversely, she was required to take as much time about her suffering as she could.

Her breathing coming in gasps she tried, unsuccessfully, not to allow her pain to show. It etched itself along her face as she frowned in anguish. Her toes felt as though they were on fire and yet she knew that the cigarette couldn't have burned down that far; she was certain that she would be the first to know when it had.

When, an eternity later, it began to roast the sensitive skin, her screams echoed and re-echoed around the cell to the accompanying chant of Paul demanding that she answer the questions which had been put to her.

She shook her head from side to side, whether in answer to Paul's demands or just from the red-hot agony which was pouring through her, none could tell. She clenched her fists so tightly that the knuckles turned white and her fingernails dug *deeply* into the palms of her hands, causing them to bleed. All the while, she screamed out her misery and Paul demanded answers to his questions.

How long this went on she could only guess. There came a time when she became aware that the cigarette had been removed and she gasped out her relief. A sharp slap across her face brought her back to reality. Paul glared furiously at her and then at her feet. As her breathing regained some semblance of normality, her screams subsided into whimpers of anguish. The assembled Cultists regarded her impassively. A slow smile appeared on Paul's features. He looked her straight in the eyes as he slowly drew another cigarette from the packet and lit it.

"*It seems,* Miss *Hunter, that you are determined to be stubborn. Think, though, of the additional pain when the skin between each of your toes has been burned — surely you don't* want *to experience that — and more besides? All you have to do is answer my questions.*"

She simply looked at him; what he was saying penetrated her mind but with so much pain flooding her consciousness it was difficult to think straight. All she wanted was for the pain to stop, for no more to be inflicted upon her. Even so, at a deeper level, she knew that she could not bring herself to cooperate with these enemies of Hayter and Tony; even though she fully realised, as far as she was able, what the result of that decision might mean for her. Slowly, her breathing still rapid, she shook her head and managed to repeat what she had said earlier. Her agony and hatred made her embellish it slightly. "Go to hell, you bastard," she whispered.

He smiled at her. She could see, below his mask, the movement of his lower lip. He took several puffs upon the cigarette, without inhaling, and merely blew the smoke in her direction. It mingled with the smell of her burnt flesh, evoking the fear of what she knew was going to happen.

He approached her, knelt by her feet, and then selecting two toes, the second and third from her big toe, as opposed to the first and second which had held the original cigarette, he inserted the smouldering instrument of torture between them exactly as before. He stood back to enjoy and savour the anticipation upon her face, and her torment when the torture actually began.

***

It was some considerable time later when her ordeal came to a temporary end. The skin between each of her toes had been subjected to Paul's peculiarly cruel form of torture, and by the time that the assembled Cultists decided to suspend her torment in order to increase her apprehensions about what their next move might be, she was in a state where nothing existed but pain. Her fetters were opened and at a motion from the Supreme Brother, they disappeared. Although she had been released, she made no attempt to move, was confined in her own world of misery and suffering. She gasped air sporadically, whimpered continually, and shuddered involuntarily without even being aware of it.

Paul approached her again and she squirmed away from him, her whimpers of pain becoming squeals of terror. After this latest torture the only thing with which her mind could associate him was excruciating pain. She managed to propel herself backwards away from him, using her hands, until she came up against the wall. He moved closer, bent towards her, until his face was *inches* from hers.

"*You* will *tell us what we want to know. You think you've experienced pain, Miss Hunter? Let me assure you, you don't know what pain is yet,*" he straightened to his full height.

He dropped his gaze to her lower abdomen. Suddenly, his eyes gleamed and he glanced from her vulva to the cigarette pack which he still held, and then back to her face.

343

For all the numbing terror and the agony which she was still experiencing, she followed his gaze and groaned. No, he *couldn't* mean...not *that*. She glanced up at him, her resistance almost completely eradicated, only pride preventing her from telling them what they wanted to know.

He had read upon her face the thoughts which had passed through her mind. He lit a cigarette, glanced again, briefly, between her legs and then back to her eyes. "*We'll see,*" he promised. "*Perhaps we can try that when I return.*"

On that nightmarish possibility / idea / threat, he turned abruptly and strode away from her. Graham opened the door and they filed out, leaving her alone again, but petrified into immobility by the fear of their return. Agony flooded her body, anguish filled her mind.

She had almost been broken.

The cell began to spin, to lurch crazily from side to side. Everything she had experienced combined together and was too much for her mind to hold. She passed out.

***

The Supreme Brother looked around the small assembly, a grim, stony smile upon his face. Brother Fidelis caught his eye and he nodded slightly, amplifying his meaning by asking, "Do you wish to attempt to worm your way further into her confidence?"

"Yes, Paternal Brother. I can claim that, in private, Paul managed to dissuade you from torturing me as you intended — emphasising in the process the fact that she has nothing to reproach herself with; that if she tells me what you want to know, I will prevent anyone from harming her further. It will, of course, be an empty promise."

"You seriously think that she might find that story credible?" queried the Supreme Brother. "I do not. When you return, the third and fourth fingers of your hands will have been removed. Miss Hunter may assume *that* was your punishment. I want her to feel that *she* is responsible for your mutilation; she might then be more inclined to answer your questions."

"You are devious, Paternal Brother. I will go to her now."

"Thank you, Fidelis; I *try*."

Fidelis left them, and the Supreme Brother watched him disappear. He turned his cold gaze upon Brother Paul, who returned it steadily. "You are to be commended, Paul. Your idea about the cigarette, your whole deportment during this torture has been of a degree of excellence which pleases me immensely. I am certain that she will tell us what we want to know next time we visit her. Graham, what do you suggest for the next phase of her persuasion?"

"I think we have been gentle for long enough, Supreme Brother. I therefore suggest that next we burn her forearms — either by smearing oil over them and igniting it, or by showering them in petrol or paraffin and setting them alight, one forearm at a time. I can't guarantee that she *will* break, but in my experience just the *suggestion* of similar treatment being applied to, say, the insides of the legs or to the breasts has the desired effect. It might well be enough in this case. The so-called tortures that have been applied so far have done little more than cause her *minor* discomfort. *This* will be different."

The Supreme Brother frowned and nodded slowly. "Paul, what do you think of what Graham advises?"

"I agree with him, although I disagree in one respect." He glanced at Graham, as though to convey that no insult was intended. Graham nodded, indicating that none had been taken. "I think that, before all of us go back to..."

He broke off as Fidelis returned briskly. "She's unconscious. I think she has simply passed out, but I suggest that Richard take a look at her."

345

Richard rose from his seat. He had thus far been a silent spectator of these exchanges but now he spoke. "Of course, Brother Fidelis. After all, we can't let her die — not yet, anyway," he added cynically, his lips curling into a smile. He located his doctor's bag and followed Fidelis out of the room.

The silence that followed was broken by Supreme Brother's voice. "You were saying, Brother Paul?"

"Yes, Supreme Brother, I was saying — I think that before we all return and carry out Brother Graham's excellent suggestion, that I accost her alone, restrain her, whip her..."

"But that has *already* been done," interrupted Graham, impatiently.

"Brother, it has *not* been done the way that I am proposing. I suggest that I reveal my face to her and renew our acquaintance. The shock and the memories which I *will* generate within her will end her resistance."

The Supreme Brother frowned again. "I had some vague idea of a similar nature earlier, but I'm not sure. Perhaps we should ask Richard's opinion," he said as Richard returned, Fidelis behind him. He deposited his bag upon the floor and sat.

"I'm glad to say that it's nothing serious," he began, "it seems that she simply passed out in reaction to what has been done to her. From a medical point of view, it would give cause for concern, but from our point of view, it's very encouraging."

"Is she conscious now?"

"No, but she will come around shortly. I didn't want to disorientate her by forcing her into consciousness, as that could have interfered with our plans."

"Give us the benefit of your expertise, Richard. Paul has suggested that he visit her alone and let her understand *exactly* who has been inflicting this upon her. He feels that this course of action might facilitate our questioning of her; that her resistance to answering will be crushed, in effect. What is your opinion?"

Richard sat for several minutes, his brow furrowed as he considered this scenario. Finally, he lifted his head, and locked eyes with Paul. "Why is that you are so positive? I take it that you weren't close?"

"Far from it. I made certain that her childhood was *far* from pleasant."

Richard accepted the admission calmly, without even blinking. "I see," he said slowly. "It's quite possible that your sudden appearance might cause such a state of confusion and despair that her stubbornness would be overwhelmed by it. Tell me, as a child, did she fear you?"

"She was *terrified* of me — *hated* me."

"Then it could well work — but take care *not* to traumatize her too much, or she might well pass out again." He looked from Paul to the Supreme Brother. "It may work; I think it might be worth a try."

Supreme Brother accepted the statement. "Very well. Fidelis, you may try your scheming and if it comes to nothing, then Paul, you may attempt what you have outlined to me."

Brother Fidelis rose and moved towards the cavern's entrance. "I think it might be as well if I were there to comfort her when she comes to," he murmured as he disappeared.

"Supreme Brother," said Martin, "have you any idea what Hayter is doing at the present time?"

"No," he answered brusquely. "Although Brothers have been told to continue their watch upon the mansion. At this stage, I don't expect Hayter to telegraph his intentions to us. All Brothers are in a state of constant readiness should he *dare* to attempt attacking us, however."

Martin nodded. "I wish I *knew* Brandon was dead. At the time, the most important thing was to capture the girl — but I wish we'd have had the time to make *sure...*"

"You acted correctly. Had you gone back complications may have ensued. I would rather Brandon be alive than Miss Hunter escaped."

At that moment, Brother Adam appeared. "I have come to report that all is quiet around the mansion. Nothing has changed, Supreme Brother."

"How is it *you* were assigned to watch the mansion?" Supreme Brother demanded.

"I volunteered, and Brother Alex ordered me to make this report, as it was so routine."

"I see," murmured Supreme Brother. "And what if your report was *not* routine? What if you were to report to Brother Fidelis that Hayter died of a heart attack — that Brandon has died of his injuries; that Tony Baron is in a state of shock and no longer poses any threat to us?"

"I don't understand," Adam protested.

"He is, at this moment, talking to a prisoner of ours. She is close to *all* three of them. What effect do you think all this news will have upon her?"

Adam hesitated and then grinned his understanding. "But how will Brother Fidelis know that what I say is false?"

"He will know it before you reach her cell," promised the Supreme Brother.

"Do you wish me to go now?"

"No, give them about twenty minutes."

***

Margaret regained consciousness slowly. Pain wracked through her, demanding that some action be taken to protect her feet. The crimson weals and welts covering her body seemed minor irritations, by comparison. She was thirsty, but that was the wrong word for it. She was *parched*. She hadn't been given anything to eat or drink since her capture — were they

348

hoping to deprive her of these as yet *another* torture, she found herself wondering.

She moved her feet and groaned at the sudden intensification of the agony coursing through her. It was unbelievable, incredible that such pain could have been caused by so simple a method.

It was as these thoughts coursed through her awareness that she became conscious of the fact that she was *not* alone: that someone was watching her; that the cell had been illuminated. The possibility that the Cult might have returned whilst she had been...she had fainted, she realised suddenly — she opened her eyes and quickly glanced around. The only person visible was seated next to her. She let out a sigh of relief, her heart slowing somewhat.

He smiled at her beneath his mask; she sat up, conscious of how tangled her hair must be, how *grim* she must look; he proffered a plastic beaker.

She glanced at the water within, wondering whether or not it might be drugged in some way. Inwardly shrugging, she realised that even if it *was* drugged they could just as easily inject her forcibly, and it would *still* be liquid which she badly needed. She scarcely hesitated, took the beaker and drank deeply.

"No, drink it slowly, Miss Hunter. Sip it if you can. You'll find that the more slowly you drink it, the more it will quench your thirst."

She nodded at him, and tried to do as he suggested. She could detect no trace of taste in the water and had to conclude, reluctantly, that he hadn't tried to trick her. A part of her mind told her that he was different from the others, that she could trust him. It was only then that she noticed the bandages around his hands — and took in the fact that two fingers from each hand had been removed. Gulping a mouthful of water which she had been about to sip, she blurted: "What happened to your hands?"

He looked away from her. "My thanks for coming here without permission." He looked at her again. "But it was *my* fault for coming to you in the first place — it wasn't as though you *asked* me to come, or as though I did any good when I got here."

Margaret felt a little dizzy, but she quickly grasped what he was saying. She thought about the danger he had obviously placed himself in to come to her, to try to help her from her own stupidity, to attempt to save her from what had been done to her. He had even asked her *not* to give him away and as soon as she had been asked, she had done exactly the opposite by glancing at him. She could have betrayed him just as easily by screaming his betrayal at the top of her voice. And through her his fingers had been amputated, presumably without anaesthetic. Despite the searing pain from her feet, she groaned at what she had caused to be done to him. And, after all that, he had *still* been here when she came round, ready with water that she would have begged for, but which he had given to her freely.

A sudden thought made her stiffen. "What if they find out you're here now?"

"This time I made sure that I got permission. I pointed out that they'd never find out what they wanted to know if you were dead, and that lack of fluid has been known to kill. Supreme Brother then gave me leave to bring you water. I guessed you had fainted and I waited for you to come round."

"And you don't hold it against me that I gave you away and that you lost those fingers because of it?" she couldn't stop herself asking.

"I...resent it, but it was more my fault than yours. Miss Hunter, Margaret — may I call you Margaret?"

She nodded.

"Margaret, why *don't* you tell them what they want to know? Why not tell *me*, and I could pass on what you

350

say to the others. If you do, I can guarantee that no one else will hurt you. I won't let them."

"But you couldn't *stop* them," Margaret replied, puzzled.

"*I* couldn't, admitted. But I have Brother Fidelis' word that if you tell them what they want to know, through me, then they will not harm you."

"Do you believe that?" she asked, sceptically. "Why should *his* word be worth anything?"

He glanced at her, apparently puzzled. "He is the Supreme Brother's successor. When he speaks, it is with the Supreme Brother's authority. When he gives his word, it is Supreme Brother's word that he gives."

"I must admit I'm not looking forward to whatever else they've got ready for me. But...Gregory, betraying your friends, people that you love...do you have *any* idea of how I'd feel about myself afterwards? And yet, I *don't* want to be hurt any more," she said, tears streaming down her face and sobs racking her as she spoke.

"Yes, I *think* I can understand how you might feel, but ask yourself this question. Do you think that any of these people whom you love, who probably love you, too, would want you to endure such torture? Don't you think they would be the *first* to understand?"

"I...I *suppose* so; I'm so confused. What is it they want to know?" she asked, desperation creeping into her voice. "Ask your questions, Gregory," she said in a flat, resigned tone, tears still rolling down her face. She knew that, in this dangerous game, she had lost.

Stifling a smile, he spoke quietly. "More or less everything about you and Tony Baron, all you can tell them about George Hayter, and anything else which they might find of interest. Tell me about Hayter first," he continued, attempting to keep the impatience out of his voice.

"Well, there isn't really much to tell...he's a *very* excellent pianist, very..." she broke off as the cell door opened and Adam appeared.

Gregory frowned. Of all the most *inopportune* moments to interrupt! Supreme Brother's message filled his mind and his irritation decreased somewhat. "Brother?" he enquired.

"I have been told to relate my news to you by Supreme Brother himself. It is a glorious day for us, as our curse is almost at an end. George Hayter is dead." He turned slightly to look at Margaret, whose gasp of dread echoed around the silent cell. "He took Miss Hunter's abduction very badly, apparently," Brother Adam continued to Gregory, "so when, earlier, John Brandon died of his injuries..."

"*NO!*" Margaret screamed at him.

He glared back at her and then continued: "As I say, when Brandon died, Hayter's heart couldn't stand the strain. It leaves only Tony Baron, and he is in such a state of shock that it will be an easy task to destroy him."

"Is that *everything* you have to tell me?" Gregory enquired.

Brother Adam recognised the dismissal in Gregory's voice. "Yes, Brother Fidelis," he replied, as he turned and left the cell, leaving Gregory *seething* and hoping that what he had been called *hadn't* registered with Margaret.

Unfortunately, although she was confused and terrified, though she had been deprived of sleep and found it difficult to think straight, she had heard *and* understood what had been said and what it portended. It diminished the scale of what she had heard about Hayter and Brandon and in a sudden flash of clarity, she saw through Gregory, realised that what she had heard was no more than a trick. In those moments, she *despised* herself for being taken in by such a simple set-up. A child could have seen through it.

She looked at him, sitting so close to her; watched as he turned his head and locked her gaze; saw the fury and disappointment as he realised that she understood *who* and *what* he was, that his disguise as her friend had been shattered beyond any hope of redemption.

"You must have been congratulating yourself on your success, *Brother Fidelis*," she snapped at him. "I hope you had a good *laugh* at my expense. God, what a fool you must have thought me — *gullible* isn't the word. Tell me, Gregory, were you *really* whipped, were your fingers *really* amputated or was that just a little demonstration of your abilities? Perhaps it's time for you to go and tell your Supreme Brother that you have failed and that I'm tired of being played for a fool. I swear to you, you will get nothing more out of me. Not one *goddamned* thing."

Gregory jumped to his feet, eyes blazing. Without another word, he left the cell and hurried to report his failure to the Supreme Brother.

Left alone yet again, the darkness returning, she steeled herself for whatever torture was to come. She didn't attempt to delude herself into thinking that this was the end, that they had given up. Her thoughts turned to Hayter and Tony, and the story which had been intended to release all the desperation which she felt.

As her anger at Fidelis began to diminish, she realised just how ambivalent her feelings were concerning what would be done to her. Her mental anguish had been stretched further than she had ever believed possible, and now that the immediate cause of her anger had been removed she sat contemplating whether or not they would be *content* with torture or whether they would kill her. Either way, she found that the thought didn't frighten her as much as it ought to.

She felt oddly calm and lucid. Even the pain from her feet didn't seem as intense, although in reality it was just as extreme as it had been earlier. She didn't know that it was simply a reaction to all that she had been through, coupled with Fidelis' duplicity and the knowledge that shortly she would be screaming again, in agony, as they intensified their torture, which dulled her perceptions.

She knew, by that intuitive part of herself which Hayter had awakened within her, that although he might be shaken by her kidnapping, he would *not* allow himself to die — not until he had succeeded in what he had to do — even if it *was* true that John was dead. George was undoubtedly alive, she told herself, and doing all in his power — however meaningless that might turn out to be — to secure her safety. Not knowing for certain was the worst part; even through her sense of apathy she longed for solid evidence that they were well, rather than just intuitive knowledge, which she hadn't yet learned to trust.

A deep sense of melancholia settled upon her, and as time passed she thought of nothing, felt nothing, *was* nothing. The sound of the cell door being opened barely registered in her consciousness. It was only when two robed figures entered and stood regarding her that their presence infringed upon her mind, forcing her to move her eyes to look at them.

Her anger churned and *surged* within her as she became more and more *aware* of their presence, at the humiliation which she had been forced to endure. Her respiration increasing as her fury mounted, she clenched her fists in impotent *rage* knowing that there was virtually nothing that she could do to vent her anger upon them.

As one of them took a step towards her, her anger erupted; it was almost as though she became another person. She saw herself, eyes closed involuntarily, a mental picture of them in her mind. Then, just as it had done with the glass, her mind seemed to reach out, took hold of the Cultist and *hurled* him to the wall of the cell, her vitriolic emotions gaining some release with that one action. The vision fragmenting, her breathing little more than gasps for air, her eyes opened weakly to register the Cultist climbing to his feet, his eyes glittering darkly. She managed to smile slightly despite the gnawing weakness which she now felt. To do what she had just done must have taken an enormous amount of energy, she guessed, and as though she didn't have enough to contend with, the weakness which she was now feeling must be a reaction to it. She chuckled. No doubt she would pay for her satisfaction in pain, but no matter how *much* they hurt her, it would be worth it just for the pleasure of that *brief* second of being able to fight back.

Richard gazed at Paul in mild reproach. "I wouldn't have believed it unless I'd seen it myself. You must have let your guard down."

Paul glared back ruefully. *"Aye, I did. It won't happen again, though. When I've finished with her we won't be able to* stop *her talking. Have you got that medication that you used on William?"*

"Yes, but I'm not sure that..."

"Give her the maximum dose, Richard."

Richard considered, wondering what Supreme Brother's reaction might be. Finally, he nodded. "I'll be right back — can you manage on your own? Sorry, silly question," he added, noticing the look upon Paul's face. It took him less than five minutes to return with a loaded hypodermic and a swab. Immediately, he noticed that Paul had not been exaggerating his ability to handle the captive. Whether he had bound her by occult means before restraining her or whether the reaction to her demonstration of anger had sapped her strength to the extent that she was unable to resist, he didn't know.

The manacles which held her arms above her head were embedded into the roof of the cell, whilst two similar restraints — embedded into the floor — held her ankles, allowing them only an inch or so of movement. Richard approached her nodding his appreciation of the

355

fact that she had been fastened as close to the centre of the cell as it was possible to get. He pulled an eyelid up, and gazed at the distended pupil.

"She's still conscious, but attacking you on top of everything else has taken its toll. I'll inject her, and leave you to it." He nodded at the syringe. "I think it'll take about five minutes to come to the optimum effect."

"How long will it last?"

"You don't have to worry about that — the effects continue for about seven hours before diminishing." Carefully, he swabbed her arm, slid the needle into a vein, depressed the plunger and swabbed her arm again. "About five minutes: you'll know when it's working fully by how alert she seems, how receptive to pain she becomes."

"Many thanks, Richard," he said, escorting him to the cell door and retrieving a five stranded whip, and a belt which he was *certain* that she would remember. He nodded to Richard as he departed and closed the cell door. He dropped the belt and whip behind Margaret, and then moved to a position where he could watch her. He savoured the moment for which he had waited for so long. His gaze travelled lasciviously over her body; it was a pity that he wasn't allowed to go *that* far...

Her mind clearing with extraordinary rapidity, she pondered what was happening; she was aware that she had been restrained in this position by the Cultist who now stood thoughtfully before her. She hadn't struggled, had known and accepted that resistance would be futile. She knew that she was about to pay for her little triumph and was in no doubt that it would be a painful price. However, this didn't cause her resolve to waver, quite the contrary. As her senses became sharper, more intense, the agony from her feet returned, a sick wave of nausea causing her to shudder and let her breath out in a gasp of pain. Bile rose to her throat.

356

The torment from her feet continued to intensify until she believed that she was actually experiencing the whole thing again. As her senses became more finely tuned, sharper than they had ever been in her life, the pain from the whipping which she had experienced what seemed like months ago resurrected itself, adding an extra dimension to her torture. She tried, but didn't succeed, to rationalise what had been done to her. She couldn't comprehend *how* she had been forced to feel the renewed stinging and smarting so intensely. She squirmed in her bonds, attempting to lessen the pain, somehow; but she succeeded only in intensifying it even more. She moaned out loud, her confidence in her promise that the Cultists would get nothing more out of her badly shaken. Apart from the unbelievable amount of discomfort that she was in she realised that, incredibly, her vision had been enhanced, that she was conscious of the sound of her heart beating — that she was hearing the noise that it made — *but from outside her body*. She could see and focus on individual cracks in the wall, could see the pale blue of the eyes that bored into hers. She finally recognised him as Paul, her principal tormentor. He inclined his head to her, almost graciously.

"Well, Miss Hunter," he said, "you and I are finally alone together. *Why* were you reluctant to bare your body for us? It's quite superb," he said, running a trembling hand over her breasts, and down, slowly, until his fingers brushed her pubic hair.

She had started at his tone of voice, for it was the first time that she had heard him speak in anything but a whisper. The voice reminded her of something — it had deep connotations of menace that struck fear *deep* into her heart, although she couldn't understand *why* that should be so, through her fog of pain. His fondling revolted her and she instinctively tried to pull out of his reach, but to no avail. All she succeeded in doing was to bring a screaming message of pain so intense that she whimpered despite herself. Paul chuckled.

"You will do *more* than sob shortly, *Miss Hunter*, I assure you. I take it that you don't care for my touch? Rather an ungrateful attitude, wouldn't you agree? If you had a bedroom here, I might send you there to await your punishment."

Again what he said struck home, aimed at a sensitive part of her mind which had *never* recovered from his original abuse of her. She frowned, wondering whether what he said was coincidental or whether he had managed to read her mind, somehow, and knew about her father.

Whilst she was struggling, mentally, to come to terms with what he had said he casually walked behind her, picked up the whip, shook its strands free and, putting all the force of which he was capable into the swing, struck her savagely across the small of her back. The results were beyond his wildest expectations. An ululation of the purest, most excruciating agony erupted from her; her whole body shook and threshed. She drew breath and screamed her agony again, all the while her body continuing its convulsions. Brother Richard *hadn't* made idle promises concerning his drug, Paul concluded, drawing the whip back and inflicting a second blow no less harsh than the first and as nearly as possible upon the same area. Her scream threatened to tear her vocal chords, so loud did it seem to Paul. He grinned at her threshing body, *fully* enjoying himself now. He drew the whip back a third time, aiming for the back of her legs. The blow, when it landed, cut viciously across them and caused a howl which sounded ghastly in the amount of pain that it vocalized. A fourth blow caused her legs to buckle, her wrists taking her full weight. The expected shriek of agony broadened his smile. He lowered the whip and listened to her laboured breath, as she gasped air only to use it to scream out the red hot agony once more pervading and filling her body and mind. His smile faded as, between gasps, she managed to speak. "Please...no more. What do you want to know? Just *tell me* what you want to know."

Paul's rage began building up. Was she doing this just to frustrate his pleasure, his *revenge*? Slowly, he moved around her, glaring his anger. "But, Miss Hunter, I told you that eventually you *would* tell us all that we wanted to know — you will simply have to *wait* and *accept* whatever is done to you, until *I* decide that the time is right for Supreme Brother to be informed of your most expected cooperation."

"You...you're *enjoying* this, aren't you?" she gasped between breaths. He nodded and his lips curled into a grin.

"Oh, *yes*, Margaret," he replied. He watched her, fascinated as she looked at him, obviously attempting to make connections, to put the threads together and failing to do so. "I have waited *longer* than you realise for *this* moment."

With difficulty she straightened her legs, taking the weight off her wrists. The agony in her back and legs became a constant in her mind. "So, you're just going to beat me for the fun of it?" she spat at him.

He frowned, "No, Margaret, I'm going to chastise you to the extent I think you *deserve*. Just think of me in a *parental* light."

He moved quickly to the belt, and swinging it as viciously as he had the whip, he applied its caress to her back, her buttocks and her legs. She was quickly reduced to a weeping, pleading wreck, her body a mass of excruciating pain, all her weight upon her wrists. Paul stood in front of her regarding her with amusement.

"Now, do you *apologise*, Margaret?"

"For what?" she screamed back at him, agony dictating her tone of reply.

He swung the belt; it landed with a sharp *smack* against her abdomen, causing another scream, another set of convulsions to rack her body.

"For all the inconvenience which you have caused me," he roared back at her, raising the belt again.

She saw the motion and before he swung it screamed out, "Yes, I'm *sorry*, I didn't *mean* to...I'm sorry."

He lowered the belt. "Then perhaps, for the present at least, you have been punished sufficiently," he said, to her intense relief. "Tell me, why did you become involved with Tony Baron? I could *almost* believe that you did it to spite me, Margaret."

Through her pain, through the stinging, smarting agony threatening to overcome her, something in the tone of what he said caught her attention. She focussed her eyes upon him and then upon the belt that he still held... upon the belt... upon the belt... the belt... *the belt*.

Her eyes jerked to his, her mind refusing to admit even the remotest possibility of the connections that she was beginning to make. Her mouth opened to shape a "No," but she could utter no sound. She recognised *that* belt all too well; but it couldn't be, not *him*. From deep inside her, a terror, deeper and more intense than the word could even begin to describe, began to emerge.

Paul smiled at her. He put his hands to his mask and slowly removed it, dropping it to the floor. "You catch on quickly," he smiled. "Well, *Margaret*! *Daughter*! *Bitch*! I have you once again in my power. Believe me, my dear, *dear* daughter, I am going to make you *suffer* in ways that you cannot even *begin* to imagine — *this* is but a prelude."

Margaret gazed at him, her eyes wide in consternation. That she should have fallen into her father's hands — he would *ensure* that she suffered. She already knew that. Death would be preferable. He was speaking to her, but the words didn't register. Her vision swam in and out of focus.

"*No, Daddy*," she muttered as her mind, protecting itself from the physical reality of a nightmare more intense and profound than it could ever have coped with, attempted to regress her to a situation where her sanity would be safe.

Her mind rapidly explored possibilities, even as its faculties began to shut down, but failed to find anywhere where that safety could be assured. There was only one other option, which came from a place in her subconscious so deep that even Richard's drug could not penetrate it. After only an instant's hesitation her mind *accepted* that alternative. As Margaret slumped in her chains, the illumination from the cell faded from her perception to a greyness, which in turn faded to a blackness which nothing could penetrate. She was aware of nothing, her mind almost completely blank. Nothing could reach her, nobody could hurt her any more.

It was several seconds before Paul began to realise that something was seriously amiss. At first he simply thought that she had fainted again, but she didn't appear to be breathing. He stepped closer and felt for a pulse in her wrist and then her neck. His gasp of dread was covered by the noise that he made as he ran from the cell. Less than thirty seconds later, he hurtled into the cavern occupied by Supreme Brother, Fidelis, Richard and Martin; whatever they had been discussing died at his precipitate approach.

"Supreme Brother, Richard, *quick*, it's Margaret. I...I *think* that she's dead."

Richard raced out in the direction from which Paul had appeared. Supreme Brother's eyes flashed with an icy brilliance as rage overcame him.

"If she *is dead*," he snapped in a voice utterly unearthly in its bitterness, "then you *will* follow her.

361

Chapter Fifteen: Prophesies

Tony rubbed his eyes irritably. He hadn't managed to snatch any sleep since using the book which Hayter wanted to read and consider as a pillow. So far, though, the sum total of what they had decided to do was zero. Hayter still felt that his hands were tied until he understood exactly what Anton Baron's message meant. He stubbornly *refused* to attack the Cult, stating that the only time they could do so with any *chance* of success would be when the prophesy's conditions were met; and that Margaret — assuming that she was still alive, which Hayter *insisted* was the case — would almost certainly be killed instantly any attack was mounted. They all found it difficult — even now — to take in the fact that she was a Baron; it tended to make the prophesy seem more obscure, somehow.

The conditions to be met, for the Barons to be united seemed, on one hand, to be impossible to achieve, with Margaret being held by the Cult. Tony fought a never-ending battle not to imagine what she might be going through, but his mind repeatedly painted lurid visions of medieval torture chambers, hot coals, thumb screws and racks until he thought he would scream. He examined his own emotions for her very closely, at that time, and was somewhat disturbed when he realised how intense they were. The realisation unnerved him, made him uneasy, for some reason which he couldn't define. He glanced at Hayter, who sat in one of the leather chairs in the sitting room, seemingly gazing into space. John sat next to him upon the sofa, fidgeting uncharacteristically. The wound on his head didn't seem to bother him. Tony had changed the dressing four times, much to John's annoyance. The concussion which he seemed to have sustained initially had disappeared abruptly after he had intruded upon them in the study. Whether or not Hayter had been responsible for that, Tony didn't know or care. He realised that John was as impatient with this apparent stalemate as he was; it was as this thought ran through his mind that he *began* to suspect John's feelings for Margaret might be more intense than he had at first believed. He glanced at him, thinking of him in a new light — as a possible *rival* despite his blindness.

"Are you as nervous as you seem?" Tony couldn't stop himself from asking.

John grinned. "Yes; normally, I'd paint and relax that way, but the way things have turned out, *that's* out of the question."

They fell silent again, fearing to disturb Hayter's concentration — although he was so deep in thought it would have been nearly impossible to do so. Tony lit a cigarette, wishing that it wasn't so silent in that room.

Hayter looked up. "As nearly as I can fathom it, I think Anton Baron is waiting for *us*."

Tony locked eyes with Hayter. Stated out of context, what he had said seemed ludicrous, almost laughable had it not been for the fact that Margaret's life might depend upon it.

"George, you've lost me. Can you explain how you got to that conclusion? I don't mean to sound doubtful, but at the moment it makes no sense."

Hayter grinned. "That's the beauty of it. If what I believe is correct, and I'm sure that it is, it means that the Cult can't have *any* inkling of what was in Anton's mind all those centuries ago. All right; I *said* to you that Anton must have had some reason for using a flawed ritual which he *knew* would bring about his death. I *theorised* that he might have been a more brilliant occultist than we at first gave him credit for being. I *speculated* that he might have used a different form of occultism and that his death was *his* manner of payment for what he intended to do…"

363

"Payment?" John interrupted, "doesn't that then imply some kind of reciprocal arrangement?"

Hayter nodded in John's direction. "I think that Anton *knew* that he wasn't powerful enough, at that time, to destroy the Cult. I think that he bargained to be returned to life at a time and place where he *could* either destroy the Cult for good, or at least *begin* that destruction."

"So *that's* why you wanted information on temporal *and* spatial relocation. You just wanted to make sure that it was possible."

"Yes," Hayter admitted. "Although I don't know that it's ever been deliberately attempted over such a *vast* stretch of time. I don't even *pretend* to understand exactly how he could be brought back to life, though. Obviously, not a *physical* resurrection — more probably some kind of spiritual one; this presupposes my first speculations that he was an excellent occultist, of course."

Tony sat thinking about what he had just heard. Anton Baron coming to their aid like the proverbial cavalry, rising from his grave — wherever *that* might be — after more than five hundred years? He looked critically at Hayter, wondering if the strain of the last few days had proved to be too much for him. Hayter returned his glance casually enough.

"You don't believe it, Tony?"

"I've never come across *anything* to imply that what you suggest is even remotely possible — unless you want to mention fairy tales."

"And because you have never come across anything which backs up what I surmise, does that make what I say impossible?"

"No," he admitted grudgingly, "but I would like *some* evidence before I put my life on the line - I'd like to have some idea of the chances of what you're suggesting actually happening."

"Tony, have you so soon lost your overall view of the situation? Your life is on the line whatever you do, whether I'm right or wrong. What have odds to do with anything at *this* stage of events? Whether we die or survive in the attempt is mostly unimportant. Even if the odds of success were only *one* in a *billion* it's still a chance; and I'm afraid that if you want to have *any* hope of seeing Margaret alive again, it's *that* chance which we're going to have to take."

He let out a breath sharply as Hayter finished speaking. He thought for a moment, before voicing another objection. "You may be right about me losing sight of the overall situation, George, but tell me this; how does this knowledge — assuming that you are right about Anton — how does it help us? We still don't know when the criteria stated within the prophesy will be met. As far as I can see, it takes us *nowhere*."

"But we are united in purpose, at least," Hayter insisted.

"How do you know that *that* is what the prophesy is referring to? It could just as easily mean that we are physically united in one location; or united in love, or a dozen other things. How can you be sure that you're right?"

But before Hayter could open his mouth to reply, John interrupted quickly. "As you're airing your various views, I would like to make a point. I seem to be more than a little redundant in this discussion. The possibility of a pact such as George is suggesting isn't as impossible as it might sound. Remember, spatial and temporal relocation *has* been successfully accomplished at least once — why not this time?

"You keep referring to this prophesy which you seem to think holds the key to our problems. I say *our* problems, because, don't forget that if the Cult succeeds in killing you, they'll want *me* dead, too. Why then is it that neither of you has once asked *my* opinion of the prophesy? You haven't even bothered to repeat the bloody thing to me. Who knows, I might be able to throw a new light upon it. At least a fresh mind applied when needed might trigger *something* off." He turned his face towards Hayter, almost in appeal, almost in demand.

Hayter frowned. "I've always considered that it was directed at the Baron family alone," he said. "It was that consideration that prevented me from disclosing what it said to Margaret — although as it turns out she had *every* right to know. It seems as though my ignorance turned out to be a blessing in disguise — at least she can't disclose what she doesn't know."

"Do you honestly think she would tell them *anything*?" Tony demanded quickly.

"Not intentionally, no. But everyone has their breaking point..." John informed him, quietly. This reference to what Margaret might be enduring renewed the urgency which they felt and emphasised to Tony his own feelings of helplessness and depression.

"I don't see what harm it can do, not at this stage," Hayter muttered. After a brief glance at Tony, seeing his almost imperceptible nod, Hayter repeated the prophetic verse without any emphasis. John frowned as he listened, his sightless eyes glittering with concentration until his eyelids closed involuntarily in an attempt to focus his attention more keenly.

"Would you repeat that?" he asked.

Hayter complied and again John closed his eyes, analysing what he had heard, trying variations, differing combinations. Tony glanced at Hayter who raised his hands in an 'I don't know' gesture.

Silence reigned in the sitting room as John pondered and devoured the prophesy in a hundred different ways. He suddenly stiffened and a gasp of surprise escaped him. A tremulous smile attempted to creep from the corners of his mouth. Hayter and Tony sat further forward in their respective seats.

"Well, John," Hayter snapped. "What do you think?"

He burst into peals of laughter. "My God, it's *so* easy; *so* obvious; I don't *believe* how simple it is!" he exclaimed.

Hayter turned to face Tony. "I think his delirium has returned," he said, drily, as John's laughter continued to flood the room. Tony found himself grinning like an idiot, as John's amusement became infectious. Even Hayter's lips trembled as he struggled to remain in control of the situation; at last his patience broke and he snapped, "John!" in a tone which indicated that his irritation was building towards anger.

John attempted to strangle his laughter, until only the occasional chuckle escaped him. He turned his face towards Hayter. "George, I'm sorry to say this, but I *think* you got it wrong."

"Got *what* wrong?" Hayter spluttered, enraged.

"If you'll calm down, I'll tell you. Just a few minutes ago, you accused Tony of losing sight of the overall situation; of being blind, in effect. I'm afraid that the same thing has happened to you. The answer was under your nose the whole time, but you didn't comprehend it."

"John, what *are* you talking about?" Hayter demanded.

"You know, you were right?" John mused, totally ignoring Hayter's demand. "Anton must have been a *brilliant* man, if he conceived everything — the whole scenario — himself. It's completely staggering in its complexity..."

"John!" Hayter thundered. "If you have an insight into Anton's prophesy, please don't be too *proud* to share it with us."

John started at the tone of Hayter's voice, and the exuberance which had appeared upon his face slowly faded. He turned his now mournful eyes upon him. "That was *uncalled* for, George."

Hayter coloured; it was the first — and only — time that Tony ever saw him embarrassed by a rebuke.

"You are right, John. It was unfeeling and cynical. I'm sorry I said it. But I *must* know what it is that you've deduced."

"And I need to know," Tony put in. "It might just benefit Margaret. John, you know that we're so desperate that *any* help is not only needed but transcends good manners. Tell us, *please*."

He turned his head to face first Tony and then Hayter. "You got it wrong, George," he repeated. "Your translation was *correct*, but Anton altered the verse slightly, so that its true meaning would not be divined too easily. But the *really* subtle part is that he did it so obviously; you were looking for a *complex* key where none existed. You should have been simpler in your approach. I said that it was obvious, and it is. Both of you couldn't see through the prophesy with your eyes wide open. Here am I, blinded, and I see what you do not. Maybe it'll start a trend." He grinned, and held up his hands. "Sorry, I shouldn't be flippant about it. The verse, prophesy, call it what you will, as you read it to me, reads:—

'When the flesh of my flesh again be united, then

Shall my kin do battle with my eternal enemies;

The days of the Brotherhood shall at last be

Numbered — my offspring, even though it mean their

Death, shall enable my victory.'

"And you have been going round and round in circles trying to make sense of it. But you failed. And you would continue to fail, *if* you left it in that form. It is quite simple. Anton must have wanted this information to be passed to his descendants, but he couldn't make the message too obvious in case it fell into the wrong hands. So what did he do? He made it a little cryptic. When slightly rearranged, it reads like this:—

> 'When my kin do battle with my eternal enemies,
> Then shall the flesh of my flesh again be united;
> Though it mean their death, the days of the
> Brotherhood at last shall be numbered — even my
> Offspring shall enable my victory.'

"*That* is what Anton was trying to tell you, all those centuries ago — you simply failed to see through his cryptic message, that's all."

He fell silent, as though embarrassed by his extended speech. The silence stretched out as Hayter and Tony looked from John to each other and then back to him again.

"Say that again," Hayter demanded, the tremor in his voice betraying the emotion which he felt. John repeated the prophesy, as he had rearranged it. The silence grew oppressive.

"Well, George, *could* he be right?" Tony asked, simply.

"I...I don't know. It's as feasible — more so — than *anything* that we've managed to dream up. It makes sense that Anton would scramble his message, making it seem as though the prophesy couldn't come to pass if the condition of unity were not met; but it would now appear that unity *isn't* what the prophesy is about. John, I think you've just solved our problem," Hayter concluded, smoothly.

"But, a second ago, you didn't know whether I was right or wrong."

"You *have* to be right. We can make no sense of it as it stands. It means that the whole prophecy hinges on *us*. When *we* attack, it signals the beginning of the Cult's end. Regardless of Margaret being their prisoner, it would seem that we have no alternative but to attack, and as soon as possible."

Tony nodded. John sat, his face unreadable. Hayter breathed deeply. He knew that he was soon to perform the most dangerous act of his life.

He glanced at them. "So, let's try to get some sleep. It's been in short supply lately. We attack in the early hours. It will be more of a surprise to them if we attack when we are least expected to. John, have you *any* idea where they are most likely to be keeping her?"

He considered, carefully. "I would think that there could only be *one* place. The ruins of the church which began this whole mess."

Hayter nodded. "I'll attempt a gentle probe around that area and see whether or not they *are* there. If they are, it'll save me having to locate them. I don't want to risk alerting them if I can *possibly* help it."

John nodded and yawned. "That suggestion about sleep seems to have stuck," he managed to say.

"And what are we to do about *you* John; you *aren't* an occultist, and I *don't* want you with us when we attack."

John's eyes opened wide. "Just try stopping me," he threatened in a savage tone which made Hayter wince. He knew, from that tone, that there would be no dissuading him.

"O.K. John," he said wearily, in a resigned voice. "But if you end up dead, don't blame me."

He stood and left them, oblivious to the suppressed and slightly hysterical laughter which burst from them both simultaneously. With Tony guiding John, they made their way towards his rooms.

Hayter slowly made his way to his study and, sitting behind the desk, began to prepare himself to exert his will. He carefully punched a hole in the barrier before forcing his consciousness out of his body and to the ruins of the church which Anton's colleague had attempted to buy, all those years ago. He was pleasantly surprised when he ran into resistance and immediately drew back, hoping that his presence hadn't been detected. Obviously, the Cult were in attendance and didn't want to be disturbed. He tried to attune his perception to Margaret but could get no response, however faint, that might have indicated she was still alive.

There was nothing.

A few seconds later he opened his eyes, looked blankly at the wall facing him, both sad and elated for differing reasons. With a *deep* sigh which seemed, somehow, to make his age more apparent, he stood and went to his bedroom, certain somehow that this would be his last opportunity, *ever*, for sleep.

Chapter Sixteen: Catastrophes

The Supreme Brother paced the chamber impatiently, throwing sinister glances in Brother Paul's direction. He made no move to follow Richard, who, he knew, would do *all* possible — and maybe a bit more besides. This preoccupation with immediate events occupied his mind to the exclusion of all else — even to failing to perceive that some force had, for a brief moment, encountered the protective circle which he had created around the ruins and had, just as abruptly, pulled away.

He stopped his pacing as Fidelis spoke: "Exactly what did you *do* Brother Paul?" he asked.

"All that was agreed between us — how could I know that the *shock* of seeing me again would be too much for her to take?"

"I suppose you've got a point there — but I *do* remember Richard telling you not to go too far. I suppose he expected you to stop at any signs of danger. Supreme Brother allows no excuses, as well you know."

Paul nodded mutely. Supreme Brother continued pacing, anger and fury radiating from him in palpable waves. The sound of rapidly approaching footsteps broke the silence. The Supreme Brother turned abruptly to face Richard as he reappeared.

"*Well?*" he demanded.

Richard's face held a serious expression. "Brother Paul's evaluation of how much terror he would instil in Miss Hunter was *extremely* accurate. I feel *I* must take some of the blame; it never even crossed my mind that *this* might happen. It's not a common occurrence, really."

"*What* isn't?" Supreme Brother demanded, in a voice which was curious and held an edge to it, as he stifled the churning emotions within himself.

"Supreme Brother, she isn't dead but she might as well be. It seems to be a condition similar to hysterical catatonia — but without exhaustive tests I cannot be a hundred percent certain."

"Hysterical catatonia?" Fidelis queried, "what's that?"

Richard sighed. "It's basically similar to catalepsy and just as unpredictable, except that it's induced by the mind being forced into a situation that it can't cope with, so it shuts itself away. To all intents and purposes, she's in a *deep* coma."

"How long will it last?" Supreme Brother asked.

"Think of a number; *any* number. Your guess is as good as mine. She may *never* regain consciousness."

Supreme Brother frowned. "Is her life in danger? Could you bring her around?"

"Without access to a hospital, I can't perform the tests necessary to answer for her *life*; it *could* conceivably be fatal. As to bringing her around, yes I could, but I *will not* take responsibility for the consequences. There are drugs which might just force her back to reality, but she could *die* in the process — of course, if you *want* me to take the risk..."

Supreme Brother shook his head impatiently. "No, she is *too* valuable to risk killing uselessly. Well, Paul, you have *not* brought about her death; calm yourself." He turned to Fidelis who had lit a cigarette. "It seems that we will get no information from *that* source. Richard, can you assure me that you can look after her here?"

Richard hesitated before answering. "Supreme Brother, she needs the kind of monitoring which could *only* be provided in hospital. I can give no such assurance."

He nodded, eyes still locked upon Brother Fidelis, who drew heavily upon his cigarette. "It would appear,"

Fidelis said slowly, "that we do not have much choice in the matter."

Supreme Brother's eyes turned several shades darker. "I *agree*," he rasped. "And yet, I recall telling you that in some ways I felt that we were being manipulated. I feel that same sense again. Things are *not* as they seem; and yet I must agree with you; we have *no* alternative. Fidelis, summon all Brothers to an emergency meeting late tonight. We will perform the Ritual Sacrifice to our Patron Demons in order that we may finally eradicate the Baron lineage — and Fidelis, *you* may have the honour of terminating Miss Hunter's existence."

Fidelis nodded, realising that he had just been handed the most prestigious part of the ceremony — he felt proud and daunted at the same time. "I will summon our Brothers," he stated, in acceptance of the Supreme Brother's declaration. Turning, he left the cavern.

"Inform the others here, and prepare for tonight," Supreme Brother ordered. "And Richard, I would like *you* to watch Miss Hunter — keep her *alive* for me until then."

Richard nodded, "I *will*," he said, leaving the chamber. Supreme Brother sat, attempting to rid himself of his feeling of manipulation but it just *wouldn't* leave him. It made him uneasy; something cataclysmic was in the air, he was certain. Things were coming to a turning point; but which way they were going to turn he didn't know and feared to conjecture. Logically, everything was in the Cult's favour, but it was the fact that the odds were stacked so unevenly which had made him decide upon caution. He had, in naming Fidelis as the person to sacrifice their captive, in effect, turned the meeting over to Fidelis' control. If anything went wrong, he, Supreme Brother would have the time to meet and counter it.

But what could go wrong? Nothing! Yet the Supreme Brother had not gained his position by taking chances; his instincts had paid off when he had assassinated his predecessor; he saw no harm in exercising or trusting it again and exposing Fidelis to any danger which might present itself.

He thought again of Margaret — Richard had told him of what she had managed to do to Paul, and *that* without any apparent preparation. '*It is obvious that she has inherited some occult ability but does not know how to wield it,*' he thought, even though she was in no position — now — to do anything. '*Does Hayter know of this? Has he in fact been training her rather than Tony Baron? It cannot be. If Hayter had known her occult potential, he would never have allowed her to leave his infernal mansion — unless this is the trap, the manipulation of which I have been aware*'. He mused upon this, standing and resuming his pacing. Whether her capture had been by design or not, Supreme Brother again felt that sense of disquiet gnawing at him.

As soon as the sacrifice was completed, he decided, they would utilize the power which their Patron Demons represented in a surprise attack upon Hayter; he was certain that the combination of the sacrifice — she being a Baron — coupled with the power of their Patrons, directed by the Cult, would be enough to smash through Hayter's barrier, maybe even kill him in the process. He thought of Hayter, what little he knew of him, and shook his head — he wished he knew what was going on inside the mansion, but the only source of information which had been available was now silenced. He was curious as to what Hayter was doing, whether he even conceived of attacking them; he was wary of underestimating his enemy, but couldn't account for Hayter's lack of response or for the lack of activity about the mansion. Did Hayter know something he didn't? Supreme Brother wondered. A feeling of vague suspicion formed in the back of his mind. If that were the case... But *what* could Hayter know? He frowned, knowing that he was simply going around in one big circle. It was an unusual experience for him, and not one that he found himself enjoying. For the first time since he had become the Supreme Brother, he doubted himself, was unsure that he had made the right decision — even though there was no other decision he *could* have made, under the circumstances.

He sat again, his sense of impending danger growing stronger. Irritation built up inside him; he was not used to being thwarted and whatever the danger, he knew that after tonight's meeting the Baron line would be obliterated. He shifted his position upon the chair and attempted to pass the time in a quiet examination of possibilities. There was one thing about which he was certain; he wouldn't be able to relax until tonight's ceremony was completed. He caught himself wondering whether Hayter had any idea of the surprise which was in store for him, this night.

***

The hours passed slowly for Hayter, who lay fully clothed upon his bed, thinking deeply. He felt a bitter pang within him when understanding came and he knew for an almost absolute certainty that whether or not the attack was successful, his time was almost at an end. It had been, so it seemed, his appointed task to keep the Cult at bay until this day, when events would conspire to the Cult's detriment. It was all the more galling that he wouldn't be allowed to see the result. After so long spent in almost total isolation, to renew his acquaintance with his great-nephew and meet Margaret, who turned out to be a distant relative, to grow to love them so quickly and so desperately — and at the end to be denied any knowledge of whether what he had done had helped or hindered — devastated and hurt him more deeply than anyone could have suspected. He knew he would not be there to watch and see if their relationship deepened into love /marriage /children. He sighed and wiped a single tear from his face. He had lived most of his life in a solitary way — it seemed that he would have to die that way, too. He determined that he must keep all knowledge of his imminent demise from John or Tony, or they might try to prevent him doing what he *knew* he must.

For Hayter, time had never seemed to drag so slowly, or to be so precious.

He knew that he would never sleep. He got off the bed, decided that a shower might make him feel just that bit sharper in mind and wash away the sludge which he felt had accumulated in his brain.

Fifteen minutes later, he made his way back to the study and retrieved Anton's book. He studied it minutely for the last time, making certain, although he already was, that he knew the incantation perfectly.

A knock sounded on the study door. Hayter shut the book before calling out, "Come."

The door opened and Tony entered, closely followed by John. "Couldn't sleep, George," Tony informed him. "I don't know about you, but I'm too nervous."

"And you're impatient for action," Hayter observed as Tony guided John to a chair, and then sat opposite Hayter.

"Anything's better than this inactivity," Tony grinned back at him. "Don't you want to attack immediately?"

"No," Hayter replied simply. "All things in their correct order. To attack now would not cause them the maximum disruption, therefore we wait until we *will* cause it." He glanced at his watch, "And that, Tony, will not be for at least two hours more."

"But aren't there things to do, things to prepare?" Tony asked. He glanced at John as a snort of laughter escaped him.

"If there is any preparation needed I'll wager anything that you care to name that all is prepared, and has been for weeks; right George?"

Hayter glared at him. "Do you know that you are just as infuriating as ever — I held hopes that the concussion *might* have had some beneficial effect upon you, but obviously it was a *vain* hope."

"So you *are* nervous," John said quietly. "I'd *never* have believed it — but you didn't answer my question," he prompted.

Hayter grunted angrily, and then laughed. "You win, John, as usual. Why is it that I never seem able to put one over on you? Everything *is* prepared."

"I don't know," he sounded honestly bewildered. "Perhaps it's just that your mind isn't subtle enough."

"I...*you*..." Hayter spluttered, at a loss for words.

"George, I'm just trying to take your mind off what's ahead," John said kindly. "I didn't mean it to sound insulting, just so ludicrous that it *might* have been amusing, *eased* the tension."

Hayter fell silent at that, his breathing returned to normal. Finally, his mouth twisted into a smile. "It *was* funny, in an offbeat way," he admitted.

"So, what do we do for the next two hours?"

"I would have thought that was obvious — we pass the time as best we can. We base our attacks upon what is written in here," he stated, waving a hand negligently in the book's direction.

"With suitable amendments, I take it," Tony added with a grin. "After all, we don't want to follow his example *too* far."

Hayter nodded and, not trusting his eyes not to betray the emotion which he felt building up within him, turned his gaze down to the desk top immediately in front of him.

"Have you thought of anything that I might be able to do by way of help?" John asked. "I won't be left out of this after waiting so long for my revenge."

Hayter sighed: "Apart from keeping still and quiet, John, I can't think of *anything* that you could do."

"But I am not entirely ignorant of occult theory — or practice, for that matter. I'm just a bit...*rusty*."

Hayter raised an eyebrow. "Without being obtuse, John, I think you might find that you are outclassed. Take my advice, stay put and keep quiet."

A frown crossed John's face, but he just shrugged his shoulders. Deep down, however, he knew that what Hayter said was right; that he would be more of a hindrance than help if he attempted to turn this battle into his own private feud. It made him feel impotent, being so helpless, but whilst he was unable to see he knew that there was very little that he could do. He thought of Margaret and wondered whether or not she *was* still alive. He had a pretty good idea of the kinds of tortures to which she might have been subjected before she was murdered — knowledge which he had made sure was kept to himself. Even when Tony hinted that he *suspected* John might know more than he was admitting, he had refused to be drawn, not wanting to add to Tony's anguish with graphic descriptions of what the Cult might be doing to her.

And the worst thing, he reflected bitterly, was the fact that *he had let her* be abducted. It was *his* fault, no one else's. Whatever she suffered would remain on his conscience for as long as he lived. He would never forgive himself: *never*. If she was dead, then...

His head dropped in utter desperation at the thought. It would be the bitterest, most soul-destroying event to come to terms with. His brother's death had been bad enough, but to be *responsible* for her capture; he cried out the anguish within him, silently, as one tormented by legions of the damned. He refused to voice his anguish;

his blindness had even ruled out his playing any positive part in the forthcoming battle, so he couldn't even perform any minor tasks in atonement for what he considered his betrayal of her. Hayter's statement was a bitter blow to a man already reeling under the onslaught of his own fears and misplaced beliefs of guilt, which in turn were generated by his love for her; a love which he only vaguely suspected the existence of, but which was there nevertheless. Acceptance of what he felt for her was, in those circumstances, *impossible*. It added *another* burden to a man already struggling under a weight that would have crushed many.

For the ten-thousandth time, he ran the memory of her abduction through his mind. He had *known* that something was wrong. If he had only turned the land rover around and come back to the mansion instead of playing the hero and failing dismally.

He managed to thrust the memory away from his consciousness. It was *too* painful, and yet he took an almost masochistic pleasure in thus punishing himself. He became aware of silence in the study, and turned his face in Hayter's direction. "Did I miss something?"

"Only if you want a drink," Tony told him.

"Yes; coffee please. I can't even help you do that, can I?"

John could hear the laughter in Tony's voice. "You should be enjoying someone waiting on *you* for a change; don't you agree, George?"

"As a matter of fact, I do," Hayter replied softly, as Tony moved out of the study, closing the door loudly behind him. Hayter swiftly glanced at his watch. "An hour or so. John, whilst Tony is out of the room, I want you to know that if...if anything happens to me. ...if I have made a mistake in attacking and you survive, I have *not* forgotten you in my Will. I have always looked upon you as a son, and I hope you'll remember me in a *kindly* light, rather than as a cantankerous old man."

"What's this?" John exclaimed. "*Defeatist* talk from George Hayter? I don't believe it, unless..." he broke off, frowning. "What is it that *you* know that we don't?" he asked slowly, his voice losing its usual tone, becoming informal, friend to friend.

Hayter shrugged but said nothing.

"I want an answer, George. Don't I deserve at least *that* much?"

Hayter looked at him, although John could only feel the piercing gaze. "Promise you'll say nothing to Tony?"

"If I must."

"It's nothing more than a feeling, John, but I've *learned* to trust my feelings over the years. Call it a premonition, if you like, but I *know* that I'm not going to live through this encounter with the Cult. Oh, I'll do my utmost, but I *know* that I'm never going to hear Margaret's voice again."

John felt a sudden return of the desperation which he had recently been feeling.

"I know that I'm *never* going to sleep again; and so it seems that this is where it all ends, for me. I suppose it's better than waiting for my heart to stop, but I'll miss all of you more than words could *ever* express."

"But nothing is *certain*," John insisted.

"True, John. But I *sense* that our association is coming to its end. Strangely, I don't fear dying, I just don't want to leave you and my family — and I've only just acquired my family, after all. If what I am saying turns out to be more than an old man's paranoia, all I ask is that you *don't* forget me."

John gulped down the lump which had risen in his throat, stood, and hesitantly walked in Hayter's direction. The old man met him half way, and they embraced. John's accumulated anguish finally erupted into silent racking sobs as tears coursed down his face and onto Hayter's shoulder.

"George, I *wish* I could say that I've known you to be wrong in the past about such things, but I haven't," he eventually managed to whisper. Hayter patted his back gently, before moving away and leading him back to his seat.

"Try to control yourself before Tony gets back," he said. "I don't want him to know, it might detract from what he will have to do shortly. He must not have anything else on his mind. If I die in front of him, he'll have to cope with it as best he can. I've gone through that scenario with him before, I've done the *best* I could in the time available."

When he returned carrying a tray with coffee pot, cups, saucers, milk jug and sugar bowl a few minutes later, Tony felt the change in the atmosphere, but put it down to nerves about the forthcoming event.

"Not long now, eh?" he said, even managing to inject a trace of eagerness into his voice. "George, I promise you'll be proud of me."

Hayter made a grimace, as though he found the remark distasteful. "I am already proud of you, Tony. I *don't* want you taking any unnecessary risks. Just follow my lead, reinforce my incantations, but don't attempt anything fancy."

"I know, George," he said, pouring the coffee. "I can be disciplined where occultism is concerned, you know."

Hayter smiled, "I'm glad to hear it. We will take our places within the circle about half an hour before attacking. I will negate the barrier at the last possible second."

"Circle?" Tony asked. "I thought you would have at least a pentagram and triangle."

"It's not a *Hammer* film," Hayter snapped back irritably. "In my experience, a circle is just as effective as a pentagram and a lot less trouble to construct. I have erected three concentric circles of differing radii, and

382

laid certain snares around each circumference. Give me *some* credit for knowing what I'm doing, Tony."

Tony grinned ruefully. "I asked for that," he said, sipping his coffee. "What types of surprises have you prepared for anything that gets through?"

"You might see if that happens," Hayter replied enigmatically.

"Action at last," Tony muttered. "The Cult is in for one hell of a surprise in about an hour's time."

***

The Supreme Brother sat facing Fidelis in the chamber they used whilst awaiting notification that all Brothers assembled. Fidelis appeared calm upon the surface, when, in reality he felt as though his stomach was churning sickly inside him. It was only by a conscious effort that he controlled the trembling which he felt.

"Nervous, Gregory?"

"Yes," he admitted. "I think this is a *first* in the history of our Cult. Have we *ever* sacrificed a Baron before?"

"Never. It will *truly* be a feast for our Patrons and it will be simple to have them attack Hayter with us, after the sacrifice. Nothing can prevent our victory. I would have liked the information about Hayter which Margaret Hunter could have supplied, but it can't be helped."

"I could have *strangled* Adam for calling me Fidelis," he said savagely. "She was just about to tell me all..."

"In a way, you have only *yourself* to blame. You did order him *never* to call you Gregory again, and he wasn't here when it was agreed that we would attempt to delude her that you were a discontented and abused Brother."

"Yes," Fidelis agreed. "I see now what you mean about not letting things take you by surprise, to *weigh* the consequences before you speak."

"Then the lesson is not lost. Take comfort in the fact that we all make mistakes — some more than others, though."

"When did *you* last make a mistake?" Gregory queried.

"When I allowed Paul to interrogate his daughter. I know we cannot foresee *everything* that *might* happen, but a Supreme Brother is *supposed* to. Before that, my last mistake was in putting Martin in charge of tracing the Baron lineage. So, you see, Gregory, I make mistakes, but my mistakes aren't *that* visible because they are actually made by other people."

Fidelis was about to reply when a robed figure entered their chamber, not giving any notice that he might want to address either of them except by the noise that he made in his progress. Fidelis met the burning, intense eyes, and nodded his permission to speak.

He had scarcely completed the gesture when, in the zealous voice he always used which tended, despite its quietness, to be heard over all the other voices in the Brotherhood, Jerome said, "Brother Fidelis, Supreme Brother, I report all Brothers are assembled. The altar is prepared, the victim in place. When you be ready, this glorious sacrificial Ritual may begin."

Fidelis nodded his acceptance, smiling slightly.

"Thank you Brother Jerome," Supreme Brother said. "Your loyalty to the Brotherhood, and the exceptional skills which you demonstrate when completing any mission entrusted to you makes you invaluable. Return to your place and assure our Brothers that they will *not* be kept waiting long."

The compliments brought a brief smile to Jerome's lips, but the effect of Supreme Brother's words could be read best by observing his eyes. It was like looking into a furnace which had been stoked to an average capacity suddenly being injected with more highly combustible fuel. His eyes burned more furiously than ever; Fidelis realised that, if he didn't know this man and passed him on the street, he would think him more than a bit unhinged.

Jerome inclined his head to them both, before turning and making his way back to the main cavern.

"What does Jerome do, in private life?" Fidelis asked.

"Jerome? I don't think you would ever manage to guess. He is a Civil Servant; doesn't sound too *grand* does it? Not until you know that he works for the Ministry of Defence, has one of the highest possible security clearances, and is a computer genius. I believe that currently he is working on a completely different type of computer guidance system for nuclear missiles. He gets hold of some *very* interesting information at times."

"I can imagine," Gregory breathed, impressed despite himself.

"I will address the Brothers, and then turn the meeting over to you," said Supreme Brother, returning to the business in hand. "After that, you must do *everything*. If you get into difficulties of any sort I can only help you indirectly. So, bearing that in mind, is there anything, *anything at all*, that you want me to clarify?"

"Yes, just one thing. At the moment of sacrifice, do I have to slide the knife into her heart?"

"No. You can use the knife wherever you like — slit the throat, sever a major artery, but the important thing is that death must follow quickly and you may only use the knife for one cut or thrust. I prefer a thrust to the heart because it is easier to locate than say an artery or vein, and it is certain. Our Patrons would grow unpredictable if these criteria were not met." Gregory nodded his understanding. "Anything else?" Supreme brother asked patiently.

"Nothing," Gregory declared. "I know exactly what to do and when to do it."

"Very well. Are you ready?"

He took two deep breaths, pulled on his mask, stood and nodded.

"Good," Supreme Brother rasped, in an icy tone, "This will be the first sacrifice that I will have been able to sit back and enjoy for nearly twenty years." His face grew sombre, colder by the second as he anticipated the forthcoming Ritual. "Make certain that there is plenty of blood, Gregory," he advised. "Twist the knife as you thrust. But come, we must not delay longer; it is time for our Brothers to be entertained." So saying, he led Gregory out of the room which they shared and slowly, solemnly, they made their way to the main cavern.

The only difference between the cavern as it was now and as it had been after William's execution was the fact that a crude wooden altar had erected upon the dais, towards the left diagonal. A table stood close by with various implements upon it. Spreadeagled and tied upon the altar lay the pale, dirty, welt-covered body of Margaret Hunter. She lay, comatose, unable to offer the slightest resistance to her impending slaughter.

With Supreme Brother leading they ascended the dais and, as Fidelis seated himself, Supreme Brother turned to face the three circles of attentive Brothers, which were more swollen than usual; the entire compliment of the Brotherhood were present, a fact that made him a little wary. That sense which warned of manipulation, of danger, reasserted itself and he ran his eyes not just over the assembly, but over every shadow within the cavern. He moistened his lips with a pale tongue reminiscent of one which might more properly have had its home inside a reptile's jaws.

"Brothers," he began, in that rasping tone that all knew and feared, "Brothers, you will have guessed the reason for our hasty assembly." He glanced pointedly and contemptuously at the figure immobile upon the altar. "You have been summoned to observe — and

386

partake — in a glorious sacrifice. I say glorious, but you may not understand why I say it — not until I impart significant news to you, my Brothers. Look upon her. Devour with your eyes she who is soon to die, to give her blood to our Patrons.

"You may wonder why it is that she is to be sacrificed at this time, when we would not normally sacrifice a human. You might, therefore, deduce that this is no normal sacrifice. No! Brothers, you know as well as I that we sacrifice for only two reasons: in keeping our bargain with our Patrons, or upon occasion when we take an enemy of our Brotherhood prisoner. She falls into *this* category, Brothers. To be brief, Martin and Richard were successful in their mission. The pathetic, filthy excuse for a human being which you see upon the altar is none other than Margaret Hunter."

He paused as a murmur of excitement passed around the assembly. He allowed it to continue for a second before drowning it out with an icy bellow.

"But this in itself does *not* make her our enemy. '*Why*', I hear you ask, '*is she to be sacrificed*?' The answer, Brothers, is simple. Thanks to Brother James, who assisted Fidelis before his promotion, I can tell you that Margaret Hunter is the *last of the American Barons*. This, Brothers, her very *blood* makes her our mortal enemy. You have been in a state of alert for the last few days, lest Hayter attack. Well, my Brothers, action is at hand. Immediately after we sacrifice this *bitch*, descendant of the Barons, then shall we, with our Patron Demons, attack George Hayter, destroy his barrier and eradicate the Baron line from the Earth once and for all!"

This was greeted with thunderous applause from the assembly. Jerome was first upon his feet as a token of his total agreement with this course of action and in respect for the Supreme Brother, who smiled at Jerome as others followed his example and stood.

The Supreme Brother stood, his face resuming its normal frigid expression as his gaze swept around the assembly. Eventually he held up his hand, signalling for the applause to come to an end.

"Brothers, you overwhelm me!" his bleak tone expressed nothing of the feeling which he claimed. "Be seated, Brothers. Brother Fidelis will shortly take charge of the proceedings; but I wish, first of all, to express in front of all assembled, the debt which we owe to James. Initially, Fidelis carried on this course of action, in attempting to trace the Baron lineage, but it was James who carried it through to successful completion. Nor does this reflect badly upon Fidelis; he had other, equally important matters to attend to. Brother James, receive the *commendation* of your Supreme Brother and be assured that your magnificent service will *not* be forgotten."

In the silence which followed this speech, each pondered the ramifications entailed as far as Brother James was concerned. At the very least, he could name his reward — and could ask for any favours he wished. It seemed that when Supreme Brother next needed a reliable Brother for a difficult mission, with lots of prestige attached, James' name would be *high* on the list of candidates.

"And now, Brothers," Supreme Brother continued, "to the matter in hand. Brother Fidelis, when you are ready, you may begin."

Fidelis nodded, but made no move to stand as the Supreme Brother vacated the dais and made his way to a chair near to, but situated a significant distance from, the third circle. He sat, again running his eyes quickly and a little nervously around the cavern. It was too late now, he knew, to stop things. He simply had to cross his fingers and hope.

At last, Fidelis stood. The cavern became as silent as a tomb as Supreme Brother left the dais, but now that things were coming to a climax the silence intensified. Fidelis spoke, his words low and calm, but perfectly audible to those assembled.

"My Brothers, Supreme Brother has spoken very clearly of the debt which we owe James. I wish to reinforce what he said. Were it not for James' tenacity, we might never have realised just whom we had captured. Brothers, join with me now in our Ritual of Sacrifice. Let your responses gratify our Patrons, and may their gratification be boundless when they receive this gift of not merely an enemy of ours, and therefore, of theirs; not only of a Baron, and therefore fit only to be slaughtered; but of a *virgin*. I feel sure our Patrons will appreciate the fact — once they have drunk her blood."

Fidelis was mildly disappointed when he didn't get the rapturous applause which had greeted Supreme Brother's speech but he had the sense to move on quickly, before the lack of response became painfully obvious.

He moved slowly over to the altar where Margaret lay helpless, unaware. He took in the tangled hair, the unnatural pallor of her skin, the almost haggard expression which seemed to remain upon her face, even when so *deeply* unconscious. He found that a part of him was rebelling against her death; a part of him regretted his role in deceiving her; a weak, sentimental part of him demanded that he leave the dais immediately no matter what risks and penalties might be incurred from such an action.

He took a deep breath and dismissed that part of his mind from his awareness. The Baron line had to be destroyed. He reached out and brushed her hair away from her forehead. He glanced at the table to his right and took from it a bottle of oil, although most people would not have recognised it as such. The recipe was somewhat complicated, but Fidelis knew that amongst other things, it contained the essence of suppurated flesh.

He managed to drag his mind from the somewhat nauseating ingredients of the oil, to the reality of what he had to do next. Dipping his thumb and first finger in the thick liquid, he proceeded to anoint Margaret's body; he drew a symbol upon her forehead, one upon each breast, one at the base of her stomach, and finally, two identical symbols upon the insides of her thighs.

He tried to avoid breathing the foul odour which the oil exuded, and had to restrain himself from grimacing. Their Patrons found the odour irresistible, he mused. There was no accounting for taste. He realised that his thoughts were bordering upon the sacrilegious and that the Patron Demons, at the least sign of squeamishness or disapproval, might augment the sacrifice with the officiating Brother as dessert.

He lifted a small bronze amulet and placed it around her neck, tying it in place, then ensuring that the medallion itself lay glinting between her breasts. All the while, he whispered an incantation to their Patrons to find this sacrifice acceptable; having completed it, he turned to the assembly and, in a much louder tone than before, repeated his incantation.

The response, when it came, was almost deafening. In perfect time, so much so that every syllable of every word could be heard clearly, the incantation was boomed back at Fidelis. It had been spoken three times when silence returned, it seemed to each member of the Brotherhood that his sense of hearing had been heightened. It wasn't so, but merely an illusion induced by the response being shouted by so many voices at once.

Fidelis returned to Margaret's inert body. Taking a pot from the table he carefully sprinkled the animal blood which it contained over her, covering her from head to foot with the crimson fluid, staining her skin a deep, vivid vermilion.

Supreme Brother watched Fidelis' actions impassively. He shook his head slightly. Fidelis was a little *too* theatrical, he thought. He didn't radiate the extreme seriousness which any Ritual Sacrifice warranted. Perhaps, he thought, he himself was too serious when conducting the ceremonies. He smiled as he dismissed the idea instantly. The Supreme Brother could never be held accountable for taking his responsibilities *too* seriously. No doubt, in time, Fidelis would take his new position with the gravity it necessitated. Until then, it seemed as though Rituals with a dash of the theatrical were going to be *in vogue*. Supreme Brother groaned inwardly at the thought. Fidelis faced the assembly and began another long incantation, paving the way for the sacrifice which he was soon to make.

Involuntarily, Supreme Brother grunted his approval of Fidelis' handling of *this* part of the Ritual. Every syllable, every accentuation within the incantation was perfect and, he realised, he couldn't have done it better himself. Supreme Brother joined the other Brothers in the ritual response.

Fidelis stood, letting the silence stretch out. It was necessary that he concentrate to his fullest during the next part of the Ritual. Apart from the sacrifice itself, this was the most important incantation — the one which would summon the Cult's Patron Demons. This would be far different to William's execution, where the Demons, had been courteously invited; the incantation which Fidelis was about to utter *demanded* their presence, in fulfilment of the Pact which lay between them and the Cult. It was this incantation which both summoned the Demons and protected the Cult's members from their Patrons' natural malevolence; any mistakes could be disastrous.

The silence grew deeper, more intense, as Fidelis gathered his concentration, took several deep breaths,

and then roared in a voice which made everyone —
including Supreme Brother — jump in their seats.

"I, Fidelis, summon D—; I, Fidelis, summon G—;
Patrons of our Cult draw near, I command, I command, *I
COMMAND*. Make haste to your feast of virgin blood..."

Supreme Brother nodded at the power and authority
which Fidelis had managed to inject into his voice; he
was suitably impressed. As the incantation continued, in
a language so ancient it was no longer spoken as such
and considered to be dead, he knew that he had not been
mistaken in his choice of successor. Fidelis would make
a *worthy* Supreme Brother, if schooled correctly.

His musings were interrupted some moments later, as
Fidelis uttered the last line of a complex and difficult
incantation. It was evident from his demeanour that he
knew he had not made one mistake, had phrased every
sentence perfectly. He stood expectantly upon the dais,
waiting for the Patron Demons to obey his summons.

They weren't slow in obeying. Drawn by their Pact,
and by Fidelis' incantation, the Demons lost no time.
The primary indication of their presence was a
deepening, an intensification of the iciness which
permeated the cavern. Even though the Brothers were
normally impervious to such considerations, each felt the
sharp change in temperature; a sudden frigidity in the
air. Slowly, in stark contrast to William's execution, they
began to materialise to the left of and several feet above
the dais, waiting.

Even after their materialisation was complete they
remained insubstantial creatures, appearing to the naked
eye to be nothing more than swirling mist within vaguely
animal/human forms. The mist continued to change hue
as though the two Demons, separated by about four feet,
were vying with each other to see which could achieve
the most nauseating effect. Any attempt to focus upon
either demon was doomed to failure by the constant

shifting of the mist, the nauseating colours they generated and their very insubstantiality.

Fidelis allowed a slight pause in order that the Demons' presence might inspire the correct amount of reverential awe upon the Brothers, an effect which the Demons always managed to instil upon those watching once they had manifested themselves. He turned to face the two swirling multi-hued, spectral entities which seemed to hover just a few feet in front of and slightly above him. He bowed respectfully, and began a brief incantation which welcomed the Demons and assured them of blood to flow for them, of a body and soul to be defiled in every way imaginable and in a few that were quite *un*imaginable.

The colours swirled and cascaded in a sick parody of excitement. Slowly, they began drifting — although they weren't carried upon air currents, the motion was entirely deliberate — in the direction of the altar, as though to view and examine for the first time exactly what delights this virginal human sacrifice might afford them. The colours swirled ever more violently as the Demons began working themselves up to a frenzy of desire to rip and shred human skin, to drink human blood, to possess and defile utterly and completely the helpless human captive soon to be theirs.

Fidelis allowed a slight smile to cross his features, despite the seriousness of his part in these proceedings. They could do *nothing* until he performed the sacrifice, no matter how much they worked themselves up. The danger, of course, was that if he kept them waiting *too* long they could conceivably turn upon him. What made the whole scene so lurid and gruesome was the fact that the only indication which the Demons gave as to their state of frenzy was the speed of the swirling colours. They made no noise as such although they could, when they chose, as every Brother knew, communicate with the Cult quite easily. The lack of noise added an eerie

393

dimension to the Ritual, a sense of unreality, paradoxically, within a very real context.

Slowly, Fidelis reached his hand out towards the table, and picked up the razor-sharp Sacrificial Knife. It was perfectly balanced. For a second he saw *himself* reflected in the long, slim blade. He moved to the altar and stood over Margaret, slowly extending both arms and then letting both hands grasp the knife's hilt. He held the knife above her chest for a long moment, heightening the tension which everyone felt. At last the moment came and he raised the knife a few inches, preparing to plunge it *deep* into her heart.

Supreme Brother watched Fidelis intently; he nodded approval to himself of Fidelis' handling of the Demons, of waiting long enough but not *too* long before preparing for the slaughter. The Demons had worked themselves up to such a fever pitch that Supreme Brother *knew* that the destruction of Hayter was going to be much less difficult than he had supposed. Their Patrons would exert themselves to their limits, if need be. He began to feel easier in his mind, as he saw Fidelis extend his arms and hold the knife above Margaret's chest. He sat almost mesmerized by that knife. After many long seconds had passed he saw Fidelis raise his arms slightly, in preparation for the killing stroke.

It was at *that* very moment the Supreme Brother realised that something had gone very, *very* wrong.

***

Tony led John in Hayter's wake, as he led them to the place which he had prepared. Tony was more than a little surprised at being taken to Hayter's bedroom.

Before he could ask any questions Hayter led them through to his dressing room, and without hesitation opened a hidden door situated immediately to the left of a wardrobe. Steps led down. Hayter descended. Tony paused for a second before following.

"Steps, John, quite a lot of them. Keep hold of me."

394

"But where *are* we? John demanded.

"Some kind of secret passage leading from George's dressing room. Did you know about it?"

"*No*," John muttered, bitterly. "I'll bet we have just found the twelfth piano."

"The *what*?"

"Nothing," he whispered.

They continued following Hayter down the steps. Tony wondered why the air didn't seem at all stagnant or stale. As they reached the bottom of the steps, a strip light flickered into life revealing a large room with three exits.

"We're actually in the cellars," Hayter stated, as he began walking towards the opening which faced him.

"I thought the garage was built above the cellar," John objected.

"Yes, but these are the *original* cellars. Very old," he replied casually.

They made their way into a second room which was almost as bare as the first except for a concert grand piano which stood in the centre of the room, a piano stool and briefcase next to it.

Hayter passed the piano without appearing to look at it but he whispered, "Goodbye, old friend," under his breath as they passed. There was only one exit from this room other than the one by which they had entered and it was through this that his preparations — what could be seen of them — were visible.

A large table holding a copy of Anton's book, a brazier, some incense, a pentagram drawn in black upon a sheet of white card and a crystal. Apart from this, the room was bare. Hayter stepped up to the table without any hesitation; Tony followed leading John, a little more hesitantly. He glanced around at the floor.

"Don't see your circles," he commented.

Hayter gave him a withering look. "Drawn circles can be erased just as easily as constructed. My circles are drawn by the power of my mind, and *nothing* short of death or unconsciousness can erase them."

Tony concentrated upon the floor and soon saw, through his finer perceptions, the circles which Hayter had placed around them, appearing as fine lines of white-hot intensity. John sat, clumsily, upon the floor, muttering darkly to himself. He had never felt more helpless. Tony moved his gaze from John to Hayter who was absorbed in checking the implements upon the table. The small brazier burst into life as Hayter pointed at it, and he grunted in satisfaction. He placed some incense upon the charcoal and it gave off a heavy fragrance as it was consumed.

"Any last questions?" Hayter queried.

"No, I just follow your lead — I only take over if you are incapacitated somehow."

Hayter nodded and looked at John, who had turned his head in the direction of Hayter's voice, for the last time. He took a deep breath and said, "Well, Tony, it's now or never. Ready?"

At Tony's nod, Hayter began to concentrate. "I'll negate the barrier first, then let's see just how well these Cultists fare against George Hayter."

Tony felt, rather than deduced, the second when the barrier was dissolved. He heard Hayter softly speaking an incantation, summoning all his concentration and will to release an intense blast of pure occult energy at the ruins and at what evil those ruins concealed. Hayter closed his eyes and smiled slightly a few seconds later.

"Destroyed their barrier at the first attempt! I'll try a direct attack upon them but I think they'll be ready for me — if that's the case, we begin Anton's Ritual of Destruction. Understood?"

Tony nodded, but realised that Hayter couldn't have seen what he was doing. "Yes, George," he managed to whisper.

Again, Hayter muttered an incantation, but as more of a chant this time; he focussed upon everything radiating vibrations in conflict with his own.

Tony felt the surge of energy building up all around them, and felt the hairs upon the back of his neck rise up. He felt the sudden discharge of power and stood expectantly, waiting for George's message of success, but it never came; instead the energy was met with a force at least equal to itself. They came together with a sound like a clap of thunder which made the walls tremble. Tony glanced around uneasily. The sound re-echoed off the walls, and at last Hayter spoke.

"We go to Anton's Ritual — there are too many of them for me to tackle alone!"

Tony nodded his understanding, and opened the book to the correct page as Hayter added more incense to the brazier.

***

What…??????
Where….??????????

I am *aware*! *My time has come*. The circle is almost complete. *Death* and *vengeance* are *mine*. But time grows short; I must intervene lest all be lost, and *that* may not happen. Waiting for so long would have blunted another's sense of what he must do — but *not* mine. The *power* which is my due *returns to me*.

I AM AWARE. I see all. I know what is happening / has happened. There is danger. *EXTREME DANGER*. One who is *close* to me needs my aid.

SHE IS HELD BY THE HAND OF MINE ETERNAL ENEMIES. NOW SHALL THEY SEE. NOW SHALL ALL SEE AND BELIEVE THAT ANTON BARON WAS/IS THE GREATEST MAGICIAN THAT THIS WORLD HAS EVER SEEN. But first, I must *protect* she whose life *depends* upon me...

***

It was the shock which came from Hayter's initial blast at the force which had been placed around the ruins which jerked Supreme Brother's mind away from the impending sacrifice. His foreboding came back to him, even as he struggled to maintain the force protecting the ruins. His shock and surprise were such that, coupled with the strength of Hayter's onslaught, the Supreme Brother could do nothing apart from allowing his defence to be shattered.

He opened his mouth to tell Fidelis to hurry with the sacrifice, contrary to all accepted rules — which didn't matter a damn now that they were being attacked — but in the end he said nothing. He stood, mouth open in amazement. As Fidelis began the downward swing which would terminate her existence, Margaret's eyes opened abruptly. They opened *abnormally* wide. Supreme Brother saw her lift her head slightly and glare at Fidelis with such malevolence that he stepped away from her. The knife fell from his hands and then, almost as though he had been physically assaulted, he jumped back from her vicinity.

The Demons suddenly added to the confusion. Enraged by the denial of the sacrifice, by the fact that they had been promised human blood to feast upon, they shrieked their anger and frustration in high, ear-piercing howls.

All Brothers realised that, although they might not understand exactly what was happening, their Patrons could turn on them at any moment; but such was the discipline inculcated in them by their Supreme Brother, such was their fear of him, that not one Brother gave way to panic, although a lot would have liked to.

Supreme Brother was furiously aware that Hayter would follow up his destruction of the protective force which had surrounded the ruins almost immediately. "Brothers," he bellowed, with the full force of his lungs, drowning out even the wailing of the Demons. "We are

398

attacked; attune your thoughts with mine, give me your support that the next attack be repulsed."

The result was almost instantaneous. He felt the concentration of his brethren unite; their will and power began to flood through him. He located the place from which the attack had been launched and was not in the least surprised that it had come from Hayter's mansion, and that now the protective barrier had been nullified. What *did* confuse him was the fact that Hayter had attacked at the *worst possible* time as far as the Cult was concerned, and at the most opportune time as far as he, Hayter, was concerned. How had he managed to time it so accurately? From whence had he gained his information? It was *not* coincidence, which Supreme Brother did not believe in, anyway. Was there yet *another* traitor in their midst? He was certain that that was *not* the case.

He remembered earlier thinking that maybe Hayter knew something which he, Supreme Brother did not; although he had been *more* than a little sceptical about the possibility at the time, he now realised that that sensitive part of his mind had been trying to give him some *intuitive* insight into what to expect. He, in his pride and arrogance, had chosen to refuse to believe such a thing; not long ago, Fidelis had asked him: when was the last time that he had made a mistake. He remembered his cynical answer that the Supreme Brother didn't *appear* to make mistakes because other people made them for him. He knew that he had made an extremely serious mistake this time, however, and saw that it might *just* mean the end of the Cult. Attacked by Hayter on one side — if their Patrons turned upon them for being denied their right under the terms of the Pact... It was certain that they would withhold their aid in any enterprise against Hayter unless the sacrifice was completed.

Whilst one side of his mind ran frantically upon these lines, another prepared the counter-attack aimed directly at the point of origin of Hayter's assault. The energy erupted from him, only to meet Hayter's second wave and both forces, he could feel, neutralised each other.

"Fidelis — perform the sacrifice, quickly," Supreme Brother yelled, as other Brothers crowded around him, attempting to form a crude circle of bodies.

Brother Fidelis was still reeling from the shock which he had sustained when Margaret had opened her eyes and glared at him. There was *death* in those eyes, deep malevolence the like of which he had never before experienced. He had been moved away from her — had felt an intense squeezing upon his wrists, forcing him to let go of the knife. And then, as though he now posed no threat whatsoever, had felt himself casually thrown to the other side of the dais, effortlessly, although he managed to keep upright and to maintain his balance.

Since then Margaret had lain still upon the altar, her eyes widely open, but totally blank as though the consciousness which she had evinced a few seconds ago had left her.

He caught the word *possession* running through his mind but couldn't imagine anything short of a demigod which could have generated the power, the *malevolence* which he had felt. It was about then that the demons had begun their insane howling, noise so intense and ear-piercing he had to clap his hands over his ears in an attempt to protect them.

Then, either their ululations had dropped in intensity or his ears had become accustomed to what they were being subjected to because he heard plainly the Supreme Brother's declaration that they were being attacked and the command for everyone to attune his thoughts with Supreme Brother's. It was an order with which Fidelis failed to comply. He knew that Supreme Brother had ample power of his own augmented by that of the

Demons, plus the combined strength of the rest of the Cult; he was *extremely* conscious of the fact that the Demons were not very far away from him and were getting angrier by the second.

He felt the discharge of power which Supreme Brother had directed at the Hayter mansion — although he didn't know for *certain* that that was where the energy had been channelled to. Then came Supreme Brother's roar to complete the sacrifice as the only simple way to pacify their irate Patrons. He nodded, rushed for the knife...and came up short as though he had run into a glass screen. Angrily, he tried to press against it, to break through, but it simply would not yield. Anxiously, he turned and locked eyes with the Supreme Brother.

"She's protected somehow. I can't get to her."

Supreme Brother directed a blast of energy at the altar — wide of Fidelis, but it simply rebounded, forcing him to neutralize it. "Damn: Hayter's creation, no doubt," he muttered.

He felt the anxious glances of the other Brothers upon him, He had to assert his authority. "Brother Martin, prepare to meet any interim attack which Hayter might make. Brother Paul, assist him. Brother Richard, prepare another attack upon Hayter — try to keep him occupied. Brothers Graham and Alex, assist Richard."

As Supreme Brother rapped out these commands, a new sense of order asserted itself amongst the Cultists. Supreme Brother glared at the Demons upon the dais and then, gently, began to talk to them.

The angry swirling of colours slowed as he caught their attention. His mind became flooded with questions and demands from these spectral visitors. '*Why had they not been given their due? Was their own Cult reneging upon the ancient Pact?*' It was the first breach of trust between them — they demanded their sacrifice. '*Why*

401

had they been denied? Who dared *to deny them their blood?*'

"Patience," Supreme Brother formed the words in his mind, seeing a chance to enlist their aid after all. "It is not our doing — but a member of the Baron family, our sworn enemies *and* yours. It is *they* who seek to refuse you your rightful due in an attempt to make you turn upon *us* and destroy us for them."

He beamed with pleasure as he felt the Demons listen to his explanation cautiously, at first, and then turn their attention and anger away from the Cult as they examined his words and found truth in what he said. They began to radiate utter fury, palpable waves of it, but Supreme Brother knew now that it was not directed at him or at any of the Brothers, but at the Baron lineage.

"Help us destroy them, and you *shall have* your sacrifice — and them as well. Let our Pact be our guide in this. I, Supreme Brother, have *never* attempted to rob you of your right and have always defended the Pact which we *both* honour. You *know* this to be true."

'*What if we fail?*' the thought flooded his mind. '*How then would you save us from being robbed? Would you give your life in place of she that was to be ours?*'

Supreme Brother trembled at the thought. "No," he sent back. "I am *too* valuable to your earthly subjects to be your sacrifice."

'*Then would your successor take her place?*' queried one of the Demons.

"Yes," he answered, thinking nothing of staking Fidelis' life against the possibility of failure.

'*Then, Supreme Brother, you have our aid. Use it wisely. We are at your command.*'

Supreme Brother glanced around at the assembly. "All Brothers join in attacking Hayter; give him no respite. Our Patrons will aid us at my command." His bleak countenance remained icy even as grins of encouragement were beamed from one Brother to

402

another. Confidence infused them — for *who* could stand against the Cult's Patrons? The answer was painfully obvious: the Demons would overwhelm Hayter and Tony Baron with scarcely a second thought.

Supreme Brother was still uneasy. He thought about the barrier protecting Margaret Hunter from becoming their sacrifice. *How* was Hayter managing to project that protection and *still* ward off the attacks that were being launched at him one after the other? Was he *that* brilliant an occultist? Or had he underestimated Tony Baron's abilities? He rubbed his chin thoughtfully. Perhaps it was time to unleash the Demons upon Hayter, before he could demonstrate any *more* surprises.

***

Hayter refused to be distracted by the flashes and roars of attack and neutralisation, even though he was deflecting and neutralising the Cult's attacks himself, almost unconsciously. The Ritual of Destruction demanded his utmost attention; its complexity was such that all other considerations were blanked out. Nothing else existed; even though Tony provided the ritual responses nervously, Hayter hardly heard him.

Attack after attack, wave after wave still saw Hayter calmly speaking invocations, preparing for the climax of the Ritual which would destroy the Cult in one almighty eruption of savage, relentless energy.

Tony turned the pages of the volume upon the table, with which he had become so familiar in the past few days. His heart was pounding, his mouth and lips dry, his responses cracked and hoarse. Bolt after bolt of red energy assaulted them, to be brought up short against the three circles.

Eventually, something *had* to give.

He became aware of the silence as Hayter ceased his invocations. He knew that there must be a period of silence before the next stage of the Ritual could commence. Another furious bolt of energy hit the circles and seemed, for a second, to overpower the outer ring. Hayter glanced at it, casually, and the energy dissipated — leaving Tony a clear view of the two remaining circles which protected them.

Two circles. He looked at Hayter, who merely shrugged his shoulders, his mind elsewhere. He began the next stage of the Ritual as though nothing had happened. Tony felt his heart hammering in his chest almost threatening to burst, so it seemed. He glanced at John who was seated upon the floor, silent and oblivious to what was happening. He reached out and squeezed his shoulder, saw a trace of a smile edge onto his features.

He became aware of silence again and knew that he had forgotten the response. Panic built up within him as yet another wave of occult energy, directed with pinpoint accuracy by the Cult, crashed into their protective circle.

He glared intently at the page and stammered out the response; saw George's eyes upon him, *reproaching* him for his lack of concentration and discipline. That moment would haunt him until the day he died. He took a deep breath and tried to appear as calm as George himself; it didn't work. Hayter's invocations took on a new pattern as he began building up to the climax of the ritual — which he had corrected himself. Tony began to feel a faint vibration beneath his feet and thought at first that it was some new manifestation of the Cult's attack; he then realised that it was the forces which Hayter was calling upon answering the summons, becoming more agitated as the invocations were instilled with *more* power and urgency. The underlying beat of the Ritual grew up and up, more and more urgent, towards an *immense* crescendo of power which Tony had never even *imagined* could exist — and which he would never again experience.

Another bolt of fire assaulted their meagre refuge as Hayter prepared to finish the Ritual with the last incantation. He knew that he was perhaps just five minutes away from destroying the Cult once and for all as the energy bolt hit, *tearing* away the second circle and forcing him to check his defences before engaging upon the most difficult incantation which he would ever attempt.

All his will-power and concentration were locked firmly upon the Ritual in hand, to the exclusion of all else. He briefly surveyed the ruins of his defences and marvelled that they had survived so long under such an intense barrage. As his absorption in the Ritual had deepened he had unknowingly relaxed his concentration upon his defences and had weakened them to the point where the Cult had managed to destroy two of them. Quickly, he decided that he could do one of two things — repair the damage and ruin the Ritual, or continue with the Ritual and hope that the final defence would stand. It was a decision which he didn't even have to think about. He opened his mouth to begin the *final* incantation, when another thought struck him.

Anton Baron had paid for his Pact with his life — and the Ancient Law demanded life for life. Could it be that Anton's resurrection was dependent upon *another* sacrifice? A life given *willingly*? He nodded slowly to himself, seeing how events could come full circle.

Suddenly, as though a connection had been made allowing light to fall where none had before, he *knew* exactly what he had to do. He had no *proof* that what he would do would save Margaret, Tony and John; it was *just* a feeling; but Hayter *trusted* his feelings.

He began the final incantation in ringing tones, startling Tony who gazed at their defence of just one circle — a line of pale white rather than the burning, brilliant light that it had been when they had entered. He turned pages, added incense, but paid no heed to the incantation which Hayter was using.

Tony looked towards the far end of the room in disbelief. Two objects had begun to materialise out of

405

the air, their shapes indistinct; the swirling colours which radiated from them nauseating him, even as he managed to make the *last* ritual response. Hayter carried on in an even tone, his eyes locked upon the two spectral visitors.

They slowly advanced towards the circle, a high pitched wailing of glee or of unholy anticipation emanating from them. Tony knew that Hayter could not reinforce their barrier himself, so he attempted it, muttering his own invocations.

Hayter's voice rose to a shriek as he reached the *final climactic line* of the incantation.

It was then that Tony finally heard what Hayter was saying, and he realised, with dread clutching his heart in a grip of ice, that Hayter had used the flawed ending to the Ritual.

He hesitated, and in that second lost the concentration needed to maintain the integrity of the protective circle. "*No*, George," he yelled belatedly as the Demons, now fully materialised, launched themselves towards the circle, negating it; a final bolt of energy flashed through the room and seemed to hit Hayter full in the chest, knocking him off balance. His arms flew backwards in reaction, and collided with Tony, who in turn stumbled over John.

The crimson bolt seemed to run up and down Hayter's body, leaving it smoking and twitching. He moaned once quietly — but that was *more* than enough to tell Tony and John, now certain that their last moments had come, that he was in *agony*.

Tony scrambled to his knees to see what was happening, and was in time to see the red bolt of energy flicker out, and Hayter lying prone upon the floor less than three yards away. Shock flooded his being. The fact that he was defenceless and only metres away from two creatures which could probably destroy him with one angry thought meant nothing. He looked upon the body of George Hayter, seeing the pale face and *open*, staring eyes. He knelt where he was, waiting for his demise, for *oblivion* to overtake him. He didn't care any more *what* happened to him.

John slowly crawled over to Hayter — or so it seemed from Tony's perception — and he cradled Hayter's head in his hands, tears running down his face only to drip upon that of the corpse which he held.

"George, did you *have* to be right about *this*, too?" he cried, turning his face up to the ceiling, despair and pain etched starkly upon it.

Curiously, the Demons made no move towards their enemies, but seemed daunted, baffled and unsure. The light began to fade, almost as though someone had decided to draw a curtain across the death of George Hayter.

***

"Brother Richard, how go our attacks?"

Richard felt confident enough to break from the circle formed by his colleagues to report to Supreme Brother personally. "Excellently well. Initially, they neutralised our energy bolts, but a few of them hit. Hayter had apparently prepared a triple circle to aid him in repulsing our attack. We have just destroyed the second of these. Hayter seems to be making no effort to repair his shields, which makes me wonder whether or not we are doing the right thing. It could be an elaborate trap, after all."

Supreme Brother thought on this for several minutes. "No, I don't think it's a trap — he's over-extended himself in protecting the Hunter *bitch*. I think that the time has come for our Patrons and George Hayter to meet."

Richard nodded, and returned to the brethren. Supreme Brother mentally contacted the still-angry Demons. "The time is now — attack Hayter and *destroy* him," he ordered them.

The Demons swirled in a chaotic display of demented eagerness, and slowly faded. The attention of the whole

Brotherhood centred upon the fact that their Patrons were taking the fight direct to Hayter, and none doubted the outcome.

Brother Richard was the first to detect that Hayter's last circle had been overcome, and he was ready for it. He instantly directed a bolt of energy towards Hayter into which he mixed all his hatred for the Baron line. Thus, it was Richard who was responsible for the demise of Hayter — *and* for what was to follow.

There was utter silence. Even the Supreme Brother was stunned. They had succeeded. Hayter was dead. Tony Baron would soon follow. Their Patrons were there, and they would play with him for a *long* time before they even thought about terminating his life — with suitable slowness and excruciating pain, of course. Brother glanced at Brother, each seeing the same look of disbelief and ecstasy upon every other face. Nobody moved, nobody said anything. It was a *supreme* moment to savour. Supreme Brother regained his composure first, and feeling wildly elated inside, glanced to the dais where Fidelis stood, several paces from the altar where Margaret Hunter still lay helpless. The light reflected off the pendant that she wore between her breasts. He was about to order Fidelis to complete the sacrifice when he felt again that sense of having been manipulated, of not being in control. Carefully, he threw a part of his awareness in Margaret's direction, only to find that he could not reach her. She was *still* protected. Frowning, he began to think of *any* possible way that Hayter could have brought this effect about, but could not think of any. If that was the case, it was obvious that someone *else* was doing it. But *who*? Tony Baron?

Abruptly, he swung back to face the Brothers, who were only now beginning to murmur their delight to each other. Throwing out his awareness he found the Demons seemingly ready to devour the two humans who remained, but Supreme Brother felt their confusion, knew that they could sense *something* which he could not — and that made him wary of ordering them forward to attack. He felt *no* occult vibrations whatsoever so he knew that whoever it was maintaining the protection around Margaret Hunter, it was *not* Tony Baron. He drew his awareness back to himself. The main chamber and the Brothers it contained came into focus. All the Brotherhood were assembled here.

All the Brotherhood.

ALL.

Danger signals began to go off in his mind, although why he could not have explained. He turned back towards the dais to see Fidelis still standing in the same position, apparently petrified, rooted to the spot. Angrily, Supreme Brother opened his mouth to shout to him to come to his senses, when he noticed that *something* had changed. He searched his mind for a second to make the connection and then it came. The pendant which Margaret wore was no longer reflecting the light into his eyes. It was then he noticed that the light had begun to fade, almost as though someone had decided to draw a curtain across recent events.

He wasn't the only one to notice. From expressions of ecstasy, the Brothers' expressions began to display concern, disbelief. The light surrounding them continued to fade until the cavern walls could no longer he seen; they could still see each other, but beyond them on every side inky blackness descended, as though beyond the perimeter which they themselves formed, no light could penetrate.

"Supreme Brother!" exclaimed a voice which he recognised as Brother David's. He looked in the direction from which the voice originated and then beyond, as his eyes took in the *impossible*.

About fifty yards away, growing clearer all the time, were Tony Baron and John Brandon, who was still cradling Hayter's body. A few yards distant from them were the Demons, still seeming distinctly uneasy. He knew of nothing which could have accomplished such a feat as he was witnessing, but his *own* feelings of imminent disaster suddenly intensified, filling him with the knowledge that he *had* to escape, somehow. He noticed Richard raise his arms as though about to release an attack of sorts but after a few seconds they fell back to his sides.

"Something *prevents* me from summoning, Supreme Brother, I don't know what it is."

Supreme Brother tried the experiment, but found that Richard spoke the truth. The Cult was paralysed, helpless. He saw Tony Baron move his head and glare a look at them so savage in its stark hatred that even Supreme Brother hesitated to meet it.

Then the glance moved beyond him and he could see Tony's expression change as a multitude of emotions coursed through him. He said something and John Brandon, who had been cradling Hayter's head all the while, turned his attention to the Cult. They both seemed as surprised as the Brotherhood at this unexpected and unnatural meeting.

"*GREETINGS, MINE ETERNAL ENEMIES,*" the deep booming voice echoed around them. Before any could collect themselves sufficiently to ask anything, the voice continued. "*I prevent you from summoning your puny power — I am your destruction, your doom,*" the voice broke into a menacing laugh, before continuing, this time transferring the menace into the voice. "*I am Anton Baron, whom you thought to have destroyed centuries ago. You did not succeed; your failure to suspect my intentions, to allow them to come to fruition demonstrates my brilliance, and* your *ineptitude. I am the greatest occultist ever to have lived and now, time having gone full circle, the payment having been made in the prescribed manner, I have returned to complete what I left incomplete. Your destruction, Brothers. Your*

410

annihilation. Even now you gloat *over slaughtering a member of my family. Your rejoicing is inappropriate, Brothers. You did* not *kill him. He sacrificed himself,* willingly, *paving the way for my return, and your destruction.*"

The voice had been coming closer and closer, and now it seemed as though it was amongst them. All glanced around uneasily to see Margaret breathe deeply and sit up; the cords with which she had been bound apparently falling away from her. Her hands located the pendant, which she tore off and threw away. She smeared the blood upon her body as though not used to this form and trying to acquaint herself with it.

She regarded the assembly disdainfully, and then looked at Fidelis. A second later he was launched from the dais towards the brethren. They prevented his landing breaking his neck.

"*Ah...your Patrons are uneasy, I see. Draw near, demons of discord; I* dismiss *you to return back to your netherworld of darkness and decay. DEPART, I say.*" The voice issuing from Margaret's throat demanded obedience, yet still the demons refused to leave.

'*If we failed, we were promised one here in place of our lawful sacrifice. Would you deprive us of our lawful right?*' Although it was not spoken, each of them heard that clearly in his own mind. Margaret appeared to consider what had been said.

"*Very well, spawn of hatred. Of myself, I would give you* nothing — *yet I, too, am circumscribed by laws. You may take your due, but depart immediately. I am not renowned for my patience.*"

Instantly, both demons disappeared into Brother Fidelis, who didn't realise what was happening before he felt his internal organs being devoured by the beings to whom he had devoted his life. He screamed more loudly and horribly than either William or Margaret had done. He opened his mouth to scream again and a crimson arc

411

of blood cascaded from him. Twitching in his death throes, he fell to the floor. There was total silence. The demons had been paid, and had departed as Anton Baron had ordered.

"You abused this body which I now wear. When a mortal, you may have been able to defeat me, but now I am more numerous than you could ever understand. It is MY time. Come Hayter, come Tony, join me in my work of destruction begun so many years ago."

Margaret/Anton stopped speaking and turned his/her eyes upon the small party huddled less than fifty yards away upon the floor. His/her eyes took on a red glow and a terrified murmur went around the assembly as, slowly, George Hayter got to his feet, followed by Tony. They advanced towards the Brothers, eyes glaring, echoing the red glow which emanated from Margaret/Anton.

John was left alone to shout, "Tony? George? What's *happening*?" He stumbled to his feet and began to trail in their wake, instinct guiding him.

Tony moved to his right, Hayter to his left. With Margaret as the apex they formed an equilateral triangle, trapping the Cultists inside. It was as they reached this position that panic finally overcame them, and they tried to flee but found themselves bound within the triangle which had been formed. Margaret/Anton glared at one Cultist and he stopped dead, desperately trying to tear himself away from whatever force held him captive. His body was slowly bent back upon itself until sinews stood out starkly against the skin. A splintering sound told of bones breaking and grinding together. His skin was stretched tighter and tighter against his skeleton until it finally ruptured and blood erupted from so many places at once it seemed as though he had exploded.

Hayter glared at another, and he exploded into flame, but from inside. He ran around wildly shrieking and screaming his agony, but only adding to the panic which the other members of the Cult were feeling.

Supreme Brother knew that this was the end of the Cult, but he was determined that it would not be the end of *him*, and whilst he lived the Cult could *not* be destroyed. He glanced quickly around and saw that only *two* Brothers shared his perception of the carnage surrounding them. Only *two* thought rationally at this moment, as did he. Only *two* were determined to escape as was he. Their glances locked. The two others came cautiously to stand at Supreme Brother's side as he chanted an obscure incantation — not one of attack or defence and therefore *not* absorbed by Anton, but one totally in sympathy with him. It was so much so that it didn't even register in Anton's awareness as three Brothers slowly faded and managed to relocate themselves from that nightmare into territory more familiar.

Several bodies lay strewn where they had fallen, the rest were yelling in abject terror, when Margaret/Anton broke from his/her grisly vengeance and considered.

"This is too slow. Let them be destroyed in one almighty cataclysm, releasing me to my rest; I am weary."

The light began to return and the cavern walls could again be discerned. The dead lay where they had died; the living scrambling madly towards the exit. Margaret Hunter was nowhere to be seen; neither were John, Tony, or Hayter.

The majority of Cultists, unable to believe that they might yet get out of this situation alive, were the cause of the bottleneck which prevented *anyone* from leaving. People fell, were jammed up against the sides of the rock wall; some were nearly suffocated. It was then that the rumbling sound began. Silence descended for a second and then yells and pleas and screams echoed around the stone walls, filling the caverns with the sounds of utter despair. The ruins of the church where they had for so long practised *all* manner of depravities was about to become — ironically enough — their tomb.

The rumbling noise came closer, became louder, more intense. The rock floor began to heave; blocks of jagged stone fell from the roof causing many of the Cultists to fall stunned to the ground, and thus they were spared awareness of their final moments of life.

With a sickening, grating sound, the floor cracked open. The walls which had supported the roof for so many years finally caved in under the strain. The remaining Cultists were buried under the avalanche of rock, mangling their bodies beyond *any* hope of recognition.

***

Several miles away, three figures sat in a car debating what they should do.

"Our only safety — *now* — lies in joining our American Brethren. We are not defeated yet," said the first, wincing slightly as he moved his arm.

"Be careful of your arm, you twisted it badly. Try to let it rest. Really, it should be x-rayed," the second commented.

"We shall yet emerge victorious," muttered the third, glaring at the other two zealously.

"My company has a private jet for important occasions. I think that perhaps this is one of them. Let us beat a tactical retreat, for the present," instructed the first.

The other two nodded agreement.

***

Tony opened his eyes, unable to believe the *intensity* of the pounding in his head. Visions poured through him; mangled bodies, him tearing them limb from limb just by willing it to happen — and yet it hadn't been *him* performing the various atrocities. He remembered when his glance had fallen briefly upon John: he had been an

414

instant away from setting him ablaze when awareness of who he was had impinged into that *other* consciousness.

He managed to glance around weakly, before he lapsed again into unconsciousness.

Chapter Seventeen: Legacies

Tony entered the white, sterile, antiseptic-smelling corridors of the private hospital some five weeks later, still feeling curiously out of place carrying a bunch of flowers. It was a ritual which he had performed every day since Margaret had been brought here. The days blurred into each other, mainly because each one was so similar to its predecessor. Although the hospital itself was more cheerful a place than he normally would have expected, each visit he made sent a wave of depression through him. For the first three weeks he had visited twice a day, but had soon realised that his resultant feelings of desperation took so much out of him that he couldn't cope with them. For this reason he now only visited once a day.

It required a conscious effort on his part to force himself to go through the daily ritual. The fact that John was ensconced in the same hospital did, at times, make the obligation which Tony felt less onerous. His feelings were mixed. He had convinced himself that he had contributed to Hayter's death by allowing him to use the flawed ending to the ritual — although how he could have prevented it he hadn't even thought about. He had accepted the depth of his love for Margaret, but this made him feel more *responsible* than he had ever believed possible, when he considered the danger to which he had exposed her without a second thought. He thought over times he had neglected her, taken her for granted, and felt the desperation which these days seemed to be a part of him, begin to overwhelm him. He couldn't get used to the idea that Hayter was dead, John blind, Margaret comatose. It seemed so grossly unfair — even when taking the fact of the Cult's annihilation into account — that they should *continue* to suffer as a result of their victory.

He thought back to the moment he had regained consciousness, of his partial memory of Anton Baron's possession of the three of them; his dimly incredulous perception that Margaret lay unconscious a few yards away from him, apparently relocated there by Anton; John groaning as he lay face down; the stiffening form of George Hayter, unmistakably dead, eyes staring at nothing. John had come to and insisted that they get Margaret to hospital — Hayter too, although nothing could be done for him. Complicated questions had ensued, which Tony and John had managed to ward off with an unlikely version of what had actually happened. A group of depraved perverts had kidnapped Margaret and held her under the ruins of the church upon the moor. Hayter had refused to inform the police, fearing for her life if he did so. Leaving Hayter at the mansion, they had attempted her rescue only after managing to follow one of the group to their hideaway, days later. They had succeeded in rescuing her, but she seemed deeply unconscious. Then the ground had begun to shake, trapping the kidnappers under the ruins.

Returning to the mansion, John had taken a turn too quickly in the land rover, causing it to overturn, and ended up concussed and blind. When they finally reached Hayter's domain, the relief and shock of these events had resulted in Hayter having a heart attack — the official cause of death. From there they had made their way to the hospital as quickly as possible — despite the fact that Tony's car refused to start. It didn't surprise him that the police didn't want to accept his story. However, after examining the ruins, where a startled police officer discovered the grisly remains of a human leg protruding from the ground — mostly stripped of flesh by the moorland birds — they had launched a full-scale recovery operation and reluctantly accepted what he said.

The primary reason for the police not being more insistent on clarification of certain details which didn't seem to tally was the identification of one of the bodies by fingerprint records. The man concerned had once been found guilty of drink-driving. He turned out to be a close advisor to certain members of the Cabinet, and the disclosure of his presence amongst a group of perverted kidnappers was, it was decided, not to be released as to do so would *not* be in the public interest.

From then on, an unofficial veil of secrecy covered the identity of those people trapped under the rubble. Whether they were ordered not to investigate the case too deeply, or whether they just accepted that perhaps they didn't *want* to know the truth, the police had casually informed Tony that their investigations were complete, and that they were satisfied with *his* version of events. He had found it mildly surprising since the day before, an Inspector had made a point of asking several questions which obviously struck him as distinctly odd. But that was the end of it — after the initial press coverage, interest died away quickly, to Tony's immense relief. His grief was a very private thing to him and he had not admitted — even to John — just how deeply Hayter's death had affected him.

His depression became a constant in his waking moments, his hours of sleep filled with nightmares of abject terror; he ran and ran from something which he had to escape but knew that he couldn't. Abruptly the scene changed, and he was surrounded by swirling colours, certain that he was about to die. Then the colours faded into the figure of George Hayter, who looked at him reproachfully as though he was disappointed that Tony hadn't believed that he could save him. At this point Tony usually woke, sweating and trembling in his anxiety. His subconscious added to his burden of guilt by emphasising — in a roundabout way, that he was the only one *not* to have suffered some

418

physical hurt. It seemed like an injustice, that the *others* suffer and not he. But he *was* suffering — and perhaps his sufferings were, in their way, more intense than the commensurate feelings under which John laboured.

The noise of his footsteps echoing as he continued down the corridor impinged upon his consciousness, forcing him out of the daze which he seemed prone to, these days. He turned off the corridor and hesitated before managing to pluck up the courage necessary to push his way through the swing-doors facing him and to knock quietly upon the first door on his right, interrupting the muted voices issuing from inside the room.

"Come in," he heard.

On entering, he found himself again facing the senior nurse who was responsible for Margaret's care. She smiled at him, a professional smile that he had come to know and expect. Next to her was the Consultant Neurologist who found Margaret's incapacitation *so* fascinating that Tony wondered, in moments of cynicism, whether he did actually want her to regain consciousness. Both seemed to be trying to think of something new that they could say to him, some hope which they could offer him. He could see in their eyes that no such hope existed, but forced himself to ask the question anyway: "How is she?"

They exchanged glances before the Consultant replied: "About the same, I'd say. There hasn't been any dramatic change. As I said after my first examination, she could stay comatose for weeks, months, years, or *never* regain consciousness. I just don't know. The shock which she experienced from the various tortures she was subjected to made her run away from reality. I can't know that she'll *ever* return from wherever she's hidden herself."

Tony nodded, feeling the familiar despondency intensify within himself. "Can I see her?"

They smiled condescendingly at him. He knew the answer, but this was a part of the ritual, seemingly something that he had to do. As permission was granted — as it *always* was — he waved away the offer they made of accompanying him to her room; it always embarrassed him if anyone was there when he visited her. He felt almost as though they might be able to see into his very mind and understand just what emotions were churning through him. The thought disturbed him. It was possible that his feelings had been perceived, as, for the last two weeks, he had been left undisturbed with her.

He entered her room quietly, taking in the various pieces of apparatus around her, monitoring her status. He shook his head as he approached the bed, laid the flowers upon the bedside table, and sat in the one chair facing her inert body. This was the part that he hated most, attempting to hold a normal conversation. He looked at her eyes, closed as if in sleep. Her arms rested upon the sheets, and he hesitantly took hold of her right hand.

"Margaret, it's me, Tony. I know you can hear me, even if you can't show me that you do. You know, you're going to have to wake up sooner or later, 'cos I'm not going to give up. I miss you, more than I ever imagined I could. The people who hurt you are dead, Margaret. They can't hurt you any more, I promise.

"I've brought you some flowers. I bet you knew that; I bring some every time I visit you. I know you like them. I'm going to see John in a few minutes. He keeps asking me how you are — at times he can't even wait for me to get through the door before the question is out of his mouth. He gets quite annoyed that they won't allow him to visit you himself, but they say he needs bed rest.

"They seem to think that his blindness is psychosomatic, that there isn't any reason for it. Mind you, they are keeping his eyes bandaged for the time being; I don't understand why. He told me to send you his love."

He broke off, wondering what he could talk about next. Nothing suggested itself — apart from Hayter's death, and Tony didn't think that would exactly help her return to consciousness if she could, in fact, hear him. He tightened his grip upon her hand slightly. He shook his head and sighed heavily.

Almost without thinking, he began talking of inconsequential things, and eventually found himself relating his newfound closeness to John, confessing that at one time he had considered him as a potential rival for her affections.

"It sounds a bit absurd in the cold light of day, doesn't it? Perhaps I was just being paranoid; after all the pressure that we were under in the mansion, it wouldn't surprise me a bit. It made me realise, though, just how much you mean to me. I don't think I ever really gave you any indication of how much I care about you. Yet, you know I care more than I ever thought I could. Now that I *want* to tell you, I don't even know whether or not you *can* hear me. All I want is for you to open your eyes, look at me and tell me that you *care* for me. It might take a long time, but I'm *not* going to give up. I'll come here and bore you *every* day until you do wake up, because I *love* you."

Tears filled his eyes, made his voice tremble on the words. He wiped his eyes absently, becoming more conscious of the stillness that had closed around them both now that he had stopped talking. She lay in the exact same position as she had done originally, giving no indication of whether or not his words had penetrated to that secret place where she had hidden her awareness. Standing, Tony looked at her face again. Gently he bent over her and brushed her lips with his. "I'll see you again tomorrow," he said, turning and heading for the door.

Once outside the room, with the door closed behind him, he tried to compose himself after the strain he felt from keeping a one-sided conversation alive.

He found it impossible to imagine anything more difficult. He found it hard enough to think of things to talk about to people in hospital who *could* respond — but this achieved almost unbelievable proportions.

He walked down the corridor, his mind revolving around his utter failure to make any demonstrable progress in bringing her back to consciousness. Almost unconsciously, he followed the route to John's room. He stopped outside the door and grinned before knocking. He knew that John had made an *exceptionally* difficult patient. Despite being told that he must have complete bed rest until the problem with his sight was resolved — which the doctors were sure it would be — he had made seven attempts to locate Margaret — never once asking for Tony's help — which he referred to as 'Escape attempts'. All had ended in failure, as he couldn't tell when his unauthorised absence had been noticed and wasn't aware of his imminent recapture until several male nurses — word had got around about his strength in warding them off — pounced on him, hypodermics at the ready.

The doctors, made aware of his attempts at wandering by several irate nurses suffering the after-effects of attempts at recapture, decided that he might cause less trouble if sedated. Unfortunately they hadn't reckoned on his strength of will, and after feigning deep sleep, he had been discovered nearly three hours later attempting to force his way into an empty operating theatre on the fourth floor. How he had evaded the various security checks was never discovered, and John himself could give no adequate account of his movements, since he had only been semi-conscious at the time.

It was after this event that the doctors decided against further sedation lest he manage to cause some catastrophe by finding his way into other forbidden areas of the hospital — such as the incinerators or the nurses' changing rooms.

Consequently, he was watched day and night, much to his annoyance. As far as Tony knew, he hadn't found a way around this latest setback.

He entered without being invited, to find John sitting up in bed, his nurse-cum-jailor nowhere to be seen.

"Tony!" he shouted enthusiastically, even though Tony hadn't said anything. "How's Margaret? Is she any better? What are they doing?"

"Slow down," Tony insisted. "How did you know it was me?"

"Oh, I don't know. I just knew."

"Where's your guard?"

John grinned. "I blackmailed her into leaving me alone for an hour or so — I promised I wouldn't wander around. But next time...I'll get to visit Margaret if it kills me."

"And it might. Why not wait until you're allowed to?"

"I'll be an old man by then. I come here blind, and what's the first thing that they do? They bandage my eyes so even if my sight *does* come back, I won't know a thing about it. Then they make me stay in bed twenty-four hours a day; they refuse to tell me *anything* about Margaret apart from: 'She's as well as can be expected', and prevent me from visiting her. I ask you, would *you* wait, in my position?"

"Probably not," Tony admitted.

"So, how is she?"

Tony grinned again, feeling his sense of the ridiculous suddenly stir within him. It was the closest he came to laughing since the battle with the Cult.

"Well, she's as well as can be expected," Tony stated, keeping his voice even.

"*Tony*! Not you, too?"

423

The laughter which had bubbled up inside him subsided just as quickly. "No change that I can see. I don't even think I'm doing any good. To be honest, John, I can't take much more. Seeing her in that state every day is *tearing* me apart."

John nodded slowly. "Sorry. I get so wound up in the fact that I can't see her, literally, and wanting to hear that she's conscious, that I forget what this *must* be doing to you."

"You can't begin to imagine..."

"No, I can't," he admitted. "Do you think that if you had a word with my doctor you could persuade him to let me come with you next time you visit her? Not just for Margaret, but to keep your spirits up, too. That's what friends are for, isn't it?"

Tony considered. "Are we friends?" he asked.

"I think so," John answered. "You can't share the experiences that *we* have without becoming good friends or mortal enemies — and I think I'd prefer *you* as a friend."

"I agree, John. I'll see what I can do. I *tried* once before, but your doctor wouldn't even *consider* it."

"Tell him I won't pay his bill otherwise," John advised. "I bet *that'll* make him change his mind."

"How are you?" Tony asked, attempting to change the subject to one which he found less difficult to talk about. "Been on any more break out attempts recently?"

"Only one since I last saw you...er I mean spoke to you. Did you know that the kitchens are just one floor below?"

Tony stared at him incredulously. "You mean you stole some food?"

"Tony!" John snapped back at him, a frown creasing his forehead. "I thought you knew me better than that. I didn't steal it...I was just *sampling* it."

"And just how much did you sample?" Tony enquired.

"This is ridiculous, Tony. They starve me. I was hungry, and just happened to follow the smell. Tell you one thing, though, food certainly *tastes* better when you're blind."

"Have they got any further? The last time we talked, you said they thought it was psychosomatic."

John grinned. "They *think* they have. I think it's just an excuse to get me to pay my bill on time. I'll literally believe it when I see it."

They fell silent. John massaged his temples where the bandage rubbed.

Tony sat looking at him, wondering what he could say next. His problem was solved by John.

"It's weird, really," he said, musingly. "I'll never be able to forget George — not that I'd ever *want* to; but I find it difficult to believe and *accept* that he's dead. I'm stuck here, *bored* silly; you're out there," he swept his arm in a wide arc, "but you're depressed about Margaret, worried about *everything* else — even about what to say to me. I can *feel* how tense you are. It's *eerie*."

"It is," Tony agreed slowly. "Did you know that *two days* before we confronted the Cult, George amended his Will?"

"No, but I'm not surprised."

"His solicitor got in touch yesterday. Apparently, George went to his offices and completely changed it. I don't understand how he did it, because he was in the mansion all the time."

"Knowing Mr. Hayter — George — as closely as I did, I'd say that he probably just relocated himself there and demanded to see his solicitor on a matter of urgency, then later, relocated himself back. We wouldn't have missed him for an hour or two."

"I have to see this solicitor about the Will, anyway."

"Gregson: George *always* used him, said he was the best solicitor in the country."

Tony stood up. "I'll get moving. Look after yourself — and no more causing mayhem. You're supposed to be ill, you know, not impersonating the bringer of chaos."

John grinned back at him. "I'll try. Are you still living at the mansion?"

"Yes."

"Do you think you could bring my CD player with you when you next come — and some CDs. They're next to the stereo in what were my rooms."

"Don't be stupid, John. They still *are* your rooms. Yes, I'll bring it tomorrow. And I'll go and talk to that doctor now — see if I can change his mind about allowing you to visit Margaret."

He closed the door on John's retort about not paying his bill, and headed towards the reception area. With a bit of luck Dr. Copeland would be on duty and able to respond to being paged.

It was nearly half an hour later when the bald-headed yet surprisingly young-looking doctor managed to find time to see him. They shook hands amicably; Tony explained what he had in mind.

Dr. Copeland shrugged his shoulders. "Difficult customer, Mr. Brandon. You say that all his wanderings are in an attempt to locate Miss Hunter? That *that's* what's been unsettling him?"

"Yes, I think it is."

"Well, we've not had much success in keeping him in his room. Perhaps visiting her with you might just calm him down a little. Yes, let's try it," he smiled.

Tony thanked him, as he turned and headed for the exit. He made his way to his car.

He drove to the mansion, his thoughts overshadowed by recent events. When, after a long drive, he pulled up outside it, he sat for several minutes thinking about all he had learned whilst a guest inside. He didn't think of using the garage but simply left the car where it was, not bothering to lock it.

426

He approached the massive door, unlocked it using John's keys. He slammed the door, locked it behind him, listened to the echoing noise before *silence* replaced it. He wandered aimlessly around, unable to get used to the quiet, the feeling that the mansion was truly *empty*, uninhabited.

He went to the sitting room and poured himself a drink. He thought over past events and present tragedies. Everything seemed to have gone wrong since their attack. Mentally, he cursed Anton Baron for his cryptic verse, the Cult for existing, but most of all himself for all the things he should have done, but hadn't.

Placing his unfinished drink upon the bar, he made his way to Hayter's bedroom, and from there to the room where the battle had taken place. He shook his head, wishing he could undo recent events. It was painful, standing alone in that room; he cast a look around, before returning the way he had come. He stopped by the twelfth piano, lifted its lid, and hit a few notes. They sounded loud in the stillness, depth and brightness at the same time. The notes faded.

As he turned to leave, his eye was caught by the briefcase next to the piano-stool. Frowning, his curiosity aroused, he took it by the handle and carried it back to the sitting room.

It opened at his first attempt and he gazed at four large brown envelopes which it contained. He pulled one out and was surprised to see that it was addressed simply, '*For Margaret, when the time is right.*'

Similar messages adorned two other envelopes — for himself and John. His frown deepened. The third envelope was marked, '*For the Baron whom I do not know.*' Even though one was addressed to him, he knew that now was *not* the right time to open it. He was curious to know what it contained, hut not so much that he could disobey the implied command from the hand of George Hayter.

He turned his attention back to the briefcase and another, bulkier package caught his eye. It had been hidden by the envelopes. He took it out and read the message: *'For Margaret: a memento from an Old Rogue.'*

Tony thought about this for a long time. Finally, he replaced the four envelopes in the briefcase, closed it and settled to opening the package bearing Margaret's name.

It was full of CDs. He counted fifteen of them. A smaller envelope — a white one — was marked, *'Margaret'*, and Tony could *not* bring himself to intrude on Margaret's and Hayter's privacy by opening it.

He frowned again, wondering what the CDs might contain. He left them where they were, remembering his promise to take John's cassette recorder with him the next day. He could assuage his curiosity regarding the CDs at the same time as keeping his promise.

He left the sitting room and made his way to John's rooms, hesitating over the route only once. He unlocked the door, entered, and a couple of minutes later located the heavy machine.

He glanced around the room, surprised at its contents. The stereo system seemed almost incongruous with what he knew of John. There were so many things that he did *not* know, he caught himself thinking. He left John's domain slowly, locking the door carefully behind him, and made his way back to the sitting room.

He looked around vaguely for a power point, eventually noticing one by the bar. He scanned the machine quickly and was relieved that the controls seemed straightforward. He plucked a CD from the pile, inserted it, and waited for it to begin playing automatically.

It seemed to take minutes, although it was only about thirty seconds, before the cassette recorder's speakers erupted into a deafening output, distorting what it was attempting to reproduce. Frantically, Tony searched for the sliding volume control and reduced the cacophony to a more acceptable level.

It was only then that he recognised what he was hearing. Ideas connected one after the other in rapid succession in his mind, and curiously enough, under the circumstances, a slow, broad smile lit up his face.

A new feeling began to manifest itself within him, sending the dark shadows of depression fleeing in the face of that *small* light of hope. He stopped the CD, ejected it, and then took in the sheer *number* of them. How? He didn't *pretend* to know the answer, he merely replaced the CD which he had been playing in its plastic case.

As he thought of the implications of his discovery, Tony almost set off for the hospital immediately, but a second thought restrained him. Would they have received Dr. Copeland's instructions about permitting John to visit Margaret?

"Sod that," he muttered, beyond caring what *anyone* said or did.

He scooped up the CDs almost without comprehending what he was doing. He only paused to consider the implications of his actions after he had deposited them upon the passenger seat of his car, and returned carrying the CD player. A faint voice in the back of his mind warned that this might *not* be the right time, but he was, perversely enough, enjoying the sudden activity, feeling that he might actually be doing some good.

He groaned as the realisation hit him that he had left the mansion unlocked. Events seemed to conspire to cause him the most irritating, petty delays imaginable. Having locked the mansion, the car *refused* to start, forcing him to trace a loose connection. Every traffic light *en route* seemed to be against him. He was still several miles from the hospital when he felt the sudden loss of power, the engine spluttered and died. He glared at the dashboard and hit the steering wheel in sheer frustration; of *all* times to run out of petrol...

Muttering darkly, he collected an old oil can from the boot, and began walking back the way he had come. He had passed a filling station about ten minutes earlier.

He lost over an hour getting the petrol. He returned to the same filling station to fill the car, annoyed at his own forgetfulness in not checking the indicator level, and praying that there might be no more delays.

In fact, there weren't. He glanced at his watch as he pulled up in the hospital's car park. He knew that he wouldn't be expected, and that John would want to be with him when he tried his experiment. He forced the CDs into his pockets, not caring about the unsightly bulge which resulted, or the irritation of the edges digging into his sides through the fabric.

Without any further hesitation he took hold of the CD player, locked the car, and entered the hospital. He made his way straight to John's room, opened the door quietly and tried to ascertain whether or not John was alone. He was. Tony entered, certain that he was asleep, but before he was even halfway to the bed, John's voice broke the stillness, making Tony jump.

"Tony, what d'you think you're doing creeping about my room?"

Tony looked at the still recumbent figure. "I thought you were asleep."

"Doesn't make sense to me," John continued, sitting up. "I didn't expect you again until tomorrow at the earliest. Did you see the doctor?"

"Yes, and he agreed to let you come with me tomorrow." He paused as a grin flashed over John's face.

"I *knew* he'd give in if you told him that I wouldn't settle his bill..."

"John, I didn't come to tell you that. I've got an idea. I found a briefcase near the piano — you know, the one that you couldn't find?"

John became quickly attentive, frowning. "Go on," he said.

"Well, inside it were some envelopes, one addressed to each of us, and another; anyway, apart from that, I found a package addressed to Margaret. I opened it, and..."

"You *what*?" John broke in angrily. "Are you in the *habit* of opening packages addressed to her?"

"No, but it felt *right*. That's the only thing I can say. Anyway, I opened it, and inside I found some CDs. It was then that I had this idea..."

It took only a couple of minutes for Tony to complete what he had to say. He looked at John, who seemed to be pondering what he had heard.

"Well, what do you think?"

"I think," said John, "that you should have found that *bloody* briefcase a lot sooner. Let's try it."

"Do you want me to find a wheelchair for you?"

John inclined his head almost comically. "Tony, I'm blind, not crippled, you know."

"Sorry, I didn't think. Can you keep hold of my arm? I've got to carry your player, don't forget."

Slowly, they made their way to Margaret's room. John seemed more nervous than Tony, and turned his head constantly, alert for any sound.

"What's wrong?" Tony hissed.

"Nothing — force of habit. I was always caught in my other escape attempts. I suppose that it was because I was on my own."

"Could have been," Tony agreed absently. "Stairs here, John: two flights."

John nodded. Five uneventful minutes later saw them outside Margaret's room. Tony followed the same procedure as earlier, making sure that apart from Margaret the room was unoccupied. They entered, Tony guiding John to the chair. He searched the room with his eyes for a power point.

He sighed with relief when he spotted one, and, heading for it, CD player still in hand, he said, "Margaret, I'm here again because I've got a present for you from George. Two presents, really, because I've brought John to visit you."

John swallowed before speaking. "Margaret? I *hope* you can hear me. You just don't know the trouble I've been to trying to get to see you. I even ended up in the kitchens, one time. Another time, I found the operating theatres. The nurses weren't too pleased about it, though. I ask you, they dive on you and then expect you not to fight back; then when you *do* they take their revenge with their bloody syringes. It's not fair."

"Ready," Tony whispered to John, who nodded, falling silent. Tony depressed the 'Play' button, and, thirty seconds later, the strains of George Hayter playing Chopin's etudes, upon his beloved twelfth piano — although they didn't know that — filled the room.

John turned his head towards the cassette recorder, whilst Tony's eyes jumped from John to Margaret and back again.

Margaret showed no response, no indication that she could even hear the music. Tony felt the tension building up inside himself. He had been so certain that this, at least, would have *some* effect.

"Turn it up," John ordered, anguish entering his voice.

"I can't, it starts to distort. It's quite loud as it is."

"It's nowhere near as loud as it can go. I know my own machine, Tony."

"I suppose you do," he replied, sliding the volume control further to the right.

"Is anything happening?" John demanded, his head turning towards the bed, although he couldn't see it.

"Nothing," Tony replied, disappointed. They waited another ten minutes, but still she showed no response.

432

"Try a different CD, Tony," John urged him, his voice now considerably more calm and businesslike than it had been earlier.

Tony nodded, and then, aware that John couldn't possibly have seen the gesture, said, "Why not?" He stopped the CD, ejected it, and pulled another from the pile which he had dumped next to the recorder.

Shortly after inserting it, the hospital room was again deluged in piano music, as Hayter played Rachmaninov's third piano concerto. Again the two of them waited nervously for *some* reaction from Margaret, but none came.

"Perhaps it *wasn't* such a good idea, after all," Tony muttered, some twenty or so minutes later, as the first movement came close to completion. He stopped the machine and ejected the CD.

"Nothing wrong with the idea, Tony — but it *could* be..." John broke off, frowning. "Your idea was that if she heard George playing, she might be drawn back to consciousness. But, Tony, if she's never *heard* George playing these particular pieces before, would she be able, comatose as she is, to recognise that it *is* George?"

"In that case..." Tony began, attempting to see what John was getting at.

"In that case, we'd stand a better chance if George has recorded himself playing something which she's heard him play. Tell me, are the CDs labelled?"

"Yes, faintly," Tony realised.

"Can you find a recording of the Grieg piano concerto? It was his favourite piece. He played it a lot whilst both of you were at the mansion."

Tony sorted through the cassettes, until he came to one labelled as having both Grieg's piano concerto and Prokoffiev's third piano concerto recorded on it. He inserted the CD, selected track four, and pressed the 'Play' button again.

The gentle strains of Grieg filled the air causing John's expression to smooth, his worried frown to disappear and his face to take on an air almost of tranquillity, as he reminisced over the years he had spent with Hayter. The effect stretched itself to Tony, who began to feel his fears and depressions melting away, as though the mere presence of Hayter, through only a machine, could banish the *darkest* nightmare.

They became so engrossed in the music that for several moments neither thought to check whether or not this latest idea had solicited any response from Margaret. Both seemed to snap out of the spell the music cast over them at the same time.

"Is anything happening, Tony? Any sign *at all* that she can hear it?"

"Not a *bloody* thing..." Tony began, and then felt his heart surge within his chest as, slowly, delicately almost, Margaret opened her eyes, blinked a few times, caught sight of them, and smiled.

*****

"What do we do now?"

The ice cold eyes, burning in their intensity, turned to the speaker. "Is it not obvious? We begin *rebuilding*. We will have powerful help in our American Brothers. Do not forget that I rule over *all*. I may need to be cautious at first, but that does not worry me. We will bide our time."

"And *then*?" questioned the second, his eyes burning with scarcely suppressed zeal.

"And then we *crush* them once and for all. But next time, *nothing* will be left to chance. I swear by our Patrons that the remaining Barons will be sorry they were ever born, that they *will* suffer for the havoc which they brought about, and for the destruction of so *many* of our Brothers. Not only do I reaffirm our curse upon them, but upon their *friends*. From this day forward, *any* friend of theirs will be considered an *enemy* of ours and, therefore, a legitimate target."

The two who heard this speech inclined their heads in acceptance and agreement.

"It will take time," murmured one.

"Let it take time! It has taken five hundred years already. We know *how* to wait, *how* to be patient, and *when* to strike. I will not rest until the Barons are destroyed, *eradicated*." His eyes burned with an insane, dazzling intensity.

"And we two will be there with you, to savour *that* victory, Supreme Brother," the other two affirmed, solemnly.

The End